"A frothy confection of sea-foam,
young love, and derring-do."
—NPR

★ "Lukens has written a richly imagined fantasy,
filled with action, suspense, and fully realized
characters, that is also a beautiful love story that will
touch readers' hearts and live in their memories."
—Booklist, *starred review*

"Pirates and princes, magic and mayhem, this book
has it all! With exciting adventure and a breathtaking
romance, I couldn't put *In Deeper Waters* down!"
—Beth Revis, *New York Times* bestselling author of
Give the Dark My Love and the Across the Universe trilogy

"An enchanting adventure, *In Deeper Waters* is a tale
of secrets, survival, and the relationships that shape us.
Lukens fills the pages with magic, humor, and waves of
breath-stealing romance. An inescapably great read!"
—Julian Winters, award-winning author of *Running with Lions*

"*In Deeper Waters* is a siren call of delightful queer
fantasy that speaks to the power of kindness and love.
Royals, bed-sharing, secret magical identities, political
conspiracies, and shenanigans abound in this immersive
vibrant adventure steeped in lore and Lukens' own
artfully crafted mythology."
—C. B. Lee, author of the Sidekick Squad series

IN DEEPER WATERS

Also by F.T. Lukens

So This Is Ever After

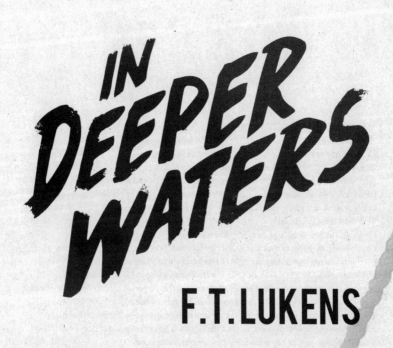

IN DEEPER WATERS

F.T. LUKENS

Margaret K. McElderry Books

New York   London   Toronto   Sydney   New Delhi

MARGARET K. McELDERRY BOOKS

An imprint of Simon & Schuster Children's Publishing Division

1230 Avenue of the Americas, New York, New York 10020

Text © 2021 by F.T. Lukens

Cover illustration © 2021 by Sam Schechter

Cover design by Rebecca Syracuse © 2021 by Simon & Schuster, Inc.

MARGARET K. McELDERRY BOOKS is a trademark of Simon & Schuster, Inc.

For information about special discounts for bulk purchases, please contact Simon & Schuster Special Sales at 1-866-506-1949 or business@simonandschuster.com.

The Simon & Schuster Speakers Bureau can bring authors to your live event. For more information or to book an event, contact the Simon & Schuster Speakers Bureau at 1-866-248-3049 or visit our website at www.simonspeakers.com.

Also available in a Margaret K. McElderry Books hardcover edition

Interior design by Irene Metaxatos

The text for this book was set in Minion.

Manufactured in the United States of America

First Margaret K. McElderry Books paperback edition March 2022

10 9 8 7 6 5 4 3 2

The Library of Congress has cataloged the hardcover edition as follows:

Names: Lukens, F. T., author.

Title: In deeper waters / F. T. Lukens.

Description: First edition. | New York : Margaret K. McElderry Books, [2021] | Audience: Ages 14 up. | Audience: Grades 10–12. | Summary: Sixteen-year-old Prince Tal is on his long-awaited coming-of-age tour when he meets the intriguing and roguish Athlen, and when he is kidnapped by pirates, Athlen is his only hope of escape.

Identifiers: LCCN 2020032400 (print) | ISBN 9781534480506 (hardcover) | ISBN 9781534480520 (ebook)

Subjects: CYAC: Coming of age—Fiction. | Princes—Fiction. | Magic—Fiction. | Kidnapping—Fiction. | Pirates—Fiction. | Gays—Fiction. | Fantasy.

Classification: LCC PZ7.1.L843 In 2021 (print) | DDC [Fic]—dc23

LC record available at https://lccn.loc.gov/2020032400

ISBN 9781534480513 (pbk)

To those who feel lost at sea, may you find a safe harbor

1

Tal closed his eyes as he bent over the bow and willed himself not to vomit. Deck bobbing beneath his boots, his belly flipped as he gripped the glossy wood of the ship's railing with white knuckles.

Don't throw up. Don't throw up. Don't throw up.

Tal hated the sea. He hated this trip. He hated that his older brother would tease him endlessly if he found him retching over the side.

He sucked in a breath through his nose, then gagged. The acrid stench of smoke from the burning derelict floating next to their warship singed his nostrils, and Tal's grasp tightened as bile bubbled in his gullet.

This was a disaster already. He'd warned his family about the dangers of him leaving the castle and gallivanting around the kingdom. They hadn't listened.

Opening his eyes, he wiped the ocean spray from his pale face with his sleeve, the fabric soft against his cheeks. He hooked a finger in his collar and tugged, hoping to relieve the pressure at his throat from the gathered fabric. It didn't work.

He should go below to his bunk in the crew's quarters and hide until they reached the port. Maybe he could write the queen a letter detailing everything that had gone wrong thus far. Maybe she'd let him come home. He had seen her vacillate when they left the docks the previous day, her usual steely resolve slipping a fraction when he waved from the stern.

"Tally!"

Tal snapped his head up and swayed away from the railing. The high sun threw sparkles on the water, and Tal squinted and lifted his hand to block the piercing light as he searched for the source of the call. His dark hair tangled and fell into his eyes, and he brushed it away only for the wind to push it back.

"I've asked you not to call me that."

His brother Garrett swaggered toward him, the laces of his own shirt unknotted, the collar flung wide open. He moved with the natural pulse of the ship, as at home on the deck as he was in their family castle. He slapped Tal heartily on the back. "Old habits."

Tal straightened his posture, and though Garrett was seven years older, they almost matched in height.

"Fine," Garrett said, draping his arm over Tal's shoulders. "Don't look so sour. I understand. You're sixteen and don't want to be babied by your older siblings."

The fourth child of five, Tal was accustomed to being teased, but now at sixteen he had a sinking feeling he'd always be coddled by his three older siblings. The trio were all set in their royal roles, while Tal's remained uncertain. His sister, Isa, was the eldest and next in line to be queen. Garrett was the head of their kingdom's navy. His other brother, Kest, was a renowned scholar.

Having been sequestered in the castle since he was a boy, Tal lived in their shadows. His coming-of-age tour would be his best chance to grow into his own, but it would be especially difficult if he never managed to arrive at the starting port. He was both anxious and eager to start. Anxious because everything could go wrong, and eager to get it over with. Of course, Garrett had had to stop to investigate a burning boat.

Tal craned his neck to peer toward the smoldering vessel they'd come upon. Attached to their ship by a plank of wood and several ropes, it drifted along their port side. The fires were mostly out. Sails hung limply from the masts, torn and singed—a lonely ghost unmoored and unmanned, haunting the inlet until a storm dashed it on the rocky shores or until it took on water and slowly sank to the depths. He didn't know why his brother had approached the ship when the crewman spotted it from the crow's nest. Duty, he guessed. For all of Garrett's gregariousness, he was staunchly loyal and followed their mother's edicts to a fault.

The derelict listed dangerously, and shouts erupted from Garrett's crew. His second-in-command strode over to them, her boot heels clicking, brown hair swinging from a high ponytail.

"Commander," she said, addressing Garrett, "we've found something interesting." Shay held up a coin between her fingers. Her dark eyes drifted to Tal. "Your Highness." She bowed her head.

Garrett raised an eyebrow as he plucked the coin from her hand. He flipped it into the air and caught it in his palm, before studying it intently. He grunted, then passed it to Tal. "What do you see?"

"It's not ours," Tal said, turning the coin in his fingers. "The stamp is from Ossetia. It's not uncommon to find currency from bordering countries this close to home." Tal squinted, running his fingers over the raised edges of the face. "It's not worn, but the seal isn't current, either. This shows the previous king's stamp."

"Good eye. You've been studying."

Not by choice. Isa was to be married to Ossetia's prince once Tal and Garrett returned. To prevent an incident, Tal's tutor had been shoving Ossetia's history and culture at him constantly. He didn't appreciate it, since there were other things more pertinent and certainly more interesting to study.

Magic, for one.

"Not newly minted, but not circulated." Garrett tossed it back to Shay.

"What does it mean?" she asked.

"I don't know yet."

"There's a chest of them."

Garrett's eyebrows shot up. "A whole chest of gold? Abandoned? Well, then, this is interesting."

"There's more," Shay said, shifting slightly. Shay was the royal house's most stalwart soldier. She'd followed Garrett into skirmishes and squalls, protected Tal as a child, and earned a seat at the royal table with her unerring bravery. To see her unsettled twisted Tal's stomach even more. "There is something you should come see." Her gaze cut to Tal and she stopped short, her eyes narrowing. "You should come as well, Your Highness."

Garrett laughed. "Tally was just puking over the side. You think he should board a pitching ship? I don't think so."

Shay straightened and gripped the sword at her side. "Of course, Commander. In hindsight, he may be too sensitive for what we've found."

That spiked Tal's interest more than a piece of pristine gold. He shrugged off Garrett's heavy arm and stepped forward. "I'm not sensitive. I'm a prince of Harth, same as Garrett, and I will decide what I see and what I don't."

"Of course, Your Highness," Shay said, bowing shortly again, her pink lips twisting up into a smile. "You know your limits. I apologize for questioning them."

Garrett laughed. "Shay, such formality. It's just Tally. You've known him since he was a squalling baby."

"I believe he's asked you not to call him that. Several times. Since we left port . . . yesterday." Shay's smile broke forth, wide and playful.

Tal frowned and brushed past them toward the plank between the ships. Other crewmen bustled around the deck and gave Tal a wide berth. They respected Garrett, as he'd been their commander for years, after having trained with most of them when he was a teenager. They didn't know Tal and didn't know the boundaries of familiarity. They looked at him, gauging his worth both aboard their ship and as a potential ruler. More than likely they'd heard the rumors, and though Tal was used to others being cautious around him, it still rubbed him the wrong way.

Sickly and spoiled. Young, untested, seasick, naïve, arrogant, *magic*. He'd heard it all since he stepped on the deck a day ago with Garrett at his side and Isa waving from the dock as they pulled away. Well, they could think those things. Tal would prove them wrong on the negatives. He'd prove them all wrong, even his siblings. And the last word on that list, the forbidden one, was for him and his family to know, no one else.

He stepped onto the plank and grabbed the rope that stretched from their main mast to the derelict's. As he was about to step across, Shay grabbed his arm and halted him.

"I'll cross first," she said, voice low. "I promised the queen I'd protect you, and I can't do that if you hurry off without me." She stepped around him on the small plank, all lithe grace and swinging hips. "Follow, young prince."

Tal scowled at the moniker but bit back a retort. They started to cross, and he squeezed his eyes shut when he glanced down and saw pieces of the wreckage pitching beneath them in the rough seas. Garrett's hand on his shoulder wasn't unwelcome then.

"Keep walking," Garrett said, voice low in his ear. "Don't look down. That's it."

Tal inched across and gladly dropped to the deck of the other ship, even though it lurched beneath his feet far more violently than Garrett's warship. His earlier queasiness returned. Clenching his jaw, he resisted the urge to clap a hand over his mouth and instead swallowed several times to keep the nausea at bay. He didn't want to give Garrett any more opportunities for teasing or any reason to send him back across.

With Garrett at his side, he followed Shay to the captain's quarters, set at the stern beneath the quarterdeck. The glass of the windows had blown out, and bits crunched beneath Tal's boots.

"Finally! Someone with authority." Stepping into the captain's quarters, Tal came face-to-face with a young man. "Well, not you," he said, addressing Tal. "You." He nodded to Garrett, standing over Tal's shoulder. "You're the commander? I demand you release me."

Garrett stroked his ginger beard. "You were not wrong, Shay," he said. "Definitely interesting."

The boy tapped his foot and crossed his arms over his bare chest. He stood tall and broad shouldered, with reddish-brown hair that flopped over his forehead. Light coming in the broken window cast a kaleidoscope of colors on his pale face, illuminating the honey brown of his eyes and the strange patterned markings that ran the length of his torso. His trousers were too short on his long legs, stopping at his shins. He had thinly boned ankles and pale bare feet with knobby toes. An iron fetter, wrapped snugly around one ankle, was attached to a chain, which was secured to the floor.

"Are you done?" the young man asked, holding his arms out to the sides. Brazen in the face of Tal's inspection. "As you can see, I'm not a threat."

"We'll be the judge of that," Shay said, moving to block Tal from the young man's sight. "What happened here?"

He flinched from her and hunched his shoulders near his ears. "What will you believe?"

"That's not a promising start," Garrett said. He nodded toward his sailors, who were gathered in the room. "Everyone out. Find him a shirt and boots." Then he asked the boy, "Do you know where the key is?"

The prisoner shook his head. "The last I saw, it was with the captain."

"And he's where?" Garrett asked. The boy pressed his lips shut into a thin line, and Garrett nodded. "That's what I thought. Well, you heard me," he addressed the sailors milling about. "A shirt, boots, and an ax. We can at least cut him from the floor before this wreck goes under. Shay, you too. Tally, stay."

Tal shuffled out of the way as the sailors left to follow Garrett's commands. He leaned against a large desk in the corner, swallowing a comment about being addressed like a pet. He gripped the furniture as the ship continued to move unsteadily beneath them, taking on water and beginning a slow descent to the depths.

The young man's gaze darted between Tal and Garrett, his brow furrowed.

Garrett sighed and scrubbed a hand over his short hair. "What's your name, boy?" He said it in the way he talked to their younger sister when she was upset, the way he used to talk to Tal when he was frightened.

The boy tilted his head to the side. "Athlen."

"Athlen," Garrett said, testing out the unusual name on his tongue. "Do you need anything?"

Athlen looked to Tal again and back to Garrett, face scrunched in confusion. "Excuse me?"

"Water? Food? Bandages? Obviously, a shirt—"

"Are you being nice to me?"

That was an odd question. "Were they," Garrett said, gesturing to the cabin, "nice to you?"

Athlen tugged on the chain. "Not particularly, no."

"We won't hurt you," Tal blurted. He prickled at the unfairness of it all. The fetter looked painful; bruises dotted the top of Athlen's foot, and the chain wasn't long, trapping him inside the cabin. Eyeing him like he was a danger, Garrett remained silent, pensive, studying the situation with a military eye, but Tal persisted. "We won't! I promise."

"And can you make that promise?" Athlen asked. "Or"—he pointed to Garrett—"are those his decisions to make?"

Tal blushed, embarrassed and indignant, and the tightly bound control he held over himself snapped. "*I* promise." A gust of hot wind swept across the small cabin, swirling debris and thickening the air like the pressure change before the rumble of an incoming storm, giving weight to Tal's words. Sparks flitted between Tal's fingertips, and he hurriedly balled his hands into fists. But the damage had been done.

Athlen whipped his head to stare at Tal, mouth stretching into a small, pleased grin. His cheeks dimpled. "Magic," he said softly.

Horrified at his slip, Tal froze.

In wonder, Athlen lifted his arm and studied the fine hairs that stood on end, a product of the crackle of Tal's magic. He took a step toward Tal, awed and unafraid, the chain slithering along the floor behind him. "You're magic." He said it with such certainty there was little use in denying it, though Tal tried.

"No." Tal licked his lips. "I'm not—"

"You're not?" Athlen squinted. "Are you sure?" Head cocked to the side, he took another step, undeterred.

At a loss, Tal looked to Garrett for assistance.

"That's close enough." Garrett's commanding voice stopped Athlen's advance but didn't release Tal from his scrutiny. In fact, Athlen stared, eyebrows drawn, more curious than scared.

Garrett pinched the bridge of his nose and sighed.

"My brother is correct. We will not hurt you, but we're not releasing you until we know what happened to this ship and where," Garrett said, holding up the coin and refocusing the conversation, "this came from."

Athlen turned away from Tal and strode toward Garrett, stopping when the chain jerked tight. "Hey! That's mine. I found it."

Garrett raised his eyebrows, his blue eyes glittering. "*You* found it?"

"I did, and you have no right to take it. It's shiny and it's mine."

"Shiny?" Garrett mouthed, brow furrowed. "Where? A shipwreck? Or was it the captain's, and you tossed him overboard and claimed it for your own?"

Athlen scoffed. "I didn't hurt anyone. And *I* found that chest in the bay, and that makes it mine."

"I'm afraid it doesn't work like that when it comes to chests of royally marked gold. Why are you bound?"

"Of course," he muttered. He crossed his arms and turned away, refusing to respond.

Despite Garrett's continued questions, they didn't learn anything else from Athlen. Minutes dragged by until Shay returned with a shirt and an ax. She tossed the shirt to Athlen, and he stared at it before pulling it over his head.

"Get him free, Shay. Then bring him aboard the *War Bird*. Tally, come along."

Tal didn't have the heart to argue. He'd sealed a promise with magic in front of a prisoner. He'd given himself away. He'd made *the* mistake his mother had warned him about within the first day of his journey.

Shay hefted the ax, and Tal scurried after Garrett, his head down, and tripped out the door. Garrett put his hand on Tal's shoulder again as they navigated back to the plank. The ship deck rolled ominously.

Garrett pointed at a skinny sailor with long hair. "Make sure that chest gets over to our ship before this one goes under. Once everyone is back on board, we'll cut her loose."

"Aye, Commander."

"He'll be your charge," Garrett said, once back on the *War Bird*. Tal opened his mouth to protest, but Garrett cut him off. "He's scared. He needs to be around someone he will see as a peer and not a threat. There's something *off* about him. Maybe you can figure that out as well."

"Wouldn't Shay be a better choice?"

"No, I trust you can do it."

Tal swallowed. He dropped his voice. "Sorry, about the magic."

"It's all right, Tally. Mother warned me it might be unpredictable, but"—he lifted his gaze and looked around the deck—"keep it a secret. You know what could happen if you don't."

Tal nodded. "I know." He ran a hand through his hair and tugged on the ends. "There are already rumors among the crew. They look at me."

"There are rumors all over the kingdoms. That doesn't mean truth, especially if you don't give them any proof. Understand?"

Cowed, Tal nodded and looked down at his feet. "Yes."

"I'm sorry your coming-of-age tour has started out unexpectedly. We'll make up for it once we reach port. And when we get back to the castle for Isa's wedding, we'll have a plethora of bawdy stories to share with Kest."

Tal mustered a smile, which earned him a hearty clap to the back. His stomach churned as he walked to the railing and watched Shay lead the young man across the plank and into the hold, carrying the length of chain still attached to his ankle fetter in her hands. They cut the derelict free and pushed it away from their side, guiding it out of the channel. Garrett's crew unfurled their ship's sails, and the *War Bird* lurched forward, leaving the smoldering ship behind to roam the shoals until it sank.

The breeze ruffled Tal's hair as they headed toward the southernmost port of their kingdom. The first day of his tour had been unexpectedly eventful. Suddenly he was to oversee the well-being of a strange boy and procure information from him about a chest of gold and a ghost ship. And his magic had flared despite all the training he'd endured over the last several years to keep it a secret. He flexed his fingers and sighed.

How could he prove himself to his family if he couldn't keep his magic under control in situations where he shouldn't even be anxious? How could Garrett trust him?

Tal took a breath, glad for the clean sea air, free from smoke. He could start with doing what Garrett had asked. Garrett wouldn't give him a task that he couldn't do. He trusted his brother in that. And following his orders would be a good first step. Steeling his resolve, Tal left the railing and strode across the deck, intent on checking on his charge.

"I need water," Athlen said, jerking his head up as Tal descended the ladder.

Tal frowned at the demand and the lack of formal greeting. His first instinct was to assert his status as a royal, but he paused. There was a strange kind of relief in not being recognized, especially aboard his brother's ship. They'd been traveling only a day, but the weight of the crew's stares and the sound of their whispers settled heavily between his shoulder blades. Maybe Athlen would treat him normally if he didn't know the significance of Tal's heritage.

"I'm Tal," he said. Not Prince Taliesin of Harth. Not Tally, youngest son of the queen. Not Tal, last mage of the royal line. "I'm going to be looking after you."

Athlen huffed. "As a prisoner?"

"As a guest."

Athlen made a face and gestured to their surroundings. "Thank you for your hospitality."

Tal glanced around. Athlen wasn't wrong. Shay had brought him down into the hold, below the crew's quarters, into the belly of the ship. The wood creaked, the sun barely penetrated the three decks above them, and damp spots dotted the floor and walls, making the enclosed space humid. Though Athlen wasn't bound, it was implied that this was where he was meant to stay.

"I'll find you a blanket," Tal said. "And a hammock. And food."

Athlen didn't respond. He sat on the floor against a small trunk, knees pulled to his chest. His knobby fingers dug into the calf muscle of the leg that was still fettered, and he flinched, features twisting in pain. He peered up at Tal, expression guarded.

"Are you going to keep me like they did? Make me do things?"

Tal reeled, dismayed. "No!" he said immediately. He held up his hands, palms spread. "No, we just want information. We're not . . . we aren't *pirates*."

Athlen raised an eyebrow. "You're going to let me go?"

"Yes."

"When?"

"When we get to the port, and after you tell us about the gold and the ship." Athlen narrowed his eyes. "Here," Tal said, offering a skin of water. Maybe a show of kindness would allow Athlen to relax. "Are you injured?"

Athlen took the water cautiously. He pulled the cork and took a long swallow, his throat bobbing, his pale neck arched. He grimaced and wiped the drops from his mouth. "This is stale."

Tal quirked his mouth. "We just left yesterday."

"I'm not injured." Athlen changed the subject, his large eyes catching the scant light and reflecting the color of honey. "I'm sore. I'm not used to being on my legs this long." He wiggled his toes. The chain clanked against the floor. "You're magic."

"Hush!" Tal said, voice shrill. He looked around, despite knowing the hold was empty save for them. He leaned close. *"Don't."*

Athlen stood, the action oddly graceful. As he stretched, his spine bent in a way Tal had seen only acrobats accomplish when they performed for the palace. He moved into Tal's space, his movements strange, like his limbs didn't quite fit with his body, in some moments awkward and unsure, and in others nimble and quick. Standing this close, Athlen smelled of seaweed and salt and crisp ocean wind. The scent reminded Tal of the depths of the blue, the cool rush of water, and the beaches near the castle, smooth stones and swirling eddies, coarse sand on the soles of his bare feet.

"Why?" Athlen tilted his head, looking toward the ceiling, indicating the crew. "Do they not know?"

"No."

He moved closer and poked Tal in the shoulder. "Are they afraid?" His lips curled into a smirk, teasing, as his gaze drifted over Tal's frame. "Of you?"

Tal blushed, the heat rising in his cheeks, his pulse fluttering under his skin. "No. I'm not—"

"Of the magic, then?"

A lump lodged in Tal's throat. *Yes*, he wanted to say. *Yes, they're terrified of magic, of me.*

Surprisingly, though, Athlen was not. While the crew gave Tal a wide berth, Athlen crowded close, with no sense of danger or regard for personal space. On the derelict, after Tal's mistake, Athlen had moved toward him, not away. He appeared more intrigued than anything, and that was . . . different. It made Tal's belly swoop, and not with seasickness.

"You're not?"

"Should I be?" Athlen asked, genuinely curious.

Tal opened his mouth, then shut it, unsure of how to respond. He rubbed his hand over his face. "It's not . . ." Tal crossed his arms, wrong-footed. "I'm not . . . there hasn't been . . ."

"Oh." Athlen smiled sadly. "Are you the only one, then?"

Sucking in a breath, Tal stared at the deck. His heart beat like a hummingbird and his palms were slicked with sweat. Brow furrowed, he pushed the words out of his tight throat. "Surely you're aware that there hasn't been true magic in a long time. And the last one, the last mage, did . . . unspeakable things." Tal's stomach twisted. His family and tutor had warned him about telling anyone what he was, and here was a strange boy with a labile mouth and large eyes, and he had drawn it from Tal in half a conversation. "I don't want to talk about it. It's time you talk." Athlen slunk away, shoulders hunched, affecting a picture of vulnerability. "What happened to that ship?"

Athlen fidgeted, worrying the buttons of his shirt with quick fingers. "Squall," he said after a long pause. "I tried to warn them. They didn't listen. They were not sailors like"—he waved his hands—"your people. Lightning struck the mast, and they fled in the small boats."

"They left you to die?"

Athlen shrugged. "I had served my purpose."

"How long have you been adrift?"

"Three sunrises." He picked up his foot. "I can't get it off. I'm not good with metal."

Bruises ringed Athlen's ankle and smattered across the top of his foot, and his skin was raw where the iron had rubbed. Tal clenched his fists. Three days. Trapped on a burning wreck for three days while it took on water and drifted, at risk of dehydration and drowning, not to mention burning to death. Tal couldn't imagine. He didn't want to imagine. It was a wonder Athlen had survived.

"Why were you on the ship? What was your purpose?"

Athlen's expression darkened and he turned away from Tal. "Tell the commander I wish to be released. I have done nothing wrong."

The change in his mood, from cautious but amiable to angry, caught Tal off guard. He tugged on his sleeves, pretending to straighten them to hide his surprise. "I'll tell him." Tal turned to go, but Athlen caught his arm. His strong fingers wrapped around Tal's elbow.

"Wait." Tal stilled. Athlen licked his lips. "Can you get it off? With your magic?"

Tal's eyebrows shot up. "I'm not supposed—"

"Please." His gaze darted from Tal to the stairs. A breeze ruffled his copper hair. "If you set me free, I'll tell you everything. You know I wasn't one of them, and they had me for weeks. I know what they were planning. I know where they got the gold." He looked up to Tal, his eyes wet with unshed tears, his expression pleading. "Please."

Tal covered Athlen's hand with his own and removed it from his arm. He shouldn't. His magic wasn't meant for frivolous things. Garrett was right, though. Athlen was terrified. He was angry. He was a victim, and the iron around his ankle was a reminder. Tal could do this for him. He *should* do this for him. This journey was about learning to make decisions, and this would be his first one. He would use his magic for a good deed.

"You vowed to not hurt me. This"—he pointed to the iron—"is hurting me."

Magic simmered under Tal's skin as Athlen invoked the promise. "Sit down," Tal said gruffly.

Athlen scrambled back to the trunk and propped his foot up on the lid, completely trusting. A pang of protectiveness lanced through Tal's gut at Athlen's bent posture. He swallowed nervously as he held out his hand and spread his fingers. He took a steadying breath and called his magic to his hand, a talent he'd mastered long ago. He focused on the band of metal, concentrated on breaking it as his magic swirled up through his body. Heat pooled in his middle, and warmth rushed up the length of his spine into the tips of his fingers. With a focused push he targeted the fetter, and a tangle of sparks leaped from his hand.

The anklet turned cherry red, glowing brighter and brighter, then burst. Shards flew outward with such force they buried in the deck.

Athlen stared with wide, grateful eyes, then a smile broke out over his features like the sun breaking through the clouds. His cheeks dimpled, and Tal's gut flipped with something other than seasickness at the sight.

"That was amazing!"

"Did I hurt you?"

"No." Athlen flexed his foot, pointing his toe, then rubbed his hand over the bare skin. "Thank you. Thank you, Tal."

For the first time since Tal had left his home yesterday, he grinned. "You're welcome."

Athlen jumped to his feet and seized Tal's hand in both of his own. Tal resisted the urge to jerk away, instead stilling, muscles tense as Athlen turned Tal's palm over in inspecting it with a somber intensity. With a furrowed brow, he ran the calloused pads of his fingertips over the smooth skin between Tal's fingers and along the underside of his wrist, his touch unusually cool. No one had touched Tal like this before, with impropriety and wonder, not even his family, and his heart pounded in his ears. Athlen lifted Tal's hand closer, his breath warm and rhythmic on Tal's skin, before he pressed a kiss to the palm. His eyelashes fluttered against Tal's fingers, and Tal exhaled in staccato.

"Your magic is wonderful," Athlen whispered. "I'll remember you."

Tal couldn't speak, but he was sure Athlen could see the thundering of his pulse beneath the thin skin of his wrist.

The sound of footsteps descending on the ladder broke the moment, and the boys sprang apart. Tal's cheeks flushed as red as the setting sun and felt equally as hot.

"You've been down here a while, Tally," Garrett said as he dropped to the deck. "Is everything all right?"

"Yes." The word came out shaky and breathless, and Tal wanted to crawl into the bilge.

"Tal freed me," Athlen said, showing off his foot.

Garrett's eyebrows twitched at the informal name, and Tal hastened to explain.

"I broke the fetter. He said he'd tell us about the gold and the ship if we freed him. He told me how the ship was destroyed beforehand." Garrett's expression remained unchanged. "He's been adrift for three days," Tal continued, feeling the inexorable need to justify himself, to reassure Garrett of his decisions and his use of magic. "He needs food and water and—"

"Light," Athlen added. He pointed up. "Light and air, please."

Garrett looked between them, hands on his hips, eyes sparkling with amusement. He pointed a finger at Athlen. "A few minutes of fresh air, then water and food in my quarters, where you will talk."

Athlen nodded quickly, and after Garrett gestured with his hand, he darted toward the ladder. "Tal, huh?" Garrett said.

Tal covered his face with both hands. "Could you not?"

Garrett's laugh boomed in the enclosed space, and he chuckled the entire way up the ladder to the top deck. Tal followed, face aflame, stomach tripping over itself in equal parts embarrassment and excitement.

When Tal emerged, he found Athlen standing next to the main mast. He threw his head back and breathed in deep, inhaling the brisk ocean breeze. The sun illuminated his exposed skin, and he appeared preternatural, like a gleaming marble statue marking the entrance to an inlet, with the sky as its backdrop and the ocean at its feet. And for a moment Tal swore he saw a flash of red shimmer over Athlen's body, as if it were reflecting the sunset.

Athlen turned to them and smiled wide and happy, his cheeks dimpling, his eyes dancing.

"Thank you, Tal," he said. Then he ran.

Tal lunged after him but missed the tail of Athlen's shirt.

Garrett bellowed at the crew to catch him, but Athlen was swift and nimble. He dodged outstretched arms and ripped away from the grasps of the sailors. He made it to the stern and hopped over the railing to balance on the edge.

"Athlen! No!" Tal pushed through the crowd, hand outstretched.

Athlen pulled off his shirt and tossed it to the deck. He gave Tal a last look and winked. Then he dove over the side.

"Man overboard," one of the sailors cried out.

Tal ran to the railing, prepared to jump after, but Garrett grabbed him around the middle. "No. Tal, no," he said as Tal struggled in his arms.

"But he jumped. He . . ." Tal peered down into the churning blue. Scanning the froth, he saw no sign of Athlen. No flash of cloth or peek of skin. He didn't resurface.

"Stay the boats," Garrett shouted. "He's gone." Garrett released Tal but kept a hand on his arm.

"He . . . why did he . . . ? What . . . ?" Tal craned his neck to meet Garrett's gaze and flinched at the sorrow and empathy he found there. "I don't understand."

Garrett shook his head sadly. "I hope you never do."

Tal swallowed and looked back to the sea. Since their sails were full, the place where Athlen had jumped was far behind them, already smoothing out from the *War Bird*'s wake. Squinting, Tal thought he saw a flash of red just beneath the water, but it was only the refraction of the sun casting on the water as it began its descent to taste the curved horizon.

His heart sank, but he stayed at the rail long after his brother returned to his work, and the day gave way to dusk.

2

Tal used his sleeve to rub the moisture from his cheek. He was a prince of Harth. He didn't need to cry over odd boys who made him smile, then disappeared. There would be other boys. And there would be other people who would live or die based on his decisions, based on his influence as a member of the royal family. Athlen was merely the first.

This was one of the lessons his mother wanted him to learn on his journey. This was his coming-of-age.

When Isa spoke of her tour, she boasted of the mischief she had dabbled in with her maids. Garrett was always loud and boisterous, and his stories were known throughout the castle as the bawdiest. Kest was reserved and quiet but talked of his coming-of-age fondly. Their youngest sibling, Corrie, was three years Tal's junior and eagerly awaited her experience.

Why was Tal the one who'd started with tragedy?

He stared at the letter he had written his mother. He hadn't minced words about the journey thus far. Tal had been bored since the encounter with Athlen. He'd spent the last two days trying to distract himself by reading a book of magic belowdecks, but he was glad they'd be pulling into port within the hour. Garrett promised things would change once they got onto dry land.

With a sigh Tal held his hand over the parchment. He called to his magic, and the letters lit with gold. Tal muttered a familiar incantation, and in a blink of sparkles the words disappeared and the page became like new.

"Handy," Garrett said, standing in the doorway. "Where does it go?"

Tal controlled his startle. He smoothed the parchment down with his palms. "To Mother's study. There's a blank parchment on her desk that receives the letters."

Garrett nodded. "I'm glad it was you," he said, "who received the gift. If it was to come down in our line again, after Great-Grandfather, I'm glad it was you."

Tal pursed his lips. "Because I'm the fourth. If anything were to happen, at least it wouldn't be to the heir."

Sputtering, Garrett entered the room fully and closed the door. "Is that what you think?" He thrust his finger at Tal. Shrugging, Tal turned on the bench seat and faced his brother. "Tally," Garrett said, sinking onto the bunk across from him, his voice soft. "I'm glad it was you because you're still sniffling over that boy two days later."

Tal stiffened. "I'm not."

"It's all right if you are. There's no harm in being sad."

Tal picked at a thread on his trousers. "You're not."

Garrett sighed. "I've seen more than you, but that doesn't mean I'm not upset. I hide it better." The sun filtered through the shutters and bathed Garrett in strands of light and shadow. "I'm glad it's you because you are a good person. You can be a little shit sometimes, but out of the five of us, you have the softest heart. It's a good attribute to have when wielding so much power."

Tal held open his hand and a small flame lit on his palm. "Not much power. I haven't mastered near enough to be useful to Isa when she's queen." He curled his fingers and snuffed the fire out. "If she has need of me, that is."

"You're young. You have time to learn." Garrett chuckled. "Don't you remember? Kest couldn't control his shift for years. We'd be out in the town and he'd see a pretty girl, and suddenly there would be feathers everywhere, and instead of my brother walking next to me there would be a squawking bird."

Their brother, Kest, had the rare ability to shift into an animal. His skill was based in magic but different from Tal's. While Tal could access his power on an innate and broad level, Kest could perform only the one specific skill. Many royal courts viewed it as a parlor trick, others a curse, but Kest considered it a gift, once he had it mastered.

Tal's lips curled up at the corners. "I do remember a lot of pheasant jokes at dinner."

Garrett snorted and slapped Tal on the knee. "Oh, he'd get so angry. And Isa would make comments about ruffled feathers."

Tal let out a loud laugh and clapped a hand over his mouth. They chuckled together, and Tal appreciated the moment. Due to their age difference, Tal had never gotten to spend much time with Garrett. When Tal was young, Garrett trained with the knights, and as Tal grew, Garrett spent much of his time at sea.

"Don't worry about Isa," Garrett said. "Our mother has been queen without a mage and without a king for many years." Tal rubbed a hand over his brow. Their father had died when Tal was a toddler, and the only memories he had were flashes of a warm voice and kind eyes. "Isa will have her betrothed. She has me and Kest. And she'll have you if your abilities are warranted, but only when you're ready. Otherwise, things will continue as they always have."

Tal flinched. "Is that my lot, then?" he asked, voice quiet. "Either to be hidden away or to be used?"

"No, that's not what I meant."

"Isn't it?" Tal frowned, twisting his signet ring around his finger. "We can't risk the other kingdoms knowing what I am, so I must be careful, and the best way to be careful is to be unseen. But I must be available for when mother or Isa calls for me, ready to reveal myself to the world. Most likely as a threat, someone to be feared, a tool for destruction."

"When there is peace—"

"My existence threatens peace!" Tal slammed his hand on the table. Garrett looked away. "Even if I become court mage, I don't want to do the things *he* did. I won't. Not even for Isa."

"I'd like to say she won't ask you to, but with political tensions the way they are right now, I don't know what will happen."

With that, the levity they shared died away, and Tal was left staring at his hands. Heart aching, he decided then he wouldn't allow his magic to become a weapon, even for his own family. He'd rather be locked in a tower or exiled off the known map than become the monster his heritage predicted he'd be.

"Tally—"

Shay poked her head into the cabin. "Docking soon, Commander."

Garrett stood. He ruffled Tal's dark hair as he passed. "Don't worry, Tal. Put these thoughts aside for now. This is your coming-of-age, and I promise it will be as rowdy as my own, if I have any say. Tales will be told. Epics will be written by bards."

Tal offered a weak smile. At least in Garrett's stories Tal would be the hero, and not the villain he was so scared of becoming.

Rows upon rows of tall ships bobbed in the harbor of the port city of Bayton, their masts scraping the blue of the sky.

But Tal wasn't looking up as he walked along the dock. He sullenly kicked a shell with the toe of his boot. "The port will be such fun," he said in a mock tone of Garrett's voice. "Now go explore the market while I do important naval things."

Shay walked a few feet behind him, guarding him as always, and he knew she could hear him. He didn't care. Strolling through the market on a hot day after three days at sea was not his idea of those epic adventures Garrett had promised. As much as he hadn't wanted to leave home for his coming-of-age, he was interested in the prospect of exploring things like architecture or ancient ruins or even magic artifacts, if he could manage to look for them on the sly. He wouldn't mind a little adventure, but walking through a seaside market that stank of oysters and buzzed with the calls of vendors hawking their wares was something he could do at home. The castle was near the sea, after all, and he and Corrie had often hidden and run away from tutors to explore the town, Shay trailing after them all the while.

That was before his magic had manifested, and he was squirreled away and forbidden to leave the castle. Before the threat of retaliation from the other kingdoms hung over his head if they ever discovered he carried his great-grandfather's legacy.

Tal shoved his hands into the pockets of his trousers. He'd left his vest and cravat back in his trunk on the ship, opting, as Garrett often did, to look less like a prince and more like a sailor. His black hair tangled around his ears and fell into his eyes, and with each kick of a shell or rock his boots scuffed.

Shoulders slumped, he could feel Shay's disapproving gaze on him, an itch on the back of his neck.

Tal's sulking was interrupted as a voice rang out over the bustling thrum of the market. "I don't understand! This should be enough. Why isn't this enough?"

He lifted his head and scanned the area. There was a commotion near a stall that sold medicinal supplies—herbs, potions, various remedies. He recognized that voice. He'd heard it in his head for the past three days every time he thought of his reckless decision to use his magic on an iron fetter. It couldn't be, though. Athlen had drowned. If, somehow, he had managed to survive, there would be no logical way for him to have arrived at the port before the *War Bird*. No man could swim that length; he would surely have given in to exhaustion. This was Tal's misplaced grief playing tricks.

Still, there seemed to be something amiss, and it was Tal's duty to investigate.

"I'm sorry, boy. If you want the medicine, you have to bring me something of value."

"They are of value. I know they are. Aren't they?"

Tal inched closer, pretending to look over the wares of a jeweler while attempting to sneak glances at the situation. A crowd stood in his way, gathering at the commotion, and he huffed. With a roll of his eyes, he pushed past a taller gentleman, then stopped short.

It *was* him.

Tal's heart constricted. Anger warred with relief at the sight of Athlen, hiding beneath the brim of a too-large hat. He stood at the counter, waving his calloused hands and arguing with the merchant. He wore trousers that didn't quite fit him but were at least long enough, his bare feet peeking beneath the hems, and a white, billowy shirt that reminded Tal of sails. His ridiculous hat flopped in his face, but it didn't hide the bright splotches of red on his cheeks. When he lifted his head, Tal caught the frustrated downturn of Athlen's pink mouth and the defeated line of his shoulders.

The merchant, short and balding, with an unfortunate mustache, leaned forward and pinched a perfect pink pearl between his fingers. "These are worthless," he said.

Tal raised an eyebrow as he stepped closer. The pearl was worth more than anything in the shop. What was the merchant playing at?

"Please," Athlen begged, a desperate edge to his voice. "My friend's mother is sick. She needs the medicine to breathe. This is everything I have."

The merchant stroked his mustache. "I'm sorry, friend."

Athlen let out a frustrated sound and clenched his hands. "I can get more," he said. "Whatever it costs. I can get more."

The merchant's eyes sparkled with greed.

So that was the game. Tal shouldered forward. Mustering every ounce of royal disdain and arrogance he could, he lifted his chin and hardened his gaze.

"What seems to be the problem here?"

Athlen startled and turned to face Tal. His expression twisted into shock and then gratitude in a blink. Standing this close, Tal caught the distinct scent of Athlen, thick even in the crush of bod-ies around the merchant's stand. He smelled of the sea—of salt and spray and foam.

"This boy is causing trouble."

"Trouble?" Tal said. He peered over Athlen's shoulder and spied myriad objects spread before him—a handful of gold coins stamped with emblems Tal didn't recognize, three perfect, round pearls, bits of multicolored sea glass, sharks' teeth, and a small rusted dagger. "I don't see trouble. I do see a problem, however," Tal said, leveling a scowl at the merchant.

The man cleared his throat and changed his tune. "No, never mind. There isn't a problem," the merchant said quickly, setting the pearl down.

Tal looked to Athlen. "Is there a problem?" he asked softer.

"My friend's mother is sick," Athlen said. He ran his sleeve over his face. "She won't stop coughing. My friend says she needs medicine. They can't afford it, so I'm trying to buy it, but . . ." He gestured weakly to the cache of objects.

Tal nodded.

Eyeing the mess, he picked out a pearl and set it neatly in front of the merchant.

"Give him everything he asks for."

"Now, sir, this pearl isn't enough for the items he wants, espe-cially the root. It's scarce this time of year and—"

Tal scowled, waving away the complaints, and the merchant fell silent. Tal reached into the small pouch at his side and pulled out a piece of family gold stamped with the royal insignia and placed it next to the pearl. He tapped it with the finger that promi-nently displayed his own signet ring.

"Royal," the merchant breathed.

"Prince Taliesin," Tal corrected. "Youngest son to Queen Carys."

The man's eyes widened, and a smattering of murmurs spread out like ripples in a pond in the crowd around them. Shay wouldn't approve. Garrett undoubtedly would.

The merchant gave a short bow. "Your Highness, it is an honor to have you at my humble stall."

"Give the boy what he wants."

"Yes, of course." He scurried away, collecting the items into a bag.

Athlen's lips twitched into a smile. "Prince?"

Tal shrugged. "It's nothing."

"No, it's not nothing." Athlen smiled, eyes crinkling. "You've saved me twice now. I should thank you."

"Please don't."

Athlen tilted his head. He studied Tal for a long moment, brown eyes soft, fingertips tapping against his mouth. "I know," he said, snapping his fingers. He sorted through his collection and picked out a jagged shark's tooth. He took Tal's hand, and Tal shuddered at the cool sensation of Athlen's skin against his own. Athlen turned Tal's hand over, pressed the tooth gently into his palm, and closed his fingers over it. "There."

Tal clutched the tooth, its point biting into the heel of his hand. It was something children found on the beach, worthless as a shell or a mermaid's purse. Certainly not as valuable as a pearl or a piece of gold or even a rusted dagger. Tal had been given many gifts over his lifetime, all lavish and expensive, meant to curry favor if from members of the court, or to look pretty in his room or on his person if from his family. This gift confused him and delighted him in a way that touched his core. His heart fluttered like a butterfly within the cage of his body, and he pressed his closed fist to his chest. "Thank you."

A flush spread over the high curves of Athlen's cheeks, obscuring the smattering of freckles that dotted the bridge of his nose.

Athlen gathered up the rest of his mess and shoved the items, including the pearls and gold and glass, into his pockets as if they were all equal. His trousers sagged with the weight of them. With Athlen's attention elsewhere, Tal tucked the shark's tooth into his breast pocket and smoothed down the fabric.

"Your things," the merchant interrupted, shoving the bag of supplies over the counter.

Athlen eagerly took the cloth sack and moved to scuttle away, but Tal grabbed his wrist and held fast.

"Oh no," he said. "You aren't running away this time. I made that mistake before."

Athlen tugged halfheartedly but grinned, and Tal had the impression he was glad to be caught.

"I thought you drowned," Tal said. "I thought . . ." His throat clogged. "I thought I'd let you go only for you to . . . hurt yourself, and I . . ."

Athlen's smile faded. Tal's heart ached for the loss of it.

"I'm sorry," Athlen said. "I didn't know you'd be upset. No one has been upset before."

"What? Why?"

Athlen shrugged. "There's no one to be upset."

Tal's throat went tight. "Are you the only one too?"

Athlen ducked his head, his hat obscuring his face. "I need to take the supplies to my friend. Her mother needs tending." He tipped his head toward Tal, expression sly. "Come with me?"

"I don't know if I should," Tal said, looking around, noting the way several gruff and greasy men nearby eyed Athlen's sagging pockets. "Shay is around, and I'm certain she won't allow me to wander away too far."

Shrugging, Athlen backed away from the stall. "I'm going. If you want to keep an eye on me, you'll have to come too."

Gulping, Tal shuffled closer, not wanting Athlen to flit away. Who was this boy who valued sea glass the same as pearls and gold? Who was he to smile slyly and tease Tal and touch him casually and make his heart race?

"Fine," Tal said, feigning annoyance. "But after this, you have to come back and talk with Garrett."

Athlen made a noncommittal noise, but Tal took it for acquiescence. More than likely, he wouldn't be able to force Athlen to come back with him, but he might be able to wheedle information from him and report it back to Garrett. He could make amends for his earlier mistake. Besides, Athlen intrigued him. Tal released Athlen's wrist, but Athlen didn't run. He stayed right next to Tal's side, his fingertips knocking into Tal's hand.

They left the shade of the stall. The walkways made of broken shells reflected the harsh light, making Tal squint against the bright midday sun. The hat cast a shadow on Athlen's features, and Tal likened it to when fog rolled in off the water at night and obscured the pale beauty of the moon.

Athlen jerked his chin toward Tal's hand. "Why did he act like that when he saw your ring?"

Tal twisted it on his finger. "It's a symbol of my family name. It identifies me as a royal."

Athlen furrowed his brow. "How did that merchant know?"

"My family is royalty." Tal hunched his shoulders. "Our symbol is on all the flags in the kingdom."

"You really are a prince?"

"Yes."

"And that ring says you are?"

"My brothers and sisters have them too, as well as anyone we consider family." He spun it again, catching the jewel on his thumbnail. "I'll give one like it to whomever I marry."

Athlen hummed, as if thinking, then stopped suddenly at a cross street. He turned, and Tal followed.

Together they made their way from the merchant area into the residential section of the port. Athlen picked his way across the cobblestone streets. Tal followed, drinking in the sights and textures of the town, the smell of the sea wafting in from the shore and mixing with the odor of horses and people. As they went deeper into the city, the air changed, as did the streets, which narrowed from the wide, straight boulevards to cramped and twisting alleys shoved between a mishmash of buildings, as if the buildings had been there first and the streets had grown around them.

As the pair went, the people of the neighborhood gave them space—Tal in his shiny boots and royal posture complete with arrogant frown, and Athlen with his bare feet, awkward gait, and hopeful smile. Shay was behind them, far enough that Tal couldn't hear her footsteps, but if he turned his head, he could catch a glimpse of her familiar frame.

They maneuvered a few blocks down a main thoroughfare before ducking into an alley. From there Athlen led Tal through a series of turns that had Tal questioning if Athlen knew his way at all. Before he could voice his concern, Athlen stopped in front of a small, shabby cottage tucked away in a cul-de-sac of other homes. The roof had seen better days, and a shutter hung at an angle.

Athlen didn't knock, but breezed through the front entrance as if he belonged there, pushing over the threshold and into a two-room home. He flung off his hat, throwing it onto a rocking chair, his copper hair sticking up in every direction.

"Dara!" he called. "I got it."

Tal didn't follow. He paused in the open doorway, one hand on the frame, the other at his side. He didn't see Shay behind him any longer, and he wondered if she had lost him in the chaos of the path they'd taken.

He was suddenly very aware of the fact that he was alone in a city he didn't know with a boy who had shown no compunction about manipulating the truth. *Foolish.*

He called to his innate magic and let it bubble at the tips of his fingers as a precaution. He could defend himself. He'd been taught as a boy how to get away from those who would do him harm. And when his magic had manifested, his tutor had made him memorize the few remaining parchments that discussed defensive magic. He could do it, but he'd never had to, not with Shay as his constant shadow around the castle grounds. But this was his first time away from his home, and he'd mucked it up already.

He should leave. He could maybe find the way they'd come. If not, he could follow the sound of the sea, at least.

Athlen looked over his shoulder and frowned when he saw Tal at the edge of the house, and his gaze flitted to the power glowing beneath Tal's skin. He crossed the room and took Tal's hand. Tal shivered at the touch, and he banked his magic, a glow of coals rather than a sparkling flame.

"Don't be worried," Athlen said, voice low, tugging Tal into the house and closing the door behind him. "Dara and her mother are very kind. They take care of me sometimes."

"Athlen?" a girl's voice replied. "Is that you?"

A curtain drew back, revealing a round-faced girl about Tal's age with brown hair pulled into a knot at the base of her neck. She wore a plain dress and an apron, and stockings full of holes barely covered her feet.

"Dara," Athlen said with a bright smile. He thrust the bag at her. "I have those things you needed for your mother."

"Athlen," she said, taking the bag. She opened it and sifted through the items. "How did you manage to afford this? What did you do?" The second question held a hint of accusation, but Tal couldn't call the tone anything other than fond.

Athlen raised his hands. "Don't worry. I traded for it. And Tal helped." Athlen gestured to Tal in the doorway, and Dara's gaze cut to him.

Tal endured her assessing stare, pulling back his shoulders, lifting his chin. Her gaze flickered to where Athlen gripped his hand, and the corners of her lips ticked down. Calmly she grabbed a fistful of Athlen's large shirt and pulled him toward her. Athlen stumbled forward, and she slid smoothly between them, staking a claim. Tal immediately missed the comfort of Athlen's hand in his own.

"Who are you?"

Athlen, who was oblivious, waved in Tal's general direction. "He's a prince. Oh, and he's the one who saved me from the bad people."

Dara's expression flashed through myriad emotions before settling on a mix of gratitude and exasperation. Tal was certain the exasperation was meant for Athlen. Though Tal noted she didn't appear *shocked* at all, as if Athlen brought home princes every day and didn't follow rules of propriety with anyone.

"Your Highness," Dara said with a bow. "Welcome to our

humble home."

Athlen rolled his eyes.

"That's not necessary. He's not that kind of prince."

Tal raised an eyebrow. "What kind of prince am I?" It was the first thing he had said since they arrived.

"Not a fussy one."

Dara smiled warmly and reached over to ruffle Athlen's hair.

"Thank you for returning him to us. We were worried. We thought he was gone when he didn't come back for weeks."

Athlen batted her hand away, his cheeks flushed.

"I was happy to help," Tal said politely. "And I was happy to help him again at the market."

"Speaking of," Athlen said, "will the items help her? Will they make your mother well?"

Tal heard a cough and a groan from the room behind the curtain. He shifted in his spot near the door and in the low light he could make out a figure on a cot along the far wall. The smell of fever sweat and sickness emanated from the area. Noting his inspection, Dara pulled the curtains closed.

"I think so," she said, turning to a small kitchen table with a low bench seat. "I can burn the root in her room and make a tea. The salve for her chest will take me some time, but. . . ." She shrugged. "I hope so."

"What's wrong with her?" Tal asked.

Dara huffed. "There's a sickness in this part of town."

"I'm sorry. I didn't know."

"If you truly are a prince, I wouldn't expect you to." She didn't face him, focused on her task at hand. "Or even care," she added under her breath.

Tal stiffened but kept his composure. His mother would be glad to know that all the royal etiquette lessons had stuck. "Is there any way I can help? Any other medicine I might be able to procure for you?"

Dara wrinkled her nose. "We appreciate your assistance, Your Highness, but we're fine. Please don't tarry here on our account."

"Are you certain?"

Dara leveled an intense glare at him. "You do understand how condescending that sounds, right?"

Tal raised his hands. "I only want to help."

"Because of him," she said, jerking her head toward Athlen. "But if not for whatever relationship you have with Athlen, you wouldn't care about our situation. We'd only be a pair of peasants in your eyes."

Tal crossed his arms, prickly at how correct Dara was in her assessment. "I care," he said, defensive. "And I would like to help. That's why I'm on this trip."

Dara frowned. "Right. You just turned sixteen. It's your coming-of-age tour of the kingdom. Just like your brothers and sister before you. I'm sure all the taverns and brothels they visited gave them a real sense of the people." She slammed a kettle on the table. "You don't look sickly, like the rumors claim. Maybe it's because the whispers about magic are the truth. Are you going to be like your great-grandfather? Is our kingdom going to be paying recompense for the next several generations because of your actions as well? Are you going to burn the land with fire from your fingertips and salt the earth?"

Tal reeled. His face lost all color and he stumbled back, the heel of his boot catching on an uneven floorboard.

"Enough!" Athlen moved between them and faced Dara. "I know you're worried about your mother, but that doesn't mean you get to be rude to my friend."

Face red, Dara pointed a finger into Athlen's chest. "It's not like it concerns you, either."

"What does that mean?" Tal asked.

Dara's gaze flickered between them, and Athlen quickly raised his hands.

"He doesn't know?" she asked. "I thought he saved you from those people."

Athlen licked his lips. "He did. And no, he doesn't."

"Ah," she said with a knowing smirk. "You don't trust him either. And you'd be stupid to. He'll use you like those others did."

Tal clenched his fists. His magic roared within him, licking up his spine in hot tendrils. "I would never hurt him. I made a promise."

She barked a laugh. "And we know how steadfast the promises of royalty are."

Athlen frowned, his expression crumpling into disappointment. "Dara . . . I don't understand why you're being unfair to me and Tal."

"You wouldn't. But trust me when I tell you that the ruling family of Harth cares little about their people."

"That's not true!" Tal's voice rose in indignation. "My sister is about to marry to form an alliance with another kingdom to help our people. My brother sails most of the year, protecting the merchant ships, to ensure our kingdom's prosperity. My mother has done everything she can to repair our relationships with other kingdoms to keep us from war."

Dara pursed her lips. "Fair enough. But when was the last time any of your family talked with a farmer about his struggles? Or a merchant about taxes? Or a tradesman? Your family is so worried about our relationships with other kingdoms, you've forgotten your own people in the process."

Tal clenched his jaw. "My mother and siblings are doing the best they can."

"Maybe they are. But what about you?"

That brought Tal up short.

A wet, rattling cough from the other room broke the gathering tension. Dara returned to making tea and turned her back on the pair of them.

"As much as I would love to continue this lively debate, Your Highness, I do have to attend to my mother."

Tal knew a social cue when he heard one, despite what Garrett said. He gave a small bow. "I'm glad Athlen was able to get what she needed. I'll be on my way." Far bolder than he felt, he reached for Athlen's hand. "Come along, Athlen."

Athlen brushed away his outstretched hand and stepped into Tal's space without a thought. Tal's breath caught at the invasion. He cast a glance over Athlen's shoulder, and Dara pretended to be busy behind him, but Tal didn't believe for a moment she wasn't listening.

"I can't leave."

"You said you'd answer my brother's questions."

"I never said that. You just assumed I agreed."

Tal furrowed his brow, and hurt lanced through him like an open wound. "I thought you died. I thought I freed you by mistake and that . . ." He swallowed around a tight throat. "I owe my brother."

"Oh, Tal," Athlen said, dipping his head. "I'm sorry. I can't come with you now."

"But—"

Athlen leaned in close. He smiled, impish and beautiful, eyes sparkling. "Thank you, my prince, for everything. I will repay you."

There was but a scant inch between them, and Tal's magic shuddered. His skin prickled with the want to be touched, straining toward Athlen's heat in a way he'd not experienced before. This close, he smelled the sea on Athlen's skin and could trace the constellation of freckles on Athlen's nose and cheeks.

"That's not necessary," he said, voice rough and strained.

"I know, but I will." Athlen's voice took on a deeper tone, and there was substance to his words, a physical quality Tal could compare only to an incantation, like the one Tal had made on the derelict.

Tal's heart thumped hard when Athlen met his gaze, the playfulness gone, replaced with a somber appreciation. He nodded, and a shiver raced down Tal's spine, as if a cold wave had splashed over him while he stood on the warm, sun-bleached shore. The weight of the moment meant something. Tal didn't know what, but red and gold rippled over Athlen's skin.

It was a pact, a promise, a declaration of intent, as if Tal had been folded into Athlen's inner circle. He likened it to the feeling of his family, when they all were together and happy, but that didn't make sense. He'd met Athlen only twice, and each time Tal had been inexplicably drawn to him. Maybe it had to do with the secret he obviously kept. A secret that only Dara and a missing captain of a ghostly derelict knew. And one of them had hurt him.

Tal took an unsteady step backward, and Athlen reached out and tugged on the cuff of Tal's sleeve.

"I will," he said again. "I will find you and answer all your questions. But not today."

Then he cocked his head to the side and smiled, wide and happy. His brown eyes caught the high sunlight, sparking amber, and he let Tal go.

"Good-bye, Tal."

Tal nodded, turned on his heel, and walked out. As Athlen closed the door, Dara instructed him to burn the root while she made the tea. Their voices faded behind him as Tal fumbled his way to the main street, Athlen's declaration echoing in the hollow of his chest.

He had no doubt he'd see Athlen again.

3

Tally spent the afternoon with a boy?" Garrett asked, grinning widely. "Alone?"

"I was in the market," Tal grumbled. "There were hundreds of people around."

Shay laughed, her head thrown back, brown eyes creased shut. She nudged Tal with her shoulder. "Nice try. You sneaked away and shook me." She punched his arm. "I can't believe you had it in you."

Tal rubbed his arm and mouthed an expletive. Shay chuckled, then took a bite of bread.

After leaving Athlen with Dara, Tal had followed the sound of the sea back to the market, where Shay was waiting for him. Her relief at finding him outweighed her anger, and when Tal explained where he'd been, her relief gave away to amusement. Escorting him back to the ship, Shay teased him the entire way and wouldn't listen to Tal's pleas not to tell Garrett. She spilled the whole story as soon as they stepped into Garrett's captain's quarters.

Garrett looked entirely too pleased about everything, and Tal buried his face in his hands, elbows propped up on the roughhewn table in front of them. The ship rocked gently at the dock, Tal's soup rippling with the waves.

"I don't want to talk about it."

Garrett leered. "Do we *need* to have a talk about it?"

"No!" Tal wanted to sink into the floor. No. He'd *had* that talk. His tutor had given it to him, and then Kest had expounded on it and . . . it was mortifying. "Nothing happened, anyway."

Garrett's eyebrows shot up. "Did you want something to happen?"

"Oh my gods, can you not?"

Shay ruffled his hair. "Aw, little Tally. Your first crush on your coming-of-age. Cute! I remember my first crush."

"Everyone knows your first crush," Garrett said, pointing his spoon at her. "You still have it."

Shay winked and brushed her straight brown hair over her shoulder. "You're right, and I'm going to make my move someday. Just you wait."

Garrett grinned, but before he could say whatever tawdry joke was on his tongue, Tal shot to his feet. "I need air." Stepping around the table, Tal abandoned his dinner and left Garrett's quarters.

He didn't go far. He crossed the deck and leaned on the railing, staring out over the water and at the port city spread in front of them. The seaside market had been packed away, the shore empty where it had been teeming hours before. Lanterns hung lit in the windows of the buildings. On the cobblestone streets Tal spied the start of fires for the night, and music and laughter from a tavern wafted on the breeze.

What was Athlen doing? Was he still with Dara and her mother? Or had he sneaked off to wherever he called home? Would he keep his promise and find Tal and tell him everything? Or would he disappear on the morning tide?

Athlen was a mystery, one that Tal couldn't figure out. It bothered him that he hadn't demanded Athlen come with him back to the ship, instead allowing him potentially to wander away. Garrett wanted that information. Tal wasn't quite sure why, but a chest of gold and a ship filled with untested sailors surely had a story behind it.

Lost in thought, Tal didn't notice the brown hunting bird that settled on the railing until it chirped at him. Tal jumped and staggered backward, while the bird chirped again and bobbed its head as if laughing. Tal smiled when he saw the familiar black eyes rimmed with gold and the brown spotted feathers along its back.

"Kest!"

The bird ruffled its feathers and fluffed its wings.

"I'll get Garrett."

"No need, I heard you." Garrett tromped out of his quarters, a robe in hand. The bird hopped down onto the deck, and Garrett tossed the garment on its head. "Hello, brother."

The bird squawked a complaint. The fabric squirmed and lumped and grew taller, and within a few moments a man stood where the bird once was. He slid his arms through the robe and tied it at the waist.

"Kest!" Tal said again, throwing his arms around his brother in a hug. "What are you doing here?"

Kest returned the hug warmly, his shoulder-length brown hair brushing against Tal's cheek. Kest was taller by several inches, and fine boned, with a large hooked nose and a small mouth outlined with a trim dark beard. His black eyes rimmed in yellow caught the sinking sun and crinkled at the corners when he grinned. He was closer in age to Garrett, but he'd always had time for Tal, and if Tal were forced to choose which one of his siblings he was closest to, it would be him. It helped that Kest possessed a kind of magic as well.

Kest ruffled Tal's hair. "Mother received your letter and sent me to check in."

Rolling his eyes, Garrett slapped Kest hard on the back. "He's fine. It was nothing."

"It was something," Shay said, stepping forward, blush high on her cheeks. "Hello, Prince Kesterell."

"Shay," he replied.

Disentangling from Tal, Kest straightened his robe and tightened the knot. A love-sick blush spread across the bridge of his nose.

"You didn't need to travel all this way. I have Tally under control."

Tal huffed.

Kest grinned. "It wasn't far for me."

"Well, you can have a brief rest and fly home."

"Are you trying to get rid of me, Garrett?"

Garrett crossed his arms. "No, but I don't appreciate the implication that I cannot look after the queen's precious youngest son."

Kest laughed. He gripped Garrett's shoulder. "There's no doubt that you can. I made the suggestion to come, and Mother approved it. To be honest, Isa's betrothed and his retinue have arrived at the castle, and I needed a break from the pretentiousness."

Garrett shrugged off Kest's hand, but his smile was genuine. "Pompous ass, is he?"

"You have no idea."

"Come along, then." Garrett gestured for Kest and Tal to follow him to the captain's quarters. "Have some soup and tell us all about it."

Shay lingered at the door and bowed out. "I'll leave you to your brothers for the night."

"Good night, Shay," Tal called, waving from the edge of Garrett's bed.

She smiled and closed the door behind her.

Garrett rubbed his hands together. "Tell us all the gossip, Kest."

Kest settled at the table and ladled out a bowl of soup. Forgoing a spoon, he brought it to his lips and sipped. After a slurp he dabbed at his mouth with the edge of his sleeve.

"Well, they arrived in a string of six gilded carriages surrounded by half their kingdom's knights, in an obvious show of wealth and power. The prince and his older sister rode separately, and not to speak badly of other royals, but I now know why. She's about as warm as a snow-fed lake."

Princess Vanessa. Tal's tutor talked about her. She was renowned for her beauty, her paintings, and her singing voice, but not much else. As the second child of Ossetia, she'd have no claim to their throne, even if something happened to her older brother. Ossetia didn't hold their women in as high regard as Harth.

"Is she nice to look at?" Garrett asked.

Tal heaved a sigh but said nothing.

"She's beautiful, but she's made it quite clear that she has no interest in our court. She said as much, to my face, right after we met."

Garrett snickered. "That sounds about right."

"With the number of jewels on her hands and the silver in her hair, it's no wonder Ossetia is fighting with Mysten over the mines along the border. They need the material and the wealth for her wardrobe alone, not to mention the rest of the Ossetian retinue."

"They don't sound as desperate as they make out to be."

Brushing back a lock of hair from his cheek, Kest took another gulp of soup, completely ignoring Garrett. "I don't know how Isa is going to suffer Prince Emerick. He has all the bearings of royalty but with none of the tact or aptitude."

"She cultivated the match herself. She knows what she's getting into."

Kest huffed. "He thinks of my gift as a parlor trick, despite Isa educating him otherwise."

"What do you expect from a kingdom with no magic at all?" Garrett said with a shrug. "He's bound to be curious."

"He tries to feed me treats."

Garrett barked a laugh, and Tal hid a smile behind his hand.

"Well," Garrett said with every ounce of diplomacy he had, "it is rather amusing to watch, especially when you're grumpy and your feathers puff out."

Kest narrowed his eyes. "Remind me to bite you next time I have a beak."

"Why don't you bite Emerick next time he asks you to shift?"

Kest's thin lips curled at the corners. "Good idea. I'll tell Isa it was all yours."

"Better not." Garrett scratched his beard. "We need the alliance. Their kingdom is rich, and our coffers are dwindling with the reparations we pay to the continent kingdoms. We can't afford for Emerick to scurry away because of a bite from one of Isa's magical brothers."

Tal bowed his head, Dara's accusations ringing in his ears. Their great-grandfather had made a mess of things between Harth and the rest of the world. This marriage was one of the many steps his mother and sister had taken to try and repair diplomatic relations. Of course, it didn't help that the queen had a magical son who bore the same talents as the man who'd started a devastating war. The mere rumor of Tal's magic was enough to threaten their alliance. He picked at a loose thread from Garrett's plush blanket.

"True. But if they break our alliance, they'll sorely miss our soldiers when their border disputes with Mysten flare up again. Though not as much as we'll miss their gold."

"Speaking of, tell Prince Emerick that we found a chest of gold stamped with an old crest on a ghost ship in the bay. See if he knows anything about it."

Kest raised an eyebrow. "A chest of gold?"

"Yes. Uncirculated, at that, going by its condition. The prisoner they left behind didn't say much before he threw himself off the stern."

Tal shifted uncomfortably.

Garrett winced apologetically. He tipped back his drink and downed a large gulp.

"There's more to the story than that," Kest said, sharp gaze darting between them.

"Tally cried."

"Hey!" Tal protested, mortified. "You don't have to tell *everyone*."

"I think Mother gathered that you were upset from the letter. Don't worry," he hastened to add as Tal paled, "she didn't show it to me. She may have also mentioned the gold to Emerick. He did say something about a lost wedding gift."

"Oh." Garrett stroked his beard. "That makes sense. Uncirculated gold from their treasury would be an appropriate present to the kingdom. Not so much to Isa."

"And not so much if it never arrived. Was it pirates?"

"According to the prisoner, it was on the seafloor. But I'm not sure I believe him. More than likely, the ship delivering it was set upon."

Kest drank more of his soup. "I see."

"Fucking marauders." Garrett slammed his empty cup down, leftover droplets splattering on the rough tabletop. "I wish I could scour the sea of them."

Kest's lips twitched. "Maybe one day when you're not taking our little brother on his coming-of-age tour."

Garrett and Kest laughed, and Tal bowed his head. His throat tightened. "Does Emerick know about me?"

"No," Kest said quickly. "He's no doubt heard the rumors, but we've confirmed nothing."

"It seems wrong to hide my talents from our brother-in-law."

"He's not married to Isa yet." Garrett wagged his finger at Tal. "Knowing about you may scare him away." He said it as a jest, though Tal didn't take it as one.

"Or entice him," Kest said. "A magical brother-in-law would be a formidable political weapon."

Garrett kicked Kest under the table. "No matter which it would be, we need this alliance."

"And when he does become part of our family," Kest hurriedly added, throwing Garrett an annoyed look, "we'll all agree about how and when to tell him. You won't have to be a secret forever, Tally."

Tal furrowed his brow. He opened his palm and a small flame

flickered over his hand. "I'm not Great-Grandfather."

Kest and Garrett exchanged a glance. "No one thinks you are, Tally," Kest said, voice soft and sincere. "But he did horrible things, and you've unfortunately been burdened with the same gift."

"It wasn't the magic that made him cruel, and anyone who knows you wouldn't believe you capable of the things he did," Garrett added.

"But I *can* do them." Tal curled his fingers and snuffed out the flame. Smoke wreathed around his fist. "I'm capable."

"We're aware," Kest said softly.

Tal didn't think they were. Only his mother and his tutor knew the full extent of his power, knew the times where it burst out of him, violent and terrifying, unpredictable and abundant. It scared Tal how easily he could destroy without thinking. Guilt rose in his gut at their blind faith. He might have promised he'd never use it to harm anyone, but he also knew that Isa was his queen and she could command it of him. His magic was there to serve the family, and once she married Emerick, that would include him as well.

"I'm tired," Tal said, shaking out his hand. "I'm going to read in my hammock."

"It was all that running around today," Garrett said with a grin. At Kest's perplexed look, Garrett added, "Tally shook Shay today and met with a boy in the market."

Kest's grin turned lascivious. "A boy in the market, huh? You've been gone from the castle for only a few days and are already embracing your coming-of-age."

Tal groaned. "Not you, too."

Kest and Garrett knocked their mugs of wine together and laughed.

"I'm leaving," Tal said.

"Good night, Tally!"

"Sweet dreams of market boy."

Tal shook his head in disbelief and closed the door behind him with more force than was necessary. He stomped his way across the deck to the port side, which overlooked the long expanse of sea. The sun had sunk below the horizon, and the last few rays of orange threw sparkles along the water. The stars slowly winked into existence in the darkening sky.

"Fools," Tal murmured. He leaned on the railing and scowled down at the depths of the ocean.

They didn't understand. They never would. Innate magic like his had disappeared from the world. The few mages that existed had been targeted and killed by King Lon to secure himself as the only power. Their knowledge had been lost, except for a few singed scrolls that had somehow survived his great-grandfather's purge. Now there was only Tal, the last mage, withering while in hiding. The rare shifters who existed were adopted into the noble houses, their gifts incorporated into the royal families.

His great-grandfather had been the last mage born of fire, like Tal, and had been unmatched in his power, able to set the continent under siege with the strength of his flames. Unopposed, King Lon had marched across the land, scorching those who stood in his way, dismantling kingdoms, and creating a legacy of fire and fear.

Tal was his direct descendant and carried the burden of his heritage. Athlen had asked if he was the only mage, the last of magic, and as far as he knew, he was.

If the other kingdoms learned of his magic, they'd demand his mother relinquish him to their mercy. They'd kill him, no matter the claims of his soft heart, to spare the continent from another ravage of fire. Out of fear for his life, his mother had hidden him away, claiming a weak constitution. It didn't stop the rumors, but it tempered them.

He'd heard a story once, when he was a child, of a mage who disappeared into the water during the height of his great-grandfather's wrath. She begged asylum in the source of her power, hoping to outlast the fire that ruled the land. Tal believed her a myth, a child's story no more real than unicorns and mermaids. Even if she had existed and survived, she would hate the descendant of the man who'd driven her into hiding, who'd forced her to leave her home and dwell in the depths of the sea.

The sound of a splash drew Tal's attention toward the bow. He moved down the railing and spied a swirl in the otherwise calm water. Squinting, Tal thought he saw a flash of red and gold, but he dismissed it as the wilting colors of the sinking sun dappling the ocean's surface.

Tal pushed away from the railing and went down into the belly of the ship to his hammock strung in the hold. After kicking off his boots, Tal hopped into his makeshift bed and settled on his blanket. The gentle rhythm of the water was a lullaby, and he drifted off to sleep with a vision of dimpled cheeks, sly smiles, and sun-kissed freckles following him into his dreams.

The following day started like all the others—with breakfast in Garrett's cabin with Shay and Garrett. Kest had flown away with the sunrise, back to the castle and his duties there. He completed one wide, lazy loop around the main mast of the ship and released a sharp cry before heading in the direction of home.

With the ship docked, only a skeleton crew was needed to oversee operations, and the rest of the sailors were off spending their coin in the port.

"Today we tour the city," Shay said with an encouraging smile. "We'll spend tonight here, and then tomorrow we'll take a carriage inland."

Tal waved his spoon. "Whatever."

"That's the spirit!" Garrett said, slapping Tal on the shoulder. "We'll tour the town and find a good tavern to spend our evening."

Tal hid a twinge as Dara's accusations echoed in his hears. They stung, but they did give him an idea. "There's a sickness in the lower town."

"Then we'll stay away from the lower town."

"What? No," Tal said, shaking his head. "We should do something about it. It's a lung condition. There are some ingredients that treat the symptoms. We should buy them and hand them out."

Shay's eyebrows rose. "That's how you want to spend your day?"

"Yes," Tal said with an authoritative nod. "Yes. That is how I want to spend my day."

Shay and Garrett shared a glance. "Okay, then. If you're sure."

"I am. I know the place to begin. Join me on the deck in ten minutes or I'll start on my own."

Tal stood and left the remnants of his breakfast. With warmth blooming in his middle, he hopped lightly down the steps to his hammock in the empty hold. He rummaged in his chest and pulled out his princely attire and changed. He wore a fine ruffled shirt overlaid with a brocade vest, and trousers cut to hug his legs. After stepping into his glossy boots, he fussed with his hair, sweeping it to one side, then abandoning it altogether when strands continued to fall into his face. He told himself the prepping had nothing to do with the possibility of seeing Athlen, and more with presenting the face of a prince who cared about his people.

Speaking of, Tal found the shirt he'd worn the previous day in the market and fished out the shark's tooth. He held it in the palm of his hand. There wasn't anything special about it at all, but just the same, Tal slid it into his breast pocket.

For the first time since they'd left home, Tal had a purpose. He liked the idea of helping others. Not only was it the right thing to do—he did have a duty to his subjects, after all—but he liked the idea of proving Dara and the villagers wrong. His family *were* concerned with their people, and they were doing their best to effect change at a high level, but Tal could understand how that might not come across to the common folk. He'd help change that today.

Finished, Tal bent to retrieve his book from where it had fallen from his hammock, and that's when he heard footsteps. The back of his neck prickled, and he spun to find one of the sailors observing him.

Unnerved, Tal cleared his throat. "Is there a problem?"

The sailor—Tal didn't know his name—stalked forward. His skin was tanned from the sun, evidence of many voyages, and he squinted at Tal, studying him.

"You may act like a prince," he said, his voice grating like the drag of wooden crates over the stone pathways near the castle. "But I know what you really are."

"And what am I?" Tal was proud his voice came out calm and even, despite the shiver of fear that wound its way down his spine.

The sailor's lips pulled back in a sneer, revealing rows of yellowed and broken teeth. "A perversion. You'll destroy us all."

Tal blanched. "How dare you address me in such a way. My brother will hear—"

The sailor closed the distance between them and pressed an arm across Tal's chest, a short dagger, no longer than Tal's thumb, clenched in his fist. Tal's heart slammed against his ribs. His magic swelled and burned, and he lit up from the inside. Struggling, Tal tamped it down and instead drew on the training the castle knights had given him as a child. He remained still and looked for an opening to escape. The edge of the knife grazed Tal's cheek, rasping across the stubble he hadn't shaved, and the man's fetid breath washed over him, setting his head spinning.

"You don't frighten me," Tal said.

"You should be frightened. The blood of your family line should not be allowed to continue, let alone pollute the other kingdoms. All of you should be dead, but especially you. I'll not allow you to—"

"Tally!" Garrett's voice drifted from above. "Your self-imposed ten minutes are up."

The sailor's gaze flickered toward the stairs. His distraction was the opening Tal needed. He lashed out and kicked the man in the knee. The knife nicked his cheek, but it was enough for Tal to get away. He ran for the stairs, yelling for Garrett as he went.

Shay met him at the top and took in his distress. She grabbed his upper arms.

"What happened?"

Tal pointed down. "There's a man. He attacked me with a knife and—"

Shay shoved him toward Garrett and drew her sword, just as the sailor sprinted up the steps and toward the ramp to the port. Shay lit after him, chasing him to the dock, and overtaking him with her superior speed.

Tal turned his head away when she engaged the sailor, knowing the bloody outcome.

"Are you all right?" Garrett asked, tilting Tal's face up. "He cut you."

"I'm fine," Tal said, chest heaving. "I don't think he was going to hurt me. He wanted to scare me." He wasn't sure that was the truth.

"What did he say?"

Tal gulped. "He said I was a perversion and that our whole family should be dead, especially me."

Frowning, Garrett wiped the blood away with a handkerchief. "Tally, that doesn't sound like he only wanted to scare you."

"He knew. He had to have seen or—"

"He probably heard about our plans for the day and didn't approve of you sowing your oats with the townspeople."

Shaking his head, Tal hid the trembling of his hands. "No. That can't be all. He said I'd destroy everyone. He said my blood would pollute the other kingdoms. He *knew*."

Garrett pulled Tal into a reassuring embrace. "Rumors," Garrett said. "They're rumors. No one knows for sure." Garrett didn't sound convinced. "No more sneaking off, though. Shay will stay with you at all times."

Tal nodded. As much as he hated to admit it, pressing his face into Garrett's shoulder was comforting. His pulse slowed, and he only slightly startled when Shay reappeared, wiping blood from her sword with the handkerchief Garrett passed her.

"Report."

"I wounded him while in pursuit, but he threw himself off the dock into the sea. He didn't resurface. The blood trail was significant."

"Dead or will be soon," Garrett said with a nod. "Food for the fish."

"Are you okay, Tally?" Shay asked. She cupped his chin and turned his head, gazing hard at the cut. "That must have been frightening."

With a breath Tal regained his composure. He pulled away from Shay and Garrett and straightened his shoulders. His cheek stung, and he swiped his palm over the cut. "I'm fine. I wish to continue with our plans."

"Are you sure? You don't want to find a tavern and hole up for the day? Rest?"

"No," Tal said. "The day has only started, and I am not going to waste it because of a miscreant with bad breath."

Shay smiled, and Garrett laughed. "Okay, brother. Where do we start?"

Tal led them to Dara's house, losing his way only once. He waved them back when he knocked on the door, unsure of his reception. The door swung inward on creaky hinges, and Dara appeared, hair pulled back under a cloth and cheeks smudged with ash from a cooking fire.

"He's not here," she said. "He left last night."

"I'm not looking for him," Tal said, blushing hotly as her gaze swept over him. She crossed her arms in the doorway. "I'm looking for you."

That caught her by surprise, and Tal reveled in it. She looked over his shoulder, and her eyes widened at the sight of Shay and Garrett.

"Why?"

"You know what items will best help the people affected by the sickness in this part of town. I'd like for you to tell me, so I can buy them and hand them out to those who need them."

She looked around. "Are you serious?"

"Yes."

"Oh," she said, then narrowed her eyes. "This won't endear you to me or to him."

"That's not my goal," Tal answered smoothly. "You weren't wrong yesterday. Sometimes we don't know what's happening in the kingdom until it's too late, but I know now. I want to help."

"I can dictate a list."

"Thank you."

"I'd invite you in, but . . ." She leaned in, and Tal heard the unmistakable sound of Shay moving closer, her sword clinking at her side—"your bodyguard looks murderous."

"She's overprotective," Tal said with a grin.

"Does it have to do with your cheek? You're bleeding."

Tal touched the cut, and his fingertips came away stained red. He pulled out a handkerchief and dabbed at the wound. "No, that's another matter. Anyway, I have a scrap of parchment in my pocket. Do you think you could let your neighbors know to come to the square near the seaside market if they need any of the supplies?"

"Yes, of course, Your Highness." She dipped into a curtsy and Tal laughed.

"He was right, you know, I'm not fussy."

"You're dressed in clothes more expensive than my home." She sobered. "I still think your family is arrogant and out of touch, but you might not be so bad."

"I'll take that as a compliment."

After acquiring a quill, Tal wrote down the items: beeswax; an assortment of oils, including peppermint and lavender and gingerroot. They left Dara, Tal waving over his shoulder as he led Garrett and Shay toward the market. Together they bought the items required with royal gold, leaving many a happy shopkeeper in their wake. For the rest of the day they passed out the remedies to the families who needed them. Shay stood watch the entire time, hand on her sword, scowl on her face, but nothing happened.

When the last of the root was handed off, Tal realized he'd forgotten to look for Athlen in the crowd. He hadn't expected Athlen to approach them, especially since Garrett stood close to Tal's side, but he'd been so caught up in his task, he hadn't had a chance to look for him on the outskirts of the crowd.

Disappointed, Tal dusted off his hands and managed a weak smile. "That was the last of it. Thank you both for helping."

"You're welcome, Tally. It was a good thing to do." Garrett slung his arm around Tal's shoulders, ruffling his hair gently.

Shay didn't agree, if the expression on her face was any indication, but she kept her opinion to herself.

"Now please tell me you've worked up a thirst."

Tal laughed. "Yes, I have. And a hunger."

"Excellent. There is a tavern right over there, and it is calling our name." Garrett tugged on Tal's arm. "Come along."

"Do the princes really think that after what happened this morning, even more time in the open is wise? And around drunkards, no less?"

"Tally's fine," Garrett said with a dismissive wave of his hand. "He did a good deed today. He deserves a drink and a fun time."

Shay rubbed her brow. "Please don't get too drunk," she said. "I don't think I can handle the pair of you."

"Relax, Shay. Nothing is going to happen."

"Someone tried to kill Tally this morning. Or don't you remember?"

"Someone tried to *scare* Tally this morning. If he'd wanted him dead, he would be."

Tal flinched. "That's not comforting, Garrett."

"I'm sorry. But you know what is comforting? Mead and ale and . . . companionship."

Tal's cheeks burned. He held up a finger. "No."

Garrett headed to the nearest tavern, walking backward, mouth in a wide, toothy smile. "Maybe we'll find you a friend for the night."

"Garrett—"

"I know it's no boy from the market."

Tal hid his face in his hands, mortified, and muttered, "Oh gods."

"But there might be a boy or girl here that will catch your fancy."

They stopped briefly in front of the tavern, and Garrett pried Tal's hands away from his face. The tavern appeared to be the oldest structure on the block. Made of stone, it sat between two wooden buildings that appeared to use its outer walls as part of their own structures. A wooden sign hanging over the door depicted two overflowing tankards. Despite its being only early evening, the crowd inside was raucous, the noise drifting into the street from the shuttered windows. From the sounds of it, the taverngoers were already well into their cups.

"You're a prince of Harth. Don't hide your handsome face." Garrett cocked his head in consideration. "Even if you can't grow a decent beard yet."

Before Tal could muster a retort, Garrett pushed open the wooden door and walked inside. Tal followed, with Shay close at his heels. He immediately winced at the noise level that reverberated within the stone walls. The building was two stories, with a long wooden bar and tables set up in the two front rooms. In the back was a kitchen, and the smell of stew made Tal's stomach growl. All they'd eaten for lunch was a bit of bread and an apple that a grateful townsperson had provided.

Unfortunately, as soon as they made their way to a table, the noise abruptly died, except for an unearthly caterwauling coming from the other room. Garrett ignored the crowd and pulled out a chair, the scrape of wood across the floor uncommonly loud in the silence. Cautiously Tal followed suit.

"Don't mind us," Garrett bellowed, taking a gold piece from his purse and flipping it toward the bar, "we're only here to buy you all a round."

That earned a few cheers, and the chatter slowly resumed, though the overall air around them remained suspicious and tense. Tal could feel the stares crawling over his skin.

"I'll order us some dinner," Shay said, hand on the hilt of her sword.

Tal stood. "No, I'll do it."

"Are you sure?"

Tal puffed out his chest, the tips of his ears going hot with indignation. "I think I can buy us food. You may come find me if I'm not back in ten minutes."

"Five," Shay replied flatly. "Five minutes. Ten minutes almost saw you killed this morning."

Tal slammed his hands on the table and pushed his chair back. He stalked off, chin lifted as he maneuvered through the maze of chairs and tables until he made it to the bar. He waited a moment to grab the barmaid's attention, but once she caught a glimpse of him, she abandoned the conversation she was having with another patron. She was older, and pretty, her blond hair falling around her shoulders in waves. Her eyebrow arched, and her smile turned sultry as she sashayed over to him, her skirt swishing, and the strap of her top falling off her shoulder. Tal averted his gaze and focused on the row of glasses sparkling behind her in the lantern light.

"What will it be, love?"

"Dinner for three." He nodded to Garrett, who was already halfway through a tankard that another maid had brought him. Shay watched him, her fingers tented on the table, her gaze steady.

"Sure thing." The barmaid's gaze roved over him, and she cocked a hip. "Anything else you want? I'm sure we can accommodate."

"No," Tal said. He pulled out a gold coin and set it on the bar. Her eyes widened. "In fact, if you keep the mead and food flowing, and promise not to bring up any other forms of entertainment for the night, this whole piece is yours."

He pushed it across the polished wood, and as soon as he lifted his finger, she had the coin stashed away.

"Royal stamp," she breathed. Then she curtsied and winked. "Your wish is my command, Your Highness."

"Thank you."

"So," she continued once all pretense of potential companionship was gone, "which one are you? Aren't there seven of you?"

"Five," Tal corrected. "And I'm the fourth."

"The sickly one. Figures," she said, pushing away. "Of course the second to last would find his way into my tavern." Tal bit back that Garrett was second in line, as that would only spur her on. "Oh well, we'll see you and your guards are well taken care of." She waved her hand, dismissing him, and Tal wasn't sure how to gauge their interaction. He'd been flirted with and insulted in the span of a few moments. Life outside the castle was confusing, and he started to miss the routine and machinations of the court.

Tal took a step toward his table but was distracted by the sound of a familiar voice. Craning his neck, he glimpsed a figure in the adjoining room, sitting on a table, empty mug in his hand, singing suggestive lyrics about sea foam.

As Tal inched toward the commotion, the young man jumped to his bare feet and spun around, stumbling to a halt when he saw Tal peering through the doorway.

Athlen met Tal's gaze and gave him a wide and tipsy smile before bowing dramatically at the waist. "My prince!"

Tal grimaced. "Oh no."

5

Tal's eyes widened, and his heart pounded double time as Athlen tipped back the last swig of his mead, his throat bobbing. The long column of his neck was bare to the lantern light, and Tal swore he saw the markings he'd seen before on the deck of the ship.

Athlen beckoned him into the other room as he continued to sing.

He was undoubtedly the kingdom's worst siren, but Tal was compelled to follow. Knowing Shay's eyes were upon him, Tal glanced around. He found an empty tin cup on the table near his hip, and he discreetly picked it up. With a quick look, he tossed it over his shoulder toward the corner where Shay and Garrett sat. He didn't see where it hit or landed, but the loud shouts and the curses told him it had provided the distraction he needed, and

Tal slipped into the room where Athlen danced and yowled like a fool.

"Tal!" he greeted, throwing his arms open wide. "Meet my friends."

The group around him clapped and snickered when Tal moved toward them.

"Athlen," Tal said, voice low and urgent. "Get down! My brother is in the other room, and if he sees you—"

"Leave him alone," a gruff voice around the table interrupted. "He ain't hurting anyone."

Athlen plopped down on his backside, causing the table to rattle, then pressed a finger to his lips. "Shhh. He's just trying to be nice, though he's bad at it."

Tal sputtered, "I am not bad at being nice!"

Athlen winked.

Ruffled, Tal straightened his shoulders. "Fine, but if my brother sees you, then he's going to drag you back to our ship and you really will be a prisoner."

Tal turned on his heel.

"Wait!" There was a clatter and a strange curse in a language Tal didn't know, but one word sounded like "swordfish." "Don't go!"

Tal spun around in time to see Athlen jump off the table and keep falling. Tal lunged and wrapped his hand around Athlen's elbow, then hauled him upright. Athlen laughed as he fell into Tal's chest, forehead lolling on Tal's collarbone. He patted Tal's shoulder, and the warmth of his touch scorched Tal even through the layer of his shirt. He could scarcely stop himself from arching into it as Athlen's fingers tightly curled over the joint.

He moved to step away, but Athlen stumbled again, and his

weight almost took them both to the floor. Tal managed to twist and right them both, his arm around Athlen's waist while Athlen held on like an octopus. This close, he smelled of mead and the sea, and his eyes flashed their strange amber brown in the lantern light.

His shocked expression morphed into a flirty grin. "You really are a prince."

Tal rolled his eyes and shrugged Athlen off but kept a hand hovering nearby in case he fell. His gait was clumsy, and he moved loosely, like his bones didn't quite belong in his skin. Despite his walk, Athlen swiped a tankard off a table and finished the contents in one long gulp.

"You," he said, dropping the tankard to the stone floor, the clay cracking. He pointed a finger into Tal's chest. "You," he said again, "are entirely too soft to be a prince. In fact"—Athlen poked Tal's chest a little harder—"are you sure you are who you say you are?"

Tal slapped the finger away. He took a step back and tugged on the hem of his vest to straighten it from Athlen's pawing. The question scrubbed against an old wound, one that Tal had constantly attempted to bandage but that always betrayed him. A wound that had been reopened when his soft heart led him to free a stranger, only to plunge him into despair over the belief that he'd been responsible for the stranger's death.

"How dare you question my parentage," Tal snapped, anger and shame welling thick and hot in the back of his throat. "You're acting entirely too familiar for someone I barely know. I warned you once about my brother. And the longer I take to return to my table, the higher the chance that my bodyguard will come investigate, and then you'll surely be caught."

"I don't think I like the idea of a royal brat threatening my new friend," said the man from before. He stood and balled his fists.

"I'm leaving," Tal said. He nodded to Athlen. "You should too."

Athlen's expression fell. He took another drunken step and reached out, but he curled his fingers in when he met Tal's hard gaze. With a sigh Athlen scooped up the broken tankard and picked at the crack with a torn thumbnail.

"Until later," he said, smile brittle.

Tal didn't answer because he didn't know what he could say that could salvage their interaction. His temper had gotten the better of him when Athlen plucked at his weakness, and he'd alienated the one person whom he longed to connect with. Ashamed in the face of Athlen's brokenhearted expression, Tal turned away. Without a word he fled.

Cheeks flushed, he danced his way through tables and patrons and sat heavily next to Garrett and Shay. His stew was waiting for him alongside a tankard of mead. He shoveled a spoonful of the stew into his mouth and followed it with a long drag of the honey wine.

"Are you all right, Tally? What took you so long?"

"Nothing," Tal said, ducking his head. He stuck his spoon in and concentrated on inhaling the lukewarm, stringy rabbit meat and the wilted vegetables.

"Tal," Shay said, "is it about this morning?"

Tal frowned. "No. It's not about this morning. It's about yesterday."

Garrett's eyebrows shot up. A barmaid swayed over to Garrett's side, and he wrapped a friendly arm around her. The laces of her shirt were stretched and close to snapping, and her cleavage was right at Garrett's eye level. Garrett tickled her side, but he stayed focused on Tal. "The boy from the market?"

"Maybe." The mead slid down Tal's throat, delicious and soothing, and between the lack of food, the influx of alcohol, and his embarrassed anger, Tal went light-headed. He suddenly understood the appeal of overindulging.

"Is he here?" Garrett craned his neck to look around.

"He left," Tal said. After draining the last of his drink, he slammed his mug down and swiped his sleeve across his mouth. His chest heaved. He addressed the maid. "Another."

Shay was spinning her dagger on the edge on the table in a game only she knew how to play, but with Tal's demand she allowed it to clatter to the wood. "Are you sure?"

Tal nodded vigorously. "Yes. Isn't that what this whole experience is supposed to be about? I'm supposed to get drunk and entangled with boys and girls, instead of trying to be nice to villagers."

Shay's eyes widened. "Tally . . . what did this boy say to you? This doesn't sound like you."

"Well, what if it does now? What if this is me coming of age?"

Garrett gently pushed the barmaid away and gave her a conciliatory smile. "Tally," he said once she'd moved to the next table and found another patron.

"My name is Tal. I don't understand why you can't get that through your thick skull."

"Okay, that's enough. You've been nothing but moody since we left the castle. I know you're upset about . . . things . . . ," Garrett said, trailing off.

Tal scoffed. Things. *Things.* Things like the secret of his magic and the crushing weight of his legacy and the fact that his mere existence could threaten his sister's wedding and their alliance with Ossetia. *Things* that preyed on Tal's mind in the dark, things that separated him from his family and marked him as truly alone.

Garrett continued, "But I'm doing my best. I know I'm not Kest, and I know we have little in common, and—"

Tal groaned. "Please don't make this about your rivalry with Kest."

"I don't have a rivalry with Kest."

Shay dropped her dagger again. "Oh, please, Commander. You two have always tried to one-up each other."

"That's not true."

Tal slurped down the remnants of his stew as Shay and Garrett argued. Once done, Tal pushed away from the table.

"I'm going back to the ship."

"We were going to stay in town tonight and get an early start with the carriage in the morning."

"Have you found a place to stay yet?"

Garrett shrugged. "We can stay anywhere. We have enough gold."

"So, no, you have not procured us a bed in town for the night. What if all the beds are taken? What if I want to go to bed right now?"

"No one is going to turn royalty away. Tal, please."

The blatant privilege made Tal's stomach turn. He put his hands on his hips and rolled his eyes heavenward. "I'm going back to the ship. The carriage can come get me in the morning."

Shay pushed away from the table. "I'll walk with you."

Tal crinkled his nose. "No."

"Tal, you were attacked this morning by someone. Be reasonable."

"Fine," he said. "You can walk twenty paces behind me. No closer."

Shay raised her hands. "Fine, but take this." She sheathed the dagger and unbuckled the belt. "In case I can't cover the twenty paces fast enough."

Grudgingly, Tal took the dagger. He strapped it around his waist, cinching the belt tight. Shay stayed in her seat as Tal made his way to the exit. The sun had set, and the streets were dark, save for the nightly fires, when Tal stepped through the heavy wooden door. The corners and alleys of the city were shadowed, and Tal's hackles raised. Maybe he should've allowed Shay to walk with him. Except she believed he couldn't take care of himself. The thought burned in his gullet.

He was magic. He had the same power of his great-grandfather thumping through his veins. He could raze cities and pull down kingdoms, grind them to dust under his boot heel. He could defend himself if someone decided to attack him, and he wouldn't leave the attacker alive to tell the tale that the youngest son of Queen Carys did indeed have the same magic that had set the world to siege.

Tal made it two steps before a cool hand stole over his mouth and yanked him backward into the shadows.

He let out a muffled shout and struggled against the strong hands that held him. He had every intention of biting down on the fleshy part of the palm that was clapped over his mouth, until a soft voice tickled his ear.

"It's only me, my prince."

Tal ceased his struggle. Unwittingly he relaxed back into the hold.

Athlen released him.

"Shush," he said, "come with me." He picked his way across the street, sticking to darkened spaces, and beckoned Tal to follow. "I'll tell you everything you want to know."

Tal's earlier anger melted into curiosity.

"Everything?" he whispered as he followed Athlen into the shadows.

"Yes."

The colors of twilight played over Athlen's pale skin as he moved. He was ethereal, and for a moment Tal thought he looked as if he didn't belong on land at all and was a creature from the sea, more used to undulating in the waves and currents than slapping bare feet on the paving stones. Then Athlen smiled, his cheeks dimpling, his brown eyes shining, and Tal couldn't conjure poetic metaphors anymore. He could only feel the thump of his heartbeat and a fluttering in his middle that was not befitting a prince.

They took a meandering path through the city, sticking to clumps of shadows and dark alleys. Tal felt like he was in one of the court fairy tales, where the curious children are led away by nymphs and fairies to other worlds, never to be heard from again. He realized he couldn't hear the familiar rhythm of Shay's footsteps behind him, but he wasn't afraid. How could he be afraid of a boy who pleaded to be freed from an iron chain? Who didn't know the difference in value between a pearl and sea glass?

Tal followed Athlen toward the docks, his boot heels making hollow thumps on the wooden planks, loud in the otherwise stillness. Anchored to the shore, the docks stretched over the sand until they jutted into the water. Halfway to the rows of moored ships, Athlen hopped off the ledge into the sand. Tal paused, admiring the view of the ships underneath the twinkle of starlight, and took a deep breath of cool, salty air. The taut pull of his shoulders loosened as the stress from the town melted away in the peace of the shore.

The sound of the sea rolling against the beach filled Tal's head, as did the song Athlen hummed beneath his breath as he strolled farther away. He walked aimlessly, wandering along the line of the surf, foam spraying over his ankles, darkening his trousers to his knees. Athlen noticed Tal had not followed, and he stopped in the ebbing water, hands in his pockets, face tipped toward the sky.

"Tal," he called as he held out his hand, palm up and open, not taking his gaze from the stars, "come on."

A shiver of promise in the timbre of Athlen's voice gripped Tal. He had been so angry only scant minutes before, but the fire of his temper was banked, and now his blood pulsed with a different warmth. Tal sat down on the edge of the dock and pulled off his boots and socks and left them there. He jumped down, the cold, wet surf a shock to the bottoms of his feet, his toes sinking in the coarse mix of sand and shells.

"Where are we going?"

"Somewhere private where we can trade confidences," Athlen said, a tilt to his lips. "But only if you want to."

Tal crossed the distance between them quickly in answer and barely resisted the urge to grab Athlen's hand so as not to be left behind in the liminal space.

Tal couldn't fathom where they were going as they meandered away from the port, jumping across tidal pools and sidestepping sharp rocks as the water seeped into the higher ground. Tal's feet would be tender the following day, and he worried he might be trapped by the incoming tide later, but he dared not stop following.

They finally paused at the mouth of a small cave. Tal turned to look toward the town and could still see the masts of the ships in the distance under the light of the waxing moon, but they were far off, bobbing gently against the backdrop of the night sky.

"Almost there," Athlen said. He touched Tal's sleeve, and Tal turned his back on the ships and ducked beneath the low-hanging rock.

As Tal emerged on the other side, his breath caught. A small amount of light poured through a hole in the ceiling of the cave, sparkling along the rocks and illuminating a calm pool of water. A shelf ran along the edge, large enough for Tal to walk. Gold, jewels, and ocean glass glittered along the path.

"Don't mind the mess," Athlen said with a grin. "I wasn't expecting visitors."

"This is where you live?"

Athlen shrugged. "When I'm not with Dara or held prisoner by bad men."

"How long have you been here?"

"A few years."

Athlen sat on the shelf and dipped his feet into the pool. He patted the smooth space beside him, and Tal followed suit. The moon rippled across the water, and small fish inspected Tal's toes before darting away.

Squinting, Athlen leaned in close and poked Tal's cheek. "What happened?"

Tal barely controlled his flinch. "Nothing. Just a scratch." He picked a jewel from a pile and held it up, inspecting it as the dark red facets sparkled. "This is beautiful."

Athlen sighed. "When I lost my family, I tried to find things that reminded me of them. That one looks like my sister's tail."

"Her . . . tail?" Tal asked, squinting at the jewel. Had Athlen's sister been a shifter, like Kest?

Athlen rubbed his fingers over his brow and pushed his copper hair away from his eyes.

Tal leaned closer, their shoulders brushing, his pinky finger slotted alongside Athlen's own. "Why did those men have you?"

"I was their courier. They had a deal with some other land folk, and they needed me to retrieve their payment."

"The gold?"

"Yes," Athlen said with a sharp nod. "The gold."

Tal paused. That didn't make sense, not if Emerick was to be believed and the gold was a gift to the kingdom for Isa's hand. "Where was it?"

"I wasn't lying when I said it was in the Great Bay. The people who paid them didn't want to be implicated, so they dropped the gold to the bottom of the bay and gave those men the coordinates. For a long time they didn't know how to retrieve it, but then they discovered me and . . . well . . . you saw the chains."

Tal furrowed his brow. "I still don't understand."

"I'm not explaining it well."

"You did drink a bit."

Athlen chuckled, the sound of it echoing in the small space. "Hardly affected me."

"You were butchering the lyrics of several songs."

"I was singing."

"You were caterwauling."

Athlen laid a hand over his heart. "You wound me, my prince." He playfully knocked his shoulder into Tal's, then furrowed his brow. "I'm trying to explain. The men who had me, they were not sailors, but people who kill others for money."

"Mercenaries," Tal said. "Are you telling me that Ossetia paid for mercenaries?" Tal's middle sank. What was Isa marrying into? What was his family allying with?

"They couldn't sail well, but they found the coordinates."

"How could you get a chest of gold off the seafloor?"

Athlen blinked. "I swam."

"How?" Tal shook his head at Athlen's blank expression and continued, "And do you know what the money was meant for? What they were meant to do?"

"They didn't say. And the squall came and many of them drowned and others left in the small boats."

"And we found you. How did you survive jumping off the back of Garrett's ship? How did you swim all the way here?"

Athlen laughed, but it was without humor. "You still don't see? You're magic. You should know there are more things beyond the human understanding of the world." Athlen stood and pulled off his shirt, revealing the faint marks that ran up both sides of his torso. He unbuttoned his trousers and Tal looked away, a high flush working into his cheeks.

"What are you doing?" Tal's answer was a splash. Water droplets hit Tal's cheek, a cool contrast to the burn of his blush. "Is it safe to swim?"

"Of course," Athlen said.

"Are you certain? The sea acts strangely in small coves like this."

Athlen snorted. "I've lived here for years, but if you're worried, I'll come out."

Tal squeezed his eyes shut and held up a hand. "No. No, you're fine."

"You land folk and your modesty."

Tal felt a familiar mix of anger and embarrassment rush into his middle at Athlen's mockery, but the sentence didn't make sense. It was the second time he'd used the term "land folk."

"Land folk? Is that a kind of designation where you're from?" Despite his reticence, Tal risked a glance, then shot to his feet at the image before him. He stumbled backward, heels skidding on jewels and wet stone until his back hit the cave wall, jarring him. He shook his head, but it didn't change the picture of Athlen with his arms crossed on the low shelf, his long red-and-gold tail arched behind him.

Tal gasped. A merman! Athlen was a merman! Mermaids were myths and legends—women who sang beautiful songs and led sailors to their death or fortune, depending on the tale. Tal rubbed his eyes, but Athlen remained. He wasn't a hallucination from the honey wine Tal had drunk—he was as real as the shell digging into the bottom of Tal's foot.

The answers to Tal's questions slotted into place. The mercenaries had used Athlen to courier the gold because he could swim to the bottom of the sea and was strong enough to haul it to the surface. That's how he'd survived the jump off of Garrett's ship.

Even in his shock Tal couldn't deny Athlen's shape was beautiful. His fins floated long and delicate, gossamer thin as they swished in the shallow water. Tal had noticed before that Athlen's shoulders were broad, but propped up as he was, Tal could see the carved muscles of his upper body. His torso was strong from swimming, and it tapered down to his hips, where his skin fused with scales below the line of his navel. Athlen rolled to his back in the pool and put his webbed hands behind his head, showing Tal the marks along his ribs—his gills, which lay closed.

Tal didn't speak for several beats, studying the way Athlen's fins moved, how his red-and-gold scales reflected the moon, the power inherent in the line of his body, built for speed among the waves. Tal didn't know he had let the moment drag on too long until Athlen's expression shuttered and he crossed his arms over his body and slid down below the line of the water.

"I've never shown anyone," he said, face turned away, and Tal could see the smattering of scales along his neck and shoulders. "Dara knows what I am and has seen me swim, but I've not . . ." He gulped. "You're magic. I thought you'd understand, since you're the last too. Alone." Athlen's gaze flicked back to Tal, and his shoulders bobbed in a shrug. "I know I look strange. I shouldn't have—"

"No," Tal said quickly. "No, don't be . . . I've never met a merman. . . . I didn't mean to embarrass you. I just . . . you're beautiful."

Athlen's smile was like the sun breaking out between clouds. "You're not afraid?"

"Afraid?" Tal's heart beat like a jackrabbit, and his palms went slick with sweat. His body's reactions were akin to those when the sailor had him pinned that morning, but in a wholly different context. It was wonder and awe at being someone Athlen trusted with such a paradigm-altering secret. It was the explosion of possibilities he might find in the world now that a fairy tale had come to life before his eyes. "No, I don't think I could be afraid of you." *Only of everything else*, Tal thought, the memory of Athlen diving over the side of the ship still a wrench to his gut.

"I wanted to tell you," Athlen said. "But those men kept me in chains, then left me to die. Your brother acted the same, like he was set on keeping me, and I knew it would be worse if he knew what I was."

Tal blinked, remembering those moments in the hold when Athlen had touched him, pleaded with him, invoked Tal's promise on the condition of providing information to Garrett. It had all been an act. Tal frowned, angry and embarrassed at how easily Athlen had manipulated him. "You . . . you *tricked* me."

"A little," Athlen admitted. "I couldn't transform fully with that fetter on my ankle. I needed it off."

Tal swallowed hard, then dropped his voice to barely above a whisper. "You told me my magic was wonderful, and you kissed my palm." Tal pressed that same hand to his chest, where a pang of hurt lanced through him. "You told me you weren't afraid of me."

Athlen surged upward and pointed a webbed finger at Tal. "That was true!" he said, voice firm. "Tal, I wasn't afraid of you because of your magic. And I do think you're wonderful. That's the truth."

Tal didn't know what to say. A wave of emotions swirled within him, but the one that floated to the surface was joy that Athlen thought he was wonderful.

"I'm sorry." Athlen ducked his head and dropped his shoulders under the water, his chin submerged. "I really am. But I didn't know you or your brother, and I saw a chance to escape. I took it."

Tal couldn't blame Athlen for his trickery, not when he saw his own insecurities echoed in the anxious curve of Athlen's spine. They shared a similar burden, a secret that marked them as different, and Tal empathized with Athlen's fear of not knowing how others would react if that secret was revealed. He crossed the small space and settled on the edge of the shelf, marveling as the moonlight played over Athlen's scales. Tentatively, he reached out and touched the back of Athlen's hand, offering comfort the best he could. "I understand."

"Thank you for saving me."

"Thank you for not being afraid of me."

Athlen's grin returned, his lips tipping up at the corners. "You're welcome."

"As are you," Tal said with a nod. "So those mercenaries . . ."

Athlen frowned and rubbed a webbed finger over the bridge of his nose. "I made a mistake that gave them the opportunity to capture me. They kept me in irons while in both forms, chaining me to either the anchor or the cabin floor. There was never an opportunity to escape, so I finally did as they asked and retrieved the chest of gold in the hopes that it would earn my freedom. But they never had any intention of letting me go. When I felt the squall coming, I tried to warn them that it was beyond their skill to weather, but they didn't trust me. Very few of them were practiced sailors, and those few were the only ones who survived. The others were swept away."

All of Tal's residual upset feelings vanished with Athlen's confession. He ached to wrap Athlen in a hug, to protect him from all the ills of the world. "Athlen—" he said, voice soft.

"I'm fine," Athlen cut him off. "Really, I am." He sniffed, rubbed his hand over his eyes, then flashed Tal a grin and a wink. "Promise."

"Okay." Tal didn't believe him but knew not to press. "Since you're the first and only merman I've ever met, I have questions."

Athlen spread his arms, showing off his fins and his gills. "Ask away. I'm an open book."

Tal spied another jewel amid the piles of trinkets. "What happened to your sister? Why do you need a memento to remind you of her tail?"

Athlen's expression shuttered. He wrapped his arms around his torso. "Several years ago the seafloor shifted, and I was separated from my family in the commotion. I went to where I knew they might rebuild if they'd survived the shift, but they weren't there." His eyelashes fluttered against his cheeks. "I've looked for a long time, but I haven't found them."

Tal bit his lip. "I'm sorry for your loss."

"I haven't given up. I'm certain they're looking for me, too, and they'll answer my call one day. Until then . . ." Athlen cocked a small smile and spread out his hands.

Tal's lip twitched up at the corner.

"So"—Athlen propped his head on his hands—"I've shared secrets with you. Now it's your turn."

Tal dangled his feet in the water, the flicker of amusement leaving him in a swell of anxiety. "Here's my secret."

He opened his palm and flames licked over his fingers. Brow furrowed, Tal concentrated the flames into a ball and willed it up and up and up until it hovered in the arch of the ceiling and cast flickering light along the carved walls of the cave.

"Magic," Athlen said with a smile. "You've shown me before."

"Yes, but there's more."

"More?" Athlen asked, eyebrows raising.

Tal nodded. "You might not know our . . . land folk history, but my great-grandfather was the last powerful mage of our kingdom . . . of all the kingdoms. He . . . he thought it was his destiny to conquer the entirety of our continent. He waged war on anyone who stood in his way. He hurt thousands of people, and his legacy is my family's bane." Tal took a breath. "No one knows what I am. Rumors started circulating when my magic first manifested and I couldn't control it as well, but it's never been widely confirmed. My mother says if people knew the truth, the other kingdoms would either attack us or force her to hand me over for imprisonment."

Athlen sank in the water. "You have to hide?"

"Yes," Tal said. He picked through another pile of shells and pearls and gold. "I've not been allowed to leave the castle. My siblings have visited all the other kingdoms in an effort to improve diplomacy, but this is my first time out in the world."

"I'm sorry."

Tal shrugged. "Don't be. This was my family's fault."

"That doesn't seem fair."

"It doesn't matter if it's fair. It is my burden as a prince. It is my family's responsibility to undo the damage my great-grandfather caused as best we can." Tal pulled his knees to his chest, his toes pruned from the water, and wrapped his arms around his shins. He rested his chin on the bend of his knees.

Brow furrowed, Athlen eyed Tal's hand. "How does it work? Is it always fire?"

"Not always." Tal flexed his fingers. "Sometimes I can will objects to move, but only if I concentrate. It's not as easy as the fire." He leaned closer. "I'm not even really good at it," he admitted, voice low. "My tutor says that with time I'll be as powerful as my great-grandfather, but he can't teach me beyond the parchments we have."

"I know a sea witch!" Athlen said. He pulled his body onto a slanted rock next to Tal and propped up on his side. "She lives in the depths and will come to any who call her name with a desire in their heart. She's powerful and beautiful and terrifying. But . . ." Athlen trailed off. "You have to bargain, and I don't . . . Never mind, I don't think it's a good idea."

Tal perked up. "How do you know a sea witch?"

Athlen blushed. "Do you think mermen have the ability to have legs whenever they want? I had to make a bargain."

"And what was your bargain?"

Athlen laughed and flopped backward, arms over his chest. He flicked his tail, making water droplets arch through the air and land on Tal's face. "I already gave you a secret. One's enough for now, my prince." Athlen crossed his arms behind his head and stretched, eyes shining in the firelight.

Tal narrowed his eyes. "Fine, but you'll tell me later." It wasn't a request and Athlen smiled.

A companionable silence fell between them as they lay next to each other on the slick rock, Tal's bare feet next to Athlen's magnificent tail. Their arms brushed, Tal's tanned skin a contrast to Athlen's pale body. There was a strange kinship between them; both were forced to hide their true selves or risk—and in Athlen's case, suffer—imprisonment.

Heaving a sigh, Tal stretched out his body and pointed his toes. He took solace in the quiet minutes and the lapping of the water as the receding tide revealed more of Athlen's home.

"Thank you for saving me," Athlen said, breaking the quiet. "I haven't had anyone looking after me other than Dara for a long time. It's nice to have another friend."

The feeling that welled in Tal was beyond description, but if forced, he'd claim it was warmth and pride.

"I have to go," Tal said, eyes heavy. "Shay is going to be so angry at me for shaking her again."

"Do you want me to walk you back to the ship?"

"I'll be fine." Tal sat up and yawned. "No need to get dressed and follow me."

Athlen huffed. "I'll use the water and swim the shoreline. You can wave to me once you're on the dock."

Tal rolled his eyes. "You're as bad as my family."

"Well, of the two of us, I have more experience with the city humans."

"Says the boy who doesn't know the difference in value between a pearl and a piece of sea glass."

Athlen puffed his chest. "I get what I need." He spread out his hands. "I have plenty to share. I don't understand why everyone is so greedy."

Tal shook his head. "You are a wonder."

"As are you," he replied, voice somber, free of teasing.

Tal's blush returned in full force, but Athlen didn't see it, as he had already disappeared into the depths of the pool.

Without his boots, Tal carefully waded back the way they had come. The tide had gone out, leaving more sand for Tal to navigate, but that also meant Athlen was farther away, beyond the surf. Tal couldn't see him in the waves, but took comfort in knowing he was there, a companion in the dark night, the stars the only witnesses to their secrets and friendship.

Illuminated by the moon, the dock appeared busier than normal. As Tal approached, a group of men detached from the shadows, accompanied by a large animal. Tal stopped, fear blossoming as they fanned out around him.

"Been waiting for you, princeling."

A glint of metal in the man's hand made Tal step back. Glad of Shay's paranoia and insistence, Tal unsheathed the dagger at his side and dropped into a defensive crouch, his toes curling in the wet sand.

"Don't come any closer."

Blade in one hand, Tal uncurled the other at his side, his magic bubbling beneath the surface of his skin. Flames licked up his spine, and heat unfurled in his belly. Defensive spells coiled on the tip of his tongue. He could defeat these men with fire and steel.

"Why? Are you going to use that blade on us? Or do you have a different weapon singeing your veins?"

They laughed as they swaggered closer. The animal—now discernable as a huge wild cat—was on their heels, ears pricked forward, lips curled into a snarl.

"Come now, princeling. Show us the sparks."

The words brought Tal up short and washed over him like a cold wave. They wanted him to use his magic. They wanted him to prove the rumors true. They thought they'd force it out of him in a conflict. He didn't have time to wonder why; he only knew he wouldn't give them the satisfaction. He clenched his fist shut, extinguishing any desire to use the flames, smoke wreathing around his fingers as he snuffed the magic out.

"Who are you?" Tal used his best authoritative voice, the one that made him sound arrogant and spoiled. "What do you want?"

"You." The sailor flipped the blade in his hand as the other men tightened around him.

Tal's pulse raced, but he steeled himself and took a breath. If not a magic reveal, then a kidnapping. He'd been trained for these—royalty was always at risk. He called upon the practices he'd learned from the mandatory self-defense classes taught by the castle knights, and gripped the dagger tight in his hand. There were five of them and one of him. He was outmatched, but he'd make them bleed for it.

He dodged the first man who lunged for him, swiping out with his blade and catching the fabric of the man's tunic. His knife sliced through cleanly, ribboning the shirt and proving his ability to defend himself. Tal ducked and rolled away from the next attack, scraping up a handful of sand and throwing it into the assailant's face. The mercenary shouted and staggered back, rubbing his sleeve over his eyes.

"Not such a whelp after all," their leader snarled. "Quit playing with him and get him."

Tal was not above running away, but they were blocking his escape to the docks, and he refused to lead them back to Athlen's cove. The sea was his only option, but the waves pounded on the shore, rolling dark as pitch, and hiding their own threats, which were known to drift inland in the nighttime. As fast as he could run, he wouldn't be able to outrun the large cat that stalked beyond the reach of the circle. It growled at him, its flashing yellow eyes marking it a shifter like Kest.

"Who are you?" Tal demanded. "What do you want with me? Whoever is paying you, I can pay you more."

They snickered. "Trust us. You are worth more to us captured than free. Maybe even more dead than alive."

Tal's body went cold. He wasn't escaping. He flipped the dagger, catching the hilt in a different grab, and maneuvered until his back was to the waves.

"Come get me, then."

They swarmed.

Tal fought. He kicked and punched. He bit down when a meaty arm clamped around his neck, blood filling his mouth until he gagged. He lost his dagger when his wrist was bent back, his fingers slacking, the weapon tumbling harmlessly to the sand. He yelled and struggled, fighting uselessly against the hands and arms that pawed at his body.

Throwing an elbow, Tal caught someone in the gut, and he

wrenched his arms away. Suddenly free, Tal stumbled along the shoreline, bare feet kicking up sand. He could make it to the dock if only he gained his balance and outran the shifter.

"Tal!"

Tal whipped his head to the side to see Athlen in the waves. In the surge of adrenaline and fear, he'd forgotten that Athlen was following him in the surf.

"Athlen!"

"I'm coming!"

Tal veered course and ran into the ocean, water soaking his trousers up to his thighs. He was almost to Athlen's outstretched hand—almost to safety.

The cat slammed into Tal's legs. With a cry Tal fell. The surf washed over him, up his nose, into his mouth, as the cat bit the fabric of his shirt, teeth scraping hot over Tal's skin, and pulled him back to the gang of men, growling. Sputtering, sopping wet, Tal gathered his feet under him, his shirt tearing, and made one last-ditch lurch toward the sea.

A swift kick to his leg stopped him. Tal's knee crumpled, and he landed hard on his side.

Get up. Get up. Get up!

Tal rolled away and blindly gripped a large shell. He swung it at the nearest attacker as he staggered upright. Blood sprayed across the sand. Athlen's voice in his head, Tal lunged for the ocean. Athlen was out there. Athlen could pull him out to sea, to safety, and he could escape. His attackers wouldn't expect it. The path would be clear. Athlen was swimming in the surf, Tal was certain, and if he wasn't, Tal would rather drown than become a ransom. He could make it. He could—

The blow to the back of his head stole his breath and sent him flat to the sand, the shell skittering out of his grip. His vision tunneled, and his stomach roiled. He tried to push onto his elbows, but he only managed to scoot his forehead across the sand. Another wave washed on the shore, and Tal wheezed as salt water flowed into his mouth.

He struggled, the sailors laughing above him as he weakly clawed at the sand.

"If he was like his ancestor, he'd have used the flames by now."

Boots filled up what was left of his vision, and then there was a hand in his hair, and his head was yanked up, neck straining.

"Come on, boy. Show us what you can do."

Tal spit out a mouthful of grit. "Die in a fire."

The punch snapped Tal's head to the side, and he blacked out.

6

Tal woke in stages, coming to consciousness slowly, like the ebb and flow of a tide, but in shades of gray instead of crystal blue. The first thing he became aware of was the lancing pain in his head. His eyes watered with it and his stomach lurched. More than once it sent him careening back into darkness, until at last it was merely a dull throb matching his heartbeat rather than a dagger in his temple. Next, he noted the rocking of the floor beneath him, the rough scrape of wooden slats and tar under his palms, and the sounds of wood creaking and water dripping. He wasn't bound, which was fortunate, but he was in the belly of a ship, of that he was sure. Maybe Garrett had found him. Maybe Shay had saved him.

He kept his eyes closed and focused on breathing, moderating the pain as best he could. Squirming, he tried to find a more comfortable position, but when he stretched his legs, his knee spasmed, and he bit back a cry. As he curled into a ball, his bare foot snagged on a steel bar. Tears gathering behind his eyes, Tal tucked his chin to his chest and reached for his magic. At first it was elusive, slipping away from him as his concentration wavered with the pain, but soon he grasped it. The familiar heat calmed him, steadied him, and he was able to think clearly.

Reaching out, eyes still pinched shut, his fingers grazed more steel near his head, and he bit back a sob at the realization that he was caged.

He'd been kidnapped.

Fear swelled in him as a hot torrent, followed quickly by guilt. Garrett and Shay would blame themselves for not keeping a better watch, and his mother, who'd pushed for Tal's coming-of-age tour, would be beside herself with worry.

He bit his bottom lip. Since they were old enough to understand, Tal and his siblings had all been warned about people who would want to harm them. Still, he'd never thought it would happen to him. They'd all taken self-defense lessons and been assigned bodyguards. But Tal was the only one with magic burning in his gut that could melt sand. How could he have let himself be taken? An ugly voice inside him whispered that he should've fought them harder on the beach. He should've allowed the flames to burst from him in an inferno. He should've . . . Tal choked back a sob. He stuffed his fist in his mouth and allowed a moment of panic, biting down on his fingers to stifle any sounds.

He counted in his head, and when he reached a hundred, he sucked in a shaky breath and pulled himself together.

He needed to figure out how badly he was injured. Tentatively he probed with his fingers, finding damp, matted hair behind his right ear and a trail of tacky blood down his neck and shoulder.

Even the light touch was enough to send sparks behind his eyes, and he pressed his forehead to the floor and gritted his teeth as his stomach crawled into his mouth. Inspection had yielded one injury thus far—a head wound that had bled considerably. Blood loss was the reason his mouth was so dry. He tested his leg and found another—a swollen knee from the last debilitating kick, which had made it difficult to run. His body ached in ways that meant bruises, and he might have a bite from the shifter on his upper arm. He'd need to wait until he was steadier to attempt escape, if there was any escaping to be tried.

Footsteps on the ladder made him tense, and he forced his body to relax. He turned his head away from the sound and hoped whoever it was wouldn't be able to tell he was faking. Despite his closed eyes, Tal could discern the change in light when the two men stood over him.

"He's still not awake? How hard did Mac hit him?"

"Not hard enough to addle him, but he's the sickly prince. He's soft."

"Not soft enough. He put up a fight on the beach. Rot has a slash we had to stitch, and Mac still has grit in his eyes."

Tal took a modicum of satisfaction at that.

"Did he use magic?"

"No, he didn't. The rumors might not be true."

"We have orders. If he does have it, we'll draw it out of him."

"Take his ring," the other said. "We'll need it if the captain wants us to ransom him."

Tal held still and didn't flinch when the sailor reached through the bars and lifted his hand, twisting his signet ring off this third finger. Tal bit back a grunt when they dropped his hand back to the deck.

They left, footsteps fading farther into the hold, and the creak of the ladder told Tal that he was alone again.

He blinked his eyes open, noting that the right was puffy and could open only to a slit. He added a black eye to his mental list of injuries. The hold was dark, save for a slant of bright sun that beamed down from the ladder opening. Above him would be the crew's quarters, and above that, the deck. From the position of the sun he guessed it was midday. He pulled his body to a sitting position and groaned as his muscles protested and his head spun. His throat was parched, but his captors hadn't left water.

He settled against the bulkhead and examined the cage. Three sides were flat metal bars bolstered by wood, and the fourth was the side of the ship itself. There were more cages like his in a row, but they were all empty. He could break the lock, like he'd broken the iron chain, but where would he go? They were out to sea—the distinct rhythm of the ship gave that away—but they weren't moving. Were they moored? Waiting for instructions? Waiting for him to use his magic?

Tal swallowed down the lump in his throat and took stock of the facts.

He had been kidnapped by people who wanted proof of his magic. They'd taken his ring, probably to ransom him to his mother or show their superior they had him. This had been planned. Someone had seen him leave the tavern and waited for him to return to the ship while Garrett remained in town, holding out for the chance to scare him into showing his power. Was this related to the man who'd attacked him in the hold of the ship earlier in the day? He'd wanted to kill Tal, but these men had kidnapped him. They could've killed him on the beach, so either the plan had changed during the hours between the two incidents or they were unrelated.

Furthermore, these men had a shifter with them—someone

who possessed that uncommon ability like Kest. Shifters weren't as rare as the type of magic that pulsed through Tal's veins, but they weren't commonplace, either. The ability traveled through bloodlines. Sought after during the time of Tal's ancestors, shifters were revered for their power by some and kept as pets by others. Many were married into noble families, and now, of the few who remained, most were of the ruling houses. Though in his lessons on the other royal families, he didn't remember learning of anyone who could turn into a big cat.

Whoever the cat was, it all pointed to a political kidnapping.

Was this related to Athlen's chest of gold? The mercenaries who'd held him?

Tal sucked in a sharp breath. *Athlen.* Was he all right? Did he get away? Would he tell Garrett what had happened? Had he followed the ship, or had he abandoned Tal to his fate—unsure or uninterested in the affairs of humans?

Tal patted the pocket of his shirt and found the hard, small lump of the shark's tooth. He fished it out and clasped it in his hand, the point of it biting into his palm. No, as different and as strange as Athlen was, he wouldn't abandon Tal to this fate. He'd made a promise at Dara's house, one that wouldn't allow him to leave Tal in clear danger. They were bound by the magic in their words. And while Tal wouldn't place his faith solely in Athlen, he wouldn't dismiss him either. He slid the tooth into his trouser pocket for safekeeping.

Closing his eyes, Tal wilted against the wooden bulkhead. The stubborn ache in his head made his vision swim. He needed to rest. He'd plan when his head was clearer and fear wasn't so tangible. Until then he knew one thing for certain—his captors couldn't find out about his magic, no matter what.

≋

The rattling of the cage jolted Tal into wakefulness. He snapped his head up from where his chin rested on his chest, and vertigo washed over him. He listed to the side and caught his body from falling with his elbow.

"Ah, the whelp is awake."

Eyes narrowed, Tal made out the speaker as the leader from the gang on the beach. He was shorter than Garrett, and his long hair hung in greasy strands. His hairline receded on the crown of his head, and his large forehead crinkled when he scowled at Tal. He had a few stitches in his cheek from where Tal had smashed the shell across his face in the scuffle. This must be Rot.

"I'm sorry, my lord, but your servants aren't here to dress you."

Tal rolled his eyes, and he would've retorted, but it would've ended in vomit.

Rot pulled a set of keys from his belt and unlocked the door. He yanked it open.

"The captain wants to see you."

He reached in and grabbed Tal's arm, pulling him to his feet. Tal stumbled, his knee protesting the movement, pain lancing through his body and his head. He gripped the cage with his free hand, the steel slats biting into his palm.

"What? Can princes not walk?"

Tal breathed heavily through his nose, sounding like the old bull the castle stewards trotted out for festivals to represent virility and prosperity, except Tal wasn't feeling very prosperous presently. He gritted his teeth and shuffled through the small cage opening.

His entire body ached from his head to the soles of his bare feet, but he gamely kept his legs despite the sway of the ship. He pulled his body up the ladder to the crew's quarters, then carried on up the steps to the top deck. Rot kept an iron grip on Tal's upper arm, squeezing over the wound from the shifter, but Tal was able to tolerate it as soon as the fresh ocean breeze swept over the deck. He tipped his head back and bared his face to the sun, his head clearing, and the nausea dissipating slightly.

Rot tugged him, and Tal lurched toward the captain's quarters at the stern of the vessel, taking in the sights and sounds around him. The sea stretched in all directions with no land in sight. Small caps on the waves rocked the ship. The ship was anchored, and sailors lazed about the deck, playing cards or sleeping. A few fished off the bow, shooing away the gulls. Squinting upward, Tal spotted a sailor in the crow's nest. The sails were furled, so he was meant to watch for incoming vessels.

Rot knocked on an ornate door. He didn't wait for a response before shoving Tal inside. Tal stumbled but caught himself before he went to his knees.

"Well, he doesn't look like a prince," an amused voice said as Rot entered on Tal's heels.

"We may have roughed him up a bit, Captain."

She nodded. "Leave us."

Rot didn't hesitate to scurry away and shut the door behind him.

Tal stood in front of the large desk while the captain leaned on her outstretched arms, studying him with a sharp gaze. Her blond hair was cut short, shaved close on the sides, and spiked with grease on top. She had a scar that ran lengthwise along her nose, another on the underside of her jaw, and faint crow's-feet around her eyes. She was dressed like a sailor in light clothes and was simply adorned, save for a length of gold chain around her neck and hoops in her ears.

She eyed him in silence. Tal locked his knees, willing his body to stay upright.

"You're the child everyone is terrified of? You don't look like much." She narrowed her eyes. "But your great-grandfather's face was said to look like melted wax, so I tend not to judge by appearance alone."

Tal clenched his hands to his sides. "I demand to know the name of the person who holds me and whom they represent."

"Strong words from a bruised and broken boy." She straightened, then strode around to the front of the desk, bracing on the edge and crossing her ankles. Her boots were old and worn, faded from the salt water and the sun. "Did my men hurt you?"

"I gave as good as I received," Tal said. That was far from true. A few stitches and sand in the eyes didn't compare with a head wound, a black eye, and a swollen knee, but he wouldn't acknowledge that to this pirate.

"My sailors said you were soft, but there is steel in your spine. I admire that."

"Release me and I'll ensure your death is quick."

"Well," she said with a smile, "I don't appreciate *that*. Threats won't work on me. I know what my potential fate is if your family realizes where you are. I took this deal with my eyes open. I also know that your safety will be powerful in a bargain."

"And where am I?"

"You're in deep water, boy. Beyond the bay and your kingdom's domain. Far away from the continent and the one ally your family has."

Tal stiffened. Had they really traveled that far? How long had he been unconscious? He licked his dry lips. "Why are you holding me?"

She smiled, hard and cruel. "Why else would I hold a prince?" She spread her palms. "Ransom. Assassination. War." Her gray eyes glinted. "Magic."

Tal didn't rise to the bait. He remained impassive. "Well," he said after a moment of silence, "which one is it?"

She chuckled. "It's not assassination for now, but test me, and it can be."

"Whatever you're being paid, my family will match it and then some."

She huffed. "Little princeling, if the rumors are true, I would not release you back to your family for all the gold on the continent and the islands. And if they aren't, well, the person who hired me will determine what to do next."

"And who hired you?"

She clucked her tongue. "It's bad business to give away secrets."

The harsh light pouring in the windows made Tal's head throb. His knee was hot and swollen, and the bite on his arm bled sluggishly. He commanded every ounce of restraint not to lunge for the bottle of wine teetering on the edge of the desk.

"It's also bad for business to treat your political prisoners poorly."

She tapped her finger against her mouth. "And what does the prince demand?"

"Water," he said, the word scraping out of his throat. "Food. A bath. Clothes. Bandages for the wounds."

She laughed, hands on her hips, head thrown back. She strode forward, the sword at her side swaying with each step. She clasped Tal's chin in her hand, nails like talons digging into his skin. She moved his head from side to side, studying him.

"Why not use your magic and summon fresh water? Or heal

your wounds? Legend says King Lon survived a spear to his throat from the power of his magic." She pressed a finger against Tal's head wound. "This should be easy."

Flames burned Tal from the inside, fierce and wild, crumbling his resolve into ash. He tamped it down, his palms sweating with the effort.

"I don't have magic," he gritted out. He flinched away from her, and this time he did fall to the deck, knee collapsing beneath him. He bit down on a cry and squeezed his eyes shut as they watered. The plush rug in the cabin muffled the thump, and he scrambled away until his back hit the wooden wall. He snapped his eyes open to find the captain staring at him with her arms crossed and her eyebrows raised.

She squatted in front of him, elbows propped on her bent knees, forehead creased in concern. Her fingertips skimmed his temple as she pushed his dark, matted hair out of his eyes. "You need to make a choice, little prince. Either you prove the rumors true or you don't. But don't be mistaken; both choices have consequences."

Tal steadied himself, then jutted out his chin. Spoiled and arrogant, that's what he needed to project, not the soft heart that Garrett teased him about. "How long do I have until that consequence?"

"Until your sister's wedding."

"It's about the alliance, then. Ensuring it fails or that it happens. Which one?"

She pursed her lips. "Ah, you are intelligent. That proves one rumor false."

Tal frowned. Isa's wedding was in less than a month. He needed to contact his family or escape as soon as possible.

"Are your orders to kill me?"

"Not today," she said. She stood and offered her hand. "You may call me Zeph. I'm the captain of this vessel, and until my employer tells me what to do, you'll be safe. But you're not a prince here. You're a prisoner and an extra mouth to feed. You'll work like everyone else."

Tal took her hand and she hauled him to his feet, but she didn't let go.

"And if I don't?"

She considered him. "Men who don't pull their weight don't foster camaraderie. You're a stranger here. You'll want all the kindness you can find."

Releasing him, she crossed back to her desk and grabbed the bottle of wine and a goblet. She poured a generous helping and handed it to him. Tal's hands trembled as he grasped the sun-warmed gold and brought it to his lips, gulping down the sweet wine.

"You'll be under guard, of course. Sailors can become restless when anchored too long. They like to start trouble, and you'll be an easy mark. And though you don't appear foolish, even smart men have been driven to attempt escape. There's nothing out there but fish and myths. I expect you don't want to become food for either." She grabbed the ornate handle of her sword, the delicate metalwork of the cross guard out of place against her simple attire—stolen, most likely. The action was intended as a threat or a show of force, but Tal was unfazed, having grown up with Shay as his shadow.

He wiped his sleeve across his mouth, panting from drinking quickly and forgoing breath. "I promise nothing."

"No. I didn't think you would." She sighed. "We have a healer who will look to your wounds. I'll ensure you have water available to you in your . . . accommodations, and you'll be fed at the next mealtime."

"I suppose I should be grateful."

"I suppose you should," she answered, snatching the goblet from his hand. She turned away from him and nodded to the door. "Rot!"

The door swung open and Rot strode in, canteen slung across his chest, holding a wrapped bundle in one hand.

He tossed it to Tal, and Tal caught it with clumsy hands. He unwrapped it to find salted pork and hardtack. His stomach growled loudly. With a ferocity unbefitting a prince, Tal tore into the food. Tough as leather and dense with salt, it was the best thing Tal had tasted in years.

Rot laughed.

"Take him and have his wounds seen to. Then back to the hold. Tomorrow starts the work, princeling."

Tal swallowed, and grimaced as the bite of food hit his empty stomach. It threatened reappearance, but before he could gag, Rot grabbed him by the arm and dragged him from the captain's quarters.

"Bite down on this," the healer said, shoving a strap of leather between Tal's teeth. He grunted in protest, but before he could spit it out, she popped the cork on a bottle of clear liquor and poured it over Tal's head wound. Tears came quick and hot, the alcohol agonizing against the open wound. Tal cried out, eyes squeezed shut, the leather falling from his mouth into his lap.

"Oh yeah," she said, prodding at the bruised and split skin at his hairline. "That had to hurt. I am going to have to stitch it. They cut you wide open, like a melon." She pushed her fingers at his arm. "I better clean this, too. Animal bites tend to go bad, you know."

Tal braced himself and hurriedly shoved the strap back into his mouth. The healer took a swig of the swill before upending the bottle over the wound.

Tal flinched, bowing his head, hands clenched tight into the fabric of his trousers. Swallowing down gasps, he ground his teeth into the leather.

Sitting on a crate in the hold right next to the cage, Tal bent double over his knees and curled his toes against the rough wood. His tattered shirt lay draped over the barrel next to him. He wasn't bound, but Rot stood watch at the base of the ladder. The healer, a young woman called Poppy, cheerfully threaded a needle.

"You're a prince, huh? Never met a royal before." She pushed his head forward. "I guess rich blood bleeds the same. Which kingdom are you from? Inland, I wager."

"He's from Harth."

"Oh," Poppy said. "The castle by the sea, then. Are you the one who can turn into a bird?"

Tal breathed through his nose as Poppy pinched his skin. The laceration burned and ached. His stomach flipped over. He was afraid to answer for fear of losing the wine and fish he'd had minutes before.

"No," Rot answered for him.

"The commander, then?"

Rot laughed. "No, he's the one been holed up in that castle— the one with magic."

Poppy hummed as Tal sat tense and still as a statue while she stitched. Tendons in his hands and arms bulged, and his body shook with restraint.

"I didn't know there was a third one of you. Magic, huh? I didn't think there was any of that left in the world other than the shifters. And even those are rare."

Tal waited until her work became bearable, then dropped the leather from his mouth. "Do you know the cat?" Tal asked, voice breathy and strained. "The one who bit me?"

"No," Poppy answered, despite Rot's hand gestures. "Never met a shifter, but if I did, I'd have a lot of questions. Like, does it hurt? And what if you get stuck? What do you see and hear? What if you die?"

Tal winced as she jabbed carelessly, unaware she had given information away. The cat wasn't part of the regular crew, then. Maybe Poppy would let other details slip.

"I can answer your questions," Tal said. "If you'd like. My brother, the bird, told me all of those things."

Rot strode across the space. "No. You're not to talk to him, Poppy. Only the captain and me. No one else."

Tal craned his neck slightly to see Poppy pout, but she nodded. "Sorry. You heard him. And I'm not going to get thrown to these currents over a boy, even one as pretty as you. I might be able to swim when we're moored closer to shore, but out here in the deep water I'd not stand a chance. Did you know there is a current near here that will drag you straight down to the seafloor, to the mermaids?"

"There are no such things as mermaids," Tal said through a tight throat.

"Shows what you know," she huffed. "There are merfolk in hiding. A few generations ago they'd come right up to the surface to play, but now they stay in the deep."

"Have you ever met one?"

"One what?"

"A mermaid?"

Poppy made a rude noise with her lips. "No. They don't come to the surface. Your great-grandfather saw to that." She addressed Rot, pointing at Tal and rolling her eyes. "Not so smart, is he? I bet he doesn't even know about the sea witch. Some sailor he is. Good thing he's not meant for the throne, or Harth would be in worse trouble than it already is."

Tal ignored the jab. "Sea witch?" he asked, perking up from his slouch. "You know her?" Athlen had mentioned bargaining with her. Maybe she'd help Tal if he asked. It was a fool's gamble, but Tal wouldn't rule out any means of escape, no matter how farfetched.

"Of course," Poppy scoffed. "She's only the most powerful being in the sea. More powerful than land princes, even magic ones."

Tal didn't rise to the bait. He wasn't vain enough to argue about who was more powerful. Though, it was interesting. The sea witch had to have some magic ability to grant Athlen legs. Could she and the mage that his great-grandfather had chased into the sea be one and the same? "Have you ever met her?"

"I will one day," Poppy said with a firm nod, tearing a bandage with her teeth. She wrapped it around Tal's upper arm and tied it off tightly. "I'll call her when I need her. All right, I'm done. Keep them clean and you should be fine."

Rot rolled his eyes.

"How do you call her?"

Poppy raised an eyebrow. "I thought you grew up near the shore. You should know these things."

Tal opened his mouth to retort but closed it when Rot leveled a glare. Exhausted and aching, Tal didn't fight when Rot hauled him up and shoved him back into the cage. He left the canteen of water, and for that Tal was grateful. Tal sank to the floor and leaned against the wooden bulkhead as Rot and Poppy disappeared up the ladder. Tal slipped his shirt on and pulled his legs to his chest. Forehead on his knees, he closed his eyes and clutched the shark's tooth hidden in his pocket.

The first full day of Tal's imprisonment started with Rot banging on the slats. Tal had spent a fitful night attempting sleep in the cramped enclosure. The sleep he managed to get had been filled with worry and nightmares. It was a reprieve from his own thoughts when Rot pulled him from the enclosure and forced him to face the day.

Breakfast on the crew deck was hardtack and a gulp of water while a group of sailors watched him with sharp eyes. He endured their amused gazes when Rot grabbed him by the back of the neck like a disobedient puppy and led him to the bow with orders to swab the deck. Tal watched the sunrise on his hands and knees, scrubbing a holystone over the deck as others threw a mixture of cold seawater and sand on the wood. It took Tal hours to complete the chore, sloughing off salt crystals and smoothing out pits in the wood and tar. By the end Tal's hands were cut and stinging. His back ached. The fabric of his trousers was shredded at the knees, and his skin was pink from the sun.

All the while the sailors taunted him, dared him to use his magic to save himself. At one point one dumped a bucket of water over his head, and he sputtered and inhaled sharply, choking and coughing until he crawled to the ship railing and vomited over the side. His stomach cramped, and his back bowed, and the sailors laughed.

He wouldn't give in. His magic surged and ebbed like the waves that rocked the vessel, but he wouldn't release it. Though he burned from the inside with hot embers, he wouldn't give Zeph the satisfaction or the leverage. That piece of himself would remain his own.

Instead Tal watched for a means of escape. He spied two jolly boats affixed to the stern, useless out in the deep water unless he knew what direction to row. He looked for a flash of red and gold in the waves and tried not to show his disappointment when he didn't spy a familiar tail. He listened to the sailors talk, hoping to pick up some scrap of useful information, but they only sang bawdy songs and spoke of myths and conquests. The crew was eclectic, a mix of skin tones and accents and genders—some, from Tal's own kingdom, stared at him with undecipherable expressions, while others, from the kingdoms Tal's family had destroyed, studied him with narrowed eyes and sneers. Rot kept him away from the openly hostile, but even with his watchful eye Tal suffered a booted kick to his ribs and a wad of spit to his cheek.

Hanging on to the railing at the stern, Tal clamped his lips shut and closed his eyes, resting his pounding head briefly on the glossy wood, breathing heavily through his nose. His mind wandered, and he hoped Isa's wedding, and the alliance she had worked so hard to cultivate, were not ruined by his disappearance. Of the five of them, Isa was the most political minded and adept, and she had no qualms about using her beauty and cunning to secure what the kingdom needed. She'd wooed Emerick with love letters and gifts, and secured the alliance despite their mother's insistence that she did not want her to enter a political marriage.

But Isa was determined to bolster their foreign support and protect their eastern border. As if a lifelong commitment to a stranger were no sacrifice.

Tal missed his older sister desperately and hoped his last interaction with her would not be him scowling while she held his hand and led him to Garrett's ship to begin his coming-of-age tour.

"Hey," Rot said, breaking into Tal's thoughts. "No rest for magic princes." He jerked Tal up from his exhausted slouch. "To the bilges with you."

In the belly of the ship, crouched in slimy water, Tal pumped the handle of the bilge pump—a device that reminded him of the bellows in the great hall's fireplace. It dispelled the water that collected in the bowels of the ship. Even the best-made warships leaked and required this task to be completed daily, but on this ship, which creaked and moaned in the smallest of waves, the bilge had to be manned continuously. Tal worked for hours, until his arms screamed in protest, and another sailor relieved him.

Dinner was fresh fish cooked over a small fire. Tal ate his share, licking his fingers when it was gone, and he guzzled the water passed to him.

"Captain wants to see you," Rot said as Tal nodded off at his spot on the crew deck.

Exhausted, Tal staggered to his feet and followed Rot to the captain's quarters. The door was cracked open, and Rot didn't hesitate to enter the captain's room. Tal followed, head bowed, shoulders sagging.

Zeph sat at her desk, cutting into a thick filet of fish, a full goblet of wine within reach.

"Leave us," she said, not looking up. She nodded to a chair across from her. "Sit."

Tal hobbled over and sank slowly into the cushions, wincing as his joints protested. He'd never hurt like this before—his entire body was tender and bruised. He'd trained with the castle knights, fallen off horses, danced for hours at balls, and run through gardens while playing with his younger sister. But he'd never been subjected to repetitive manual labor as he had that day.

"Why didn't you use your magic to complete the tasks?" Zeph asked around a mouthful of food. "It would have been easier."

"I don't have magic."

"Pity." She gulped her wine. "It would make your life here better. What's left of it."

"Which kingdom doesn't want the alliance between Harth and Ossetia? Who would risk kidnapping me?"

Zeph's fork scraped across her plate. "What makes you think that's the reason?"

"You're the one who mentioned the wedding."

Zeph shrugged. "Maybe it's to ensure the alliance goes through. Or maybe it's to see what we're all dealing with—another madman like King Lon or the soft, sickly prince your mother-queen has pushed to the rest of the world." She pointed her fork at him, flinging bits of fish across her desk. "Maybe it's to keep your dangerous magic away from Emerick so he won't find out and dissolve the contract. It's why your family sent you away before his retinue arrived, isn't it?"

Tal narrowed his eyes. "It's my coming-of-age tour of the kingdom. It's our family tradition."

"Convenient that the wedding was planned for the same time."

Tal . . . hadn't thought of it like that. Had his family scheduled it that way? Made sure he wouldn't be around to jeopardize the alliance? No, no, they wouldn't do that to him. He had to hold on to his faith in them. He was exhausted, physically and mentally, and Zeph wanted to manipulate him. Poking holes in his confidence and making him question his family would be an easy way to break him.

"What do I have to do to return home?"

Zeph smiled, lacing her fingers together. "I've already told you—it all depends on you. Show us your magic and I'll tell my employer, and he'll determine what happens next. Resist, and you'll stay here, working, until your family collects you or you die." The cork popped when she pulled it from the bottle, and she poured herself another goblet. "It makes no difference to me. I get paid either way."

"When my family comes, they'll kill you."

"They might try, but I'll make a deal. I always do." She returned to her dinner. "Have a good night, princeling. Rest well. You have another day of work tomorrow."

Tal stood on shaky legs and let himself out onto the deck. He obediently followed Rot to the hold and into the steel cell, head down. His wounds itched and his body shook, but he stood until Rot had ascended the ladder to the crew's quarters.

Once he was gone, Tal gave into the despair that haunted him. He collapsed to the floor and allowed the tears that had threatened all day to fall. As he curled into a ball and cried, he felt all the new physical hurts he'd accumulated, from his aching back and sunburned skin to his scraped knuckles and throbbing knees. His mind filled with the jeers and taunts of the crew and with Zeph's questions about his family.

Were they looking for him? Or was this better? He wasn't there to risk or ruin everything. They wouldn't have to continue to lie for him.

He should never have left home. He should've stayed with Garrett and Shay in the tavern. He should've fought harder on the beach. He should've used his magic and escaped. He should've said good-bye to his sisters and brothers. He should've kissed Athlen in the cave.

Sniffling on the floor in the dark, Tal turned his head to the side and paused. Eye level with the deck, he could see something snagged beneath a crate. Squinting, he shuffled toward the metal slats. Was that a parchment? Sure of his solitude, he carefully opened his palm. A flame appeared, casting light and shadows as it danced above his skin.

Squirming closer, he could see it wasn't parchment but cloth. The scrap of sail was tucked beneath a crate. It was badly damaged, but he could use it. He could send a message to his family!

Closing his fist, he extinguished the light. He reached his hand through the bars, his shoulder pressed hard into the steel slats. He gritted his teeth as his muscles strained and ached, but his fingers didn't reach, not even close. Tears of frustration pricked behind his eyes, spilling over onto his already dampened cheeks.

He took a breath. He could do this. He *had* to do this.

Reaching within himself, he found his magic. Usually it came to him in the form of fire, but this time he begged for the force of will. He focused on the power and grabbed it, willing the cloth to come to him.

"Please," he whispered. "Please. Please. *Please.*"

The scrap twitched.

Letting out a breathless laugh, he focused, drawing his eyebrows together, face red from exertion, and he *willed* the sail to his hand. It tugged from beneath the crate and, in a sweep of wind, slapped into Tal's palm.

He pulled it through the bars and clutched it to his chest. Giddy with hope, Tal smiled.

Spreading it out on the floor of his cell, Tal grasped the shark's tooth in his pocket. The serrated edge would make a fine point, but he needed ink.

Gulping, Tal looked to his battered hands. One more wound wouldn't make a difference. He pricked the tip of his finger with the shark's tooth. A bead of blood welled out, and using the pointed edge of the tooth as a rudimentary quill, he pressed it to the cloth. He wrote.

Kidnapped. Deep water. Strong currents.

After the first few letters Tal squeezed his finger again, and after a few more he pricked the tip of another.

Continue wedding.

It wasn't much, but it might give his family a starting point.

He held his hand over the message and concentrated. He called to his magic, and the letters burned like embers. He muttered the incantation, and slowly the words faded until all that was left was the scrap of sail and the bloodied tooth.

The achievement was small and the message vague, but Tal squeezed the tooth in his hand, hope a flickering flame in his belly. Someone would find him—Athlen or Garrett or Kest or Isa.

Exhausted, he closed his eyes and fell into a dreamless sleep.

The next day was much of the same, and in his brief reprieves from the backbreaking work, Tal peered over the gunwale of the ship and wished for a glimpse of Athlen's tail. He kept his eyes and ears open for more information, but the crew was tight lipped, and water stretched as far as he could see.

After dinner Zeph called him to her quarters and taunted him with rest if only he used magic. He attempted a glimpse at the maps spread on her desk, but she was savvy and blocked his view.

"They're not coming for you," Zeph said, swirling the wine in her glass. "Word is they stopped looking and have given you up for dead."

Tal bit down on his lip. It wasn't true. It wasn't true. It wasn't true. His mother wouldn't allow them to stop searching.

That night he took out the scrap of sail. With no one around, he touched the tip of his finger to the tar between the planks and heated it until it bubbled. He dipped the tooth into the viscous liquid and dragged it across the fabric. For a moment he imagined setting fire to the ship, escaping in one of the jolly boats, and rowing away. But his body was weak, and he had no supplies and no earthly clue where he was. He wouldn't last long. He licked his cracked lips. He could endure. He would last until Garrett and Shay found him.

Same place. Cpt Zeph. Cat shifter.

Tal paused, breathing hard, before he added, *Injured.*

Days bled into nights, and time passed in a cycle of work and sleep. Tal gathered no new information. He hunched in the bilge and pumped the handle until the muscles in his arms bunched and burned. He worked on the deck, scrubbing the wood or coiling rope, until his skin scorched and peeled and his hands oozed with blisters and blood. He weathered Zeph's bold declarations that his family wasn't looking for him and had given up. The days flew by, as did the time before his sister's wedding. His body and resolve slowly withered, and the flame of hope he held on to dimmed with every passing day.

Each night he sent a message that he didn't know if his family received. Since he had no new information to share, Tal's messages only served to assure his family that he was alive and to beg that they keep looking for him. Then he slept hard. Some nights he didn't dream. Others he dreamed of Athlen, of the frisson of magic and intimacy they'd shared in the cave. He dreamed of his sister Corrie urging him to play with her and her dolls. He dreamed of Kest flying in to save him. He dreamed of Garrett's laughter and Isa's kind eyes and Shay's stern expression when he shook her in the port town. When he woke, and the dreams dissipated in the dust and closed air of the hold, Tal's heart would stutter and sink as despair crept back in.

He didn't know what day it was when Poppy woke him well before dawn with a touch to his face through the bars.

"Prince," she whispered.

Tal stirred, his eyes cracking open into blurry slits. She smiled and slid a canteen through the slats. Confused and exhausted, Tal pushed himself up. He popped the top and carefully tipped the canteen to his mouth. He wet his lips first, then gulped, the cool water soothing to his raw throat and cracked skin around his mouth.

"Where's Rot?" he said in a sleepy slur.

"Not awake. He'd be upset if he knew I was here." She nudged the water. "Drink more. You need it."

Tal didn't question her and slurped more of the water until it sloshed in his empty belly. He took a breath, then poured the remainder of it over his feverish face, rivulets cutting lines through the grime.

"Why are you here?"

She frowned. "I don't like what they are doing to you." She looked away, the shadows obscuring her face. "I'm sorry your family isn't coming for you."

Tal wiped his tattered sleeve over his forehead and didn't answer.

"They want to break you. They say you are dangerous, and you have this power that could send all the kingdoms careening back into war." She shook her head, light brown curls bouncing over her cheekbones. "But you don't seem dangerous, and you keep taking the punishment the sailors give you."

"I'm not dangerous."

"I didn't think you were." She covered his hand with her own, her skin dry and cool. "You're handsome and spoiled, but resilient. You're the kind of royal the fairy tales talk about."

Fogged with exhaustion, Tal stared too long at where she touched his hand, dredging up the memory of the last person who had dared to be so familiar with him—Athlen. Athlen, who had confessed his secrets and loneliness to Tal with no agenda, who had openly listened to Tal's burdens rather than press a reveal for his own purposes.

Tal pulled his hand away from Poppy and tucked it close to his chest, her touch feeling like a betrayal to that memory.

"I'm not dangerous," he repeated.

"But do you have it?" She pinned him with a thoughtful stare. "Do you have magic?"

Despite the water, Tal's tongue lay thick and heavy in his mouth. "What does it matter?"

Poppy's eyebrows shot up. "Because if you have it, show them! The work and insults will stop!"

"And if I don't?"

She leaned in and wrapped her hands around the bars. "Do you?"

Tal laughed, the sound scratchy and dry. He did. He *did*. He could burn the ship down around them and send them all to the depths. He could boil the sea. He could wrap Captain Zeph in chains of fire and taunt her as she'd taunted him. He could blast the lock open and waltz out of the cage onto the deck. But that's what they *wanted*. He might be as soft hearted as his siblings claimed, but he was stubborn. He shook his head. "No."

Her face fell. "I would like to see magic," she whispered. "Like in the stories of the great mages, and the unicorns, and the merfolk. My grandmother used to tell me about swimming with them in the waves when she was a girl." Poppy leaned in closer, as if imparting a secret. "Sometimes I dream about diving all the way to the depths and staying there, waiting for them, and living in the sea."

"You'd drown."

"No." She shook her head and shifted on her knees. "I'd make a bargain with the witch."

"And what would you have to offer in a bargain with a powerful witch?"

She wrinkled her nose. "My servitude, of course. I'd pledge my life to her if she'd let me live in the sea with her."

Tal sighed. That actually didn't sound terrible at all. He wouldn't mind living on the ocean floor with Athlen if it meant escaping. *Athlen.* He missed Athlen. "Tell me more about the merfolk."

"I already told you what I know from the stories. They hid when the land burned because they knew they'd be next. They stay below the waves now, never to emerge lest they be stolen for their magic. Now, I shared about the sea magic—you tell me about your fire."

Tal pressed his lips together.

She sighed. "It must be terrible to carry that secret. Not being able to tell anyone about the things you can do."

"I know what you're doing."

She furrowed her brow, puzzled. "What do you mean?"

"The water and the promises." He waved his hand. "You came to me as a friend, someone to confide in, and when I let my guard down, you'll run to Zeph as a hero. This is part of it. You're part of it."

"You're out of your head." She pulled a wrapped package from her pocket and slid it toward him. "Here. You must be hungry to be having delusions. I took it from the stores when no one was looking."

The small bits of tough red meat smelled awful, but Tal shoved them in his mouth anyway, barely tasting the salt and the sinew before choking them down. They scraped his throat as he swallowed, then sat leaden in his gut.

Poppy eyed him. "I don't want to see you die, but that's what's going to happen. You're not eating enough and you're not drinking enough. Your wounds aren't healing. They'll turn."

"If you're so worried about me, tell me where we are."

She wrinkled her nose. "I can't do that."

"Why not?" Tal rubbed a hand over his eyes, knuckling away the grit. He perked up, sleep sloughing away with the extra food and water, and with the way Poppy peered at him with wide blue eyes.

"I can't betray Zeph. She's my captain. My family."

"Family?" Tal huffed. "She's a tyrant."

"She *saved* me." Poppy slapped her hand against the bars. "She is fair and good to the crew, and that's all that matters. The opinions of princes be damned."

"Then why do you dream of the bottom of the sea?"

That brought Poppy up short. She narrowed her eyes. "This is why Rot didn't want me talking to you." She wagged her finger. "You're trying to trick me."

"Please," Tal said, voice cracking, "just tell me where we are."

"How will that help you? How does knowing where we're anchored stop them from working you to death?"

"I'm not magic," Tal said. Denying his truth *hurt*, but he forged on. "I'm the fourth child of Queen Carys of Harth, and I'm not a threat like the rumors would have everyone believe. I'm not the heir to our throne. I'm not strong or smart like my brothers. I'm not cunning or beautiful like my sisters. I'm *nothing*."

Poppy sighed. She bowed her head. "You're still a prince. You're still worth more than my life ever will be."

"That's not true. Everyone is of worth." Tal closed his eyes and sank back against the bulkhead. "I just want to go home. But if I can't, I'd at least like to know where I am when I die."

"We're in the Morreline Sea."

Tal's throat clogged. He opened his eyes to peer at her. "What? Are you certain?"

"Of course I am. I've been sailing these waters all my life." She cocked her head. "Now tell me you have magic. Show me. I want to see."

Tal laughed. "If I had magic, don't you think I would have used it by now?"

"I think you're not as good of a liar as you think you are." She stood. "But Zeph was wrong. She thought that if you wouldn't break from the physical demands, you might crumble at a show of kindness." Poppy kicked the cage. "Maybe I wasn't kind enough, or maybe you're too smart for your own good." She turned her back on him and walked to the ladder. "I hope it's quick when you die."

Once she was gone, Tal scrambled for the cloth and the tooth. He didn't have much time, but he scratched "Morreline Sea" into the scrap of sail and hovered his hand over the words. With a muttered incantation, it lit in gold, then disappeared.

Tal closed his eyes and slumped. The Morreline Sea was indeed open water, beyond the bay that surrounded their kingdom's southern border. But it wasn't large, nor uninhabited. Several island nations called the sea home. For Tal not to be able to see land on either side meant they must be located right in the middle.

Tal touched the tip of the tooth back to the sail to add details, but the sound of Rot's footsteps on the ladder interrupted him. After tucking the tooth into his pocket and jamming the cloth into a small space between the wood and the metal cage, Tal stood and waited.

He crossed his arms over his chest and schooled his expression as hope rekindled in his chest. They'd find him. His family would find him, and until then he would endure whatever Zeph and the crew doled out.

Then he'd ensure that Garrett and Shay repaid them in equal measure.

Two nights later Tal tossed and turned in the small area of the cell. He finally slipped into a light doze, only to be awakened by a sound that wasn't the gentle rocking of the ship, the creaking of the wooden boards, or the bilge pump squeaking. No, this was something from his dreams of home, of the castle.

Tal smiled idly when he heard it again, a soft trill, followed by a ruffling of feathers. He stirred and peered through the gloom. Squirming, he wrapped his hands around the slats, metal biting into his abraded palms, and saw a bird. With a hooked beak and sharp talons, the bird fluffed its brown feathers and turned its head.

Tal clapped a hand over his mouth, muffling his gasp of joy, spotting the black eyes rimmed with gold.

"Kest," Tal whispered. Hope sputtered in his chest. "Kest, is that you?"

The bird hopped over, clicking its beak, feathers puffing up in surprise. One moment it was a bird, and the next, with a crackle of magic and a transformation of muscles and bone, Kest manifested in his human form. He knelt at the bars, movements cautious.

"Tally?"

In the low light Tal couldn't be sure that this wasn't another dream, another vision spurred by his fatigue. The vision cracked a smile, and Tal lunged for his brother. Kest returned the gesture, reaching through the wood and metal and grabbing Tal in an awkward hug.

"Tally," he breathed. "You're alive."

"Is it you?" Tal choked on the words. "Are you real?"

"Yes. It's me."

Tal sobbed and scrabbled closer, grasping Kest's forearms in a bruising grip. Kest's long hair tickled Tal's cheek, and the small, familiar detail broke the dam inside of him. Relief flooded his body and soul. Yet it was all tinged with fear. Kest was vulnerable, naked and unarmed. He could easily be captured alongside Tal, but he was there, warm and corporeal.

"Shhh," Kest soothed. "I'm here. I'm here." He smoothed a shaky hand through Tal's hair. "Garrett's ship is over the horizon. He'll be here by sunrise."

Tears dripped over Tal's cheeks, sliding down his chin to splatter on Kest's bare skin. "You've been getting my messages?"

"Yes," Kest said. "What have they done to you?" he said softly, eyeing Tal, forehead furrowed. "Can you run?"

Tal nodded frantically. "Yes. I can break the lock and we can go. They have jolly boats at the stern. We'll row."

Kest stood, frowning. "There are sailors on the deck."

"I'll kill them," Tal said in a fit of desperation, straightening on shaky legs. He ignored Kest's look of surprise—his mouth dropped open, his eyes wide. "I'll use magic and we'll escape and—"

Footsteps cut Tal off. They echoed overhead, moving toward the ladder that led to the hold.

Kest whipped around. "Someone is coming."

"Don't—"

"Garrett is nearby, and now that we know your exact location, he'll be here soon. Hang on for a few more hours, Tally."

Tal's gaze darted to the ladder, then back to Kest. His stomach sank. "Don't leave me." Kest backed away, and Tal threw his body against the bars, bruising his chest and torso, hand outstretched, fingertips brushing Kest's skin. "Don't leave me. Please, Kest." His voice broke. "Please."

"I will be back at dawn with Shay and Garrett. I promise you."

Despair clogged Tal's throat. His breathing hitched on painful gasps and sobs as tears streamed from his eyes. He shook, clutching the bars to keep his feet.

The footsteps stopped at the top of the ladder. The wood creaked, and a pair of feet appeared on the top rung.

"I can't be seen. I *promise* you, Tally."

In a blink Kest transformed. The bird took flight, wings outstretched, feathers flashing in the broken moonlight. The sailor on the ladder sputtered and cursed as Kest shot up the shaft to the deck above. With a short but piercing cry, Kest disappeared from Tal's sight.

Tal fell to the deck, legs crumbling beneath him. He buried his face in his knees. His brother had left him. His brother had *left* him locked in a cell on an enemy ship, injured, feverish, and crying.

Zeph wanted to break him. She'd tried by punishing his body. She'd tried with taunts and goads. He'd held out, kept his magic tucked close to his chest, and lied and lied, clinging to hope for rescue by his family or by Athlen. He'd endured for days, but inadvertent as it was, Kest's appearing, then leaving him behind, was much crueler than anything Zeph had done.

Tal curled into himself, and his soul ached with betrayal. In that moment, if Zeph asked him to confess, Tal wasn't sure he'd turn her down.

Zeph stood over Tal as he knelt on the deck near the stern, holy-stone in his battered hands, a sludge of sand and water spreading out before him. Her boots had been polished and her buttons shone. The short locks of her hair tousled in the wind, and the sun glinted along the row of gold earrings in the shell of her ear.

"Rot says there was a bird in the hold." She raised an eyebrow. "Was it your brother?"

Tal had woken that morning with tear-stained cheeks and a vague memory of Kest hugging him through the bars before flying away. Feverish and exhausted, Tal couldn't trust himself. It wouldn't have been the first time he had dreamed of rescue.

"No," he said.

She cocked her hip and leaned on the railing. "Did you think it was?"

"For a moment," Tal answered.

She clucked her tongue. "I told you they weren't coming. No one knows where you are. And your family is embroiled in a political dance that has no room for missing magic princes."

Tal didn't answer.

The sun had yet to rise over the horizon, but the sky had lightened considerably. The ship rocked with whitecaps, the roughest seas they'd experienced thus far. A large splash had Tal glancing to the water, his breath catching when he spied a flash of red-and-gold scales. He shook his head. First he'd imagined Kest in the hold, and now a phantom Athlen.

A hysterical laugh bubbled out of his throat.

"What's so funny?" Zeph snapped.

Tal craned his neck and met her hard gaze. He licked his dry lips. Maybe he'd show her. Maybe he should burn the ship, condemn them all to the depths.

"Ships!" the sailor from the crow's nest cried, pointing off the bow. "Three of them on the horizon. Heading this way at a clip."

Tal whipped his head around to follow the line of sight.

"What flag?" Zeph called from her position at the stern. "Friendly?"

The lookout raised the spyglass. "Harth's."

Garrett? It . . . hadn't been a dream.

"Hoist the anchor," Zeph shouted. "Loose the sails. We'll outrun them."

No! Tal jumped to his feet and ran toward the bow, dodging the outstretched arms of the crew. "Grab him!" she called. "Don't let him get away!"

Tal made it to the bow unscathed and threw one leg over the railing before he was grabbed and wrenched backward. He struggled and cried out, determined to break free, kicking and biting as they dragged him toward the hold.

"Captain, they're breaking course."

Tal's heart leaped to his throat. Why? Why would they turn away? Would they leave him again?

"No matter. They're too close for comfort. We're moving to the next location."

Zeph grabbed the lapels of Tal's shirt and jerked him toward her. "Calm down, boy. You're making a scene."

Tal wrapped his hands around her wrists. "Let me go," he pleaded. "Please, let me go back to my family. I've done nothing. I've done what you've asked. I'm not magic. I'm not magic." He choked on a desperate cry. "I'm not magic."

Zeph's features softened. "Oh, poor princeling. Magic or not, you were never going back alive."

"What?" Hot, fresh tears spilled down Tal's cheeks, her words a punch to his gut.

She shook her head, pink mouth turned down. "If you were magic, we were to hand you over to Ossetia to use as a weapon in Prince Emerick's name. But you're not. I believe that now. Thus, our orders changed. We're to kill you and frame Mysten. They've protested the alliance for months. Your death will force your mother to war and settle the dispute over the border mines."

His mouth worked uselessly, no sound coming out save the smack of his lips as the significance of Zeph's revelation hit him. "I . . . I . . ."

If he died, his family would still be in danger, manipulated into a war they didn't need. All his life he'd hidden his magic—under guard and under threat. He'd denied his true self, tamped the flames down, smothered them until it *hurt*, until smoke rolled in his gullet and his tongue burned with ash, all in the name of protecting his family. And it had been for *nothing*.

Zeph caressed his cheek. "Shhh," she said. "It's okay, princeling. I'll ensure your death is quick when the time comes."

Tal gasped and flinched. "I don't . . ." He paused as realization sank in. He needed to live, and for that he needed magic. He didn't have to hide it now. It boiled up within him, sparking into a flame, then rising into an inferno.

"It will be a loss to your family, but you're fourth in line. Your kingdom will live on and your death will be the reason. Think of it—a strong alliance for your family and prosperity through war and conflict."

Tal swiped his sleeve over his eyes. Smoke wreathed around him in the rising light. Embers sparked at his fingertips. "It's a good thing."

"Yes," Zeph said with a sharp nod. "It's a good thing."

"No." Tal took a step away, and in her kindness, she allowed him. It was a mistake. "No, I meant, it's a good thing, then," he continued, flicking his gaze to her, "that I have magic."

She paled.

Tal thrust his hand to the sky. Magic burst from him, raw and uncontrolled, as he unleashed a pillar of fire. He poured his spirit into it, willed it higher, hotter than the breaking sun, and brighter than the watchful moon. It tore through the air, a beacon to his brother's ships. The intensity of his innate fire sliced through the predawn sky like a flaming sword, rending the very air, a signal flare proclaiming proof of life and magic. In his abandon he singed the mast and set the sails ablaze.

The canvas caught and flames licked the beams. Wood sizzled and popped. Embers rained as Tal ducked out of Zeph's reach and scrambled to the stern, toward the jolly boats, intent on escape in the aftermath of his display.

"Stop him!"

A knife whizzed past his ear and embedded in a beam in front of him. He skidded to a stop as a line of crew blocked his path, weapons drawn. He whirled around, and even as the ship continued to burn, Zeph pursued him.

"Let me go!" Tal yelled over the sounds of the tumultuous seas and the creak of catching wood. "I don't want to hurt you!"

"You are not leaving here alive. The world will thank me for it!"

Surrounded and out of time, Tal licked his cracked lips. He'd never wanted to hurt anyone, but he was left with no other choice. He shot a blast of magic at the men nearest him, sending them scattering like ashes, then funneled the blaze to the deck, coaxing and pushing the fire where he wanted until the whole ship burned and blackened and curled with heat. Smoke twisted upward in a billowing mass, sweeping from the stern to the bow, obscuring sailors and equipment from view. Heat bubbled up beneath Tal's feet as timbers and planks popped and crackled. Sweat beaded along his hairline and rolled down his spine in rivulets as all the secrets and worries he'd held back for so long ripped from him in a torrent.

He could escape now. No one would stop him. No one could. But as his fire flashed in front of him, wild and raw, so did the memories of the last few weeks, the taunts, the torture, the cruel manipulations. Tal chose to lean into his power, his rage, and burn the ship to cinders, leave nothing behind of those who had made him helpless and afraid. He was done being hurt. He was done being used. It was his turn to wrest control of his life from the whims and machinations of others. It was his moment to turn the tide in his favor. The ship rocked, and wood creaked and splintered. Ropes fell, and ash swirled as Tal rained destruction. He tipped his head back and breathed in the hot, hot air. His body shook with adrenaline and joy, all wounds forgotten, his parched throat raw from a cathartic scream.

If he was going to die, he'd take Zeph and her crew with him in a cruel spectacle of power and light and flames.

He took a breath, banked the fire that raged within him, and clenched his hands to survey the chaos he'd wrought. The sailors he could see through the thick smoke scrambled about the deck like ants, trying to put out the fires, while others fled in the jolly boats, jumping overboard to the relief of the sea. Beams that had burned to cinder cracked and fell, breaking through the deck and the railing. The ship pitched as it took on water.

Zeph stared at him, mouth open in surprise and horror, until her lips curled into disgust.

So this was what it was like to be feared. People who had heard the rumors had always been suspicious of Tal, wary of the possibilities of his blood, but they'd never cowered before him. They'd never shouted in panic and scurried away like they did now. The pulse of power was heady, warm and filling, a match to his pounding heartbeat. Intoxicated, Tal finally understood the appeal. He'd never felt as close to his great-grandfather as he did right now, with embers fluttering on the hot wind and terror seizing the minds of those who'd hurt him. He was no longer powerless and weak. He was in control.

A hard tackle from behind sent him sprawling to the deck. His cheek scraped along the grain as a knee pressed into his spine. Zeph's shiny boot stepped on the nape of his neck.

Rot's voice was harsh in his ear. "What have you done, whelp?"

Tal struggled and gasped as Rot wrenched his hands behind his back.

"My family is coming."

"Too bad you'll be dead before they get here." Zeph pressed harder and Tal choked, the apple of his throat pushing into the wood. "Clap him in irons. Be careful of his hands."

Tal called to his magic and lit his palms, causing Rot to curse, but iron rings encircled his wrists anyway. Zeph released her hold and nudged him over to his back with the toe of her boot. She leaned down and sneered.

"What did you hope to accomplish? You're still going to die."

"Yes," he said, voice strained. "But so will you."

Features twisted in fury, Zeph tugged him to his feet and threw him hard against the railing.

The ship burned, listing to the side. Sailors scrambled along the deck, tossing buckets of water on the fire to no avail. Three warships approached, flying flags with his home's emblem, skidding across the water with sails full of wind and vengeance.

Tal's chest heaved.

Zeph grabbed his chin, her nails digging into his flesh. She yanked him close. Her gray eyes glinted. "I am going to kill you myself." She released him and unsheathed her sword, pressing the tip to his breast. He steeled himself for the pain and hoped his family would find his body amid the wreckage.

A sharp cry pierced the air. A flash of talons and a flurry of brown feathers filled Tal's vision. Kest dove, clawing his way between the trio. Blood splattered. Zeph cried out. Her sword clanged to the deck. Kest shrieked again, his beak clacking, claws swiping, raking across skin to the bone. Tal staggered away, ducking his head as Kest eviscerated Zeph with beak and claws, and Rot cowered in fear.

Amid the scuffle and shouts the ship pitched, throwing Rot sideways into Tal. The collision sent Tal reeling, his feet sliding across the slick scrubbed deck.

Battered by waves and fire, the ship shuddered in its death throes and rolled to its side. Between one moment and the next Tal lost his balance and fell.

The cold water hit him like a slap, stealing the breath from his lungs as he slid under. Kicking wildly, Tal pushed upward and broke the surface, breath heaving from shock. He bobbed barely above the waterline, waves lapping over his face as he struggled to stay afloat. With his hands bound behind his back, he fought to tread water in the rough seas, tilting his body to keep his nose and mouth above the whitecaps. Sputtering with each toss of the waves, Tal struggled to stay near the ship, but the strong current swept him away.

Staring into the dawn, smoke wreathing in thick, dark tendrils against the orange sky, Tal laughed at the destruction he'd wrought, salty spray filling his mouth. At least he'd die knowing his family had come for him, that they hadn't left him as he'd feared.

He inhaled a mix of smoke and water, then slipped beneath the waves.

His chest burned with his last breath. Senses muted as he sank in the murky depths—his vision blurred, his ears flooded with the rushing sound of water mixed with his own heartbeat, a tattoo of fear. A plume of red bloomed in front of him as his shoulder leaked a steady stream of blood. Adrenaline and detachment had made Tal unaware of the wound until then, but it stung now, a throb of pain to equal the pressure building behind his eyes and in his chest.

Even if he weren't bleeding, he was significantly weakened from the injuries from the fight on the beach and the ill treatment by the crew. He couldn't fight his way upward to air, and he couldn't swim away from the currents leading him down to the ocean's depths. This was his death, marked only by a splash.

Looking up, Tal barely made out the shadow of ships above him, the hulls rocking violently. Good. Something positive would come of his death. Maybe his captors would soon follow at the hands of Shay and Garrett. A smaller shadow dove toward the sea, an image of madly flapping wings, but Tal was too far down to be certain.

Tal's struggles slowly gave way to feeble twitches—his limbs too sluggish and uncoordinated to break free of the shackles. His magic danced away from him, elusive with his ebbing consciousness. His vision darkened, black spots growing in front of his eyes.

Death, he discovered, was simple, not the terrifying and daunting fate that had loomed over him during his time on the ship. It was easy to give in, to let his eyes slide half closed, to let his body drift in the rhythm of the sea. His pain dulled—the scorch from his chest and shoulder became distant, as if it weren't happening to him at all. But he still felt regret over the thought of never seeing his family again, of never seeing Athlen again. . . .

His imagination must have taken pity on him in his last moments, because a vision of Athlen suddenly appeared before him, staring at Tal with his wide sunlight eyes, his pretty red mouth open. But the feeling of Athlen's webbed hands holding Tal's face was shockingly real, soft, and gentle.

Tal's first kiss was rough and frantic, Athlen's mouth bruising against his own, a tight seal on Tal's lips. A burst of oxygen followed, filling his lungs like sails. Tal surged back to awareness. Athlen broke away, gaze roving over Tal's body, then he hooked one strong arm around Tal's torso. With a flick of his tail and an undulation of his body, Athlen pulled Tal through the water at a dolphin's pace. Even Garrett's ship couldn't move as fast in the condition of the seas, but the rolls and froth didn't hinder Athlen as he powered Tal through the water.

Tal didn't have much time to appreciate Athlen's mobility and speed before they broke the surface.

Tal gasped, sucking in heaving gulps of air as Athlen held him close. His arms ached from their odd position, and his wounds burned from the salt water. But he was alive.

He was alive!

"Athlen." The name punched out of him as his head lolled on Athlen's collarbone, foam splashing his chin.

Athlen gave him a tense smile. Water beaded along his bare shoulders, his own copper hair wet and dark and matted around his ears and forehead. They floated above the waterline, Athlen's arms snug around Tal's body as Tal leaned heavily on Athlen's chest.

"Are you all right?"

"You saved me."

He shook his head. "Not yet."

Athlen's gaze was far away and Tal followed it. Stunned at the distance they'd covered, Tal could barely discern the ships on the horizon, the only indication of any disturbance being the thick columns of smoke.

"My family," Tal said.

Athlen nodded. "I'll get you back to them. But not yet. It's too dangerous to swim near ships, especially ones ramming each other."

"I trust you." Tal coughed, then grimaced at the wet sound, water dribbling from the side of his mouth.

Athlen's brow creased in concern. "We need to get to shore."

Tal stared at the hard line of the underside of Athlen's clenched jaw. "How did you find me?"

"Followed your brother's ships." Athlen swallowed. "We'll talk more when we're not in the middle of the Morreline Sea with a storm brewing. We need to get you to the beach." He looked over his shoulder. "Even merpeople tire."

"There's a storm coming?" Tal glanced at the clear sky. The sun had fully risen, casting rays that hurt Tal's head and sparkled on the frothing water.

"Yes, and—oh! That will help."

Tal craned his neck. A jolly boat floated nearby, loosed from one of the ships. Athlen sliced through the water, carrying Tal with ease.

"Can you grab the . . ." Athlen trailed off. "Your hands are bound and you're bleeding."

"Yes."

"What did they do to you?"

Tal laughed. He ached down to his marrow. Every piece of his body that he could feel *hurt*. He didn't know how to answer that question.

"Can you use your magic to break free of the shackles?" Athlen asked, his shoulder bumping against the side of the boat. "Like you did for me?"

Tal considered it, but he was weak all over, and his fingers were numb. His eyelids grew heavy with each passing moment. His thoughts slugged through his brain. He was cold and hot all at once. He'd almost drowned. His chest hurt, and he couldn't feel much below his knees.

"I don't think it's a good idea for me to try right now."

"Okay." Athlen had one arm wrapped around the side of the boat and the other around Tal, and he looked between the two with a furrow in his brow. "Take a deep breath."

"What?"

"Trust me."

Tal sucked in a breath and Athlen released him. He sank like a stone for the second time that morning. Panic choked him for a gut-wrenching second, but then he was back in Athlen's arms and propelled upward.

He fell into the bottom of the small vessel with a yelp. His face scratched on the wood and his body twitched, and he'd never been happier to be back on a boat in his life.

Athlen's head popped over the edge. "All right?"

Tal rolled to his side to ease the pressure on his wrists and hands. "Sure," he said, voice a rasp.

"Fantastic. There's a rope here. I'm going to pull you to shore."

Swimming on the edge of consciousness, finally feeling safe, Tal nodded, eyes sliding shut. "Thank you."

Athlen's response was a splash. The jolly boat jerked into motion. Tal relaxed into the sway and passed out.

9

Tal woke up shivering. He squeezed his eyes shut, curled into a tight ball, and cursed whoever had left the door to the royal wing open. His chambers were down a long hallway, between Kest and Corrie's bedrooms, with Garrett across the way. In the winter fierce breezes whipped off the ocean, and the stone corridors became wind tunnels. Tapestries would inevitably fall no matter how many fasteners the stewards used, and the sharp gusts howled, scaring everyone with the promise of ghosts. The doors helped to temper the chill and strength of the breezes, but only if they were closed and latched.

The last time the door had been left ajar was when Kest sneaked into his rooms in the small hours after spending the night with someone. He wouldn't say who it was, but Tal guessed it might be Shay. Her crush wasn't a secret to anyone except maybe the queen. Though Tal wouldn't put it past his mother to know too.

She'd known about Tal even before he told her that he was attracted to the athletic squires and the beautiful ladies of the court and those who identified somewhere between. She'd merely smiled and cupped his reddened cheeks in her jeweled fingers and told him he was fortunate to have so many people to choose from for his potential spouse—when and if he wanted one. And whoever he did choose would be lucky to have him.

That was before the magic, before his life changed irrevocably and his dreams disappeared in a puff of smoke. Thoughts of a future had vanished when he set a tablecloth on fire while arguing with Corrie at the dinner table. From then on he was confined to the castle, hidden away from staff and nobles alike. The whispers spread as fast as the wind barreling through the corridors—sickly, shy, melancholic, *magic*.

"Tal?"

Furrowing his brow, Tal attempted to curl further into a ball, knees to his chest, but his arms were stuck behind his back. A burst of pain lanced down them into his hands, and he groaned.

"Tal?"

"Kest?"

"No. It's Athlen."

Tal cracked open his eyes. They were crusted, salt clinging to his eyelashes. "Athlen?"

"I'm here."

Tal's chest ached. His throat was raw. His lips were split. His skin felt flayed, stretched tightly over his joints. His head throbbed.

"Help."

"I . . . what? Tal?"

Athlen's face blurred above him. His mouth turned down in a deep frown. Dark lashes framed his wide honey eyes. He leaned in close over the lip of the jolly boat, droplets of water sluicing over his shoulders.

"Cold."

"Oh. Hold on."

There was a splash of water. Tal's bed wobbled. He lifted his head and shook off the remnants of his dream. But he couldn't shake the fever or the chill that had sunk into his bones. He blinked. He was still in the boat.

"Where are we?"

"My home," Athlen answered. He reappeared at Tal's side and draped a damp sail over Tal's body, jabbing the fabric around him. "You've been here before. Don't you remember?"

Tal did. Vividly. But being tucked into the bottom of a jolly boat in the shallow water of Athlen's cove was much different from sitting next to him on the trinket-strewn shelf.

"I do."

"Can you use your magic now? On the irons? I don't have a key, and your fingers don't look as they should."

Tal flexed his fingers, then wished he hadn't as pins and needles pricked along his skin. He needed to free his hands, or risk permanent damage, but he'd have to use magic. The thought made him sick to his stomach, and he closed his eyes. An image of the boat aflame lit behind his eyelids, and he clenched them tighter to will it away. But he couldn't; the vision seared in his memory. He'd done that. He'd destroyed Zeph's ship in anger and despair. The cries of the dying crew members rang in his ears.

"Do you have anything that could break them?" Tal's voice was rough and weak.

"No. I looked. Just use your magic like you used it on mine."

Filled with guilt, Tal gritted his teeth and concentrated on the flicker of magic in his belly and channeled it to his fingertips. They stung with the sudden heat. He flinched, gasping as his fingers curled in toward his palms. He opened his eyes and met Athlen's worried gaze. "I can't."

"You can," Athlen said, moving the tarp to squint down at Tal's hands. "I know you can."

Tal bit his lip. He didn't deserve Athlen's faith, but he couldn't deny him, so he tried again. Tears of frustration and pain and overwhelming regret pricked behind his eyes. His rising fire sizzled painfully down his nerves. Wrapped in a sail and surrounded by wood, he imagined igniting it all by accident, hurting himself—or worse, hurting Athlen—especially with how unfocused he was. He'd need another way.

He had used the power of will to snag the sail from beneath the crate to send his family messages. Maybe he could . . . maybe if he . . . Tal gathered his magic. His core flooded with blessed heat and power, but it was different from before, difficult to wield. He tried to will the cuffs to break, yearned for the iron to become brittle, but his magic skittered away from him in a wash of dizziness.

Taking a deep breath, he focused on his decorum lessons. He'd learned to be *royal*, to demand respect and command attention. He'd had teachings drilled into him from an early age—squared shoulders; straight spine; flat, intimidating gaze. He was a prince. His birth and blood demanded obedience and deference, but it was his integrity and character that would command loyalty and respect. Except nothing about his recent decisions made him feel like he deserved loyalty or respect. Yet Athlen was still here, supporting him, believing in him. Perhaps whatever small part of Tal that had shown kindness to a stranger was still there, deep inside. Perhaps a small part of him was still good.

Tal throttled his feelings of self-loathing and concentrated on recalling how he'd felt when he helped Athlen escape his shackles, reaching farther than he ever had for his magic. He could do it. He could do it. He had to do it. He *would* do it.

He demanded the metal to *break*.

A crack like a whip echoed in the cave, splitting the silence. Tal gritted his teeth and stretched his arms, and the cuffs snapped.

Tal cried out. He was stiff from cold and being bound, so moving his arms was agony, but he persevered and managed to arrange his limbs in front of him. His fingers were colored from lack of circulation, and bruises ringed his wrists. Despite how utterly wretched his body felt, he was giddy with the thought that, through some miracle, he'd escaped. He blindly searched for the edge of the sail, grabbed it, and burrowed beneath, cold and wet and miserable, but free.

"You did it!" Athlen poked Tal in the arm until he opened his eyes. Athlen beamed above him. "I knew you could."

Nodding, Tal didn't try to move further. His senses hovered at the edge of exhaustion. He wanted to sleep again but was afraid.

Athlen's smile faded. "You don't look well." He tilted his head. "Are you . . ." He bent closer. "Are you ill?"

Tal lifted an eyebrow. He shivered, but his body burned. His head pounded. "What?"

Athlen's fingers were cool as they slid over Tal's forehead, then down his cheek and the line of his jaw. "You're hot, and you're pale except your cheeks." He gently pushed on Tal's shoulder, and Tal bit down on a shout. "Your shoulder is bleeding." He licked his lips. "Does it hurt?"

Tal laughed, the sound a scrape from his raw throat. "Yes."

The boat rocked as Athlen took a closer look, peeling back the sail and Tal's wet shirt. "Merpeople heal much faster than humans. Our skin is thicker and knits quickly, so I'm not sure how to fix you. Were you stabbed?"

"There was a scuffle before I fell in. I think that was when it happened."

Athlen frowned. Without thinking, Tal weakly raised his hand and traced the curve of Athlen's mouth with clumsy fingers. Athlen clucked his tongue when Tal grimaced at the action, but Tal wasn't sorry for it, not when Athlen took his hand, wrapped his own knobby webbed fingers around Tal's, and held them close to his chest.

"You saved me," Tal said.

Athlen mustered a grin. "You saved me first, remember? I was returning the favor."

"That was a lifetime ago."

Tal smiled lazily, and his eyes fluttered shut. A smart smack to his cheek startled him back to wakefulness. He scowled.

"Don't fall asleep yet. I think you're sick. I need to get help."

Athlen heaved his body from the water with a grunt, his beautiful tail creating ripples in the otherwise smooth surface. Once on the shelf, Athlen transformed, grimacing as his fins fused into body and his scales smoothed. His tail split and Tal looked away, unwilling to watch the rest.

A rustle of fabric followed, and Tal craned his neck to see Athlen dressed in trousers and a shirt. He shoved the wide-brimmed hat on his head.

Panic caught in Tal's throat. "Don't leave me." His voice was plaintive, bordering on a whine, not at all befitting a prince.

"I'll be right back with Dara. I promise."

Athlen crossed the area and picked up a bundle of fabric. He shook it out, scattering gold coins, sea glass, and jewels across the narrow floor. He pulled the boat, Tal's bed for now, closer to the shelf and spread the blanket over Tal's body. He tucked it in, as he had the sail, and though it was musty, it was infinitely warmer.

Tal sighed into the heat.

"I've lashed the boat. You won't drift away."

"Take me with you."

"Can you walk?"

Tal pointed his toe and his muscles spasmed. He gritted his teeth to keep from crying out. His head was full of wool and he wanted to sleep, and he was losing snatches of time, reality fuzzing in and out. It was irrational to want Athlen to stay when they both knew he needed to go, but Tal was afraid. Afraid his rescue was all a dream. Afraid of recapture. Afraid of *himself*, of the monster he'd become in his rage and grief.

Athlen knelt next to the boat. His palm was heavy and cool on Tal's hot skin. "I can't . . ." Athlen's throat bobbed. "I don't know how to take care of a sick human. I've not done it before. I need to get help. You've been bleeding the entire time it took me to drag the boat here. You could be dying, and I wouldn't know. I can't . . . I can't lose you, too."

Tal swallowed down a thick sob. "I'm being childish."

"No." Athlen shook his head. "You're not. But you're safe here. And I promise, I will return as quickly as possible."

"Okay." Tal blinked, and his eyelids stubbornly stayed closed. "I trust you."

"Good," Athlen said, his voice close.

"Don't . . . don't tell her about the magic."

"I won't."

"Thank you," Tal said on a sigh.

There was a wet, warm press to Tal's forehead, followed by the scent of a salt breeze. "You're welcome."

Tal fell asleep to the sound of trinkets scattering across stone, the rustle of fabric, and the fade of footsteps echoing off the rock walls.

"Why won't you just tell me where you're taking me?"

Tal woke from his fitful sleep. He had dreamed again, visions of his home mixed with that of the ship to create a patchwork of warmth and terror. They left him unsettled and afraid.

"Dara, could you trust me, please?"

Athlen. He'd returned. Grateful and relieved, Tal felt the strangling panic release its hold, and his tense and sore muscles eased, as did the furrow of his brow.

"I do, sometimes, but you're not good at being truthful."

"If this is about not showing you my tail—"

"No, I know that's a special thing."

Tal had seen Athlen's tail. It was beautiful—red and gold with gossamer fins and scales that sparkled—and powerful enough to cut through frothing seas and deliver Tal to safety.

"But . . . we've been friends for a while now," Dara continued, "and you flit in and out of my life with no notice. Where have you been? I thought you'd been captured again. I was worried."

"I didn't mean to worry you, but I really need your help now. Watch your head."

The voices moved closer, and Tal craned his neck to find Athlen leading Dara into the cave. Her long brown hair was plaited and hung over her shoulder. She wore trousers and boots and a stiff blouse with long sleeves and a high collar that laced at the throat.

She reminded Tal of Shay, except with a rounder face and lighter skin, and his eyes pricked with tears.

He missed Shay. He missed her blush when Kest teased her. He missed her disapproval when he and Corrie sneaked away. He missed her laugh when she and Garrett engaged in one game or another. He'd lost her dagger. He'd have to buy her a new one. If he ever saw her again. If she even wanted to be near him after what he'd done.

"What is this place?" Dara asked, toeing a golden goblet out of the way.

"My home."

"This?" she asked. "This is where you sleep?"

"No." Athlen motioned to the water. "Under there. It's nice and calm, and there's a nook right in the side of the cave wall, and . . ." He waved his hands. "It's not important." He pointed to Tal in the boat. "He's important."

Tal saw the moment Dara realized who he was, and her eyebrows jumped, and her jaw clenched, and twin spots of red appeared on her cheeks, then bled to her temples and down her neck.

"The missing prince! Athlen! What have you done? Did you kidnap him?"

Athlen scoffed and placed his hands on his hips. "No. I saved him."

"He saved me," Tal echoed. "From mercenaries."

Dara's eyes widened at the raw sound of his voice, and she dropped to her knees at the edge of the water. Leaning over, she reached for him, then hesitated.

"Um . . ."

"You may touch me."

Athlen crinkled his nose. "You have to ask?"

"He's royalty. Of course you ask."

"I didn't."

"I make exceptions for myths from the sea," Tal said with a loopy smile.

"I'm not a myth," Athlen muttered.

Dara rolled her eyes, then laid her palm on his forehead. "You're burning up. What happened to you?" Tal opened his mouth to respond, but she shook her head. "Never mind. Don't talk. It'll be nonsense with a fever this high."

"He's bleeding, too. His shoulder."

A wrinkle appeared on Dara's forehead as she pulled the blankets away and found Tal's bloody shirt. She pursed her lips as she inspected the wound. Tal grimaced when she skirted her fingers over his shoulder, then she shushed him when he groaned. "We need to clean and bandage it, as well as the other wounds." She lifted Tal's battered hand. "Even small cuts can go bad. Then we need to get him out of these wet clothes and warmed up." She nodded to Athlen. "Hand me my bag." Then to Tal, "Can you sit up?"

Grabbing the side of the boat, Tal struggled to sitting, but his body shook and his head spun.

Dara's frown deepened, and she steadied him with a hand on his back.

Tal stayed stiff and still as Dara inspected and bandaged him. She poured a foul-smelling liquid over the puncture wound that stung and burned, and he gritted his teeth to keep from flinching. Then, using a bundle of cloth from her bag, she tightened a bandage around his shoulder and bound his arm to his chest. She rubbed a salve on his blistered hands and bandaged them as well. She checked his weeks-old head gash, and he grimaced as she clipped the crude stitches. She stabilized his swollen knee with sticks laid along either side of the joint, then wrapped it in cloth. She gave him fresh water in a canteen, and Tal resisted the urge to gulp it down.

"He needs dry clothes. Athlen, do you have any stashed here?"

Athlen scurried to the other side of the cave, and in a dark corner sat a chest. He flung it open and pulled out a pair of trousers and a shirt that were finer than anything Tal had seen him wear. Tal blushed when he needed both Athlen and Dara to help him change while he stood shivering in the damp air of Athlen's home, his toes curled on the wet, chilled shelf of rock, and goose bumps blossoming over his skin. With his face flushed red from fever and sunburn, he hoped they wouldn't notice his embarrassment. If they did, they didn't comment. Athlen had no compulsions about nudity anyway.

Dara held up Tal's tattered shirt between her thumb and forefinger. "I'm going to throw this away."

"Wait." Tal lunged forward, stumbling over a cache of trinkets. Athlen caught him by the waist as Dara handed over the shirt with a raised eyebrow and a wrinkled nose.

With trembling fingers Tal dug into the chest pocket, and despite the fight and the rough water, the shark's tooth was miraculously still tucked inside. Tal clutched it in his palm, the comforting edge blunted by the bandages.

"The tooth?" Athlen asked. "You kept it?"

"Yes." Tal's mouth went dry. "It helped me when I was captured."

"Oh?" Athlen's gaze flitted to Tal's hand, then to his face. "Oh." His lips curled into a small smile. "Really?"

Tal's cheeks blazed as he nodded. His knees trembled and Athlen clasped him tighter. This close, Tal tipped his head back to meet Athlen's unwavering gaze. He spied the light line of freckles that spread over the bridge of Athlen's nose, and the dimple in his cheek, and the slope of his neck as the collar of his shirt slipped sideways. Tal's blood pounded and his head swam, and he didn't know if it was due to illness or something else, something about Athlen's proximity and the strong cage of his arms and the salty smell of his skin.

"You need to lie back down," Dara said. "Before you fall."

Athlen jumped, and Tal grasped his shirt in his free hand to keep from sliding to the ground.

"I'm sorry!" Athlen said, grip bordering on painful. "Are you all right?"

Tal shook his head, but the dizziness persisted. "I don't feel—"

"You're dehydrated and feverish," Dara said, interrupting. "And with your arm bound, your balance will be off. Let's get you back in the boat. It's the only level and uncluttered place in here."

As much as he disliked the notion of sleeping in the jolly boat, there wasn't much choice. Settled back against the hull like cargo, in fresh clothes and bandages and wrapped in blankets with a cushion under his head, Tal was finally warm. He didn't feel strong by any means, and his belly sloshed with water and no food, and his hands itched, but he was safe.

He was safe, even if he didn't want to consider what he'd done to escape, how he'd blazed his way free. He clamped down on the feelings of weakness and shame that welled in him, banished them as best he could, and closed his eyes against the images of fire and smoke. Instead he focused on the tight wrap of clean bandages against his skin and the musty smell of his borrowed shirt. Tal squeezed the shark's tooth in the clutch of his hand, the point digging into his palm, securing him to the present and to Athlen like a tether. He listened to Athlen and Dara whisper to each other, the soft sound of their voices a comforting hum. Tal breathed deeply;

the fresh air of Athlen's cove was a far cry from the ash-laden, hot air that had bubbled from the scorched planks of Zeph's ship.

After a few moments Tal felt grounded, and he slid the tooth into the pocket of his trousers and opened his eyes to peer at the hole in Athlen's ceiling. The stars twinkled above him, and the half-moon was partially obscured by clouds. The dawn was so long ago, and the events of the morning seemed more like a dream than a memory, as blurred as he had been. How long had he slept? How long had Athlen towed him through the seas?

"What happened to the storm?"

The fierce whispered conversation between Athlen and Dara ended abruptly.

"The storm?" Dara asked. She leaned over, blocking Tal's view of the sky, and brushed the back of her hand over his cheek. "His fever has gone down, so he shouldn't be delusional."

"He's not," Athlen said, his voice hinting at amusement. "I told him this morning there was a storm brewing. It's already passed by on the sea."

Tal furrowed his brow. "Oh."

"I'll let you know if another one is coming."

"You can do that?" Dara asked, braid whispering over Tal's chin as she turned away.

A passing cloud spliced the moon in two. The cavern darkened, awash in shades of blue and droplets of gold.

"Yes. When I'm near the sea. I haven't traveled far enough inland to try it on land." Athlen splashed his toes in the water. "You should rest, Tal. Dara and I will keep watch, if you're worried."

"Not worried. I know I'm safe here."

"Good."

Tal's eyes slid closed. The gentle rocking of the boat soothed him, and the rhythm of the waves beyond the cave reminded him of home and of the sounds of the waves on the beach outside his bedroom window. Bundled in warmth, he slipped along the edge of sleep.

"What was your plan?" Dara whispered. "You can't keep him here forever. He's sick, and this damp cave isn't going to do him any good. What if he gets worse?"

"If he gets worse, then I'll bring him to your house."

"Across the town where the missing prince was last seen? He'll be recognized in an instant."

"Is that not a good thing? It'll get him to his family. That's what he wants. That's what he needs."

Dara huffed. "A group of mercenaries tried to kill him! It's not safe for him to be seen in public, much less with a boy who has a reputation for being strange. You don't know who else is after him or what people might say or think. He's a prince."

"Is that a problem? That he's a prince?"

"You don't understand." Dara's tone wasn't condescending, but fond and gentle. "I don't know what it was like where you're from, but princes don't cavort with commoners. And certainly not *that* prince. According to rumor, this is the first time he's left the castle in years, and he's already been kidnapped and almost killed."

Tal squirmed and shifted in the boat. Dara wasn't wrong, but that didn't mean he liked what she was implying.

"Two people," Tal mumbled, tongue thick in his mouth.

"What was that?" Athlen's voice went sharp. "Two people?"

"Zeph and her crew kidnapped me, but before that, one of my brother's sailors tried to kill me too." If that sailor had succeeded, then Tal wouldn't have killed Zeph and her crew, and his family wouldn't have to worry about him any longer. Maybe that would've been better, if Tal hadn't yelled for help, if Shay hadn't intervened. It was an unsettling thought, and one Tal entertained only briefly, because despite his inner turmoil, he knew he needed to live to save his family. But the ache of his decision to hurt and to destroy teased at the back of his mind. It left him feeling hollow.

"See?" Dara said, voice bordering on shrill. "His brother's own crew tried to kill him. He can't trust anyone except his family. You have to get him home."

"I'll take him now. We'll get a boat and we'll—"

"He's too weak to move. He needs a few days to recover before you go galivanting around the kingdom."

"No boats," Tal said. "No more boats."

"Fine. No boats. We'll go by land."

Tal cracked open an eye. "Will you be okay on land?"

"I'll manage."

Dara sighed. "Go to sleep, princeling."

Tal winced at the moniker, panic thumping hard in his middle, and he roused out of his drowsiness, Zeph's sneers and taunts echoing in his ears. "Tal please. Just . . . call me Tal."

"Tal," Dara said, tone going soft. "Get some rest. We'll talk more in the morning. You too, Athlen. You swam for hours—you must be exhausted."

Athlen's shoulders relaxed and he wilted forward, propping his head on his hands, his elbows on his knees. Fatigue was evident in the line of his body and the circles under his eyes. Tal hadn't noticed before. "You'll watch over him?"

"Of course. My mother won't start to worry until the morning."

Athlen nodded, his eyelids lowering. He tossed his hat into a rounded corner. "I'll be right here. I won't go into the water. Just in case you need me."

He didn't move to another part of the cavern, merely curled into a ball on his side, his head pillowed on his hands, a testament to his exhaustion. Lying on the shelf, he was level with Tal. Their faces were a scant foot apart, the side of the boat the only thing between them. In the low light and shadows Athlen appeared otherworldly—cold and beautiful and beyond Tal's reach. But his smile was warm.

"Thank you," Tal whispered. "Thank you both."

"Go to sleep, Tal."

Tal nodded and closed his eyes, face tipped toward Athlen, secure in the knowledge that both his new friends would watch over him in the night.

"Tal! Wake up! I brought food."

Tal startled, body jumping, boat rocking beneath him. His eyes flew open, and he groaned, clenching them shut as the high sun blinded him. He attempted to throw up a hand as a shield but found himself bundled in a way he couldn't move. He squeezed his eyes shut, intense orange bleeding through his eyelids.

"You've been asleep for hours. It's almost midday."

A shadow passed over him, and cautiously Tal cracked open an eye. He'd slept the morning away, yet he could have continued sleeping if Athlen hadn't been so loud.

Athlen stood above him, wearing his wide-brimmed hat and a shirt and a pair of trousers with tattered hems and a hole in the knee. His pale toes wrapped around the edge of the ledge. He held a tin pan of food that smelled hot and delicious enough to rouse Tal. His stomach rumbled as he untucked his blankets and pushed his body to sitting.

"Here. It's from the tavern. I asked for everything they had for breakfast." Athlen set it on Tal's lap with a wide grin. "I have to return the plate when I go for lunch. And I promise to clean off a spot today for your bed. I know you don't want to be in that boat any longer than you have to."

Athlen rambled while Tal stared down at the pile of fluffy eggs, sausage links, and two large biscuits. His stomach cramped with hunger and nausea. He balanced the plate on his knees, and using his unbound hand, he scooped the food into his mouth with abandon. The eggs were salty, the sausage was greasy, and the biscuits were a little hard, probably a day old, but it was the best meal Tal had eaten since leaving the castle. He shoveled it in, uncaring that he was staining the bandages on his fingers or that all sense of decorum had been tossed aside in favor of food.

"Here's water."

Athlen's voice startled Tal, so focused was he on the plate in front of him, but he took the canteen gratefully and sucked down the cool, clean water between bites.

"Dara left before dawn, but she'll be back this afternoon to check on you," Athlen said as he moved gracefully around his home. He had a pile of blankets at the entrance that he'd brought with the plate of food. He moved to the spot closest to the wall and cleared a space, pieces of gold, jewels, and earthenware plunking into the water or rolling along the rocky ledge. Athlen hauled the blankets over and laid them out with care, straightening the edges and smoothing down the plush fabric. "I heard that princes are used to thick beds. Is this good, or do I need to get more blankets?"

Tal smiled, and warmth that wasn't related to his fever spread through his chest. "It's fine. Thank you."

Athlen grinned. "How's the food?"

"It's good. It's the most I've had in days." Tal flinched as soon as the words tumbled out, and he was awash in the memory of the gnawing hunger and unceasing thirst that had plagued him while he was on the ship. He absently licked his fingers, then bit into another sausage as his thoughts raced inevitably toward the circumstances of his escape and his mind's eye replayed cruel images of the choices he'd made. He drank more water, and it sloshed down his throat, hitting his filling stomach. He grimaced, feeling the food as well as his guilt stack up in his gullet, his next bite lodging at the top. Everything soured and was rejected, and Tal clapped a hand over his mouth, willing the food to stay down. It didn't work, and he doubled over before vomiting into the water. His back bowed, and his stomach heaved, and tears streamed from the corners of his eyes.

He hated boats. He hated water. He hated throwing up. And he hated that this had become a common occurrence.

Once it was over, he dropped heavily back into his blankets. Sweating, he breathed deeply and swallowed several times to keep another incident at bay.

Athlen stared at him, clutching his hat, skin pale. "Is that normal?"

A laugh bubbled up at the ridiculousness, and Tal clutched his stomach with his good arm. "No, it's not. I think I ate too much too fast. I'm sorry I wasted it."

Athlen waved Tal's concern away. His mouth tilted in worry and uncertainty. "Should I get Dara?"

"No." Tal shook his head. "I'll be fine."

"Maybe we should get you out of the boat?"

"That's a good idea." Tal's head ached from the light pouring in, and the spot Athlen had cleared was in a darker corner, where he could easily slip back into sleep.

With Athlen's help, Tal was able to step from the boat to the ledge and walk to the pile of blankets. He eased down onto them, and Athlen fussed, covering him with another bedspread and tucking him in. He placed a cool palm on Tal's forehead.

"I should've found you quicker." He sat by Tal's side. "I should've intervened on the beach."

Tal squinted. "No. They would've hurt you."

Athlen slid his fingers to Tal's overheated cheek. "They did hurt you."

"There was nothing you could've done." Tal leaned into Athlen's touch. "They were prepared."

"I could've pulled you into the waves. I tried, but there was that cat and . . . I feared those humans. They acted like the ones who trapped me."

"That cat . . ." Tal trailed off. "That cat had to be someone from one of the royal houses, but I don't know which one. Zeph said that if I had magic, I was to go to Prince Emerick to be a weapon."

Athlen shrugged. "Who is that?"

"The prince from Ossetia my sister is to marry."

"Do you think he was behind your kidnapping? Why would he do that? He'll be allied with you after their marriage. He'll . . . have access to you?"

Tal scrubbed a hand over his face and pushed his hair from his eyes. "The whole time I was on that ship, the sailors tried to get me to reveal my magic. We hadn't told Emerick about . . . my power, and we weren't sure if we were going to at all. Maybe this was his way to figure it out, to draw it out of me so he would prove the rumors true and know for sure."

"Except they tried to kill you."

"They tried to kill me to force a war. When I didn't give in, they decided I couldn't have magic. And when I couldn't be a weapon, they were going to blame my death on the kingdom that borders Emerick's land. That would push my family to war, and it would only benefit Ossetia. Ossetia engages in border disputes, but their army isn't large enough to handle a real fight. The addition of Harth's army would allow them to challenge Mysten."

Athlen shook his head. "Your land politics are weird."

Tal shot to sitting, ignoring the pain in his shoulder. "I have to send a message to my family. I have to tell them I'm alive and to stop Isa's wedding to Emerick. He has to be the one behind this."

"Can you do that?"

"Yes." Tal swallowed. "With . . . with magic." He flexed his aching fingers. Sending a message would be a simple use of his power, even simpler than breaking his chains, but disgust welled inside him at the thought of tapping into that part of himself again. The same part that had wrought destruction and killed the crew. That had been surprisingly simple as well, unleashing a torrent of fire, and watching in grim satisfaction as sails burned and wood bubbled and curled from the intense heat and sailors screamed in panic. Tal imagined sliding down the slippery slope from breaking chains and sending a message to burning the countryside in his want for home and in defense of his family.

"Tal?" Athlen asked. "Are you okay?"

Tal balled his hands into fists. His breaths quickened. "I'm fine."

"All right. How can I help? What do you need to send your message?"

Tal shook his head. His chest was tight, and he knuckled a spot on his breastbone. "I'm not. It's too dangerous." *I'm too dangerous.* What if he implicated Emerick in a message and someone other than his mother saw it? Would that put his family in danger? And if he told them he was alive, would that send more people looking? What if he had to defend himself? What if he had to use his magic again? Was it better to remain missing or presumed dead until he could get to the safety of his home, where he could hide and lock himself away? "Emerick is at the castle right now. He could have spies that might intercept the message."

"Oh, good point. What should we do? How soon is the wedding?"

"I . . . don't know what day it is. A few days?" Tal picked at a loose thread. His hands trembled. "I don't know. I told my family to go ahead with the alliance when I shouldn't have. I made a mistake. I need to fix this. I need to get to them. I need . . ." Tal choked on panic; his throat clogged. All he could think about was how he'd doomed Isa to a marriage unlike her romance stories. And how Emerick could use Tal to fight his wars. He'd be a murderer like his great-grandfather. He already *was*. There was no escaping his legacy now, not with the taste of ash on his tongue and the burn of cinders on his fingertips. "I killed them." The words slipped out in a whisper. "I killed them with magic. My magic."

Athlen gripped Tal's shoulder. "Tal," he said, voice soft.

"I killed them." Tears rolled down his flushed cheeks. "Zeph. Her crew. Poppy. All of them. I'm no better than my great-grandfather." Tal curled into himself and buried his face in the crook of his elbow. Sobbing, his shoulders shaking violently, he gave in to his anguish. He'd promised himself he'd never use his magic to hurt or destroy, but he had. He had, and oh, how easy it'd been.

"Hey." Athlen's voice was low and calming in his ear. Athlen's hand on his shoulder slid into his hair and gently pulled Tal until his forehead rested against Athlen's chest. "Shhh. It's okay. It's okay."

"But I—"

"I know. I know. It must have been terrible." His arms tightened around Tal. "But I know you, and I know you wouldn't have done it if you'd had another choice."

"You don't know that," Tal said, voice thick.

"I do, actually." Athlen rested his chin on the crown of Tal's head. "I know you saved me when you didn't have to. I know you love your family. I know you care for the people of your kingdom. I know that something that is a part of you could never be bad."

Tal sagged farther into Athlen's embrace, his cheek pressed against the stiff fabric of Athlen's shirt. Athlen's heartbeat was a soothing rhythm under his ear. "You don't understand," Tal said bitterly. "I chose to destroy the ship. I made a choice."

"So did they, when they chose to hurt you."

Tal bit his lip against another wave of tears, but he couldn't stop the rising tide of his emotions, not in the face of Athlen's sincere faith. Athlen's assertions didn't absolve Tal of his guilt, but they were a balm to his tattered spirit.

"We'll get you home," Athlen said. "We'll fix this. I promise." Tal clasped Athlen's shirt in his fist and held on, desperate and afraid. He focused on the reassurances in his ear and the closeness of Athlen's body while he shuddered and sobbed. Time passed in a haze of panic and visions, until exhaustion surged and Tal slumped forward, his body and tears giving way.

He came back to himself in moments. Athlen's hand rubbed up and down the length of his spine, and his voice spoke slow and soothing, though Tal couldn't make out the words. He hiccoughed and leaned heavily into Athlen's body.

"Tal?"

"I'm sorry."

"Don't be." Athlen held him tighter. "Don't be. I was waiting for it to happen."

Tal frowned. "For what?"

Athlen sighed and Tal moved with the expansion of his chest. He should've been embarrassed, sagging as he was onto Athlen's body, but he was too tired to move.

"When the seafloor shifted all those years ago, and I lost my family and my people, I looked for them for weeks. No, months. I spent all of my time swimming, looking for anyone who was still alive. Parts of our home were too hot, and I could see the . . ." He shook his head, his hair sweeping across Tal's cheek. "When I finally took a moment to rest, everything crashed down. It was the first time I cried over losing them. It wasn't the last, but it was the most . . . visceral."

Athlen pulled away but kept his hands clenched on Tal's shoulders, peering into Tal's face with his wide honey eyes, his lashes dark and wet.

"You've been through a lot in the past few days. It was bound to catch up to you."

Tal bit his lip. He nodded. "Thank you." He released his grip on Athlen's shirt, the fabric crinkled from force and sweat, and wiped his sleeve over his eyes. "I'm sorry there wasn't anyone there for you when it happened."

Athlen looked away and he sniffed. "Maybe next time I'll have someone."

Tal's middle fluttered. Athlen could've meant any number of situations with that statement, but Tal hoped it meant that they would be friends far in the future, whenever that unknown next time would be.

"You saved me again. We're even."

Athlen smiled and his eyes crinkled. His gaze cut back to Tal, and he brushed a wayward strand of hair from Tal's forehead, his knobby fingers cool and smooth on Tal's flushed skin.

"You need to rest. Especially if we're going to get you back to your family before your sister's wedding."

Tal didn't argue. He settled back on the cushion in the nest and closed his eyes. Athlen rearranged the blankets and hovered nearby as Tal drifted in and out of a restless sleep.

10

We have a problem," Dara said when she returned late that afternoon. She startled Tal into wakefulness while he was in the middle of a snore, which turned into a loud snort. He rolled onto his side and peered at Dara over the edge of a blanket.

"What?"

"Great. You're awake. Where's Athlen?"

Tal yawned and stretched his good arm over his head, his injured one bandaged to his chest. "I don't know. He was here when I went to sleep." He sat up and accepted the canteen of hot broth Dara shoved at him. "He might be swimming."

She twisted her hands. "Oh no. He needs to get back here right away."

Alarm lanced through Tal. "What's wrong?"

"We have a problem," Athlen said, popping up from the water, surprising them both. Tal dropped the canteen and Dara let out a yelp. "Oh, hi, Dara. What's wrong? You look upset." He pushed his body from the water with his strong arms, his gills closing and his tail morphing as he emerged, water sluicing over his muscles as he stepped onto the shelf.

Tal and Dara both looked away as he stood dripping. Dara's cheeks were as red as Tal's felt.

"Trousers!" she snapped.

"Right. Right. Land modesty." A rustle of fabric and a soft curse later, Athlen was dressed. His hair was flattened to his head, tendrils sticking wetly to his cheeks.

"Like I said, we may have a problem."

Tal pointed to Dara. "That's what she said when she walked in."

"What's your problem?" Athlen asked, using the edge of a tattered sail to wipe off the remaining droplets of water, his torso flexing in the golden light of the late afternoon.

A lump lodged in Tal's throat, and he squirmed in the makeshift bed.

"There was a royal messenger in the next town over who made a proclamation. Rumor has already spread, but the kingdom is in mourning." Her brown eyes zeroed in on Tal. "You're officially dead."

"Oh." He unplugged the canteen and took a drink of the broth. It was hot and thick and hinted at flavorlessness. It was better to his stomach than the eggs and sausage had been. He swallowed. "Did they say how?"

"Murdered."

"Oh," he repeated. Tal picked at the edge of the canteen. Murdered. Not assassinated. There was a slight difference. The latter being politically driven. His family either hadn't made the connection or hadn't found evidence to support a declaration of assassination. They'd be reluctant to declare anyone an enemy when they had so few allies.

Either way, his mother thought him dead. Tal hugged his stomach.

"That's not all." She tugged on her braid. "The proclamation says that the perpetrators have been captured or killed, but there is a bounty for information about anyone who may have helped them." She shifted her gaze to Athlen and gestured to him. "The townsfolk have implicated you."

Athlen pushed his head through the fabric of his shirt, then pointed to his chest. "Me? I didn't help them. I saved him."

"I know that. Tal knows that. But you were seen with Tal at the tavern before he disappeared. You've been gone since that night and then show back up and spend large sums of gold around town. You must know how bad it all looks."

Athlen's mouth fell open. He looked to Tal, then back to Dara. "But I didn't . . . I am not . . . oh no."

"Yes, oh no. The village people are stricken over the loss of the kind young prince who handed out supplies during the sickness. Everyone is tense and looking for vengeance. You'll be the first target. You better stay out of sight until the both of you are ready to travel back to the castle."

"I'm sorry," Tal said. He studied the grooves in the floor of the cavern, where the tide had seeped in for centuries and worn a pattern into the rock. He traced one with the edge of a fingernail.

"It's not your fault," Athlen said, padding over. He crossed his arms over his chest, and the sleeves of his shirt billowed out, wrapping his slim torso in an excess of fabric.

Tal didn't believe that, but there was nothing he could do to change the situation. "So," he said, "what's your bad news?"

Athlen grimaced. He pointed at the water. "I was at the docks. Well, under them, listening to the sailors and . . . well . . . they talked about your family."

Athlen hesitated. Tal took another long drink of the broth. "I'm dead. I can handle it."

"Your sister . . . is married."

Tal went cold. "What?"

"Why is that bad?" Dara asked. "That was part of the proclamation too. The wedding was held early so it wouldn't conflict with the funeral rites. I didn't think that was as bad as Tal being *dead*."

Tal set the canteen aside and drew his legs to his chest, the blankets sliding off. He ran a hand through his hair, then gripped his knees with white knuckles.

"We have reason to think that Prince Emerick was behind Tal's kidnapping. And our plan was to stop the wedding."

"Oh," Dara said. "That is bad."

Tal shuddered. He closed his eyes and drew on his lessons. Composure. Regain composure. Don't let them see the cracks. "My plan hasn't changed. I need to get home. I need to expose Emerick. But I will go alone. Athlen, you should hide until this storm blows over."

"No."

"Athlen."

"No." He put his hands on his hips in an eerie mirror of Isa. "I didn't save you from those"—he waved his hand—"pirates to have you turn around and be hurt by someone else. You're not going alone and you're not going to brush me aside."

Tal scrambled to standing, careful of his tender leg. "I'm not brushing you aside. But I don't want to be responsible for you being jailed for a bounty. Or worse. You never told my brother why you were on that ship and how you came to possess that chest of gold. And if he gets to you without me there, he'll hang you."

"I'm aware of all the risks. I make my own decisions, and I'm choosing to take you across the land and get you back home."

"No. I will not allow it."

"You can't stop me."

"Yes, I can. I am a prince of Harth."

"Technically, you're dead," Dara said, nose wrinkled.

"I'm not going to fight about this. As soon as I'm well, I will find a horse and ride home."

Athlen's face went pale save for a splash of red on his cheeks. "You'll abandon me, then?"

That brought Tal up short. He floundered. "What?"

"Why am I always the one left behind?"

"I'm not . . . I'm not . . . I wouldn't do that."

In the short time Tal had known him, he'd seen Athlen happy and sad and drunk and brave, but not *livid*. With his brow furrowed, he stood with clenched fists, and his nostrils flared and his body shook. He pointed at Tal and opened his mouth but stopped. He snapped it shut, and in one fluid movement he stripped off his shirt and dove into the water.

Tal hobbled to the side and peered into the half-moon basin of crystal water that plunged deceptively deep. He caught a glimpse of red-and-gold fins, then they disappeared. The abandoned trousers floated to the surface.

"Wow," Dara said.

Tal jumped. He'd forgotten she was there.

"I've never seen him like that." She shuffled over to Tal's side and peered into the depths. "You must have touched a nerve."

"I'm not abandoning him."

She huffed. "You're protecting him. But he doesn't see it that way. He's been lonely for a long time, and your dismissal hurt him."

"I didn't mean to."

"I know. And he knows that too. It's easy for him when he is the one doing the leaving. I think that's why he comes and goes as he pleases. He'll visit and help when he's needed, but he doesn't stay around. It's why I've never been here before, despite knowing him for years."

"He doesn't let anyone get close." In that they were surprisingly similar. "He can't afford to be hurt again."

"No. He can't." She rested her hand on his shoulder. "It's why I tried to warn him away from you. He likes you, but we both know that once you are home, there isn't going to be room for a wayward merman in the life of a prince."

"You don't know that," Tal snapped. He shrugged off her touch and fiercely met her gaze. "You don't know what my life is like, or what I do or do not have room for. You don't get to make that decision."

She raised her hands in surrender. "So you will have time for him? You won't have to become an advisor to your now-married sister or be married off yourself for another alliance? What about dinners and balls? What about courtiers? Is he going to fit into that life?"

Dara wasn't wrong. Could Athlen fit in at the castle? Would he even want to?

"This isn't the time to ask these types of questions. I've been declared dead. My sister married the person I suspect of organizing my kidnapping and torture. Athlen is implicated for these crimes. And our kingdom is on the brink of war."

"Brink of war?"

Tal frowned. "You don't think the death of a prince by another kingdom is an act toward war? If my family figures out this was political and not about . . ."

"The rumors."

"Right, the rumors. Then we'll end up in a war manipulated by Prince Emerick and Ossetia."

"I didn't think of that." She grimaced.

"Yeah, well, I am a prince. It's more than dancing and dinners. We do have to know how to navigate political quagmires."

She raised an eyebrow but didn't rise to the bait. "Drink your broth and go back to sleep. You're snarky when you're tired. I have to go home, but I'll be back tomorrow to change your bandages. We'll discuss finding you a horse then."

Tal sighed, his anger draining quickly. "Thank you," he said, thumbing the edge of a bandage. "I mean it," he added when her expression remained dubious. "You didn't have to help me, and I realize keeping our secrets places a strain on you as well."

Dara tucked her hands into her apron. "You're welcome." She rocked back on her heels and her nose crinkled. "You're important to him. So you're important to me, too." She blew out a breath. "And I may have made a harsh judgment of you when we first met."

"Arrogant and out of touch," Tal parroted.

She winced. "Yes, that. I appreciate that you listened to what I had to say. You did something about it, even if I questioned your motivations."

"You were right to. My family isn't perfect, but we're trying." Tal fiddled with the cuff of his sleeve. "I also appreciate how difficult that was for you to say," Tal said, meeting her gaze, a teasing smile curling the corner of his lip.

She pushed his shoulder and laughed. "I see why he likes you."

Tal glanced back to the swirling water. Small fish chased bubbles at the surface, and the tide ebbed, revealing more of the rock shelf. But there was no sign of Athlen.

"He'll come back."

"I know," Tal said. He didn't doubt that, only what would happen when Athlen did. He didn't have the strength of character to refuse Athlen again if he asserted his place by Tal's side. He was too selfish. Athlen's continued faith and support made him feel better, helped him assuage his feelings of self-loathing, and Tal couldn't lose that, not if he was going to move forward and save his family.

Dara left in silence, and Tal gingerly walked back to the bed and lowered down into the warmth and thickness of the blankets Athlen had bought with his gold. He drank the broth, followed by a cup of water. He rubbed the salve Dara had left into the sores on his hands and the peeling places he could reach.

Tal kept his eyes open for as long as he could, anxious that Athlen had yet to return, until he fell asleep.

Movement beside him had Tal jumping out of a nightmare. He shot up in the bed, teetering on the edge of panic from his dreams, but Athlen's soft voice soothed Tal before he was fully awake.

"It's only me."

Tal blinked in the low light. The cave was near full dark, and he could barely make out Athlen's features save for his wide eyes. His first instinct was to open his palm and light the area with a small flame, but he paused and stared at the clench of his fist, unsure and afraid.

Athlen crouched next to Tal's makeshift bed. His fingers were cool when they nudged Tal's gently. He nodded in encouragement. "Go on."

"What if I—"

"You won't hurt me."

"How are you so certain?" Tal asked, his voice small.

"Because I know you."

Tal's heart skipped a beat. His pulse raced. With a steadying breath, he opened his palm, and a feeble flame flickered to life over his trembling hand. Gently he pushed it above them, and it hovered in the air, lighting the area in a warm, wavering glow. For a silent moment they both watched the flame float harmlessly.

At Athlen's soft and awed expression, a sense of peace settled over Tal. Athlen wasn't afraid. Athlen still thought him wonderful, and an innate piece of Tal slotted back into place.

"See? Nothing that is a part of you could ever be bad."

Tal ducked his head because that was the crux of it all. Magic was a part of him, and he couldn't separate from it even if he tried. He could bottle it up, but it would always be there, simmering beneath his skin. He could either embrace it or forever be at war with himself. He'd already spent most of his life hiding, and that hadn't worked. Denying such an integral part of his being had only made it worse when the time came to use his magic in his own defense. Maybe it was time to try something new. Maybe it was time to heal and trust himself, as Athlen trusted him.

"Thank you."

"For what?"

"Believing in me."

Athlen met Tal's gaze and gave him a lopsided smile, uncertain. "Of course."

Tal cleared his throat. "So you're back."

"Yes." Athlen placed a dripping dagger next to Tal's bed. "I brought you this."

"Shay's dagger?" Tal picked it up by the ornate hilt. The blade glistened in the darkness, and the metal was slick and cool on Tal's palm. "You found it."

"It wasn't far from where you lost it."

"I'm sorry." Tal dropped the knife—it clattered on the rock—then grabbed Athlen's sleeve. The fabric was damp but not wet. Athlen's hair was dry as well, fluffed into an untamed mess. He'd been back for a while. "I'm sorry."

Athlen's eyelashes fluttered as he peered intently at the place where Tal touched his arm. He gently laid his hand over Tal's. The last time they were together like this, quiet in the cave, the tide receding, something thick and magical like a secret between them, Athlen had talked about losing his family. He didn't say much, the wound still raw despite the years, but Tal wanted to know. He needed to know.

"Why are you afraid of being left behind?"

Athlen frowned. He turned Tal's hand over in his own and drew lines down the length of Tal's fingers. When he spoke after several minutes, his voice was low and shaky.

"I was away exploring despite my mother and father warning me not to wander too far. While I was out, the seafloor rumbled and I was caught in the sea wave. I was pulled leagues away. Once I was freed, I swam home as fast I could, thinking about how much trouble I was in, but . . ." Athlen's brow furrowed. "My usual way home was blocked by rubble. The walls of the tunnel had caved in because of the quake. I went around to another passageway and . . ." Athlen swallowed. When he continued, his voice was thick with grief. "The seabed was cracked. Molten red bubbled up and scorched the water, boiled it into steam. I tried to find my family, but the closer I swam, the harder it became to breathe, and my scales burned." Athlen rubbed a hand over his eyes. "There were bodies floating, merfolk who'd tried but didn't escape in time. I didn't see my parents or my sister, but . . ."

Tal gripped Athlen's fingers. "I'm so sorry."

Athlen's eyes glittered with tears. He shook his head. "They may have been able to get away, and if they did, they may have thought I was one of the trapped, especially if they couldn't find me. I'm certain they didn't mean to leave me behind on purpose, but . . ."

"Athlen—"

"I looked for them for months, but I never found them." Shrugging, Athlen studied their entwined hands. "I had to force myself to confront the fact that I might not see them again. I was lonely."

Athlen paused. Tal tightened his grip.

"So you made a bargain?"

"Our people often talked of the sea witch as a legend. I was afraid and awed by the stories. Those who called her name and had a desire in their heart could barter with her. I was desperate, so I tried. She came to me and offered me the ability to walk among the humans so I wouldn't be alone."

Tal leaned closer. "What did you give her?"

Athlen didn't respond right away, and the quiet stretched between them. Finally Athlen looked up, his mouth turned down; the expression he wore was something Tal could only classify as regret.

"Something I thought I would never find." He reached out and touched Tal's chin, the tips of his fingers cool and tentative, then he slid them along the line of Tal's stubbled jaw and cupped his cheek. "I know you want to protect me, but I don't need protecting. I'd rather be in danger with you than left behind."

Tal rested his forehead against Athlen's. His heart beat wildly.

Magic and desire scorched through his veins, his body set aflame. "I won't leave without you. I promise."

"Thank you."

Tal didn't know what awaited them beyond this moment, but this was the chance he thought he'd missed. He wouldn't miss it again.

Closing the scant distance between them, Tal tilted his head. His pulse thudded hard under his skin as he brushed his chapped lips over Athlen's, trembling and unsure, terrified in equal parts that he might be pushed away or pulled closer. It was the briefest of kisses, and Athlen's mouth was slippery and cool before Tal inched away, breaking the gentle suction. He shivered as Athlen cradled his face in his hands and drew him back to kiss again. Tal surged forward, bold and eager, hungry for every sensation, his fist clenched in the fabric of Athlen's shirt. Athlen returned each fervent press with an intensity of his own, lips parted, mouth hot and willing, and as clumsy as Tal felt.

Athlen gasped, his breath a shock on Tal's mouth, and they kissed desperate and wild until Tal pulled away, chest heaving as he tried to catch his breath. Athlen's hands slipped down to the sides of Tal's neck, fingertips grazing the sensitive skin behind his ears. Tal stared intently at Athlen's chin, embarrassed at his inexperience and enthusiasm, while his body burned and his breath punched out in stutters.

With wide eyes, his mouth open, lips wet from Tal's kiss, Athlen ducked down to meet Tal's eyes with a shy smile, his eyelashes fluttering. "We will find a horse and ride to your home. Together."

Tal nodded. "Together." Then he darted in and kissed Athlen again, his ferocity tempered. They kissed slow, dragging kisses that left Tal light-headed and raw lipped. Despite his wish to continue,

Tal felt his eyelids droop, and Athlen laughed into his mouth.

"You are tired, my prince," Athlen said, head tilted to the side, pensive and quiet. "Move over. I've not slept in a bed before."

Tal blushed fiercely but smiled. He scooted toward the wall, leaving a wedge of space for Athlen to slide into. Their shoulders knocked, and the blankets barely fit over them both, and Tal smelled of fever sweat, but Athlen didn't seem to mind. He squirmed along Tal's side.

"I sleep in the water," Athlen said, running his fingers over the blankets. "Because it's safe and quiet there. But I've slept on the deck of the ship and on the shelf here when watching you."

If possible, Tal's face flushed hotter.

Athlen tucked his hands under his cheek. "But never in a bed."

"Welcome."

Athlen laughed. He poked Tal in the side. "To be honest, I don't see the appeal."

"This isn't quite a bed. When we return to the castle, I'll show you the finest beds in the whole kingdom. Then you'll understand."

Athlen laughed again. The sound echoed off the walls, and Tal would gladly have drowned in it.

"Well, until then, rest and heal."

Tal closed his eyes and, for the first time in days, fell into a deep, restful sleep.

Tal recovered in Athlen's cove for the next several days. His fever finally broke and his wounds slowly healed. His knee didn't ache as badly as before, though it twinged if he stepped the wrong way. His food stayed down. The periods between his rests grew longer. And his magic came back to him, as strong and as hot as before.

In his lucid moments he came to terms with his death and with the implications of it. He ruminated over the information he had—the things he knew, the pieces that he didn't—and came to the same conclusion again and again: Prince Emerick wanted a war with Mysten, and he had used Tal and Isa to get one. And that made Tal angry.

He also thought about the way Athlen made him feel. The shivers that started in his belly and worked their way down his limbs and into his throat. The jump of his pulse when Athlen tucked close to him at night. They hadn't engaged in any more sessions of kisses, because Tal was distracted and Athlen was satisfied with curling next to him at night in the pile of blankets.

Standing in a shaft of sunlight, Tal flexed his hands as he and Athlen waited for Dara to return. Fire danced along his fingertips while Athlen splashed in the water nearby. Dara was reluctant to declare Tal fit for travel, and although Tal was under no obligation to follow her advice, she was integral to their plan. Neither Tal nor Athlen could leave the cavern, especially with the steep bounty Tal's family had placed on information. They needed her to procure supplies and a horse.

Before Tal could burst from impatience, Dara squeezed through the opening, cursing as she stumbled into a pile of Athlen's things. Tal snuffed out the flames and crossed his arms, wincing as the movement strained his injured shoulder.

"I have news," Dara said.

Athlen swam over, tail flapping in the water. He crossed his arms on the ledge, water droplets beading along his shoulders, his copper hair flat on his head.

"Hello, Dara. How are you?"

She rolled her eyes. "Great. Here is your food." She passed over a parcel. Tal sat on the floor and spread it out between himself and Athlen.

"This morning we heard rumors from the next town over about a procession. I went to see, and there were kingdom knights riding in a line, followed by a group of marching soldiers."

Tal shoved a biscuit into his mouth. "Knights?"

"Yeah, and instead of flying Harth's banner flags, they had black ones."

"Oh. It's a funeral procession," Tal said around a mouthful of food. His shoulders slumped. "Though I don't know why they'd be way out here. Custom dictates services be held wherever the person was born."

"Could one of your brothers or sisters be with them?" Athlen asked. "We could take you to them."

"Doubtful. But I don't know. I was so small when my father died, and that was the last funeral I attended. I don't much remember what happened, other than traveling to the town of his birth for his rites." Tal bit his lip. "Did the knights give any indication as to what they were doing?"

"I don't know. No one stopped them to ask. But I did see something you might be interested in."

Tal lifted an eyebrow. "What?"

"Your scary bodyguard was at the head of the line."

11

W hat?" Tal straightened from his slouch. "Shay? Here?"

"I think? She has the brown skin and the long brown hair. She was leading the retinue, wearing armor and riding a white horse."

"With a braided mane?"

"I guess so."

"That's Shay!" Tal jumped to his feet in his excitement. "Where are they now?"

"Camped a little bit out of town. They're heading east."

Tal paced. "You have to contact her for me."

Dara raised her hands. "No."

"Yes! Tell her you have information about me. Tell her you know the boy who was on the derelict in the Great Bay. Lure her here."

"Not here," Athlen said. He crossed his arms over his chest as he bobbed in the water, though not defensively, protectively—as if he was hugging himself. "Not my home."

"No, you're right. I'm sorry. Is there somewhere nearby we can meet her? Somewhere discreet?"

"There's an inlet not far that's hidden by large dunes."

Dara nodded. "I know it. But I'm not doing it! What if she skewers me?"

"She'll recognize you," Tal said. "She saw you when we came to your house. She has an excellent memory for detail, and she'll follow you."

"And if she doesn't?"

"She will." Tal put his hands on his hips and spun on his heel to face her. "But if she doesn't, tell her that you know about her crush on the second prince."

Dara's eyes widened. "I'm *not* saying that!" She threw her hands in the air. "In fact, I'm not doing any of it."

"Fine. I'll do it." Tal crossed his arms. "Lead me to them and I'll lure her away. I know how."

"Great. She won't know it's you, and you'll antagonize her, and she'll stick the pointy end of her sword through you. Then you'll really be dead."

Athlen's tail slapped the water. "I'll do it."

"No," they said in unison.

"I think we established what happens when you try to order me around, my prince."

Tal dropped his arms and his shoulders slumped. He knew better than to argue. "Fine." He raised a finger. "But we'll do it smart and you'll be careful."

≈

Athlen sprinted around the dune, legs churning, sand kicking up as he skidded in the turn. His shirt flapped behind him, and one hand held his large hat down on his head, while the other clutched a woven bag of apples. His eyes were wide, but his mouth was an open smile, laughter loud and teasing as he barreled toward Tal and Dara.

The sea lapped against the shore at their backs. On either side were wild beach grass and slopes of high dunes. And following Athlen between the break in the large mounds of sand was Shay, running full tilt, arms pumping, high ponytail swinging behind her.

"Thief!"

Athlen ducked behind Tal, hefting the apples over his shoulder, chest heaving.

"I brought her," Athlen said on a laugh. "Now it's up to you."

Shay slowed her steps when confronted by the trio, and Tal saw the moment her body language changed from annoyed to defensive. Her boots left deep indentions in the soft sand where she stopped, eyeing them from a distance.

"If this is a poor attempt at a trap, know that I can gut all three of you within seconds." Shay unsheathed her sword, the blade gleaming in the falling dusk. She leveled the tip at Tal and Athlen. "Which I may be tempted to do. Now, who are you? Speak."

Tal stepped forward and threw back the hood of his cloak. "I didn't know you had a flair for the dramatic, Shay. But bravo. You should join the traveling theater group that visits the castle in the summer."

Shay crossed the distance between them in two strides, shoving the point of her sword into the sand, then grabbing Tal in a fierce grip, her strong hands wrapping around his biceps and holding him still. Her gaze roved over his features, her mouth open, her eyes wide and pleading. When she had found what she was looking for, she pulled him into a bruising hug.

"Tally," she whispered as she crushed him to her leather armor.

Tears clogged Tal's throat, and he embraced her as hard, if not harder, tucking his face into the sweep of her dark hair.

"Tally," she said again, her voice thick. "How? Where? Kest saw you drown. He saw you fall over the side, and we searched for you. We searched and searched, both Kest and Garrett dove into the water and swam through the fire and the bodies, looking for you, until they almost drowned themselves."

Tal clenched his teeth. His eyes watered.

She thrust him away, holding on to his shoulders, then cupping his face. "Is this really you? Or are you a doppelgänger? A ghost come to haunt me for failing?"

Tal flinched. "You didn't fail, Shay. You didn't."

"I let them take you."

"They were waiting for me. It was planned. It was all planned. If they hadn't taken me on the beach, then they would've grabbed me on another point of the tour."

"But *how*, Tally? Kest saw you!"

"I saved him." Athlen stepped forward. He gestured to Dara. "And she healed him."

Shay yanked Tal to her side and eyed Dara and Athlen with narrowed eyes.

"You're the boy from the derelict, and you're the girl from the lower town." She thrust out her chin. "What is going on here?"

Tal pulled his arm from her hold—he'd have finger-shaped bruises—and stepped between her and the duo, his back turned to Athlen in a show of trust. "It's far stranger than anything you can think of," Tal said. He smiled broadly at her unimpressed expression. "Relax, Shay. These two have taken care of me. They're not going to hurt me."

She shook her head. "You look awful."

"I was worse. I promise you."

"What are you doing here?" She retrieved her sword from the sand and sheathed it. "Why haven't you sent a message to your mother?" She waved her arm. "Kest blames himself for leaving you there. You know how he has bouts of melancholy, but now he's inconsolable. Garrett is ready to murder anyone who was involved. It was almost impossible to get him to take prisoners instead of killing them all on that marauder's ship. Isa is about to declare war. And Corrie hasn't stopped crying since you went missing."

Tal rubbed his chest, his heart aching. "Why are you leading a royal retinue? Why aren't you at the castle?"

Shay dropped her hands. "Answer the question, Tally. You're not cruel, so why have you left your family believing you've been murdered?"

"I have been ill. I haven't been able to send a message." That wasn't the entire truth, but it was easier than explaining his struggle with using his magic after what he'd done to Zeph and her crew. "Also, I didn't know how safe it was. There is far more at work here than you might realize." He stuck out his chin. "Now you."

"We're invoking sympathy for the impending war. Drumming up support for the queen's and Isa's decision once they declare your murder a political assassination. The queen knows that you were killed on orders from another royal family. The only hard evidence we have is the word of that captain who had you before Garrett killed her. She said it was Mysten."

Tal shook his head. "No. They're wrong. Mysten was framed."

"By whom?"

"Emerick. That's why I haven't sent a message. It was safer for me . . . for everyone to think I'm dead. And I couldn't be sure that it wouldn't be intercepted. Kest said their retinue was large, and they're all staying in the castle."

Shay raised an eyebrow, then laughed. "Emerick?" She brushed her hair over her shoulder. "Are you certain?"

Athlen stepped forward, shoulders straight, and stood next to Tal. "Yes. It was him."

"As much as I want to believe the word of a known liar"—Athlen winced—"Emerick couldn't find his way out of a barren rose garden. Tally, he's not planning a coup."

"What?" Tal exchanged a glance with Athlen and Dara. "We found Ossetian gold on the ship where Athlen was chained. And Zeph, the captain Garrett killed, told me that Ossetia was behind it. They kidnapped me to be a weapon, and when I wouldn't . . ." He trailed off, then cleared his throat. "When I wouldn't give them what they wanted, they planned to kill me and frame Mysten."

"Emerick is a pile of rocks. He's beautiful, don't misunderstand me, but do you know the reason Isa chose him of the siblings of Ossetia?"

Tal toed a hole in the sand. "No."

"Because he would be the easiest to manipulate. Isa loves him, bless her, but, Tally, he's not a mastermind behind anything."

"You're wrong, Shay. All the evidence we have points to him."

She put her hands on her hips and rolled her head back to look at the sky. "Come along, then. I'll take you back to the knights, and one of them will take you home. I would, but I have to lead this group to the border and wait for the queen's command to invade Mysten."

"No."

"What?"

"One of Garrett's sailors tried to kill me, or don't you remember? Emerick has invaded our household, and I know in my bones that he arranged my murder. I'll get home on my own, thank you. Until then you cannot tell anyone that I'm alive. It will endanger my family and you."

Shay thrust her arm in the direction of the encampment. "We are marching to war, Tally! Our kingdom, as weak as it is, is about to strike against another on the premise of *your* death. You cannot shirk your responsibilities to your kingdom and hide here with these two."

Narrowing his eyes, Tal hobbled forward. "How dare you."

Shay didn't back down. "You've had your fun, whatever that was, but now it's time for you to return to your family and stop this conflict before it begins."

"Fun?" Tal's voice cracked. He stalked forward. "Fun?" Anger burned through him. Smoke curled from his fists. His body warmed with fire and flame. "You have no idea what I've been through. I have been kidnapped and tortured and hidden away, all to protect my family and our kingdom. I am not the young boy I was when we first set out on our journey, and I most definitely was not having *fun* at the expense of those I love. I am Prince Taliesin of Harth, fourth child of Queen Carys, and you will obey my command. Is that clear?" Shay's dark eyes glittered with anger, and her jaw clenched.

Shay bowed at the waist, keeping her eyes locked on Tal's. "Yes, my prince."

"You will not tell my family any details of this conversation. You will not tell them I am alive. You will not give them my location. And you will not implicate either of these individuals in information you share with them."

"You are making a mistake, my prince."

"Then I will make that mistake on my own. When you move on in the morning, you will leave a horse behind, a fast and sturdy steed, tied to a tree with a saddle and supplies. Do you understand?"

"Garrett was right. You are a little shit when you want to be." Tal scowled. "Yes, my prince. It will be done as you command."

"Good." Tal shed the royal facade, the tension of his spine loosening. "It was good to see you, Shay. I . . . uh . . . well . . . Athlen found this."

Tal untied the dagger from his belt and, holding the blade, thrust the hilt toward her.

She didn't move. "Keep it."

"I shouldn't. It's yours. I thought I lost it on the beach when I fought them—"

"Keep it, Tally. You will need it on your foolish quest."

Tal wrapped his hands around the hilt and pulled the dagger to his chest. "I'm sorry for not listening to you. I'm sorry for yelling at you and sneaking away."

Shay shook her head. "I was devastated when we lost you. I never want to feel like that again. I disagree with the plan you've laid out, but I will do as you command. Just . . ." She reached out for him, and Tal accepted the touch to his arm. "Don't die." Shay looked to Dara and Athlen. "Look out for him. He may be pretending to be ready for the road ahead, but he's been sheltered inside a castle with siblings and servants for his entire life. He doesn't know the ways of the world outside the walls."

"I'll watch over him." Athlen stuck out his chest. "He'll make it home."

Shay gave him a sharp nod. "Your horse will be waiting for you."

"Thank you, Shay."

"Good luck, Tal. Be safe. Stop this war as quickly as you can."

"I will."

Shay gave him one last lingering look, a small smile teasing the edges of her lips, then she turned on her heel and stalked off, hand on the hilt of her sword, hair swinging behind her.

"She's frightening," Dara said, coming to stand by Athlen's side. "You're scary too, when you transform from Tal to Prince Taliesin."

Tal shrugged. "She wouldn't have listened to me if I hadn't demanded it."

Athlen frowned and tapped his finger along the seam of his mouth. "You're a prince." He said it, brow furrowed. "And you can order others around to do your bidding." He studied Tal. "She would have to do anything you asked of her?"

"Shay swore an oath to my family. She must do what the family commands. But it's also understood that we would not ask of her anything that would violate laws or her moral code."

Athlen raised an eyebrow. "Then, we may want to hurry to get back to the castle. She may find that being ordered to keep your secret is against her moral code."

"She won't." Tal tucked the dagger in his belt. "But we should hurry."

"Tal, why would Ossetia want you as a weapon?" Dara asked, frowning. "That's the part I don't understand."

Tal stiffened. His mouth went dry. He hadn't told her about his magic while she tended to him. She'd seen the evidence of his torture, but she didn't know about his breakdown and his subsequent torrent of fire. Only Athlen knew. But Tal trusted Dara, and maybe it was time for his secret to be shared. Athlen knocked his fingers into Tal's and gave him an encouraging smile.

"It's complicated," Tal said. "But you weren't wrong about me when we first met."

Dara's eyebrows drew together in thought, then she paled and pressed her lips together. "The rumors are true, then. You're like your great-grandfather."

"I'm not him," Tal said quickly. "I'm different."

"How?" she asked, no accusation in her question, only genuine curiosity and concern, which Tal appreciated.

"Because he wanted to start a war. I'm going to stop one."

"Are you certain it's Emerick?" she asked. "Could you be wrong? Could Zeph have lied to you?"

Tal pursed his lips. Zeph had revealed the plan in a moment of unexpected pity, when Tal was broken down to his marrow. She hadn't been lying. That had been the most real exchange between them since the minute he was brought on board.

"I'm not wrong."

"I trust you," Athlen said, gripping Tal's shoulder.

"For what it's worth," Dara said, resting her trembling hand in the bend of Tal's elbow, "I do too."

"Thank you." Tal bolstered under Athlen's touch and Dara's tentative acceptance. For the first time since he left the castle by the sea, Tal was confident in his choices and his course of action. He would save his family and his people. He would complete his quest. Now, if only he could convince his heart to stop racing.

Tal and Athlen left the cave in the wee hours, when the night was coldest. Wrapped in a dark cloak, Tal followed Athlen along the shoreline.

Athlen picked his way across the shallows, his bare feet nimble in the low water, while Tal's boots skidded across the smooth stones.

The docks loomed in the distance, the masts of ships bobbing against the dark sky, the stars the only witnesses to their trek across the sand. Tal pushed down the emotions that rose in response to the sight of the docks, and focused on the path in front of him.

They skirted the town and met Dara at the inland edge.

"Here," she said, shoving a wrapped parcel into Tal's hands. "It's food for the journey, in case your bodyguard was mad enough not to leave any." She fished around in the pocket of her apron and pulled out a folded piece of parchment. "A map with the fastest route. Just follow this road for a few days, then take one left to head back to the sea. Any fool can follow it, but I know the both of you, so please remember to check it once in a while."

Tal cleared his throat. "Thank you."

"Well," she said as she twisted her hands in the fabric of her apron, her voice watery, "don't eat it all at once. Don't stop on the road, and make sure when you camp to at least hide in the woods. Small fires only, so you don't draw attention." She pushed a tendril of hair away from her face. "Once we get to the horse, I guess you won't want a lengthy good-bye. And I'm not sad you're leaving. You've been a pain in my neck since you showed up at my door with the things my mother needed."

"Dara," Tal said with a roll of his eyes and a slight smile, "that's the nicest thing you've said to me."

Dara laughed and punched Tal in the arm. "You're an ass. But if I had to know a magic prince, I guess you're as good as any."

"You were right, you know." Tal cleared his throat. "My family and I should do better for our citizens. We'll do better. I promise."

Dara's expression softened. "Thank you."

"No. Thank you," he said. "For everything. I wouldn't have made it, if not for you."

"Neither of us would have," Athlen said, standing at Tal's side. He closed the distance between himself and Dara and enveloped her in a hug. "I'll be back, I promise."

"Okay." She pulled away. "Come on, boys. We're almost there."

She turned on her heel and ducked her head. They followed her to the outskirts of the city, where the buildings thinned and farmland became more plentiful. The sky lightened toward dawn by the time they found the flattened grass and fire circles that marked the clearing where the regiment had camped. They traveled over a short hill and spotted a horse tied to a tree.

Shay had listened despite her disdain for Tal's plan. The horse was a spotted white mare with a worn leather saddle and bags hanging on either side. She didn't dance away from Tal's touch, which was good, since Tal didn't think Athlen would be able to stay atop a skittish animal. She sniffed his hand and ate the proffered apple, her broad tongue licking over the flat of Tal's palm.

"Good girl," he whispered. He patted her neck and she tossed her head. Tal mounted the mare, boots sliding into the stirrups. He took the reins and patted the horse's neck, soothing her with a low voice.

Athlen's lips thinned as he approached. He cast a look over his shoulder toward the port city and the sea beyond before allowing his shoulders to sag. His large, floppy hat obscured his features, but his posture showed how skeptical he was about riding.

"Come on," Tal said, offering his hand. "It'll be fine."

Dara laced her fingers and urged Athlen to step. Gingerly Athlen took Tal's hand. Between the three of them, Athlen was able to swing his leg over the horse's back and settle in the cradle of the saddle behind Tal. He clutched Tal's waist and rested his forehead on the back of Tal's neck.

"Be careful," Dara said. "Only use the road during the day. You're sitting ducks at night. Follow the route I gave you. It's the shortest way to the castle by the sea."

"Thank you, Dara," Tal said. "When I get home, I'll make sure to tell the queen about your kindness and bravery. You'll be compensated."

Dara smacked his leg. "Just get home safe and take care of him." She jerked her chin to where Athlen clung to Tal like a limpet. She tugged on Tal's trousers, and he bent over the mare's neck. She leaned in close. "Protect him by any means necessary."

Tal nodded. "I will."

"Good." She stepped away and sniffled. "Good-bye, Athlen."

Athlen trembled behind Tal but lifted his head high enough to smile, his chin digging into Tal's shoulder, the brim of his hat hitting the back of Tal's head.

"Good-bye, Dara. Thank you."

Tal clucked his tongue and the horse jerked forward. Athlen scrambled and grabbed Tal around the shoulders, his hands splayed over Tal's chest.

Tal stifled a laugh and turned his attention to the road in front of them. They had several days' journey ahead. He had a merman who had never left the sight of the sea and who had a bounty on his head, a forbidden magic under his skin, a family in mourning, a snake in his household, and a kingdom on the brink of war.

He had more to think about than the puffs of breath skirting across the skin of his neck, and the lean body pressed to his back.

Tal kept the mare at a brisk pace but slowed every hour or so to give her a break, allowing her to clop leisurely down the packed dirt of the road. The landscape spread out in front of them, a picture of spring. Vibrant green grass poked through the thawed soil in lush thatches, and carpets of wildflowers decorated the hills, the petals basking and open to the sun. Small animals scampered in the brush along the road—squirrels and groundhogs and one nosy fox that followed them for a few miles, until it found something more interesting than two quiet boys.

They encountered a few other travelers—lone riders on horses or families walking to and from villages that dotted the landscape, visiting friends and family on the bright day. They passed a trader with a laden cart and a stubborn donkey and turned down the offer of a trade for their mare.

With each interaction Tal kept his head down and spoke softly but firmly to affect the airs of a man with a brusque manner who was in a hurry, which he was. Athlen didn't speak much at all, only to the girls of the families, who giggled at the color of his hair and the brightness of his eyes, and to politely frown at the trader, who tried to sell him a pair of boots. But his grip on Tal eased and he perked up, taking in the scenery as much as Tal was.

They rode for the entire day, eating from Dara's bundle in the saddle, and passing the canteen between them when needed. When the sky darkened, Tal led the mare off the road to a small grove of trees.

"We'll stop here for the night."

Athlen shifted behind him. "I don't think I can get down," he confessed after a moment. "How should I do it?"

Tal turned slightly and held out his arm. "Hold on and swing your leg over."

Swallowing, Athlen gripped Tal's forearm and, with the grace of a cow, slid off and fell to the grass.

Tal burst out with a laugh.

Athlen hobbled to standing and wobbled into the grove. "I'm glad I could be your entertainment for the evening," he said as he disappeared.

Tal disembarked and took care of the mare, tying her to one of the nearby trees in a spot with plenty of clover for her to eat. He removed her saddle and blanket and took one of the cloths Shay had provided to wipe her down.

After Athlen returned, Tal made camp while Athlen watched, tilting his head. Around a small fire they shared rations as the night birds hooted and the crickets chirped; then they lazed peacefully.

"Tell me about them," Athlen said, hands laced behind his head, bare feet flexing as he stared up into the branches above them. "Your brothers and sisters. I'd like to know them before I meet them."

Tal sat cross-legged by their fledgling fire, leaning against the trunk of one of the trees. He tossed a twig into the flames. "You met my brother Garrett."

"Tall fellow with the red beard and the squinty eyes. He didn't like me much."

"He wasn't quite sure what to make of you," Tal said. "It was strange to see him unsure."

Athlen lifted his chin. "You understood me."

"You tricked me."

Athlen laughed. He held up his thumb and forefinger, squeezing them close. "A little."

"I thought you threw yourself off the boat because of the horrors you'd been through on that ship."

Athlen ducked his head, the fire casting shadows on his face, his copper hair glinting with the flickers of the flames. "I'd say I'm sorry, but that wouldn't be true. But yes, I met Garrett."

Tal shook his head at the unsubtle change back to the subject. "My older sister, Isa, is the crown princess. She's going to rule like my mother. She's smart and tactical. Regal. She would like you."

"Why?"

As shrewd as Isa was as the future queen, she had a love for stories about romance and kissing and damsels. Maybe it was because she couldn't afford to be a woman in distress, swept off her feet by circumstance and a charismatic stranger. Isa would sigh as she read, and sometimes she would entertain them all with retellings. Tal had thought romance absurd. How did the princess or the servant or the warrior always end up swooning in a lover's arms? How did the right moment always find them between battles or after escape or right as the sun set? It all seemed ridiculous and farfetched and contrived. But he understood now—that moment of awakening, the heady rush of realization, and the beautiful ridiculousness of it.

Tal blushed. "Because I do."

Athlen's expression melted into a smile. "She loves you."

"Yes," Tal said. "I think she was upset at first when she found out she had a third brother, but she was always kind to me, and when she wasn't busy, she was fun to be around. She was occupied a lot, though, what with lessons and training to become queen."

"She must be lonely."

Tal shrugged. "Maybe. I don't know her well. Garrett does. Kest, my other brother, he might too."

"He's the bird."

Tal half smiled. "Yes, the bird." Since he'd seen Shay, Kest had centered in Tal's thoughts. He was prone to melancholy, times when he would sleep for days, wouldn't eat, and wouldn't smile. When those times came along, he complained that his body ached and that his thoughts wouldn't quiet. He would wrap thick shirts and cloaks over his hunched shoulders and shuffle along the corridors, servants trailing behind him to ensure his safety. And around the colder months, when the days were darker, Kest often struggled. He had been hit hardest when their father died, and Tal hated that he might be a cause of one of Kest's spells.

"Kest is the smartest of us. He is a great scholar and loves to read books. I . . . I always felt closer to him. We share magic, where the others do not. And he was there for me when I didn't understand what was happening to me."

Athlen's smile tempered. "He sounds like a good man."

"He is." Tal snapped a stick in half and tossed it into the flames. "The youngest of us is Corrie. She's a spitfire."

"What does that mean?"

"Hotheaded. Um . . . feisty. She talks back to her tutors and to our mother—the queen. None of the rest of us dare. But Corrie"—Tal shrugged—"she does what she wants. We all let her get away with it too, because she's the youngest. She never knew our father. He died a few months before she was born."

"She doesn't sound like you at all."

"No, but sometimes I envy her, I think. As do the others."

"Why?"

"She gets to be carefree. She's not an heir or a commander of the navy or the royal shifter-scholar or the one with . . ." Tal curled his fingers.

"Magic," Athlen supplied.

"Yes. With magic."

Athlen crawled closer and propped himself next to Tal on the tree trunk. His knee banged into Tal's thigh. "I like your magic. It's beautiful. And nothing like I've ever seen. Even the sea witch . . . her magic is borne of the water. She was able to gift me with legs, but only because I'm a creature of the sea." Athlen nudged his shoulder into Tal's. "We don't really have fire in the ocean, you know. We can float just below the surface and feel the sun, which we were strictly forbidden from doing in case we were seen."

The corner of Tal's mouth curled up in a smile. "Which means you did it, didn't you?"

"Of course. All the time. The only other way to feel heat was to find a vent in the seafloor." An expression of sorrow flickered over Athlen's face, but it was fleeting. Tal's stomach dropped in sympathy all the same. "But it's nothing like this." Athlen held his hand over the flames, and his eyelids fluttered close. A dreamy smile stole over his features. "I like it on my skin."

"Is that why you like me?" Tal asked with a laugh. "Because of the heat?"

"Maybe." Athlen's smile grew, and he opened his eyes to give Tal a coy look. "Or because you're a prince."

Tal huffed. "You don't care about that."

"No, I don't. I think it has to do with how you stepped in to save me, twice, when you didn't have to."

"I snapped a fetter and kept a merchant from taking advantage of you."

"And you didn't have to," Athlen said with a firm nod. "You could've left me chained up, but you intervened because you didn't like the way I had been treated. And you saw me in trouble in the market, and you bought the items I needed."

Tal bit his lip and lifted his good shoulder. "What of it? You saved me from drowning, remember? Death and fire and a stab wound trump chains and some baubles."

"Don't discount yourself. You saved me," Athlen said with

finality. He scooted closer. "But if you must know, it helps that you're nice to look at."

Tal laughed, his unease melting away. He knocked his shoulder into Athlen's. "You're nice to look at too."

"Of course I am. I'm a merman." He winked.

Tal licked his lips. He darted in and pressed a kiss to Athlen's dimpled cheek.

Athlen's mouth curled into a smile. He leaned in with intent, mouth open, eyes hooded. Tal prepared for a kiss, his blood aflame, his stomach fluttering, and he closed his eyes and waited.

And waited.

And waited.

Face scrunched, Tal opened one eye to find Athlen grimacing and clutching his leg, swallowing a gasp.

"Athlen? What's wrong?"

Fingers digging into his muscles, Athlen rubbed vigorously, features twisted with pain. "I guess," he said, voice a strangled sound, "that I'm not used to being on my legs this long."

"They hurt?"

Athlen nodded, then gasped as he stretched both legs out in front of him and pointed his odd toes. He squeezed his eyes shut and gripped his thighs.

"Do you need me to—"

"I'm fine," he said after a moment. "I'm fine." He shuddered. "I'm fine."

"Repeating it doesn't make it true."

Athlen rolled his eyes. "It was a cramp. I'll be okay."

"Drink water." Tal slapped the canteen to Athlen's chest. After training, the knights would ply Tal with water and fruit, saying it helped with soreness. Tal didn't have fruit. But he could supply water. *Water.* Maybe Athlen needed it in more ways than one. "Do we need to find you a stream? Or a lake? For you to stretch your fins?"

Athlen took a few gulps and considered the proposal. He set the canteen aside, then he kneaded his leg above his knee. "No." He shook his head. "No. I'm sore from the horse. That's all."

"You'll tell me if you need anything. That's not a request."

"Is that an order from Prince Taliesin?" His mouth quirked up. "I hate to remind you, but I'm not one of your subjects."

"It's not an order. It's a . . ." Tal trailed off, then crossed his arms. "Fine. It's an order, but it's me taking care of you. You took care of me in the cove, let me take care of you now."

Athlen twitched, and his hands went to his calf. He squeezed the muscle, his mouth flattening as he stifled a groan, lines of pain crinkling around his eyes. He bowed forward, his back heaving with stuttered breaths.

"Athlen?"

"Sleep," he said, squirming. "I need rest. That will help."

"Okay. Let me set up our . . ."

Athlen crawled away from him to where their supplies lay on the ground. He shook out the horse blanket and rested his head on the curve of the leather saddle, tucking the blanket over him. It wasn't long enough, and his feet poked out of the end.

"I'll sleep here," Athlen said. "Good night."

Confused and hurt at the abrupt dismissal, Tal stood and grabbed his own bedroll as Athlen closed his eyes and pretended to fall asleep. The twitches of his eyelids gave him away, as did the jerk of his legs.

Tal spread out his blanket under the tree. He banked the fire and curled up without removing his boots, the necessity of a quick retreat a very real possibility. Tossing and turning until he found a spot without a rock or a tree root, Tal second-guessed his relationship with Athlen. Had the bed sharing just been a new experience for him? Had the kissing been a way to distract from their argument? Did Athlen not share in Tal's feelings? Athlen was in pain. Maybe he thought it would be better to sleep apart in case he hurt in the night. Maybe he didn't want Tal to know how bad he felt. Tal would be sure to find him a private stream or brook to swim in soon, even if it was only for a few minutes.

Exhausted, Tal tucked his hands under his head on the thin blanket and closed his eyes. This was only their first day. He couldn't afford to worry about Athlen's idiosyncrasies when his family was in trouble. He needed to press on, and he couldn't do that with a bad night of sleep, moody merman or not.

Things would look better in the morning.

12

The mare's hooves beat a steady rhythm as Tal and Athlen crossed the countryside. The packed dirt road ribboned out in front of them, over rolling hills and flat farmland. Tal had never seen this part of the kingdom. He'd studied their northern and eastern borders but knew them only as lines on a map, and not as the ridges of mountains in the distance, snowcapped even in the spring.

Tal didn't love the sea, despite growing up overlooking the foam and waves, but he had a new appreciation for it after days of riding a horse across the landscape. His hips and bottom were sore from the saddle. His back ached from Athlen holding on to him no matter their pace, and from sleeping on the unforgiving ground.

Athlen wasn't faring much better. In fact, his pain only worsened the farther they traveled. His face grew pinched and pale, and his lips went bloodless. Circles spread under his eyes, and he hobbled when he walked, gingerly stepping and biting back grunts. When he thought Tal wasn't looking, he rubbed his muscles—his thighs and calves and the bottoms of his feet.

"Let me find you a river," Tal said on their third day of travel, the map Dara had given them spread on the ground. "Please." He reached across the small distance between them and touched Athlen's hand.

Athlen startled, then stared where Tal's fingers rested against his own. Slowly, and deliberately, he pulled away and tucked his hands in his lap. Tal's heart stuttered.

"It won't help," Athlen said, unsuccessfully hiding a grimace.

Pushing away his own hurt, Tal took his best guess. "Because it's not the sea?"

Athlen's jaw set as he stared at the parchment, his gaze lingering on the jagged coastline. He gave a small, reluctant nod. "We should keep moving," he replied. "You need to return home as quickly as possible if the rumors we've heard are true."

Tal didn't argue. Athlen wasn't wrong.

"That's the closest coast to here anyway," Tal added, folding the map.

Athlen nodded. "Yes, it is."

Tal swung back onto the mare and pulled Athlen up behind him, noting the stark lines of pain around Athlen's eyes. They rode for the rest of the day, skirting the towns they encountered. Tal's stomach growled at the thought of stopping at a tavern for a hot meal, but it was too dangerous, especially with the black flags that flew, memorializing his death, instead of the usual kingdom banners.

Food aside, Tal wouldn't mind a conversation to disrupt his own cyclical thoughts. Athlen had become as silent as the grave, answering Tal's questions with phrases so short Tal eventually stopped trying to engage with him.

Other things had changed over the days of travel as well. He didn't touch Tal unless he had to. He didn't sleep next to him by the fire, opting to crawl as far away as possible and curl into himself. It was as if all the intimacy built between them in the shadows of the cove had disappeared once exposed to the inland sun. It *hurt*, and while on the surface Tal could attribute Athlen's strange behavior to being in pain and away from his home, he couldn't help but feel as if there was another reason lurking beneath Athlen's forced smiles and distant stares.

Tal slept little that night under a clear sky and a bright moon. Athlen tossed and turned in his sleep a few feet away, while Tal's thoughts tumbled through his head. His family was in danger. Shay might already be engaged in battle. Ossetia might already be benefiting from their deception. He was running out of time.

On their fourth day of travel, Tal regretted his decision not to travel by boat. It was foolish of him. They'd be pulling into port that day if they'd sailed through the Great Bay. By horse, they still had three more days' journey ahead of them. Maybe he *was* too soft to be a prince, so upset by the thought of traveling by boat that he'd put his family, his friend, his country, and himself in greater danger.

Late in the afternoon the silence that had become their constant was broken when Athlen looked to the cloudless sky and frowned. "There's a storm coming."

Tal lifted an eyebrow. He twisted in his seat and gave Athlen an incredulous look. "There's not a cloud in the sky. There's no breeze. And we're inland."

Athlen shrugged. "I don't think I'm wrong. There is going to be a storm."

"How do you know?"

Athlen looked away, not meeting Tal's eyes. "I have a feeling."

Frustrated and confused, stressed and exhausted, Tal turned back around in the saddle and focused on the road ahead. "My family is in danger. We still have two days until we reach the castle. We're not stopping because you have a *feeling*."

Hours later the wind whipped through Tal's tousled hair, and his cloak pulled at the clasp at his throat, choking him. Soaked to the bone, hunched over the horse, Athlen shivering and clinging to his back, Tal regretted not stopping at the farm they'd passed an hour or so back. Angry with himself, he cursed his own stubbornness for ignoring Athlen's warning. Athlen had merely tried to help, and Tal had dismissed his concerns because of Tal's own tangled emotions. If only he'd listened, they could've bedded down in the barn for the night with the horse, safe and warm and dry. Instead they were riding down the muddied road, and Tal gripped the reins with white knuckles, terrified that the horse would take a misstep and send them sprawling, or worse, injure herself.

The thunder rumbled above them as clouds rolled in dark, ominous clusters, obscuring the stars and tumbling over the low light offered by the moon. Athlen jumped when lightning forked above them, and Tal gritted his teeth.

With a soft kick to her sides, Tal spurred the mare onward, hoping the storm would blow over or they'd find a place to rest. The path curved through a small wood, then widened, and Tal straightened from his hunch when they came upon the outskirts of a town.

"Up ahead," Tal said, his voice drowned out by the rain and the wind, "there's an inn. We'll stay there for the night."

Athlen didn't question the intelligence of stopping in a public place where Tal might be recognized, small as that chance was, and

Tal took that as acquiescence to the plan. Perceiving the potential for a respite from the storm, the horse picked up her pace with minimal urging as the mud beneath her hooves transitioned to stone at the border of the village.

Within minutes they stopped in front of a bustling tavern and disembarked. Athlen slid off the mare's back and collapsed into the mud, his legs unable to hold him. Tal jumped off and hauled Athlen to his feet, throwing Athlen's arm over his shoulders.

"I'm fine," Athlen said, clipped and impatient.

"You're not. You need to rest." Tal slipped the dagger from the saddlebags and into the back waistband of Athlen's trousers. "We should be fine in here," he said, "but you shouldn't be unarmed."

"What about you?"

Tal clenched his hand, smoke blossoming from the creases of his fist. "I'm prepared."

Together they hobbled up the three short steps. Tal flipped a coin from Athlen's stash to the boy waiting on the leaky porch.

"Take care of her. She's had a long day. Then bring the saddlebags up to our room."

The boy held up the gold in the light. He bit it, wiggling it between his teeth, before leaping off the porch to lead the docile mare to the stable.

With the pair of them sopping wet and Athlen grunting in pain with every step, they drew far more attention than Tal wanted as they stumbled into the tavern, but there wasn't much to be done for it. Tal dumped Athlen into a chair right inside the door and squelched his way to the first barmaid he found.

"Room for the night," he said. "And dinner."

She gave him a once-over. "Can you pay?"

"Yes." He slipped a coin into her palm.

She then jerked her thumb over her shoulder. "Up the stairs. Second door on the right."

"Thank you."

Tal hauled Athlen to his feet by his upper arm and dragged him up the stairs. Every step was a chore, and by the time they reached the landing, the boy from the stable had run past and dropped their bags into the room.

"For another coin I'll tell you the day's news. Royal messenger came through. I heard what they said."

Interest piqued, Tal fumbled for a coin while Athlen leaned hard into his side. He found one and tossed it to the boy. "Go on. Tell us."

"The prince was assassinated. We might go to war, but the royal family is doing what they can to find a 'diplomatic option.'" He said it as if reciting a lesson from school, making sure to get the words correct. Tal sagged with relief. They weren't at war yet. They still had time. The boy continued. "My dad said the prince was sickly and he died, and the queen just wants a war. My grandpa said that he was killed because he had magic. Actually, the baker said that too. And the farmer over the hill. Oh, and the tavern keeper."

Tal's eyebrows climbed. "They all said that?" The rumors had grown, and they weren't wrong.

The boy nodded his head like a puppet on a string. "Yes, sir." He held out his hand, palm open. "I can find out more if you want, for another coin."

"That won't be necessary. Thank you."

On his way out the boy wrinkled his nose. "You look awful, mister," he said to Athlen. "My mum is a healer. She's got a tonic that'll fix you up, if you need it."

Athlen sagged against the wall. "No, thank you."

The boy shrugged and ran out, his shoes slapping down the hallway.

Tal's thoughts spun with the information the boy had provided. His focus shifted, though, when Athlen made a noise of pain and grabbed his leg, his bare toes curling against the wooden floor.

Tal gripped his arm and steadied him.

"You should rest," Tal said, gesturing to the single narrow bed along the wall. "I'll get us dinner."

Athlen stared at the bed. Rainwater dripped from his hair, ran along the soggy planes of his shoulders, and pooled on the wooden floor. The skin around his eyes was dark, and his expression was pinched. He was obviously weary from travel and in pain. He was far from his home and the sea, but none of those things should make him push Tal away. Not after what he'd shared in the cove, about his loneliness and his fear of being left behind. No, there had to be something Athlen was hiding. Tal was certain of it.

"Athlen," Tal said, nudging him, "please rest."

Athlen didn't make a move other than to pluck at the ties of his shirt. Exhausted and irritated, Tal didn't have the wherewithal to dissect Athlen's mood. He turned away and stepped out of his boots and socks. Wiggling his wrinkled and pruned toes, he unbuckled his belt and dropped his trousers. They plopped to the ground. He pawed through the saddlebags and pulled out a slightly damp pair and slipped them on.

Next went his shirt. He flung the sodden fabric over his head, glad to be free of it.

He found a light shirt in the supplies from Shay and slipped it on. It was a size too large, and the collar slipped down his collarbone, but it was dry and warm. Straightening, he stopped short when he found Athlen staring, a blush across the line of his cheeks, and his eyes fever-bright.

Oh.

Tal raised both eyebrows. "Athlen?"

He startled and stepped backward, banging into the bed. He shouted a curse and grabbed his leg, flopping onto the hay-stuffed mattress.

"Athlen? Are you okay?"

He nodded, mouth clamped into a thin line. "Fine."

Tal sighed. He rummaged through the bags and found a pair of dry socks. He crossed the room and sat on the bed. The mattress dipped dangerously beneath the pair of them.

"Are you going to tell me what's wrong?"

Athlen fluttered his eyes closed. He rubbed his feet, pressing his fingers into the soles and rubbing his odd thumbs over the tops. "I'm sore. That's all."

"That's not all. You're not telling me something."

"Some things you shouldn't worry yourself with, my prince. Especially with all the other burdens you carry."

Tal bowed his head. "It wouldn't be a burden. You're important to me. I want to help."

"Not as important as your family, as your kingdom." Athlen shook his head. "We should focus on getting you home."

"Athlen," Tal said on a sigh. "Please." Sitting close, their thighs bumping together, Tal felt affection and concern stir in his middle. He'd been upset at Athlen's distance and closed himself off in return, which had led him to ignore Athlen's warning, but he hadn't forgotten their time in the cave, and how Athlen's lips tasted, and how Athlen's hands had cleverly caressed his skin, his touch cool and soothing over Tal's aches.

Tal trailed his fingertips over Athlen's cheek. Athlen didn't flinch away this time. Instead he nuzzled into the touch, eyes remaining closed, but the wrinkles of pain around his eyes eased. Tal leaned in and kissed Athlen's jaw, then the corner of his slight smile, then he pressed his open mouth to Athlen's parted lips.

Athlen sighed into it, melting into the kiss, mouth open and pliant, head tipped back as Tal cradled it, his fingers running through the thick copper hair. Tal pressed a little harder, a little more urgent, a fierce want brewing in his veins.

"I shouldn't," Athlen said, lips pink and wet. He brushed Tal's hair from his eyes. "I shouldn't."

"Why?" Tal said. "What has changed?"

"You're a prince."

"You knew that from the beginning. I didn't think you cared about that."

"I don't care, but that doesn't mean that you aren't one, Tal. You have duties and a life that I don't understand."

"You can have a place in the castle—in my life. Once we stop Emerick and save my family and stop this war . . ."

Athlen smiled. "That's a nice sentiment."

"You didn't want to be left behind. I thought that meant—"

Athlen sighed. He scooted away, then stood, grimacing as he stepped toward the door. "I'll get our dinner."

He left without changing out of his wet clothes and with no further explanation. Frustrated, Tal flopped backward onto the sagging mattress and threw his arm over his eyes. He was content to lie there until Athlen returned, but then there would be an awkward conversation about bed sharing, and Tal wasn't in the mood for that, either.

And who knew what kind of trouble Athlen could find in the span of a few minutes?

Tal sat up and put on the dry pair of socks, then slid his feet into his damp boots. He stomped out of his room and down the stairs.

The tavern had a layout similar to that of the one he had visited with Shay and Garrett. There were two main rooms divided by a single wall near the stairs. A corridor led to the back door and out to the kitchen. Thick red curtains adorned the walls, hanging in parallel lines. Eyebrow raised, Tal guessed the curtains were there for much the same reason that tapestries lined the cold stone of the castle, but after seeing two of the curtains with multiple pairs of feet poking out beneath, and hearing low moans emanating as the fabric moved, his cheeks reddened. Scandalized, Tal turned back toward the main dining area, but he didn't make it far before a cool hand stole over his mouth. He grunted as he was jerked backward and behind a curtain hung on the wall.

"It's me," Athlen whispered low in Tal's ear.

Tal nodded and Athlen let go.

"What is going on?"

Athlen peeked around the corner of the curtain, then ducked back into the shadows. His face had gone paler, if possible, and he pressed his lips into a thin, bloodless line.

"It's them."

Tal shook his head. "Them who?"

"The captain." Athlen's throat bobbed, and he flailed his hands in the small space between their bodies. "The ones who had me. The ones who chained me to the floor." His chest heaved, breaths stuttering out in rapid pants; he was on the verge of panic. He twisted his fingers into a knobby knot.

"Athlen," Tal said, placing his hand on the center of Athlen's chest, "did they see you?"

"I . . . I . . ." He trembled. "I don't know. I don't think so."

"Okay. It's okay. We'll leave."

"We can't."

"We can. We'll go get our things and get out of here before they see you. I won't let them have you. I will protect you. Understand?"

Athlen's gaze was far away, honey eyes peering into the middle distance. Tal pinched his arm, and Athlen flinched.

"Listen to my voice," Tal said, inching closer until his lips were next to Athlen's ear. "I will shield you. Do you trust me?"

"Yes."

Tal needed to get them out of there. The stairs to the upper floor were across the room from where they hid by the back door, which led to the detached kitchen. The men sat around a table, drinking ale and eating stew. They wouldn't recognize Tal if he walked past the group to gather his and Athlen's things.

Athlen clutched Tal's hand. "Don't leave me, please."

"I won't."

Crossing the room with Athlen latched to his arm like a hunting bird was out of the question; with his hair and his distinct way of moving, he would be recognized instantly. They could leave their belongings, but all their money was upstairs, and they might need it on the rest of their journey to the castle by the sea.

"We'll hide." He patted Athlen's hand. "We'll stay right here until they leave."

"That could be all night."

"Then it's all night."

"What if we're discovered?"

"Then we act drunk and pretend. I'll do the talking. But we're safe right here, right now, and—"

The front door banged open with the driving wind. The curtain blew and shifted, and Tal saw her as she strode in. The hood of her traveling cloak fell in a gust of wind, revealing her wet hair pinned back in an elaborate knot. She kicked the door closed with her heel, then turned, her black eyes ringed with gold alighting on the men at the table. Her features twisted into a feral smile.

Tal's heart banged against his ribs.

"It's her," Tal said.

"Who?"

"The cat shifter from the beach."

"The one that bit you?" Athlen's voice went high, and Tal nodded his head sharply.

He shoved Athlen between himself and the wall. He grabbed the edge of the curtain and tucked it around his body, nudging Athlen to do the same on the other side. Luckily, there was a threadbare patch of cloth at Tal's eyeline, and he peered through it as they huddled together. He strained to hear the conversation over the music and the laughter and the squeals of the revelers.

"My mistress and her family are not pleased."

"Now, that's not a proper greeting from a lady, especially not one with such close ties to royalty." The man Athlen had identified as the captain smiled and tipped back his chair. He thumped his muddy boots on the table, crossing his ankles. "Good evening, milady." He waved his hand. "See? Not so hard. Your turn."

Her red lips turned down sharply. "You failed your mission."

"Well, if your mistress wanted the mission to be a success, she shouldn't have left payment at the bottom of the Great Bay."

"You found a way to retrieve it."

"Yes, we did, and got nothing but trouble. We didn't know his kind could conjure a squall, but I bet you did."

Athlen shook his head. "I can't conjure anything," he whispered sharply, breath hot on the back of Tal's neck. "They didn't *listen*."

"Since you failed, and my lady was forced to hire another to complete your task, she wants repayment."

"Do you hear that, boys? She wants her gold back."

The group around him laughed timidly, their bravado tempered in the face of her impressive scowl.

Her dark eyes narrowed and her perfectly arched eyebrows drew together. "I'm here to collect either in gold or in flesh." She drew her hand from underneath her cloak and held it open, palm up. Her black manicured nails grew and curved, sharpening as her skin darkened and furred. Her hand reshaped into a massive paw. "It's your choice," she said, her voice low and guttural. A shiver slid down Tal's spine.

"We lost the gold." The captain spit on the floor. "Rumor is that fucking Commander Garrett has it. Ask him. Your lady and he are related now, aren't they?" Tal stiffened. "And I heard that you've already gotten your flesh. Zeph's dead. That could've been us."

"It will be you," she said, tucking her hand into her sleeve, "if you don't do what my lady wants next."

"And what's that?"

"The boy's body wasn't found. The royal family believes him to be dead. They've sent a band of knights and soldiers to the border, but they are reluctant to engage Mysten's army. They're not convinced by the word of a kidnapper and mercenary about who hired her to kill their youngest brother. At least, not enough to prod them to war."

The captain shrugged. "What does that have to do with us?"

"My lady wants the border of her kingdom expanded. She wants Mysten's mines. War is the way to get them, but the royal family of Harth needs one last push." She leaned in and dragged the tip of her claw down the captain's scarred face. "You complete the job and your debt is paid. Be warned, however, that there are others who, if they get to him first, will reap the rewards. And you"—she seized his chin in her hand, pinpricks of blood beading where her nails dug into his skin—"will be dead weight."

"What did you have in mind?"

"Another assassination should do the trick."

"Which one do you want us to kill this time?"

"The bird."

Tal's gasp was loud amid the general noise of the room. Athlen clapped a hand over Tal's mouth and pulled him back into the swaths of fabric. The pair of them waited with bated breath while Tal's mind reeled with anger and fear. Those mercenaries were going to murder Kest! They were going to hurt his family again!

Tal and Athlen didn't have to wait long for a response. Footsteps quick and light-headed in their direction, and a pair of heeled boots appeared beneath the sway of the fabric before the curtain was violently swept aside.

The woman stared at Tal with dark, wary eyes, the tip of her sword held solidly between them. The point stood steadfast under Tal's chin. She was a lady, that Tal could see, not only from the fact that she was a shifter, but also in the bearing of her posture and the way she peered down her nose. She didn't wear any adornments— no signet ring or necklace with a crest, and thus no indication of her family—but she was noble.

Tal didn't recognize her.

And she didn't recognize him, either. As her gaze roved over him, there was no moment of surprise or acknowledgment at seeing the dead prince of Harth, just suspicion at finding two boys amid the red fabric.

Her gaze flickered between the two of them, questioning, and Tal acted before he thought. He boldly grabbed Athlen's hand and leaned back into the warmth of his body.

"Do you mind?" he asked with a roll of his eyes, affronted and impatient. "My boy and I would like a little privacy. Unless . . ." He looked her up and down, from the soles of her well-made boots to the thick tangle of her hair at the crown of her head, and tried his best for a leer. "You'd like to watch."

Athlen caught the hint and wrapped his arm around Tal's waist, pulling him closer and placing a loud, openmouthed kiss on Tal's neck.

Her pouty lips curled in revulsion. "Disgusting commoners," she said with a sneer, dropping the tip of her sword.

The group of mercenaries behind her laughed.

"Run along, peasants. Find a room or a barn." She reached into a purse at her hip and flipped a coin toward them. Tal caught it, the cool edge of the gold biting into his palm.

He smirked. "Thank you, milady."

Her eyes flashed, but before she could comment, he ducked his head and dragged Athlen toward the stairs. They hurried up the creaky staircase, not once looking back, and banged into the shared room.

"Pack everything," Tal commanded, slamming the door and throwing the bolt. "We need to leave and get home. I have to warn Kest."

Athlen's hands shook as he stuffed the saddlebags. "They saw me," he choked out. "They saw me. They won't let us leave."

"They might not have recognized you."

Athlen nodded quickly as he grabbed the thin quilt from the bed and balled it up. Tal didn't stop him from stealing the blanket, especially as they were about to go back out into the cold, wet weather.

Tal opened his palm, and Ossetia's stamp gleamed in the low lamplight. He twirled the gold in his fingers. No scuffs. No chips. Uncirculated gold, just as was found on the derelict. Ossetia had hidden shifters among their royal house, and they had paid to have Tal kidnapped and were planning Kest's murder.

The pounding at the door broke Tal from his thoughts, and he stashed the coin away in his pocket, the gold clinking against the shark's tooth.

Tal backed away from the door and cast a glance behind him. Athlen clutched the quilt to his chest, his expression blank, his face drained of all color except the bruiselike half circles under his eyes. The only other escape was the shuttered window, and while they might be able to squeeze their way out, the drop was too dangerous.

"Toss the bags out of the window," Tal said low, jerking his chin to the shutters. "We'll pick them up on our way out."

Athlen gulped. The pounding became fiercer, the door shaking in the frame.

"Athlen!" Tal snapped, and Athlen jerked, blinking at Tal, fear a cloud over his features. "It'll be all right. I promise. Now pull the dagger, and toss the rest out of the window. Understand?"

Athlen shivered, but he nodded. He busied himself with his tasks, and Tal faced the door.

These people had hurt his friend. These people had planned to kill him. These people were after his family. He had hoped he would never be in a situation where he could lose control of his magic again, not after he'd condemned an entire crew to froth and flames, but as the wooden door heaved inward, that eventuality appeared inescapable. Yet in the face of it, cornered with no way out, the choice was startlingly clear. In a game of kill or be killed, Tal would live, and he would ensure anyone he loved would as well, by any means necessary. He wouldn't allow anyone to hurt him or Athlen again.

He fanned the flame of his magic. It roared to life, kindling from the ever-present flicker of flame in his belly to a wildfire burning down his arms, until his fingers glowed like molten steel.

"Tal?"

"Be ready to run."

The door shattered inward, the lock giving way from the wood, splintering it, before breaking and falling. A mercenary from the group squeezed through the opening, gleaming weapon in his hand, grim smile twisting across his mouth.

Tal crouched in a fighting stance.

"Oh, what do we have here? Are you going to fight—"

Tal didn't wait for him to finish the taunt before he conjured a ball of flame and thrust it across the small space, hitting the man in the chest. He screamed and fell backward, short sword falling from his limp hand and clattering on the floor. Tal rushed forward, picked up the weapon, and stabbed the next man who dared try to enter. Blood sprayed when he wrenched the sword free, splattering across the walls and misting Tal's face.

Tal leaped back when a bull of a woman broke through. But at the sight of Tal with sword in one hand, flames dancing up his other arm, the mercenary stopped in her tracks.

"By the dead gods," she breathed. "*Magic.*"

Tal didn't deny it as he once would have, as he'd been compelled to on Zeph's ship. No, it was time to start controlling the narrative about magic, even if this pirate didn't know who he was. "Step aside and I won't kill you."

She didn't hesitate. Raising her hands, she stepped over the body of her fallen compatriot and moved to the corner.

"Is there anyone behind you?"

"No. We thought three would be enough."

Tal kept his sword point leveled at her. "Don't look at him."

She turned her head and stared at the wall.

Tal extinguished his flames, then tossed a glance over his shoulder to spy Athlen holding the dagger close to his chest with both hands, trembling, pale, and unsure.

"We have to run. Can you?"

He nodded, gulping. He reached out and fisted his hand in the back of Tal's shirt. That was the only signal Tal needed.

They crept from the room into the hallway. Finding it clear, they ran for the stairs. Tal jumped down them, turned sharply, and ran for the back door and the kitchen courtyard. Together, they made it outside into the misting rain, but Athlen's hold on Tal's shirt abruptly gave way as Athlen let out a cry.

Tal spun in the mud just as the captain caught Athlen by the arm and swung him into the exterior wall.

One large hand splayed across Athlen's chest and held him pressed into the daub, while the other twisted Athlen's wrist, weakening his grip on the dagger. It fell harmlessly to the mud.

Two others charged Tal from the side. He swiped with the sword and met steel in return. As the first man deflected his blow, the second dodged and grabbed Tal in a bear hug, pinning his arms down to his sides. Tal struggled, grunting and twisting, but the larger man had him in a vise grip. Breath squeezing from his lungs, Tal dropped the sword.

"I knew that was you," the captain said with a deep growl. He gestured to the storm. The rain had calmed to a drizzle, but lightning lit up the clouds as the sky rumbled. "And in the company of a squall, no less. Who are you trying to drown this time?"

"I'm not." His voice was tinged with fear and desperation, a plea.

Athlen trembled and turned his head away when the captain leaned in to sneer, "Where's the gold?"

"Gone," Tal said.

The captain cast a glance over his shoulder. "And how do you know that?"

"He told me."

"He's a liar." He pressed harder on Athlen's chest, and Athlen's hand grasped the captain's wrist. He struggled, breath punched out in a gasp, mouth open as he gulped helplessly. "You'll pay, boy. I'm certain I can find a use for you."

"I won't do it. I won't go with you."

"Who says I want you on a boat, where you can sink us again? I'm sure there is a traveling spectacle that would pay money for your kind. An actual merman. It would give me great satisfaction to see you spend your life in chains in a tank of your own filth."

Athlen fought weakly.

Tal lifted his chin. "Let him go."

"Or what?" He laughed. "Who are you? His protector? Did he promise you riches? Or was your time behind the curtain riches enough?"

Tal's gut twisted with fire. "Last warning. Let him go."

"You're annoying, protector." The captain nodded at the man holding Tal. "Kill him. And bring me the chains for this whelp. We'll take care of the bird, then we'll figure out what to do with the fish."

Tal dipped into the embers of his magic. Fire danced down his arms, wreathing his hands in flame. The mercenary holding him yelped, releasing him as his skin burned. Tal dropped to the ground and rolled away in the sludge, grabbing the hilt of the sword and finding his feet. The blade was covered in mud, but it would do, and Tal willed fire to engulf the metal.

"What in the blazes?"

Tal raised his other palm, a ball of fire hovering at his fingertips. "Let him go. And I promise I won't hurt you."

Tossing Athlen to the ground, the captain turned and focused his full attention on Tal. In the storm-filtered moonlight Tal appeared as a demon, wreathed in flame and misted with blood. Rain hissed when it hit his skin, and a thick steam surrounded him like ether. He was a wraith, a spirit called forth from beyond to exact vengeance on those who would hurt his family.

"Who are you?" the captain demanded, unafraid despite the specter Tal made. "What are you?"

"Like you said, I'm his protector."

"I think someone would pay a price for you as well." He narrowed his eyes. "Not much magic left in the world."

"I have plenty."

"I see that. They didn't find that boy's body—the magic prince." He jerked his head to where Athlen lay in a puddle. "Maybe it's the other way around and he's your protector."

"I don't need protection." Tal dropped his gaze. "He doesn't need much either."

Athlen surged up from the ground, dagger in hand, and plunged it into the meat of the captain's side. He cried out as Athlen ripped it free and struck him again. Tal threw the fireball at the mountain of a man who had held him. It struck him in the shoulder, and he toppled backward. The third took off running into the night, and Tal let him, concerned only with the two twitching in the mud.

Athlen staggered toward him, face as white as the moon, hands trembling, holding the dagger streaked with dark heart blood. Tal took it from him and wiped the blade on his trouser leg before tucking it into his waistband.

He took Athlen's hands in his own, squeezing them, pulling him close. His skin was ice. "Are you okay?"

Athlen nodded shakily. "I think so. I don't . . ." He swallowed, throat bobbing. "I don't know."

"We can't stay here. There's more of them and we're bound to attract attention."

"Okay. Okay."

"You're safe. Understand? You're safe and we're running. Let's get to the mare."

Tal laced his fingers with Athlen's and tugged him into action, sword in one hand. They ran to the side of the building and scooped up their saddlebags and the quilt. The mare awaited them in the stable, and between the two of them, they made quick work of saddling her. It wasn't the safest rig, and the saddlebags had to be wedged between them, but they took off into the night, the shouts of Athlen's would-be captors echoing behind them.

They rode. An hour turned into two and bled into three. The night darkened, but the storm cleared, and the moon and the stars lit their way. Once Tal deemed them far enough away, he reined in the mare and coaxed her to the side of the road.

He needed to regroup. They both did.

Tal slid off her back and held his hand out for Athlen. He took it, and Tal helped him to the mossy ground.

"I'm sorry," Athlen said, voice tight. "I'm sorry I couldn't help you."

"It's all right, Athlen." Tal wiped his face with his sleeve, staining the fabric with a mixture of blood and mud. He grimaced. "Are you okay? Do you need anything?"

Athlen twisted his hands into knots and pulled the quilt tighter around him. "I don't know. I don't—I want to stop shaking. I want to stop thinking about being chained to the deck and thrown overboard whenever they wanted me to search the seafloor. Or being trapped in a tank for the rest of my life." He shuddered.

"Can I touch you?" Tal asked, stepping closer.

"Yes."

Tal wrapped his arms around Athlen's shaking body and held on. "I've got you."

"I know." His breath was cool on Tal's neck. "For how long?"

"Until you tell me to let go."

"Oh." Athlen rested his forehead on Tal's shoulder. "We need to get to your family's home. There are others after your brother."

"Yes. And we'll start again in a few minutes, but let me hold you."

Athlen melted into Tal's embrace. "Okay. But only for a few minutes."

Tal swept his hands along the line of Athlen's spine. "A few minutes, then."

As the adrenaline bled off, Tal's aches and pains returned in full force, and fatigue settled across his shoulders like a weight. Resting against Athlen, Tal closed his eyes and dreamed of the time when they would reach the castle, and everything would be behind them, and they could be together without the fate of the continent looming over them.

Tal was loath to release Athlen when he deemed their respite completed, but he finally did. Together, they fixed their awful saddling of the mare and reattached the saddlebags. Tal changed his shirt to rid himself of the mud and tacky blood clinging to his skin. Athlen rewrapped himself in the quilt and perched at Tal's back.

With a cluck of Tal's tongue, they were back on their journey, racing toward the castle and their fate.

13

Athlen clung to Tal's back as Tal pushed the mare to her limit. They hadn't stopped for more than a quick rest since the scuffle at the tavern two nights prior, and since they'd learned the news that Kest's life was in danger. The mare galloped as fast as she could carrying two, her barrel heaving with breaths, lather gathering under the saddle. Tal bent low over her neck. Her mane whipped his face, stinging away the exhaustion gathering heavy in his eyes.

The tempo of her hooves beat in rhythm with the thoughts in his head. *Save Kest. Stop Ossetia. Save Kest. Stop Ossetia. Save Kest. Stop Ossetia.* The words filled his head and body and spurred him onward.

His family's castle loomed over the landscape. At first it appeared as a blocky shape against the horizon, but as the mare ate up the distance with her long strides, the image sharpened into walls and turrets. And as she approached, the very atmosphere changed, the smell of the sea permeated the air, and the breeze was sharp and cool rolling in off the ocean. Athlen perked up, resting his chin on Tal's shoulder, his mouth close to Tal's ear, and he inhaled.

"The sea," he said, his breath a tickle on Tal's skin. "I miss the sea."

Tal's heart clenched.

Tal reined the mare in at the town's outskirts, where the buildings clustered close together and the road was narrow and made of stone. The only thing between them and his home was the city that surrounded the keep's outer wall.

"Why are we slowing?"

"This will be tricky. Hold on."

Athlen's grip tightened. Tal patted the mare's neck. "One more push, darling," he said, bent low to her ear. "Then rest for days."

Clicking his tongue, he spurred her forward, her hooves loud in the otherwise silent town, beating a fast rhythm as he maneuvered her through the twisty, narrow streets toward the main entrance to the castle. They galloped past the open-air market where he and Corrie would buy sweet pastries from the stalls with coins given to them by Isa. Tal banked a hard turn at the apothecary with the pungent herbs and candles and boring books with pictures of plants. He sped by the public stockade, where punishment was meted out for small offenses. Memories and ghosts flashed by Tal in the last moments of their journey as he drew the remaining energy from the mare.

He reined her in at the large central gate. They skidded to a stop at the heavy door leading into the main keep. The portcullis was lowered, as it was the middle of the night, and the guard towers were shut. But there should be at least two guards right on the other side, standing watch. Tal blew out a breath and maneuvered the mare until his leg bumped the steel grating. He reached through the bars and pounded on the wood with his fist.

"I demand you open this door!" he yelled. "I have an urgent message for the queen!"

The mare pranced beneath him, nervous, feeling the tension in Tal's legs. He held his breath, waiting for a response. After an eternity a small door within the wood swung open. A guard's face appeared in the frame.

"The castle is closed for the night, young sir, and you'd do well to find a place to sleep until these doors open in the morning."

Tal frowned. "I have urgent news about the murdered prince."

"As do a lot of folks, but they're not trying to wake the family, who are in mourning. Come back in the daylight if you truly have news regarding Prince Taliesin."

Frustrated, Tal yanked back the hood and pointed to his face. "I *am* Prince Taliesin."

"Well, that's a new one. I think the royal family would know—"

Another guard shouldered into view. "Go away, boy. Before you anger our captain of the guard."

"The captain of the guard is named Bertram, and he'll be furious to learn that you turned me away."

The guard's expression filled with unease.

Tal turned the screw. "Furthermore, your punishment will come directly from Commander Garrett. And you'll face his wrath when he finds out you denied his brother entrance to his family home."

The guards exchanged a look. The small door shut, and after a moment the larger creaked inward. Tal dismounted, leaving Athlen, pale and exhausted, clutching the pommel of the saddle.

The guards raised a lantern and peered through a space in the portcullis. Realization dawned across both of their faces. "By the stars, it is you."

"Raise the portcullis and ring the warning bell. Wake the household."

"Yes, my prince."

They swung the door open, and the heavy iron grid raised inch by inch.

Athlen smiled, fatigued and tight. "You're home."

"I am," Tal agreed. "There is much to be done."

Once the iron grate was high enough, Tal took the mare's reins and led her inside through the archway and into the keep proper, her hoofs ringing against the stone. In the dark the keep was shadows and sharp angles, formidable and frightening from the perspective of an outsider, but to Tal it was a comfort. He was home.

Sprawled before him was the central courtyard, made of stone and bordered by walls, with paths like spokes of a wheel that led to the stables, gardens, knights' quarters, and other areas of the castle. With purposeful strides Tal crossed the open area in the direction of the throne room. A wide set of stone steps, guarded at the base by a pair of imposing statues of knights, rose into a series of parallel arches that led into the castle. Tal stopped his hurried pace at the bottom of the steps and turned to Athlen. He offered his hand and Athlen took it, sliding off the mare on unstable legs.

Tal handed off the reins to the gate guard who'd followed them. "See she's taken care of. She's had a rough few days."

"Yes, sire."

Tal caught Athlen's elbow and guided him toward the steps. "Stay behind me."

Athlen looked as a ghost, and his wide honey eyes reflected the moonlight. Otherworldly and beautiful, Athlen shrugged off Tal's grasp and gripped his hand instead, his skin cool against Tal's sweaty palm.

"As you command," he said with a slight lift to the corner of his mouth.

Tal laced their fingers and squeezed, hoping Athlen took the gesture for what it was, a sign of affection and hope.

The peal of the warning bell broke the moment, the sound echoing across the keep, ringing sharp in Tal's ears. It was used in times of urgency, and it hadn't rung in years, not since the last great storm had battered the coast when Tal was a child. Now the bell sounded ominous as Tal tugged Athlen up the steps and into his home.

Passing through one of the arches, they entered the common area of the castle. Protocol required the royal family, which would include Emerick, to regroup in the safest part of the castle, which was the formidable and near-impenetrable throne room. One long corridor and a set of large ornate doors sat between Tal and the moment he'd been running toward since his rescue. Magic surged to life in his belly, lighting behind his eyes, but he tamped it down, wrenched it under his control. Athlen stumbled behind him, dropping Tal's hand in their hurry, but he remained close on Tal's heels as Tal broke into a desperate run. He hoped with all his being they'd made it in time.

Tal didn't allow the doors to stop him for a moment; flicking his hand, he willed them to open, and they did in a blast of wind. They banged hard against the stone.

With fire simmering beneath his skin, his body trembled, exhaustion hovering on the edge of his senses, but determination overrode all else. He entered, striding down the purple carpet that led to the twin thrones of Harth.

The room was dark, save for a single brazier near the queen's seat. Tal thrust out his hands and the rest flared to life, and fire roared in the large fireplace, flooding the room with light and heat.

The other occupants of the room startled, spinning to face him.

A pair of guards stood with Isa by the throne. She wore her nightgown, a robe hastily thrown over it, her long red hair in a braid over her shoulder, her feet bare. An unfamiliar man stood next to her, her husband—Emerick—looking just as disheveled, his eyes wide as he stared in wonder at the blazing fireplace.

"How did that—"

"Halt!" a guard yelled, raising his weapon. "Stop right there!"

Tal stalled his approach, pausing in the middle of the room, several feet from the throne.

Isa clasped her robe closed with one hand and peered around the guard. She gasped and brought the other hand to tremble over her open mouth. "Tally?" she said, pushing the guard out of her way. "Tally? Is that you?"

Emerick stared at him, stunned. "Was that . . . was that magic?"

A flurry of footsteps sounded on the stone as others filed in behind Tal, and he quickly checked over his shoulder. Athlen had shuffled off to the side, leaning heavily on the wall, watching the scene unfold. Garrett was there as well, hair and clothes in disarray, a regiment of guards behind him.

His mouth dropped open when he spied Tal. "Tally?"

Garrett walked toward him, and Tal held up his palm, halting Garrett's progress. "Where's Kest?"

His voice was hoarse, but he was loud enough, even over the

clang of the warning bell.

"Tally?" Garrett said, his name choked out around a sob. "What . . . what happened to you? How are you here? Where have you been?"

Tal shook his head. "Where is Kest?" he demanded, the words scraping from his throat.

Brow furrowed, Garrett stood, his hand twitching at his side, as if he wanted to reach out and grab Tal, confirm that he was real. "In his quarters."

Tal staggered in relief, his knees weak with it. He'd made it. He'd made it. Garrett crossed the distance between them and caught Tal by the elbow. Tal didn't shrug free; instead he welcomed the surety of Garrett's grip and the steadiness of his presence. "Place him under protective guard." Tal fisted his hand in Garrett's shirt sleeve. "Please, Garrett. You must."

Garrett tilted his head to the side. "He already is, Tally. How do you know about that?"

Tal didn't answer. Kest was saved. That had been his primary goal. Now he could move on to the second. Stop Ossetia. Tal narrowed his bloodshot eyes, turning back to face Emerick.

"You," he breathed.

Emerick's brow furrowed and his expression was one of confusion. "Me? I . . . I don't believe we've met. You must be Isa's youngest brother. I'm Prince Emerick, or just Emerick since we're brothers now. No need to stand on formality. I'm happy to see you've returned." He pointed to the braziers on the wall. "Was that . . ." He gulped. "Magic?"

Slipping from Garrett's grasp, Tal took a step forward, allowing a tendril of power to crackle in the air. Emerick took a step back, bumping into the dais behind him.

"Did you know?" Tal jutted his chin in Emerick's direction. His heart beat a rabbit's rhythm. His palms were slick with sweat.

Emerick exchanged a glance with Isa. "Did . . . did I know what?" He squinted. A bead of sweat rolled from his temple. He pressed his palms together. "Did I know about the magic?"

"No. Did you know what your sister had planned?"

Emerick blinked. "Vanessa?"

Tal gave a sharp nod. He'd finally understood after hearing the conversation in the tavern, and the clues had fallen together as Tal tore across the countryside to save his brother. Emerick hadn't met a shifter before Kest, regarding his power as a parlor trick, and the cat shifter had referenced her mistress when speaking to the captain. The gold was indeed Ossetia's stamp—uncirculated, unmarked, from the royal coffers. But there was more than one royal visiting Tal's home, a woman uninterested in Harth's court, second in line to her own throne, blocked from power in her kingdom because of their culture's misogyny, but not uninterested in power herself.

"Did you know what she had done in your name? In Ossetia's name?"

"Tal," Isa said, her voice a regal warning. "What are you doing?"

"Saving our kingdom from war." Despite his fatigue and his haggard appearance, Tal exuded power, the picture of cold calm, though a fire raged within him. He took another step forward. "Where is she?"

Emerick fiddled with the cuff of his nightshirt. "I don't understand what's going on. How do you know my sister?"

Garrett joined Tal by his side.

"Tally? You're not making sense. It's obvious you've been through something awful. You need a good rest and a hearty meal.

We can talk this through in the morning."

"I was first," Tal said, licking his cracked lips. "Murdered, since I wouldn't give them what they wanted. Then it was to be Kest to force us to war." He glanced to Garrett. "Ossetia planned it. Not Mysten. The unmarked gold on the derelict was blood money."

A tense silence fell over the room, the only sound the clanging of the bell in the courtyard. Tal thought for sure there would be a vocal reaction, bluster, retorts, denials, but there was nothing except Isa pulled taut as a bowstring and the clench of Garrett's jaw. Something had happened.

"What did they want from you?" Garrett asked, his tone stern, his gaze shrewd as it cut to Emerick.

"My magic. They wanted me to be a weapon. But I didn't give in. I wouldn't give it to them, so they tried to kill me on the ship."

Garrett's brow furrowed, and Tal saw the moment he pieced together all the information. His hand fell to the hilt of his sword, and the very atmosphere in the room changed. The guards behind them moved as one, following their commander's lead.

"Is this true, Prince Emerick?"

Emerick's mouth opened, then shut. His face turned red, and he pointed a shaking finger at Tal. "How dare you? These are baseless accusations! This is ridiculous! Where did you come up with these . . . these . . . lies?"

"I'm not lying!" Tal snapped, losing the tight control he had. The fires in the braziers roared, casting the throne room in blinding light, flames licking up the stone. He smothered his magic immediately, but it was enough for Emerick to pale and for the guards' low chatter to increase.

Garrett's hand was heavy when it landed on Tal's shoulder, and it helped to temper him. "Men," Garrett called, "take Prince Emerick under guard. And find his sister. Alert the queen. I'm certain she will have questions for them. And tell the gate guards to stop ringing that fucking bell!"

"This is preposterous! Isa, my dear, tell them they're wrong. I would never try to hurt your brothers."

Tal stiffened. *Brothers.* If Kest was under protective guard, why hadn't he been escorted to the throne room?

Isa stepped to the side and allowed the guards to grab Emerick. "We'll review my brother's claims. Until then I think it's best you go with these fine men."

Tal grabbed Garrett's arm. "What's happened?"

Garrett's answer was cut off as hurried footsteps announced more of the household joining them.

"Emerick!" a woman screeched. Tal glanced to where two women appeared from the inner chambers on the left side—from the wing for honored guests. One looked like Emerick—his sister, Vanessa. The other wore a cloak, head bowed, the hood obscuring her face despite the brightness of the room, but Tal recognized that cloak and the heeled boots she wore.

"What is going on?" Vanessa yelled as she took in the scene. "Have your guards unhand my brother at once! What is the meaning of this?" She pointed at Tal. "Who is this?"

"I'm under arrest!" Emerick wailed. "Vanessa, tell them you didn't try to kill this child! That you didn't pay mercenaries for his magic and that you didn't frame Mysten!"

Vanessa stared at Tal, her expression hardening. She was as beautiful as the rumors claimed, even as she regarded Tal as if he were a bug under glass.

"Vanessa," Emerick prodded. "Tell them!"

She huffed. "Whatever you think Emerick has done, you're

wrong. He's not smart enough." She tossed her hair and narrowed her eyes at Tal. "You must be the little prince. I'm surprised Zeph couldn't wring the magic out of you. I paid her well enough, though it looks as if she didn't finish the job."

Tal clenched his fists. His anger swelled like an incoming tide as he remembered his days on the ship. He tasted cinders on his tongue, and smoke curled from between his fingers as he reined in every desire to turn her to ash. "She tried." He moved toward her. "I have the scars."

"I'm sure. I can only imagine what the other kingdoms will say when they hear that King Lon's great-grandson shares his gifts. Will they march on Harth and overthrow your mother, or will they take you in the shadows and bury you so far under the ground only the worms will know you?"

Garrett crowded behind Tal's shoulder. "They'll do neither."

"Vanessa," Emerick said. "What have you done?"

Vanessa smiled, cold and cruel. "What you couldn't, brother. I have put us in a fine position. I've started a war we sorely needed to wrest control of the border mines from Mysten. And I've secured us a powerful ally, right, little prince?"

Tal bristled.

"Oh"—she waved her hand—"don't look like that. I gave you a choice. You could've easily given up and died on that ship. You were meant to when you wouldn't prove the rumors true. But now that you have shown the magic that burns inside of you like the rising sun, you'll be essential in our war. The war that started this morning."

Tal froze.

"Oh yes," she said, nodding, jeweled fingers tapping her angular chin, "you are a smidgeon late."

"Kest," Tal said, his brother's name a breathless whisper from his tight throat.

"The assassin may not have killed him, but it was a near thing, and it gave your queen the push she needed to invade Mysten this morning."

"Arrest her," Isa said, voice flat with rage. "Arrest her and throw her into the darkest dungeon you can find."

The guards advanced in tandem, but the cloaked figure moved swiftly and barred the way between them and Vanessa. She pushed up her sleeves to reveal dark, sharp claws, which lengthened as she dropped into a crouch. Conjuring a gust of wind, Tal snapped her hood back and met the dark eyes ringed with gold.

"I should've known you weren't a commoner," she said, smirking. "You have the stench of royalty all over you." She sniffed, lip curling in disgust.

"Maybe if you were a dog, you'd have recognized my scent from when you helped kidnap me on the beach."

She shrugged and studied her claws. "Cats don't see fine details, especially when their prey struggles and cries as much as you did."

Garrett unsheathed the sword strapped to his side, the metal sliding through the leather. "Arrest them all."

Vanessa's maid bared her teeth. In a blink her clothes shredded as she shifted into her cat form and jumped over the advancing guard. She growled, guttural and fierce, and Tal shuddered, the bite from her jaws fresh in his mind. With attention drawn elsewhere, Vanessa tried to make her escape.

Garrett shoved Tal to the side, sword drawn, but the cat dodged away and ran straight to where Athlen slouched in the corner, unarmed and silently watching everything unfold.

"No!" Tal yelled.

With a jerk of his arm, Tal conjured a wall of flame from the floor. It erupted from the stone in a riot of red and orange, flames like spikes creating a barrier between the cat and Athlen. He thrust out his other hand and, with the force of will, grabbed Vanessa and pulled her backward by her hair.

She screeched. The cat yowled. Athlen skittered away from the flames as the cat skidded to a stop, claws raking across the stone, to save herself from barreling into Tal's magic. The chamber exploded with movement. Isa ran for Vanessa, tackling her to the floor, and Garrett and his guards sprinted toward the singed cat, swords at the ready. Isa and Vanessa rolled over each other, scratching and fighting, tumbling in a flurry of silk and hair, Isa gaining the upper hand to allow the guards to intervene.

Garrett and his men encircled the enraged cat. She stalked in a line as they approached, eyes focused on Tal, lips curled back over her fangs. She growled when the guards closed in, backed to the wall of the throne room. In a last-ditch effort to escape, she charged, vaulting over the line of raised weapons and landing in front of Tal. She pivoted and took off at a sprint toward the open side door.

Tal shoved his hands outward and the doors slammed shut, blocking her exit.

"There's no way you're escaping," Tal said, sparks popping from his fingertips. "Surrender, please."

"Run!" Vanessa yelled, struggling against the guards. "Run! They'll kill you if you're caught."

The maid didn't hesitate. Dodging the guards, she sprinted right toward Garrett, her furred body hurtling toward him. Garrett dropped into a fighting stance, his sword drawn. She didn't slow. They would collide, and Tal saw the bloody end for one or both if he didn't act.

Without hesitation Tal cracked a whip of fire that sizzled and sparked. He caught her by the back leg and yanked her off course. She screamed, writhing, but Tal held fast.

He fell to his knees, grunting as his bones banged on the stone.

The doors from the royal household chambers wrenched open, and his mother barged in, a picture of fury in a brocade gown. She was followed by knights, with his little sister, Corrie, right behind them.

She surveyed the scene, sharp gaze settling on Vanessa and Emerick, both in the grip of castle soldiers, and the growling, snapping cat wrapped in a rope of fire. The scent of burned fur filled the room, and the queen wrinkled her nose.

"Detain them all!" she shouted, arm sweeping regally over the scene. "Lock the siblings in the guest quarters under heavy guard." She pointed to the cat, whose struggles had weakened but who still swiped her massive paws at anyone who dared venture close. "Kill it or throw it in the dungeons."

Tal jerked on the cord of magic binding the cat, and she shrieked. In a ripple of skin and fur and a cascade of sparks, she transformed back to her human form, and Tal immediately released her. Glaring at Tal, she lay on the floor, on her hands and knees, dark hair draped over her naked body. Garrett tossed a cloak over her, and she clutched it to her as the knights surrounded her and dragged her to the dungeons.

The rest of the guards easily subdued Emerick and Vanessa, escorting them to the guest wing, swords and spears aimed at them. Emerick pleaded with Isa. And Isa, with arms crossed over her chest, agony written in her features, turned away, red braid swinging. Vanessa remained stone-faced despite the cruel curl of her lip, and with head high, she peered down her nose at Tal as she strode past.

"You lost, little prince," she sneered. "The war has started, and your magic is at the mercy of Ossetia."

Shaking with fatigue and rage, Tal stood and faced her from the other side of a cross of spears. "I'll die before I let anyone use my magic for war."

"A bold claim, but as you've proven, you're exceptionally hard to kill."

"Enough," the queen snapped. "Take her away until I can deal with her and him," she said, indicating the wrecked Emerick. "Thank goodness they finally silenced that blasted bell. The whole kingdom doesn't need to know what happened here tonight until we're ready to tell them."

Once the hall had cleared and all that remained were Tal's family and Athlen, the queen's visage softened, and she crossed the floor in a flurry of skirts. She cupped Tal's face in her hands and stared at him with rapidly filling eyes.

"My son," she said, voice trembling, her thumb smoothing over the line of his cheek. "My son. You're alive."

"Kest," Tal said. "Is he . . . ? Did they . . . ?"

Her face shadowed. "They tried," she said. "But your brother is strong. He's resting under guard."

"But the war—"

"Shh, my son," she said, touching her forehead to his. "Let me see you first. I thought you were gone."

Tal leaned into her touch, eyes closing at the gentleness of her hands, her familiar fragrance washing over him.

"I'm here," he said.

"How?"

Tal opened his eyes and smiled. He pointed to where Athlen had slid down the wall, sitting on his haunches. Athlen looked as tired as Tal felt, his eyes sunken, his skin pale, his cheeks hollow. Tal's stomach fluttered as Athlen raised his weary gaze and gave Tal a small, fond smile.

"Him." Tal placed a hand over his heart. "Athlen saved me. And there was a village girl, Dara, who healed me."

"I owe them both my gratitude."

"As do I."

His mother smiled and kissed Tal's forehead. "I'm so very happy you're home, my son. But your entrance has stirred a hornet's nest. You accused another royal house of treason against our family. Not to mention the display of forbidden magic."

"She was going to ram me," Garrett said, coming behind Tal and resting his hand on Tal's shoulder. "His magic saved me. He saved me."

Tal gulped. "I'm sorry. It was the only way I could—"

"Hush now." She lifted his chin with her finger. "I'm so proud that you have come into your own. But we will have much to discuss in the morning. For now you need to refresh and rest. And I need to send messages to our borders immediately and stop a war." She squeezed his hands. "I'm certain your siblings want to talk to you as well."

Garrett, Corrie, and Isa took her words as permission to crowd him. Corrie's hug punched the air from Tal's lungs, her arms wrapping around his torso in a vise, squeezing him until his ribs creaked. Garrett slapped his back, almost toppling him, and Isa grabbed him around his shoulders and kissed his cheek.

His mother smiled, then turned on her heel, waving at her own guards a few steps away to follow her, and disappeared through the doors leading back to the royal chambers.

"I didn't know," Isa whispered, tears glistening. "I didn't know. I should've known. If I had, I would have killed him in our marriage bed for what he's done to you and what he tried to do to Kest. This is my fault. I was the one who—"

Tal shook his head. "No, Isa. Please. Don't."

"Tally," Garrett said, wiping his eyes. "Kest saw you fall overboard. We searched for you until we almost drowned. How are you alive?"

"Athlen." Tal gestured to him. "He saved me. He pulled me from the waves."

Athlen leveraged to standing, using the wall. His legs trembled. He lifted a hand in a wave. "Hi."

Garrett's eyebrows shot into his hairline. "The boy from the derelict."

"The one you cried over?" Corrie asked, tilting her face upward.

Tal winced and ran his hand down his flushed face. "How do you know about that?"

"You cried over me?" Athlen knotted his hands, cheeks flushed. "Why?"

"You jumped off the stern." Garrett crossed his arms. "We thought you were dead. That seems to be a theme. How are *you* alive?"

Tal disentangled from his sisters' arms and staggered across the room to the where Athlen leaned on the wall. He took Athlen's arm and settled it on his shoulders, wrapping his other arm around his waist.

"Questions later." Tal waved his hand, fatigue catching up with him. He couldn't remember the last time he'd slept well, and he looked forward to collapsing into his bed. "We need baths and beds and rest. I should see the court physician. And I want to see Kest."

"So demanding, Tally," Garrett said, smiling. "We'll wake the steward; he can get everything sorted and find Athlen his own quarters. But *we* can bother Kest. He'll want to see you."

Corrie took Athlen's other side. "We can walk together, and while you're visiting Kest, Isa and I can take care of your friend." She winked at Tal, then turned to Athlen. "We'll take you to Tally's room while we wait for the steward."

Athlen's eyes widened. "Spitfire," he mouthed.

"Corrie," Tal said, rubbing his hand over his eyes. "I'm too tired for your antics and so is Athlen. He's fragile and in pain, and I don't want you to pester him." Tal tightened his grip as Athlen staggered and his eyelids drooped.

"I'll be fine. We've survived much worse than your nosy sister. Please go see your brother."

"Are you sure?"

Athlen gave Tal a light push. "Yes. Go. I'll see you when you're done."

Despite his misgivings, Tal left Athlen with Isa and Corrie in Tal's quarters and followed Garrett into Kest's bedchamber. They passed several guards along the way, all alert, all bowing their heads to Garrett, and all prepared to defend Kest.

"There are more," Tal said as they entered Kest's room.

"More?"

"I ran into Vanessa's handmaiden in a tavern when she was bargaining with the mercenaries who fled the derelict. She told them she'd paid more than one assassin. They thought the death of a different prince of Harth would push Mother to war with Mysten."

Garrett stopped in his tracks. "Tal," he said, voice choked, grabbing Tal by the elbow. His grip was unforgiving. "You must know. . . . It wasn't that we weren't devastated and enraged. I wanted to . . ." Garrett took a breath. "I would have walked into Mysten with only my bare hands as weapons if I'd thought for a second it would have brought you back. You know that, right?"

Tal had never doubted his family's love for him, not once. He might be a burden, the fourth in line for the throne, and a prince with the same magic that had destroyed the continent and his family's legacy, but his family truly loved him.

"I know."

"Good." Garrett shook his shoulder. "We'll protect Kest. We won't allow anyone near him who means him harm."

"I'm worried." Tal knuckled the sleep from his eyes. "Isa was manipulated. We've invaded another kingdom. There are others after our family. And I've revealed my magic to the world after keeping it a secret for years." Tal's chin dropped to his chest. "I'm scared of what's going to happen next."

Garrett's hand landed heavy on his shoulder. "Tally, you're forgetting something."

"What?"

"You don't have to face any of these things alone. You're home. We're here. Whatever happens, we'll be together."

Tears gathered in Tal's eyes. "Thank you."

"No, thank you, for being a stubborn shit and surviving. Your return was the best gift I've ever received." He cleared his throat. "Now, are you sure you want to see Kest? I'm not going to lie—you look like one stiff breeze could knock you over. He'll be here in the morning."

Shaking his head, Tal continued farther into Kest's room. "He'll be mad if we don't wake him. And I can't be the source of his despair for another day."

Garrett sighed. "You're right. Come along."

Kest lay in his bed, fast asleep, dark hair spread out on the pillow. Crisp sheets covered his bare chest. Tal sat next to Kest's hip, and Kest roused at the shift of the mattress.

"What?" His eyelids fluttered, voice heavy with sleep. "Who's there? Garrett? If this is a prank, I swear on my feathers—"

"Kest."

His brow furrowed. "Tally?"

"Yes."

Kest's eyes snapped open. He shot to sitting but groaned and fell back to the nest of pillows. The coverlet slipped, revealing bandages around his ribs and a bruise that spread from his armpit to his hip.

"Hey, be careful! Don't hurt yourself."

"Tally," he breathed. "Am I dead? Or is this a dream?"

Tal smiled fondly. "Neither."

Kest's expression didn't ease. With a shaking hand, he slid his fingers along Tal's cheek. "How? I watched you die."

Tal leaned into the touch. "I didn't. I promise you."

"You fell. I saw you. How are you here?"

"There's a boy who helped me. The one from the derelict. He's also the boy from the market."

"You didn't tell me that!" Garrett said, gripping Kest's bedpost.

"I haven't had the time."

Kest smiled. He touched Tal's chin with his thumb. "I'm glad to see you."

"I'm glad to see you, too. Are you okay?"

"An archer tried to shoot me from the sky this morning, but he didn't have the best aim. Merely grazed my side."

"Don't listen to him. He stuck Kest like a pheasant, but our brother is an obstinate bastard."

Kest swatted at Garrett, who danced away, laughing.

Tal's body warmed. His brothers—he was back among his brothers. He was home.

"This belongs to you." Kest tugged on the chain around his neck, and a gold ring slid from beneath the blankets. "They sent it with no ransom note." Kest frowned at Tal's signet ring, running his thumb along the line of the family's crest. The emerald, denoting Tal's birth month, shone in the low light. "We knew we had to find you quickly. The messages you sent helped."

"You got them?"

"Yes. Mother was frantic when the first one arrived written in blood. The tar was a better idea."

Tal grimaced. "Sorry."

"Here." Kest took off the necklace and dropped the ring into Tal's hand. The chain pooled in his palm. "I'm glad I don't need to wear it any longer to remember you by." He smiled tight, pain in the lines around his mouth and tears in the shadows of his eyes.

"You should rest."

"As should you. If Garrett hadn't confirmed it, I'd think you a ghost come back to haunt me for my failure."

Tal shook his head. "You didn't fail."

"I *left* you." Kest gripped his hand. "I never should have left you."

Tal's throat went tight. "You did what you thought was best. Neither of us knew their intent was to kill me."

Kest closed his eyes and fell back to his pillow. "I shouldn't have left you."

"I forgive you." Tal didn't know why he'd said it. Kest didn't need forgiveness from him. But maybe it would help him forgive himself.

"Thank you."

"We should allow Kest to sleep," Garrett said, abandoning his spot by the door, which he'd taken up to give Tal and Kest space to have a moment. "Come along, Tally. We'll visit again tomorrow."

Tal squeezed Kest's hand. "Good night."

Tal was half asleep by the time he made it back to his room. He pushed open the door and sighed deeply at the sight of his bed within his reach. The pillows and coverlet looked the same as when he had left, maybe a little tidier, and he wanted to sink down into them and sleep for days. He shuffled forward, head bowed, and so focused he nearly forgot that he'd left Athlen in the care of his sisters. They were gone, as was Athlen. They must have found him quarters. Despite the appeal of his own bed and his utter exhaustion, Tal wanted to talk with Athlen before falling asleep, just to ensure he was all right. Tal moved to exit, but the sound of a small splash caught his attention.

"Athlen?"

Tal pushed the curtains to the adjoining chamber aside and wearily smiled at what he found.

Athlen was in a long tub, brilliant tail flopped over the side, his upper body submerged, arms crossed over his chest. He was fast asleep, copper hair floating in the gentle waves created by the flex of his gills.

Tal trailed his fingers over the water's surface, finding it warm to the touch. His sisters must have woken the servants to draw a bath, then left Athlen to his own devices. Though it wasn't salt water, maybe a good night's rest would help Athlen to feel better. Maybe in the morning he'd be in less pain and he'd be ready to talk about his future. Their future together, if there was to be one. Tal wanted one. He wanted one desperately, and he'd do anything to show Athlen how much. He'd promised he wouldn't leave Athlen behind. Hopefully, Athlen would promise the same.

Despite his fatigue, Tal took a moment to observe him—the peaceful state of his features, the freckles along his nose from his time in the sun, the webbing between his fingers, the scales that scattered along his torso and shoulders until they fused and over-lapped beneath his navel into the pattern of his tail.

He was beautiful.

Tal's heart lurched. Athlen missed the sea. Tal was home in a castle made of stone.

It was too much to think about right then, and Tal returned to his bed. He shucked off his disgusting shirt and trousers and crawled into the plush covers. With a sigh Tal closed his eyes, finally home, and fell into a deep, dreamless sleep, the shark's tooth clutched tight in his palm.

14

Tal was on the verge of waking when he heard the voices. They were low, nearby, but he couldn't quite make out what they said. His name? He scrunched his eyes and curled tighter, knees to his chest, remaining still in the hopes that whoever it was would pass him by and allow him to sleep a bit longer.

Except the voices wouldn't allow him to sink back into the darkness. He tensed when footsteps brought them closer, and when his arm was touched, he snapped his eyes open. He shot out of sleep between one heartbeat and the next. He grabbed the intruder's wrist, bent it backward, and using his weight, flipped him over. They fell in a tangle of blankets and limbs. But Tal had surprise on his side, and he gained the upper hand, his knees thudding on either side of the intruder's body. He didn't hesitate to light the fire in his veins. Kneeling above, chest heaving, he splayed his right hand across the other's chest, left hand raised above his head, steeped in flame.

Corrie screamed. Garrett shouted his name.

Tal blinked. Garrett sprawled below him, hands up, face blanched, and eyes wide, reflecting Tal's magic.

Sweat dripped between Tal's shoulder blades. Throat tight, he stared down at his brother, panic real and acrid, thudding hard beneath his skin.

"Tal," Athlen yelled, running from the adjoining room. He was dressed and awake. "It's okay! You're okay!"

Tal gulped and nodded. He closed his hand, snuffing the flame. "I'm sorry," he croaked.

Garrett patted the outside of Tal's thigh, his expression troubled, but he forced a laugh. "Well, no more playing pranks on you, then."

"I'm sorry."

"Don't apologize. We shouldn't have sneaked in here," Garrett said.

"We didn't mean to frighten you." Corrie tangled her hands in the folds of her skirt. "But you've been asleep for an entire day, and we wanted to see you."

Tal winced. "Oh."

"It's all right. But how about letting me up?"

Tal scrambled off Garrett and moved to Athlen's side. Athlen appeared well rested, but he still wasn't well. The bruises beneath his eyes had lightened, but the stiff way he held his body remained. Athlen brushed the back of his hand against Tal's in a gesture of comfort, and Tal melted into it, the knot of terror easing with the gentle touch.

Garrett brushed off his trousers and straightened his shirt. "We have a council meeting this evening after dinner." He looked to

Athlen. "All of us." Athlen shifted, bare toes flexing on the stones. "You need a bath," Garrett said, wrinkling his nose at Tal, "and to change. Then we'll have a very late lunch or an early supper."

Tal's stomach growled. "What time is it?" Heavy curtains hung from ornate rods divided the interior of his quarters into sections, and as a result, they blocked the light from his two windows.

"Late afternoon." Corrie bounced on her toes. "You both must have been exhausted. Kest slept through the day as well, but the physician says he will be able to join the meeting for a little while."

"That's good."

"What's this?" Corrie picked up the shark's tooth from the floor.

Tal stiffened. "It's a tooth."

She rolled her eyes. "I see that. Why is it on your floor?"

Tal chewed his bottom lip. "It's mine." He held out his hand. "Give it back, Corrie."

She rubbed her fingers over the edges, wincing when the serrated side bit into her skin. "Make me."

Athlen watched the scene silently, though there was a clench to his jaw and a wrinkle between his brows.

"That's a bad idea." Garrett plucked the tooth from Corrie and gave it back. "Tal brought me to the ground over waking him. I'm not about to see him crisp you over a trinket."

Corrie made a face.

Garrett ignored her. "We'll send the servants in. Don't take too long. Mother wants to untangle this mess as soon as possible." He paused, uncertain. "She'll want a full accounting." He frowned, gaze cutting to Athlen. "Best get your stories straight. Whatever they may be."

Tal nodded. Athlen stood silent while Garrett and Corrie left, and a handful of servants bustled in. They emptied the tub Athlen had slept in and filled it with hot water. They laid out clothes for them both.

After they left, Tal walked behind the curtain and sank into the steaming water and sighed. His cuts and blisters stung, but otherwise, it was heavenly. He could've stayed there forever, but he didn't have much time. He bathed while Athlen sat on the floor just on the other side of the curtain.

Suddenly Tal realized their mission was completed. Athlen had promised to see him home, and he had. His obligation was filled. After the meeting with the queen, Athlen could leave if he wanted. Athlen could *leave*. Tal's heart clenched at the thought. A lump formed in his throat as tears threatened, and he swallowed it down as he hastily scrubbed the soap over his skin.

He cleared his throat. "Did you sleep well?" he asked, rubbing soap through his hair. "In the water?"

Athlen sighed. "It was wonderful. Better than the ground."

"Did my sisters treat you well?"

Athlen huffed a laugh. "They were fine, Tal. They offered to find me my own quarters, but I told them I'd wait for you. The servants drew a bath and I . . . fell asleep."

Tal's cheeks heated. His sisters would no doubt tease him over the fact that Athlen had stayed in his room overnight. It hadn't been like that at all, though not for Tal's lack of want.

Braver than he felt, Tal continued. "You could've crawled into the bed."

There was silence, and Tal pictured Athlen shrugging and wrinkling his nose. "I didn't want to impose."

Right. A small part of Tal had hoped that Athlen's distance was due to the urgent nature of their journey, but now they were out of immediate danger and the distance remained—an invisible wall Athlen had erected since they left the cavern.

"We don't have to tell them about you."

"Then how will we explain your rescue?"

"You stowed away on Garrett's boat and jumped into the water when I went overboard. Then we used the jolly boat."

"That's ridiculous, Tal."

Tal sank up to his chin in the warm water. "I don't want you to feel forced into revealing yourself. Even if they are my family."

"It's all right. I chose to help you, and I knew it meant telling others what I am."

"They may not believe us. You might have to show them . . . something."

Athlen sighed. "Yes. I know that, too."

They were interrupted by a knock on the chamber door.

After the creak of the hinges, Athlen said, "The physician is here to see you, my prince."

"Right. Let him in."

Tal rinsed the soap and wrapped a towel around his waist. He suffered the indignity of an exam, being poked and prodded and bandaged. His shoulder was healing well but would scar. His knee was painful and slightly swollen, and he allowed the physician to wrap it to stabilize the joint. The smaller cuts and bruises and aches and pains would diminish with rest and time.

After the physician toddled off, Tal sat on the edge of his bed and dressed.

"They brought you clothes as well," Tal said, nodding to the extra folded pile.

Athlen picked up a shirt between his thumb and forefinger. He raised an eyebrow. "I think I prefer what I have on."

"These are nicer."

Athlen dropped the shirt. "And these are what I prefer," he said, sweeping his hands down his body and wiggling his toes. "If your family is about to learn that I'm of the sea, then I should keep to the aesthetic."

Tal laughed. "Fine."

They left the room to find lunch, and Tal's stomach growled when they sat at a table laden with food in the kitchens. His mouth watered, and all decorum disappeared as he dug into the meal of smoked turkey, baked ham, fresh fruit, green vegetables, and soft, warm bread.

Athlen lifted a perfect red apple and took a tentative bite before diving in, munching the crisp flesh and peel.

"Couldn't wait?" Garrett asked, ambling in and plopping into a seat.

"No," Tal said around a mouthful of food. He shoved a slice of fresh bread dripping with butter into his mouth. "We haven't eaten in days."

Garrett paused in loading his plate. "Days?"

Athlen nodded, nibbling around the core of his apple. "Days," he echoed.

"Well," Garrett said, clearing his throat, "here. Let me help you." Garrett took Athlen's plate and piled on the food. He slathered cakes in syrup and jam, speared sausages with a fork, and plopped a heap of potatoes onto the side. He set it in front of Athlen and nudged it with his fingers. "No need to be shy. Eat your fill."

"I don't think I can eat all of that." Athlen exchanged a look with Tal.

Tal shrugged, a small grin tugging at the corner of his mouth. "It'd be rude not to try."

Athlen raised an eyebrow but grabbed his fork and joined Tal in stuffing his mouth full.

≈

"I think I'm going to be sick," Athlen said, holding his stomach as he and Tal walked to the queen's council chamber. "I ate too much."

Tal groaned in agreement. His belly was uncomfortably full.

Garrett laughed at the pair of them. "Don't throw up on the rug. It's mother's favorite. Aim for the stone."

"That's not funny, Garrett," Tal said, hand hovering near his mouth.

Garrett's expression turned solemn. His gaze raked over Tal's skinny frame. "No, I guess it's not." He glanced at Athlen at Tal's side. "Are you injured?"

Athlen lifted his head from where he'd been studying the paving stones and rugs under their feet. "What?"

"You're moving . . . oddly."

"Oh." Athlen rubbed the back of his neck. A blush painted his cheeks. "I'm not used to riding. And we've been on a horse for days."

Tal frowned. Not quite a lie and not quite a truth. Athlen was good at that, hiding his thoughts and feelings, tucking them away behind a congenial smile. The night in the bath must not have helped as much as Tal had hoped.

Athlen avoided looking at Tal and ducked his head again, his bare feet padding silently along the ribbon of thick carpet leading to the queen's council chamber.

A few minutes later the trio stopped in front of a set of large, ornate doors. Several guards stood across the hallway, hands on their swords, sharp eyes boring holes into Athlen as he approached. Athlen paled and slowed, angling behind Tal.

Tal reached behind him and took Athlen's clammy hand, squeezing it in reassurance.

Garrett gestured with his arm, and the line parted to allow them to pass. A steward opened the door to reveal the council room. A large, glossy table sat in the middle, its legs and trim covered in designs. Several high-backed wooden chairs with plush cushions encircled it. A sprawling rug covered the stone, the design a tangle of blue and purple threads radiating outward from the center of the room. Tapestries adorned three of the four walls, cushioning the sound and breezes from the windows in the fourth wall, and depicting some of Tal's favorite fairy tales—unicorns frolicking with maidens, a manticore fighting a knight, a large black bear with horns and red eyes howling from the top of a mountain, and a scene of mermaids near a beach enticing sailors to swim in the froth of a tumultuous sea.

Tal hadn't noticed that one before, not in the scant few times he'd been in this room, or the one that hung behind his mother—a picture of a mage with flames entwining her limbs and fire in her eyes, mouth open in a scream, her enemies crushed under her feet, a sword thrust through her middle from a knight behind her.

His grip tightened on Athlen's hand as they entered.

The rest of Tal's family already sat around the council table. His mother, the queen, presided at the head, her dark hair piled beneath her crown. Isa sat at her right hand, demure, the gold circlet around her forehead glinting in the light from the high windows in the stone wall. Kest was next to Isa, right arm in a sling, his tangled hair hanging in his pale face. Corrie leaned close by his side, ready to jump in if Kest tipped over. The seat at his mother's left was open for Garrett, her second-born, and those next to Garrett's were empty, presumably for Tal and Athlen.

The occupants of the room all swiveled to stare as the door swung shut behind the trio.

Tal followed Garrett and eased into his seat, pulling Athlen to the one next to him.

Athlen's eyes were wide, his mouth slightly open as he took in the opulence. His hand trembled in Tal's, and Tal noted the moment Athlen noticed the tapestries of the mermaids and the mage, as his body shuddered and his throat bobbed. He ducked his head.

"I'm glad you could join us," his mother said, addressing Athlen. "I am honored to meet the man who saved my son."

"Thank you," Athlen said softly. He cleared his throat, eyes firmly on the table. "I'm happy to meet Tal's family."

Her eyebrows shot up at the familiarity, and Tal hid his wince.

"We've much to discuss regarding the treason and subterfuge committed by Princess Vanessa of Ossetia and her handmaiden, including what this means for our relationships with the other kingdoms, especially Mysten. First, I'd like to hear an account of Taliesin's . . ." She paused, eyes fluttering shut, her fingers gripping the edge of the table. She took a steadying breath. "Of Taliesin's misfortunes."

Tal took a sip from the goblet in front of him to bolster his resolve, thankful it was filled with sweet wine. He licked his lips and, with a slight nudge from Athlen, began his tale. Under his family's scrutiny, he recounted finding the derelict and freeing Athlen from the fetter. He told them about the sailor in the crew's quarters who'd tried to kill him, before Shay chased him to his death. He spoke about the kidnapping on the beach, the shifter who'd chased him and dragged him from the waves when he tried to escape. He talked of the days on Zeph's ship, the work and the pressure to reveal his magic, and how in the end he'd broken after seeing Kest in the hold and Garrett's ships on the horizon. He told them how he'd fallen into the sea and would have drowned save for

Athlen, and of his days in the cave healing with help from Dara, and their journey across the countryside—running into the men who'd held Athlen captive and the shifter from the beach, Vanessa's maid.

The words tumbled over themselves, and while he left out the wonder of Athlen's reveal, and the kisses they'd shared, and the despair he'd felt sending messages in blood and tar, they were all there in the telling, in the hitch of his breath, the stutter of his tongue, and the moisture on his cheeks, which he wiped away with his sleeve.

"Tally," Isa breathed when he'd finished, tears glistening in her eyes. "You are so brave."

"I'm not," Tal said quickly. "I merely did what was needed to survive, to see you all again, to ensure our family would not come to harm."

"You did well, Tally," Garrett said, grasping his shoulder and squeezing. "You did well."

Tal studied the table. "I was ashamed for what I did to Zeph's ship and for my lack of control. I still am." His voice cracked. "But I know that if I hadn't, I wouldn't be sitting here with you now. And we'd be in a war that would hurt our kingdom, orchestrated by someone who doesn't care about our people."

"You did nothing wrong," his mother said sharply. "They tortured you and you *survived*. That is what is important."

Tal wilted under his mother's scrutiny and nodded.

Kest tapped his fingers on the table. "How did Athlen save you from drowning? Garrett and I . . ." His words went quiet, his jaw worked, and his next words sounded thick with grief. "We searched and searched and almost drowned ourselves trying to find you."

Tal shot a look to Athlen.

Athlen bit his lip, appearing small and intimidated in the presence of the royal house. He cleared his throat. "I'm a . . . I'm . . ." He licked his lips. "Well, I'll show you." He disentangled from Tal and lifted his hand, his long knobby fingers spread apart, and slowly they transformed, scales rippled over his skin, and webbing grew between the digits.

"Oh," his mother said, fingertips at her throat, her expression one of delighted surprise. "A merman."

Stunned silence followed, broken only by the sound of a shutter on the high windows shifting in the ocean wind. They stared, and Athlen dropped his hand and tucked it under the table, while a high blush spread into his cheeks.

"Yes," Athlen said, voice wobbling high into a question.

Tal's siblings erupted with questions. Tal ignored them, instead staring at the way his mother glanced wistfully at the tapestries in the room, settling on the one with the mermaids on the beach. Mind whirring, he took in the cadre of fantastic creatures—unicorns, mermaids, a manticore, a howler—and experienced his own epiphany.

"You knew," he said.

The chaos died down at his words, and his mother smiled softly. "Yes."

"I don't understand," Isa said.

Corrie squinted. "Knew what?"

His mother waved her hand toward the tapestries. "King Lon did damage to more than just the other kingdoms. He attacked all magic not his own, either killing it or driving it into hiding. The merfolk dove to the deep, where my grandfather could not follow, and remained."

Poppy hadn't been lying. She'd known. King Lon had killed the creatures, which meant he did drive the mage into the sea. The water mage and the sea witch were one and the same.

"The myths," Kest said, leaning forward, Corrie's hand on his arm to keep him from toppling. "The ones you made us read as children. They're real?"

"In more ways than you can imagine."

"How could you not tell me?"

"Ever the scholar," Garrett said on a sigh. "If you'd spent more time at sea, you'd have heard the stories."

Athlen's eyes grew wide. "You know about merfolk?"

"Very little," the queen said, "and only what my grandmother told me before she died. Unfortunately, the creatures were the first of Lon's conquests, completed when he was a young man, before my mother was born. I'm afraid all their history is lost here on the continent. He saw to that." Her words sat heavy over the group—a reminder of the ruthlessness and cruelty of their ancestor. "But I wonder," she said, tapping her lips. "How are you able to traverse land? I wasn't aware the merfolk could change at will like the shifters. It's a different kind of magic, isn't it?"

"We can't. I made a bargain with a sea witch for legs. I was lonely after my family disappeared. That was several years ago."

"And what was this bargain?"

"That's not for discussion." Athlen's voice was clipped and strained, the little composure he'd gathered stripped away.

The queen frowned, and a tense silence settled in the room.

Athlen's chin lifted in defiance.

"Athlen is the last," Tal blurted.

Athlen startled, head whipping around to stare at Tal, then he hunched in his seat and confirmed Tal's statement with a sharp nod. "It's true."

"I'm sorry to hear that, Athlen," his mother said. "That's unfortunate."

"Well," Isa said, hands clasped tightly on the table. "This has been enlightening, but it does not address the fact that we are on the brink of war with Mysten and that Tally has shown the world that he is capable of carrying on Lon's legacy."

"What do you wish to do, my daughter? We can annul the marriage with Emerick. The alliance will stand, since they will be indebted to us after Vanessa's treachery."

"No, it's stronger with the marriage ties. I don't believe Emerick had anything to do with the plots against us." She rubbed her brow, the first sign of her fatigue, her composure cracking slightly. "I don't believe he's capable."

"We'll need to be certain."

"I'll question the captives," Garrett said. "I'll wring the truth from them. Tally will accompany me. They've seen what he can do; they may provide more information under threat."

Tal swallowed. "I'll not hurt them."

"You won't have to," Garrett said.

Isa straightened her posture. "And I'll have Emerick send a letter to his brother, King Rodrick, and demand an apology and recompense for what their sister has done to my brothers."

"And Tally?" Kest asked. "His magic?"

"Tally can stay behind the castle walls, right?" Corrie asked. She clutched Kest's arm. "It was a mistake. We'll say it was a mistake."

"I'll not hide," Tal said, frowning. He studied the grain of the table, his brow furrowed, his words slow but true. "Not again. I'm not him. I thought, maybe, that I would be, because we share the same fire. But I'm *not*." Tal had made mistakes. He'd burned the pirate ship in his weakest moment, but he'd resolved he'd never do anything like that again. He *wouldn't*, because as freeing as it had felt, as desperate as he'd been, it was terrible and terrifying. "I won't do the things he did. Never. Not even at the order of my queen. And I'm not afraid anymore." Tal met the gaze of his mother. "I'm not afraid of myself." He lifted his palm, and fire danced along his skin and dripped from his fingertips, sizzling the wood of the table where it landed. "Of what I can do."

"I don't believe hiding is an option now," his mother said. She did better than Corrie at disguising her fear, but Tal could see the sorrow etched in her features, the weight of the decisions ahead of them.

"There are rumors in the towns about me. And I know you've always said they're just rumors, but if enough people speak them, if enough people believe in them, then they aren't just rumors. They are truth. Those same rumors are why I was taken and why we're in this situation. Hiding me may have been the right choice when I was young, but it's certainly not anymore. Now we must control the narrative. We have to change the misconceptions about magic, and to do that, I have to reveal myself. I must show the world that I'm not another Lon."

"I agree," the queen said, eyes shining with pride. "The other kingdoms will want to meet you, Taliesin. They will want to hear this all from you to allay their concerns."

"Then invite them," Tal said. "Invite them here or I'll go to them."

"That's too dangerous," Garrett said, elbows on the table. "We've seen what happens when you travel. They'll come here."

"A celebration," Isa said. "Some kind of celebration."

"What kind? We've just had a wedding," Kest said.

Isa's lips thinned. "That was an alliance. And rushed, at that, due to . . . unforeseen circumstances. We'll have another. A celebration of joy."

"Yes," the queen said, her shrewd gaze settling on Tal. "The king of Mysten has a bastard daughter. He's been looking for a way to make her legitimate. If we provide one, he may forgive our transgressions against them." Her jaw clenched. "I promised myself I would never ask any of you to marry for an alliance, but I'm afraid I will have to break that promise."

Kest cleared his throat. "How old is she?"

His mother sighed softly, then raised her head, opened her eyes, and addressed the table with her usual regal bearing. "She is seventeen."

Tal froze.

Athlen clamped his hand down on Tal's wrist on the table, chilled fingers wrapping firmly around Tal's arm.

His mother zeroed in on the gesture.

"Corrie," she said softly, "I think it's time our guest was shown to the quarters he'll be using while he is staying with us."

Corrie frowned. "Hey, I'm a part of this family! I want to know what happens."

"You'll be informed as soon as we've discussed it. But as you're too young to be considered, it's not your concern. I require this other task of you. See to our guest. Treat him with the respect you would a hero who saved your brother."

Corrie grumbled but stood and curtsied.

Athlen looked to Tal for guidance, and with a breaking heart Tal patted Athlen's arm. "Go with Corrie. I'll find you later."

He tilted his head, eyes narrowed, but stood all the same and allowed Corrie to loop her arm through his.

No one at the table spoke until Corrie whisked him out the door, chattering all the while.

Tal shared a glance with his siblings, then swallowed. The duty should fall to his shoulders. He was the obvious choice, being the closest in age, and it would be a gesture of good faith, especially if he was to reveal his magic. But . . . he didn't want to, not if Athlen would have him, not if there was any chance for them to be together. He wished they'd resolved the tension between them before he was confronted with this choice. A deep sense of loss pierced him for what might have been. He took a breath, then faced his mother, choosing his words carefully.

"If you ask me to, I will do it. I know this is my fault for—"

"No." Garrett's fist hit the table. "No. Did you see the way they look at each other?" he said to their mother. "No. It's not fair to ask Tally."

"I'll do it," Kest said. He picked at the tablecloth runner with a fingernail. "I am the next closest in age. It would be a good match."

"What about Shay?" Tal asked.

Kest reddened. "It'll be fine. We were not—"

"You two act like I have one foot in the grave," Garrett said, crossing his arms. "I'm commander of our military. I am second in line to the throne. I'm only twenty-three. I'm a damn fine prospective husband."

Tal fidgeted in his seat. "You don't have to do this for me."

Garrett puffed out his chest. "Who says I'm doing it for you? Maybe it's time I settle down."

"Settle down?" Kest huffed. "This coming from the man who spends most of the year at sea."

"Yes. Settle down. Give Mother some grandchildren. The sea knows she'll not have any from you if you don't ever let Shay know you adore her."

Kest sputtered in embarrassment.

"Grandchildren? Hellions, more like," Isa said, mouth pulled into a smile. "But you're certain, Garrett? This isn't a decision to be made lightly."

"You married for an alliance, Isa, to help our family and the people of our kingdom. I will do the same because it's the responsible thing to do, but also because you know I can't allow you to be better than me at anything."

"If that were the case, you'd be much better at politics," Kest shot back. "And wouldn't run into every situation with a sword drawn."

Garrett grinned, and there was no doubt he had a pun about marriage and swords on his tongue before their mother cut him off with a sharp glance. She couldn't hide her smile. "It is decided. Isa, ensure Emerick writes to his brother and reminds him of the seriousness of the transgressions against our family. Vanessa will be returned to them if they relinquish their hold on the mines along their border. The handmaiden will die for her role in kidnapping my son, but not before she is questioned. I will send my regards to the royal family of Mysten, offer my apologies, and propose an alliance through marriage if needed." She folded her hands. "You are dismissed. Except you, Taliesin."

Tal plopped back into his seat. His mother remained silent while his siblings shuffled out. Kest moved slowly, and Isa stayed by his side, and it felt like an eternity until the doors closed. Once they were alone, his mother stood from her chair and settled in the one Garrett had occupied. She took Tal's hands in hers, the many jeweled rings on her fingers flashing in the light from the high windows, her skin warm on his.

"Do you love him?"

Tal bit his lip. "Yes."

"He's a merman. You are a human."

"Yes."

"Does he love you?"

Tal shrugged. "I don't know."

"Is he truly the last?"

"Yes."

She regarded Tal for a few long moments. Her expression revealed nothing, and Tal stilled under her assessing gaze, waiting for her judgment.

"My darling son," she said, voice soft and kind. She brushed a lock of hair from his forehead. "You will ask him to stay. Provide him with what he needs to live in the castle, and if he decides to do so, then we will discuss this issue again after a further courtship. If he cannot stay, then end it. Do you understand?"

"Yes, Mother."

Seeing his troubled expression, she cupped his cheek. "I hope he stays, darling."

Tal's stomach ached. Since that moment in the cave, when his heart thumped, and his middle dropped, and his skin burned with the fiercest desire to be touched by Athlen's fingers, he'd wished for a way for himself, a magic prince, and Athlen, an orphaned merman, to live together in the castle by the sea. Now his mother was providing him with one.

If only Athlen would choose it.

15

When Tal emerged from his meeting with his mother, Garrett was waiting for him, leaning against the castle wall, ankles crossed.

"Are you all right?" he asked, stroking his beard. "You look like you could fall over if I poked you with a feather."

"I'm fine," Tal said. He rubbed a hand over his eyes. "Just tired and hungry again."

Garrett pushed away from the wall. "You don't have to come with me to question the prisoner if you don't want. I can do it on my own."

Tal shook his head. "No. No, I want to come. I want to hear what she has to say."

Garrett nodded. "Let me know if it becomes too much."

"Thank you."

Tal followed Garrett down the winding hallways and staircases into the deepest part of the castle. It was dark and damp and cold below the ground, the carefully carved stone giving way to rough-hewn rock. Guards stood outside the main entrance to the dungeons, sitting in chairs around a fledgling fire in a grate, tossing dice on the floor in a game.

They jumped to their feet at the sight of Garrett.

"Commander," the first one said, breathless.

Garrett ignored the dice rolling across the dips and divots of the floor. He jerked his chin toward the large wooden door. "Open it."

A jangle of keys later, the door swung inward, and Tal followed Garrett inside.

Harth rarely used its dungeons. There was a prison near the outer wall for holding those awaiting trial, but otherwise, justice was swift and there was no need for the dank chambers.

Tal had never been down there before, and he trembled as he crossed the threshold. The ceiling was low, the walls were carved of rock, and a row of iron bars lined a dark walkway on either side. At the end of the corridor was a gentle curve.

Garrett grabbed a torch from the wall and passed it to Tal. "Light it."

Tal tentatively held the shaft of wood and iron. "Really?"

"You're not hiding any longer. That's what you said, right? Light it."

Tal blinked, and the torch roared to life, a burst of flames illuminating the closed-in space. Shadows flickered on the wall, casting eerie shapes that made the atmosphere substantially creepier.

Garrett didn't flinch and grabbed the torch from Tal's hand without pause. "Handy." He turned his back and raised the torch high. "This way."

Acceptance was a strange thing, and Tal's knees went weak with it as he staggered after his brother. Garrett wasn't afraid of him. Even after his display in the throne room on the night of his return, Garrett trusted him.

Tal smiled at the realization he'd be unfettered now, in the castle, in the village. He could be his true self for the first time since he was a boy.

Overjoyed, Tal ducked his head and thought of all the things he could do with his magic, all the people he could help. He could integrate into his family again, not be hidden away when important guests arrived or during council meetings. No longer would he have to disappear to the walled gardens to practice, or study the few remaining texts of magic in secret. Lost in thought, his steps slowing, he drifted too close to the cells.

A hand shot out from between the bars and grabbed his arm in a vise grip. He jerked away, heart in his throat, but another hand reached out, grasping his vest and yanking him close.

His chest slammed into the bars, punching the air from his lungs. He craned his neck, searching for Garrett in the dark, but he'd turned a corner and disappeared, taking the warm, flickering light with him.

"Garrett," Tal said on a breath, the sound no louder than a whisper.

"You," she said. Her voice sounded scraped raw, low and accusatory. "You didn't die. How are you alive? How?"

Tal squinted into the gloom, then his eyebrows shot up. "Poppy? You're alive?"

Her hair fell in a wild tangle across her dirt-smeared face. Her breath blew stale, and her lips cracked when she grimaced. Tal grabbed her wrists and twisted his body until her grip slackened, and he skittered away.

"You're not dead." She pointed a shaking finger. "I didn't murder you."

He'd had the exact same thought about her. "How are you here?"

"Your brother," she spit. "He pulled me from the waves after the ship sank. He saved me. Said I was too young to die. Reminded him of you, I wager."

"You're lucky he spared you."

She scoffed. "I didn't want to be spared. I'm the last of the crew now. The last of the family Zeph made," she snapped. "You saw to that." She spread her arms, gesturing to the empty cell. "I'm just like you now." She walked around the cell, bare feet padding on the stone. She had a mattress in the corner and a thick blanket and a bucket. Far more amenities than he'd had on Zeph's ship, but he still found it cruel. "Let me out. I belong on the sea, not locked in a cage."

"Why should I do that?"

"I was kind to you," she said. "I stitched your wounds. I took care of you."

"You tried to manipulate me for Zeph. You would've allowed them to kill me."

"I helped you as best I could. What could I have done against them all? I told you about the Morreline Sea. I told you about the mermaids. I wished you a quick death. Have mercy."

Tal crossed his arms. "I'll talk with my brother."

She smirked. "You have no power here, either, then."

"I can't just let you out," Tal said on a sigh. "You were an accessory to a kidnapping. But you did show me some small kindness. I will talk to my brother on your behalf. It's the best I can do."

On a yell, she lunged, arm spearing through the space between the bars, fingertips grazing the fabric of Tal's shirt. "You lied to me.

You have magic. I saw you burn the ship. I saw you drown. How did you survive?"

Tal shook his head. "Are you getting enough to eat? To drink? I'll make sure you're comfortable until we can figure something out."

"Was it the mermaids?" she asked, voice small, brow furrowed. "Did they save you? Drag you to the depths, then spit you out on land?"

Tal paused. He didn't know how wise it was to glean information from someone who would obviously say anything to be set free, but if she could provide insight about the merfolk, maybe it would help him figure out what was causing Athlen pain. Maybe he could find a solution that would allow Athlen to stay. "What if I said they did? What could you tell me about them that you haven't already?"

Her gaze went sharp. "Every child born on the islands knows of the merfolk and the witch of the sea. I know all the stories. I could tell you. Let me out and I'll tell you."

"You mentioned the sea witch before. What do you know about her?"

"She was a water mage driven into the waves by fire. Call her name with a desire in your heart. She'll bargain with you."

Tal's heart thumped hard as Poppy confirmed his suspicions. The mage and the witch were the same! And her description of how to bargain matched what Athlen had told him. If bargaining with the witch would allow Athlen to stay, then Tal would gladly do so.

"How do you know that?"

She put her hands on her hips. "That's for me to know. Unless you release me."

"Tally? Where did you go?" Garrett's voice echoed down the

dark corridor.

Tal turned back to Poppy. "Please."

Shaking her head, she smiled and batted her eyelashes. "Come closer. I'll whisper it in your ear."

His hackles rose, but Tal shuffled forward, tilting his head toward her. She leaned in close, her lips a scant inch from her ear.

"Tally!"

Tal jumped backward as Poppy snapped her teeth as if to bite him. She howled with laughter as Tal staggered, surprised.

Garrett appeared from around the corner, torch held high. "What are you doing?" he said as he snagged the back of Tal's shirt and jerked him away. "Never mind. Come along. We're leaving."

"What? I thought we were to question Vanessa's maid."

"We'll get nothing else out of her."

Tal tripped over his feet, Garrett's grip the only thing that kept him from falling. "Are you certain? She said she'd contacted other mercenaries than the ones I saw at the tavern. Who knows how many more are out there with the same purpose?"

Garrett strode back to the main door. "Then we'll prepare."

"Why are you so angry? What did she say to you?"

Garrett's brow furrowed. His mouth pinched. "You didn't tell us she bit you."

Tal absently rubbed his shoulder. "What?"

"You didn't tell us that she dragged you across the beach, that you almost drowned, that you fought them until you bled. What else did you leave out, Tally?"

Tal glanced toward the door and the spill of light from the crack near the lock. He licked his lips, then shrugged. "You don't need to know all the details."

"I do!" Garrett's nostrils flared, his cheeks reddening under the firelight. "What else are you hiding?"

"I'm not hiding. And what does it matter? I'm home now. I'm safe."

"It matters to me!" Garrett's voice bounced off the stone walls, full of anguish and grief. "I was supposed to look after you. Our family entrusted your safety to me, and I . . . I *failed*."

"Garrett . . ." Tal touched his shoulder, and the coiled knot of muscle jumped beneath his palm. "It's okay. I'm okay."

The torch clattered to the ground when Garrett swept Tal into a bone-crushing hug. Tal's ribs creaked as Garrett's large arms yanked him close. Tal sank into it, the warmth and the safety, and grasped Garrett just as hard.

"You are so much stronger than anyone gives you credit for," Garrett said, giving Tal one last hard squeeze. "We were wrong to think your soft heart was a weakness."

"The world isn't kind," Tal said as Garrett held him at arm's length, the flames of the torch flickering from the ground, casting them both in eerie shadows. "But that doesn't mean I can't be."

Garrett shook his head fondly, a small smile tipping up the side of his mouth. "You're a wonder, little brother. And I don't just mean the magic." Picking up the torch, he quickly wiped his eyes. "Come along. It's late. You're tired and hungry, no doubt. And I'm sure there is someone waiting for you."

Tal's cheeks heated, and he was grateful for the low light.

Garrett walked with him the entire way back to his chambers, teasing him gently about the way Athlen had held his hand during the audience with their mother, Tal teasing back about Garrett's potential upcoming marriage.

By the time Tal entered his room, he was exhausted. His upper arm ached from phantom pains, and his knee spasmed in warning of overuse. Tal was disappointed that Athlen was nowhere to be seen, sequestered in his own chambers, most likely. He had hoped Athlen would want to stay the night again, even if not in Tal's bed but in the tub. And Tal desperately wanted to talk with him, tell him what his mother had offered, figure out their future, either together or apart. The fact that Athlen wasn't waiting for him was a reminder of the distance between them, despite the moments they'd had in the council room, holding hands, bolstering each other in the face of Tal's family.

Tal would have looked for him, but as it was, it took everything he had to halfheartedly eat the fruit left behind on his table, then toe off his boots. He didn't have the strength to handle a potential rejection at the moment either, if Athlen chose to return to the sea and his cavern of trinkets.

After shucking off his clothes, Tal crawled into his bed. He fished the shark's tooth out of his pocket and held it up between his fingers—the tip stained with blood—then folded it into his hand. He fell asleep dreaming of the glittering walls of Athlen's cove and the swell and ebb of the tide.

16

"You don't have to marry her, do you?"

Tal blinked sluggishly as he closed his chamber door behind him. He yawned and didn't bother trying to hide his open mouth behind his hand.

"What?"

Athlen twisted his fingers, pacing along the hallway outside Tal's room. "The princess of the other kingdom. Do you have to marry her?" He shook his head. "Maybe it would be better that way. Easier. For you. To marry a princess. But if you don't want to, I'll help you run away. Your family can't make you marry if you're hiding. We'll go by the sea this time, though. I don't think I can handle any more horseback riding."

Fogged with sleep, Tal couldn't comprehend half of what Athlen said as he sputtered and paced. Corrie had come to visit Tal in the very early morning, waking him before the sun rose, to talk non-sense, and he had nodded off midconversation. He supposed it was her way of reconnecting with him, the same way Garrett had done the day before.

When he'd woken for the day, he'd had a mild panic when he couldn't find his shark's tooth in his bed or on the floor nearby. When he did find it, it was on his night table, wrapped in a length of cord and threaded on a long string of leather. The necklace was tangled with another, the gold chain that looped around his signet ring. It hadn't been placed by accident—Corrie's small way of showing her approval and understanding. Tal had clasped the leather necklace around his neck, and now the tooth sat snug against his breastbone. He'd pocketed the other.

"Tal?" Athlen said, poking him in the shoulder. "Did you hear me?"

Tal ran a hand through his hair, pushing wayward strands from his face. Hope swelled in his middle at Athlen's concerns and his offer to run away together. He smiled in spite of himself. "I don't have to marry the princess."

"Oh, good," Athlen said, visibly deflating in relief. "Unless you wanted to marry her?"

"No. I didn't want to marry her." Tal rubbed his knuckles in his eyes and squinted. "You're wearing boots," he said. "And trousers that fit and a waistcoat." Tal furrowed his brow. "I can't believe it."

Athlen smoothed his hands down his front. "Corrie made me. She said it wasn't proper for a royal guest to wear clothes with holes and no shoes."

Tal cleared his throat. "It suits you." Tal couldn't take his eyes off him. Corrie had talked Athlen into wearing a crisp white shirt with a high, stiff collar and brocade down the sleeves. His vest was a deep blue, and his trousers were tan. His ankle-high boots were a soft brown and had three shining buckles. His copper hair had been cut and styled, the wild tresses tamed with wax but still uniquely Athlen.

Athlen tugged on the collar of his shirt. "I can't breathe." He picked up his foot and rubbed his toe along the length of his leg, the leather creaking. "And I can't feel the floor."

"You look like a prince."

"I'm not a prince."

"But you're the favorite of a certain prince," Tal said with a fond smile.

Athlen's expression turned vaguely mortified. He jerked on the hem of the waistcoat. "Is that what this means? Is that what everyone will think?"

"No," Tal said, shaking his head. "That was a joke. But would it be so bad if everyone knew that, well, that you're my—"

"I'm your what?" A blush painted the high line of Athlen's cheeks.

"Maybe we shouldn't talk about this in the hallway." Tal frowned and took Athlen's hand in his. He laced their fingers. "But I'd like for you to be . . . I want you to be . . ."

"Yes?" Athlen stepped closer. He licked his lips. "You want me to be what?"

"Mine."

Athlen smiled, eyes crinkled at the corners. The leather of his boots creaked and Athlen's gaze shot to his feet. His smile slowly faded.

"But I'm not yours," he said. "I have a debt to pay."

"Whatever it is, I'll pay it. Call the sea witch. I'll give her whatever she wants."

"No!" Athlen placed his hand over Tal's mouth. "No. Don't ever say that. Never say that. Do you understand?"

"I don't." Tal's voice was muffled by Athlen's palm. He gently pushed Athlen's arm away. "I don't. I've been trying to understand. I've been patient, Athlen. But you are clandestine when it comes to your bargain."

Athlen sighed. "I want to tell you, Tal, but . . ." He turned away, shoulders hunched. "It'll hurt you."

Throat tight, Tal took Athlen's hand in his own. "Come on. I have something to show you."

The castle by the sea was just that—a large stone fortress built on the rocks overlooking the swirling ocean. Tal's ancestor had leveled the cliffs and built her castle from the stone. And from there, each generation had added.

The west wall was the longest and overlooked a thin stretch of land that disappeared during the high tide. The water was plagued with sharp juts of rock that only small boats could navigate, making it near impossible to mount an assault on that part of the castle. Facing east, the front wall was tall, with turrets and a massive entrance with a steel portcullis, the way that Tal had entered upon his return. The south wall faced the entrance of the Great Bay, while the north butted against a set of hills.

Within the massive structure were built gardens to sustain the residents and the staff, as well as hanging beds of flowers, and spring-fed pools and fountains.

Tal led Athlen to one of the hidden gardens—a small place that wasn't used much other than when Tal had practiced his magic so long ago—away from prying eyes, and with plenty of water in case of mistakes. Hand in hand, they walked down a set of narrow stone steps and through a wooden door into a bastion of peace and quiet interrupted only by the soothing sound of flowing water.

"This is my favorite place," Tal said, stopping in front of a basin of clear, cool water. He dipped his fingers in and created ripples across the surface. "It's a little overgrown. I guess I hadn't come in a while even before my coming-of-age tour. But I love the quiet."

Athlen touched a budding flower. "It's beautiful."

"It's yours, if you want it."

"What?"

"You can use the large pool to swim. This water comes from the sea. And no one will bother you here. It's quiet. I'll have the stewards build shelves for your collection of trinkets, if you want, and if you don't want me here, I won't bother you either. It can be just for you."

Athlen sat down on the ledge of the fountain—a fish with an open mouth spouted water in a high arc until it splashed into the wide pool. He trailed his hand over the surface.

"You'd give this to me?" Athlen asked, gesturing to the garden and the shimmering pools. "All of this? To stay?"

"I know we're young," he blurted. "I know that we met under stressful circumstances. I know that I'm a prince and you're a merman. But I also know that I've never felt this way about anyone else. I know we're both the last, and we've felt alone. But we could be alone together."

Athlen looked out over the walled garden—the blooming flowers and the swirling water and the lush green carpet of grass. "Tal," he said, "I don't want to be on land without you."

"Is that a yes?"

Athlen stood. He cupped Tal's cheeks, his skin cool and smooth on Tal's skin, and gently drew him close. He rubbed his thumb over

Tal's bottom lip, then closed the distance and kissed him, soft and sweet.

Tal sank into it, but Athlen broke away, mouth red and wet, amber eyes reflecting the morning sun.

Without hesitation, Tal reached into his pocket and took out his signet ring. He looped the chain over Athlen's head, and the ring dropped to the center of Athlen's chest.

"This is also for you."

Athlen cradled it in his palm. He sucked in a breath, staring at the round piece of gold and the dark jewel in the center.

"Your ring. I don't have anything for you," he whispered.

"You already gave me a present. Remember?" Tal lifted the tooth from beneath his shirt.

Athlen's smile trembled, and his eyes filled. "I want to be alone together with you."

Tal drew Athlen close, and their mouths met again in an inelegant and enthusiastic kiss. Tal's heart hammered beneath his ribs. His lips tingled where Athlen pressed a little deeper, a little harder. Tilting his head, Tal opened to the soft pressure, wanting everything that Athlen could give him, wanting it so badly his body shook. He clutched Athlen's thin hips, and Athlen responded, wrapping his arms around Tal's shoulders and pressing their bodies together until only the layer of their clothes was between them.

"You promised once"—Athlen's lips grazed Tal's cheek—"that you'd show me what the bed of a prince was like."

"I didn't mean it like that."

Athlen smiled, coy yet fond, while he played with strands of Tal's hair. "I did."

"Oh." Tal's blood thudded hot in his veins.

Athlen kissed him again, backing Tal against a stone pillar and giving no quarter, each pass of his lips heavy with intent. Tal's passion surged, every inch of skin begging to be touched, every breath a gasp, even the smallest gap between their bodies a canyon.

"Do I need to ask again?" Athlen said, the words a playful murmur on Tal's lips, the vibrations a sting.

Tal smiled, tucking his red face against Athlen's neck. "Come on." He laced their fingers, and loath as he was to slide out from the crush of Athlen's body on the pillar, he did. He tugged Athlen back into the castle, flushed and aching, and the seconds they were not kissing were agony. Once at his chamber, Tal guided Athlen inside and then locked the door behind them.

Tal stretched in the warm sheets. He was on the edge of sleep, in the heavy intermediate space where he could drop back into the comforting depths of slumber or allow his eyes to flutter open and wake. It was a blissful place, a moment to laze in the coziness of the bed and the warmth of another's body next to him, with the ability to acknowledge and appreciate the sensations.

He didn't know the time, only that it was early in the morning. He could faintly hear the roar of the sea below his windows and the sound of the birds combing the beaches. With the shades and curtains drawn, the sun couldn't pierce the inner room of his chambers, but Tal was rested well enough to know they'd spent the entire day together, then slept through the night. Soon servants would knock on his door and summon them to start the tasks of the day.

Athlen shifted next to him, his preternatural body cool against Tal's skin, in contrast to the fire that thrummed through Tal's veins, a pulse of magic as innate as the rhythm of blood.

He grumbled something under his breath, and Tal huffed a laugh, draping his arm around Athlen's ribs and pulling him close.

Tal buried his face between Athlen's shoulder blades, palm flat over Athlen's heart, fingers splayed along the gentle curve of his collarbone.

"Quit moving," he said, voice muffled in the pillow and Athlen's skin, words slurred with sleep. This—this was perfect, and Tal wanted to give in to the tug of dreams and rest, pressed along the length of Athlen's body.

Athlen threaded his fingers though Tal's. "Are you awake?"

"No."

Athlen's body shook. "Are you dreaming, then?"

Tal sighed. "It's a good dream."

"I'm sorry to ruin it." Athlen's voice was strained. His body shuddered again. "Go back to sleep, my prince."

Tal cracked an eye open. "Ruin it?" He propped up on an elbow, all vestiges of sleep slipping away. "Athlen?"

Athlen shifted again, expression pinched with pain, teeth digging into the red flesh of his bottom lip. He gasped when Tal shot to sitting, jostling the mattress.

"What's wrong?"

"Nothing," Athlen breathed. "Go back to sleep."

Tal furrowed his brow. "You're in pain."

Squirming, Athlen rolled over to face Tal, his face half hidden by the pillow. "I didn't know it would happen so quickly."

"What would happen? Athlen? What's going on?"

He gasped again, eyebrows drawing together. "She's calling in my debt." Scales rippled over his body, and he curled into a ball, one arm around his middle, fingers spread over the shifting and fluttering of his gills, and the other hand clasping his shin. "I have to go to the sea. I have to face her."

"No," Tal said on a breath. "No. Not without me."

Athlen shook his head vehemently, mouth curled down into a frown. He lurched to sitting and fumbled in the blankets until he extricated himself and stood. He held up a webbed finger. "You cannot. Tal, please."

"What was the bargain?"

Athlen shook his head as he pulled on a pair of trousers. He walked as if on needles, hand over his mouth, breathing heavily. Scales glittered along his skin, then disappeared in waves. Drops of blood were smeared on his ribs as his gills opened uselessly, then fused.

Tal knelt, watching helplessly as Athlen fought his own body. All the happiness from before was sucked out of the room, and Tal's heart broke seeing Athlen in pain and not knowing how to help. "Please. Athlen. What was your bargain? Just tell me! I'll pay it. Whatever it is!"

"Don't say that!" he snapped. "Don't."

"Why not? I'll do whatever I can to help you."

He grimaced. "Tal," he said in warning.

"I don't understand. I'll do anything. You know that. Anything to keep you from pain. Anything to keep . . . *you*."

"I can't."

"What's so terrible you can't tell—"

"It's you!" Athlen blurted.

Tal stopped short. "What?"

Athlen hobbled away, tear tracks on his cheeks. He whimpered in pain with every step, and he tugged on the strands of his hair in frustration. "It's you." His voice cracked.

"Me?" Tal swallowed around the sudden lump in his throat. "I don't understand."

"I promised her the blood of my beloved." He bowed his head, face scrunched in agony and misery, cheeks red. "I gave it away freely because I never thought I'd find someone to love, someone who loved me. My family and my people were gone, and I was alone." His voice broke. "I was so alone."

Tal reached out, but Athlen flinched away.

"I thought . . . I thought if I kept away from you, she wouldn't know. But then you were kind and then you needed me. And then I thought if we were inland, she wouldn't be able to feel how I'd started to love you. But my legs hurt the more my affection grew, and I knew. I knew I couldn't keep it from her. And last night"—he gestured to the bed—"I wanted one night with you, to be loved, to not be alone anymore. And it was selfish, because it would be the end."

Tal's heart stuttered, then shattered. "The end?"

Athlen nodded. He rubbed his eyes, expression twisting into grief.

Jumping from the bed, Tal shook his head, refusing to accept Athlen's truth. "It's only blood."

Athlen snapped his head up, his face paling in an instant. "No! Stop what you're thinking. She doesn't make fair bargains. It's not a drop of blood. It's the blood of my *beloved*. It could be your heart, Tal. It could be all the blood in your body. It could be the blood of your family. It could be your magic."

"I'd gladly give my magic up for you." Tal opened his palm and a flame danced along his skin. He closed his fist and snuffed it out. "That's an easy decision to make."

"No! Don't you understand the consequences of blood magic? Blood is a powerful substance. She could use it against you. Against your family. Against your kingdom. And she would. She would."

"Because my great-grandfather drove her into the sea?"

Athlen stilled, gaze on the floor, legs trembling. He gave a sharp nod.

"She's the mage he didn't kill. The one who fled."

"Yes," Athlen whispered. He wobbled and grabbed Tal's sleeve. "I didn't know. I promise you, I didn't realize. Not until after I already loved you."

Tal slipped his hand over Athlen's. "There's nothing I wouldn't do for you. I'd face her a hundred times over. I'd give her all the blood she wants."

"Don't say that." Athlen let out a high noise of frustration and tugged on his hair again. "She's dangerous. It . . . it was forbidden to seek her out. But I . . . I had no other way to—"

A sharp rap at the door interrupted Athlen. He skittered away to the alcove by the windows, stifling grunts of pain.

"What?" Tal barked.

The door opened and a steward appeared. "Your presence is requested in the courtyard, Prince Taliesin."

"Not now. Tell them I can't."

The steward cleared his throat. "The response from King Rodrick has arrived. Princess Vanessa is to leave the castle at once and face justice in Ossetia."

"Now?" Tal asked. "Can't they wait?"

The steward shrugged. "I'm only the messenger, Your Highness."

"Right. Fine. I'll be there shortly." Tal dismissed him, focus already back on Athlen, who hid from the steward's sight behind the long curtains.

"Go," Athlen said after the door closed. "I'll be fine."

"You're coming with me."

"No. I can't. Not like this." Athlen lifted his hand and spread his fingers, highlighting the webbing between and the scales trailing up his arm. "Be with your family, Tal. Being with them as your true self has been your goal since the beginning. You can do that now."

Tears pricked behind Tal's eyes. "I won't leave until you promise you won't do anything until we talk again."

Athlen looked away. His body shook. He squeezed his eyes shut. "Don't be too long."

"That's not a promise."

He bit his lip. "I promise."

Tal relaxed his shoulders, then ran around the room throwing on clothes. He kept his eyes on Athlen, and the lines of pain around his mouth, and the way he moved gingerly, clutching the wall as he limped back to the bed.

Tal shoved his feet into his boots. "I won't be long."

Athlen bowed forward, the line of his back an impossible curve, his hands white-knuckled on his knees. "I'll be here."

That was the only confirmation Tal needed. He opened the door and left.

When Tal emerged from the castle, his brothers and sisters at his side, the crowd that greeted them was far larger than what he had expected for the short notice. Rumor had spread quickly. The courtyard was packed to the brim; the only clear space was the path for the carriage to take Vanessa from their home back to her own kingdom and to her brother, who was, in Emerick's words, quite angry. Knights and soldiers ringed the perimeter, guarding the royal family, and courtiers and nobles filled the empty spaces behind Tal's family, milling about to watch the spectacle. With the keep's doors flung wide, people from the village flocked in, and they whispered behind their hands as they saw Tal in the line of his siblings, very much alive, if not worse for the wear.

Standing at the top of the stone steps, surveying the courtyard packed with hundreds of onlookers, Tal was filled with a kind of dread he hadn't experienced before, the kind that he'd been fortunate to avoid, sequestered away all the years prior.

"You look like you're going to faint," Kest said from Tal's right, voice dipped low.

Tal glanced at him. "So do you."

"Well, I *was* shot with an arrow a few days ago."

"Good point."

Kest huffed a laugh at the unintentional pun. "Is everything all right?"

No. It wasn't. Athlen was hurting. The sea witch's magic was failing. His debt was due. And he wouldn't allow Tal to pay it, even if he could.

"Nervous," Tal said in reply.

Kest nudged him. "I'm right here. As are Isa and Garrett and Corrie. You're not alone."

"I know."

Corrie elbowed him, and he shot her a glare. She jerked her chin, and Tal spotted Athlen slipping from the doors behind them, joining the gathering of castle residents at their backs. He looked awful, his skin translucent save for the feverish bright spots on his cheeks. His hair was wild and untamed from Tal running his fingers through it, and he hobbled and grimaced with each movement.

"What did you do?" Corrie whispered with the bite of accusation.

Tal frowned. "It's none of your business. Pay attention to what's happening in front of you."

A murmur ran through the crowd as Queen Carys stepped through the castle arches. Her crown sparkled in the sunlight, as did the swords of the knights on either side of her. Chin lifted, shoulders back, her dress flowing behind her as she walked, she was the picture of royalty—steel and grace personified.

Tal straightened his own posture as she took her place over the proceedings.

A hush fell over the crowd as his mother spoke. She talked of the treason, of Tal's kidnapping and presumed death, of Kest's injury by a failed assassin. She spoke of the evidence against Princess Vanessa of Ossetia and her handmaiden.

She didn't speak of magic or mermen.

After the queen finished, guards brought Vanessa from the castle, her wrists clapped in iron chains, her hair unkempt, her dress tattered and dirty. The crowd greeted her with jeers and rotten fruit.

Corrie laughed when a tomato hit Vanessa in the cheek.

Tal's stomach churned at the parade as she was trotted out and humiliated. His skin crawled with every taunt, the memories of his time on Zeph's ship still fresh.

The guards paused at the doorway to the carriage and waited for the queen to grant permission for the prisoner to board.

"Any words before you depart?" she asked, a courtesy, a chance for Vanessa to begin healing the rift between their kingdoms.

"Yes, Your Grace. I would like to express my apologies to the prince," Vanessa said thinly, the words ground out. Her smile was more a grimace, but she inclined her head in Tal's direction primly, deliberately.

The queen narrowed her eyes. "Very well."

Tal descended, leaving his family at the top of the stone stairs, and the small crowd dispersed around him, the way a school of fish react to a shark. He stopped at the bottom.

"I am sorry," she said, eyes glittering, "that I didn't kill you myself."

Tal was not surprised. "You've lost," he said evenly. "I survived. My family survived. And we're stronger for it."

"Yes, you did, unfortunately," Vanessa breathed, features twisted in a snarl reminiscent of that of her maid. Her voice dropped to the sound of a breath. "What will all these people do when they find out what you are? Do you think your mother can stop the other kingdoms when they storm in to kill you? To take you away? No. She cannot, and your magic will be your family's downfall."

"I'm not hiding anymore. I'm not afraid."

"You should be. People fear what they don't understand. Fear becomes hatred so easily."

Vanessa wasn't wrong. He and his family were at the beginning of a hard few months as the political landscape changed and Tal's magic became known, but they had one another. "I have my family."

Vanessa's expression hardened, and her sharp gaze cut to the carriage that awaited her. "Yes, they've already killed for you once." She clenched her jaw. "I'm certain they will again."

Tal stiffened.

"I'm not usually so petty," she said, lifting her chin. "But you took someone from me. It's only fair I return the favor. A sister should do."

Tal's blood ran cold. He followed her line of sight to a turret and caught the glint of the sun on an arrow tip.

"Isa! Corrie! Get down!"

He couldn't move fast enough. He thrust his hand out and released a blaze of fire, but he merely singed the arrow as it thrummed through the air.

Chaos erupted. Women screamed. Guards swarmed. The knights

swept the queen away into the castle and tried to corral Tal, blocking his view of the stairs, where the rest of his family stood. He fought through them, pushing people aside, shouting orders until they parted, and Tal ran to the steps.

He skidded to a halt, heart seizing. Blood spattered the stone. Corrie screamed, hysterical, blood spray across her face, pinned to the ground, Athlen sprawled across her.

"He pushed me," she sobbed. "He pushed me."

Athlen.

Tal gained his senses and vaulted up the steps, meeting Garrett at the top. Garrett slid Corrie from beneath the limp weight of Athlen, then passed her off to a guard standing by, and they both dropped to Athlen's side.

Tal's world narrowed, his senses fuzzing out save for those focused on Athlen, the absolute chaos around him mere background noise. The bolt was as brittle as ash from traveling through Tal's magic fire, smoke curling around the wooden shaft. But the head of the arrow had struck true and lodged deeply in Athlen's chest. Blood bubbled around the wound, slowly spreading across the fabric of Athlen's shirt. Tal's signet ring lay in the hollow of Athlen's throat, the gold chain coiled around his pale neck, a rivulet of blood pooled in the dip of his collarbones, staining the emerald crimson.

"No," Tal breathed, hands fluttering over Athlen's body splayed across the stone, limp as a doll. "No. No. No. Athlen?"

His eyes were half open but staring at nothing. Tal gripped Athlen's hand in both of his own, pulling it to his chest.

"Athlen, please. Garrett? Do something. Can you do something?"

Garrett's expression was grim as he tapped Athlen's cheek with his thick, calloused fingers. "Come on," he said. "Come back for a moment before you go to your rest."

His words shivered down Tal's body. *Come back to say good-bye.* Garrett's words confirmed what Tal feared—it was a mortal wound. For all the magic that lived under his skin, for all the power that inhabited his body, he couldn't defend against a single arrow, he couldn't rewind time, he couldn't save Athlen from bleeding out from a sharp point of metal.

Athlen blinked sluggishly, eyes roving until they settled on Tal, gaze slowly focusing.

"Tal?"

Tal squeezed Athlen's hand. "Yes. I'm here. I'm here. Why did you do that? Why would you do that?" He brought Athlen's knuckles to his lips, tears slipping from his eyes and cutting tracks through the blood staining Athlen's fingers.

"For you. Your family." He grimaced. "Had to leave anyway." Each word was a labor, stuttering out of him in tortured gasps. "Bargain . . ." He trailed off, coughing, red bubbling in the crease of his lips.

These were the last moments between them, and Tal wouldn't be plagued by their argument from that morning. He shook his head. "No. Please. Athlen. I love you. I love you. I love you."

Athlen's fingers spasmed in Tal's hand. "Beloved," he murmured. His expression twisted in pain, and his body jerked.

"Can the sea witch save you? Athlen? What should I do?"

Athlen's eyes rolled in his head and his body went limp.

"Athlen?" Tal gasped. He shook Athlen's shoulders. "Athlen?" Tal held his hand above Athlen's parted lips and cried at the soft, slow puffs against his skin. "He's breathing."

She'll bargain with anyone who calls her name with a desire in their heart.

"Take him to the beach."

"Tally," Garrett said, voice sad and full of resignation.

"No!" Tal lurched across Athlen's body and grabbed the lapel of Garrett's shirt in his bloodied hand. "Take him. He's a merman, which means he is hardier and heals faster. He will survive a little longer. Take him to the closest beach, the one by the castle wall. You must! Promise me."

Garrett's mouth was a grim line. "I promise."

Tal shot to standing, tense as a bowstring, desperation and grief compelling him forward. He stumbled on the stone stairs, trusting Garrett to complete his task.

Her name.

He needed her name.

"Whoa, Tally." Kest caught him as Tal ran through the arches. "What's happening? Are you injured? Why are you covered in blood?"

"Let go. I need to know her name. I need her name."

"Whose name?"

"The sea witch!" Tal twisted out of Kest's grip and ran. Athlen's blood grew tacky on his hands, and it smeared along the stone as Tal stumbled toward the dungeons. His heart raced and his legs were weak, but his resolve only grew as he ran down the twisting steps and burst into the dungeons. He ignored the guards, called fire to his hand, and concentrated on the lock. It shattered under the force of his panic and despair.

"Poppy!" he yelled as he shouldered through the door, the guards yelling at him. "Poppy!"

He skidded to a halt in front of her cell.

She stared at him through the tangled strands of her hair. "What do you want?"

"Tell me the name of the sea witch."

She narrowed her eyes into slits. "Why?"

"I don't have time, Poppy. Do you know how to call her?"

Shrugging, she stood from her mattress and walked to the bars. "You're covered in blood, but you're still not dead."

"Poppy, *please*." Anguish welled in him. She didn't know. Or she wouldn't tell him. He'd wasted precious time. He'd run away on a fool's quest, and Athlen was going to die without him.

"Let me out and I'll tell you."

Tal didn't hesitate. As he had with Athlen's fetter, as he had done with the door, he concentrated fire on the metal lock until it heated to a cherry red, and it melted from the iron bars. He wrenched the door open, the fire licking across his skin.

"Tell me, *please*."

"Morwen. Most call her Morwen."

Tal turned and ran.

18

B lood soaked the sand.
  Tal skidded to a stop, chest heaving, heart racing so hard he was light-headed. But it didn't matter, he had her name.

Garrett had placed Athlen at the edge of the surf, the incoming tide wetting the hem of Athlen's trousers. His face was gray. His chest didn't move.

Tal clutched the shark's tooth on the cord around his neck, the serrated edge biting into his palm.

"Tally," Garrett said, voice soft and solemn.

"Lift him."

"What?"

"I said lift him. We have to get him back to the sea. We don't have much time."

There were others crowded on the beach, murmuring, crying, no doubt watching for their prince of fire to shatter in the waves. But he wouldn't.

Not here.

Garrett lifted Athlen into his arms, and the way his legs hung over Garrett's elbow and the angle his neck rolled and the complete lack of tension in his body made Tal grip the tooth harder. Athlen's vivid copper hair stuck to his cheek and forehead, and blood was smeared along the gray-tinged skin of his neck, into his ear. Hints of his gold-red scales glinted in the bright sun, a reminder of the sunset, and of the preciousness of Athlen himself.

Tal wasn't strong, especially after what he'd endured these past weeks, but he gathered Athlen in his arms and held him close. He didn't dare listen for breath or a heartbeat. He didn't need to. His resolve was strong even if his body wasn't. He avoided Garrett's gaze, knowing he would cry if he saw the sorrow and pity in them, and instead turned away and made for the surf.

The first wave knocked him to his knees, and he almost lost his grip on Athlen's body, but suddenly there were strong arms behind him, lifting him as the next break rolled in.

"I've got you," Garrett said. "Keep going."

They waded out farther, past the rolling foam and froth. Tal's boots filled with water, his clothes soaked through, weighing him down. But he kept going until his toes lost touch with the sand at each ripple of the waves.

Crimson bloomed around them like petals of a flower. Athlen's hair fanned out like a halo. His soaked shirt clung to the hard lines of his torso. He was beautiful and macabre, death and magic merged in one being, in one moment.

Tal cleared his throat. "Morwen," he whispered. He squinted his eyes shut, trusting in Garrett to keep hold of his shirt so he wouldn't float away on the current or drown in his anguish. He clenched his teeth. "Morwen. Please. Please. Please."

He poured his heart's desires toward the sea—the life he'd envisioned with Athlen in the castle, the happiness they'd share, the family they would have together, joining as the last two of their kinds, alone together. He let the grief wash over him like the ocean and allowed his salty tears to stream down his face, adding his own small drops to the deep vastness of the sea.

Bowing his head, Tal grasped Athlen close, buried his face in the bloodied, ruined chest of his beloved.

"Morwen. Hear me. *Please.*"

Nothing.

Only the cries of the gulls above them and the crash of the waves on the beach behind them filled the thick air.

"Tally," Garrett said. "I'm so sorry."

Tal sobbed, great heartrending sobs that wracked his body and tore from his throat on punches of air. He felt cracked in half, broken open so his insides were raw to the sun and the salt. Everything *hurt*, from the stinging of his eyes to the throb of his heart to the white-knuckled grip he kept on the body floating in front of him.

As his last hope sank, a pulse of magic rent through the water, slammed into Tal's chest, and suddenly the familiar push-pull of the sea stilled.

Tal lifted his head.

"Did you feel that?"

Garrett nodded. "I think we should swim to shore."

Another shock of magic rippled toward them, and suddenly the water receded as fast as a blink, sucking everything out to sea violently. Tal lost his footing, yelling as a wave crashed over his head from the wrong direction, water funneling into his mouth and nose.

Garrett grabbed him, wrapped his arms around Tal's waist, and yanked him above the waterline.

"Hold on!" Garrett yelled, clutching Tal to him as the water rushed away from the shore, sand and shells and fish pummeling around them. Only Garrett's strength kept them both standing.

As it was, Tal scrabbled to keep hold of Athlen's limp body, but he was ripped from Tal's sore fingers, swept away in the tumult.

"No! No! No!"

Tal wrestled out of Garrett's arms to follow, but Garrett reeled him back.

"No. I'll not let you drown for a dead man."

"Let me go. Let me go. Let me—"

Tal gasped when both he and Garrett fell to ocean floor as a great pillar of surf and foam and water rose from the sea. The chaos coalesced into a figure before their eyes, and the ocean itself formed into a body. Fish swam through her torso, seaweed tumbled from her head and over her shoulders. Her eyes glittered as scales, and her mouth was red coral. Her arms were as strong as the tides. She wore driftwood around her neck and a string of shells around her waist. Pearls adorned her fingertips. She was magic incarnate, terrifying and beautiful.

Towering over them, she bent forward, examining Tal and Garrett as if they were insects.

Tal stood slowly and brushed the clinging wet sand from his hands.

"Which of you called my name?" Her voice was the song of the sea, the gentle lapping of water against the hull of a ship, the scream of a waterspout, and the crash of the waves all in one.

Tal's hair stood on end, and he curled his toes in his soggy boots. "I did."

"You are made of fire. Have you called to fight me? Finish what your grandsire began?"

"No!" Tal held out his hands. "No. I'm not him. I didn't call you to fight. I came to bargain."

She pursed the coral of her lips. "And you are?"

"I'm called Tal."

"That's not your true name. You are wise not to share it. What do you desire?"

"Athlen."

She smiled, but it wasn't kind. It was shrewd and full of shark's teeth. She scooped a handful of water from beside her and held it close to her mouth, Athlen's body floating in her palm. She blew a breeze, and the water glowed as if the sun had dipped below the surface and lit the blue from within.

Athlen's body shuddered and his clothes shredded as his legs fused into his long red-and-gold tail.

"He owes me a debt, beloved. Are you here to pay it?"

Garrett wrapped his hand around Tal's forearm in a vise grip. Tal ignored him, dared not take his eyes from Athlen, buoyed in the pool of light and magic.

"Only if you can save him."

She tilted her head and regarded Athlen. "You wish to renegotiate the terms of his bargain?"

"Yes."

She tapped her lips. "And what are you willing to give?"

"I . . . I'd give anything I could. But he . . . he doesn't want that."

Her lip curled. "You are magic, like me." She set Athlen onto a plateau of surf and spread her fingers. "But I gave up my mortal self to hide in the sea, to hide from the fire that awaited me on land. I've lived as magic for longer than you have been alive. It is a piece of me, and I will not give it away freely."

"I understand," Tal said. "What are the terms of the bargain?"

"A life for a life, beloved. Your blood for his legs."

Tal swallowed. "I don't—"

"Hurry. I can save someone who still lives. I cannot resurrect the dead."

Squeezing his eyes shut, tears leaking from the corners, Tal took a shuddering breath. "No. He . . . he wouldn't want to be without me on land. He told me. He doesn't want to be alone, and I won't doom him to that."

"Oh, beloved," she said, tone sad and kind.

Tal felt the sweep of cool water over his cheeks, wiping his tears away. Tentatively he opened his eyes, then flinched back when he found she'd moved closer. Her face was inches from his, small fish swimming behind her eyes, then down the tunnel of her neck, her expression sorrowful.

"You love him."

"I do."

"Enough to let him go?"

Tal wiped his sleeve over his cheeks. "If I must. Yes."

"I am sorry, beloved. A life for a life. Blood for blood. That is the cost of my magic."

Tal fell to his knees and covered his face with his hands. His heart broke anew. A fresh wave of tears streamed down his cheeks. Garrett wrapped his arms around Tal and held him close as he cried.

"Good-bye, little fire. You are a better human than most." She caressed his hair, then turned away.

"Wait! Morwen! Wait!"

A yell from the beach, followed by the rapid squelch of someone running toward them, pierced through the sounds of Tal's grief.

He twisted around. Poppy broke through the substantial crowd that had gathered and ran toward them, full tilt, her curly hair blowing behind her. Shouts from guards followed her, demanded she stop, but the guards didn't dare broach the shoreline. Poppy had no such fear, and upon reaching them, she fell to her knees and clasped her hands in front of her.

"Morwen! Queen of the sea! I wish to bargain."

"Poppy—"

"And what do you want, child?"

"Take me with you."

Morwen's mouth ticked up and her eyes widened. "What?"

"I pledge my life in servitude to you. I always believed in the merfolk and in you. I am the last of my crew. There is nothing left for me on land. I want to live with you in the sea."

Tal whipped his head around to stare at her. He broke from Garrett's grip. "Poppy, you'd really pledge your life?"

"Yes. My life is the sea."

"A life for a life!" Tal pointed at Morwen. "You said a life for a life. *A* life. And I'll give you my blood." Tal grabbed the shark's tooth and snapped the cord from around his neck. He plunged the tip into the crook of his arm.

"Tally! What are you doing?" Garrett yelled.

Tal grunted with pain, wrenching the tooth free. Blood ran freely down his arm. "Take it! Save him!"

Morwen scowled. "Your life for the merman's life?" she asked Poppy.

"Yes! Just take me with you!"

"The bargain is struck," she said in a biting, begrudging voice.

A tendril of water grabbed Tal's wrist, while another held half of an oyster shell beneath his elbow. She twisted his arm, and blood ran into the cup of the shell, staining the sheen crimson. Morwen peered at it.

"More."

The tendril squeezed right above the wound, and more blood welled to the surface. Tal went dizzy and swayed on his knees.

"Enough," she said when the shell was nearly full, and the tendrils released him.

Tal fell against Garrett.

"Tally?"

"I'm fine." He blinked away the dark spots in his vision. "Where's Athlen?"

Morwen turned away from them and grabbed Athlen from where he lay on the surf. He flopped like a rag doll in her grip, and Tal's belly flipped and his throat tightened. She passed her hand over Athlen, said words in a language Tal would never know.

Athlen's tail twitched.

His back arched as a tendril of water probed the wound and yanked out the arrowhead. The water glowed and shifted. Tal squinted, unable to make out what was happening, but after a minute she dropped Athlen into the water with a plop.

"He is yours," she said. She leveled her gaze at Poppy. "And you are mine."

"Yes. Yes. I am yours." Poppy stood and walked into the wall of water in front of them. It opened for her, then wrapped around her body, encasing her entirely in a blue glowing cocoon of Morwen's magic. After a moment the water released her, and Poppy emerged, a spirit of the sea, composed of salt, surf, and foam. She held up her hand and flexed her fingers, giggling at her new form. "I'm of the sea," she said, her voice the sound of a splash. She smiled wide, then turned, dove into the water, and disappeared.

Morwen stared at the pair of them left on their knees in the sand, Tal's arm covered in blood, Garrett clinging on to him.

"If you call again, I will not come."

"I understand."

"Good-bye, Tal, beloved of water and fire."

Tal bowed. "Good-bye, Morwen, queen of the sea."

She smirked and sank into the waves.

The wall of water that she held at bay broke at once, and the sea that had receded rushed back in.

Tal sucked in a large breath and allowed it to wash over him.

19

Tal woke on the beach.

He coughed, turned on his side, and vomited seawater onto the sand.

Someone pounded on his back, encouraging him to cough as his lungs squeezed and his chest heaved. He clenched his hands in the sand. His back arched, and he threw up again, before collapsing onto the wet earth.

"That's it, Tally. Cough it out."

"There he is. He's coming around."

"Tally?"

"Isa?" Tal blinked the salt and foam from his eyes and craned his neck to find his sister kneeling in the sand next to his head, and his brothers on either side of him. Isa ran her fingers through his hair and brushed the limp strands off his forehead.

"Yes," she said, voice tender.

"You'll ruin your dress."

She smiled, soft and sweet. "There are worse things."

Tal rolled to his stomach and pushed up to his knees. His clothes were sodden and his feet swam in his boots and his head ached from crying.

"Whoa." Kest grabbed Tal to keep him from toppling. "Give yourself a moment. You're bound to be light-headed."

Kest was not wrong. The corners of Tal's vision blackened, and his arm hurt.

"What happened?"

"You made a deal with a sea witch, then nearly drowned," Garrett said, his voice holding a tinge of awe.

Tal's world snapped back into focus, and he lifted his head to scan the beach. "Athlen?"

"Right over there."

Tal pushed all the way to sitting. His head spun, and Isa steadied him. "He's fine. Look there."

Down the beach a few feet, Athlen lay in the sand, Corrie next to him. He was on his stomach, propped up on his elbows as his tail splashed in the surf and his scales sparkled. A crowd of onlookers stood nearby, and Corrie glared at them when they ventured too close.

"He's handsome," Isa teased. "I see why you almost died for him."

"Are you going to swoon into his arms?" Garrett asked, nudging Tal's shoulder, grinning madly. "As soon as you can stand and run to him."

Kest snorted behind his hand. "You will run, right? It will be an epic ending to your love story."

Isa threw her hand over her eyes and collapsed into Garrett's arms. "It'll be like a scene from my favorite novel. Except you're both soaking wet and covered in blood."

Tal covered his face with both hands. "Oh no. You're going to tease me forever, aren't you?"

"Oh yes, Tally," Garrett said playfully. "Or should I call you beloved?"

Tal pinched Garrett hard in the side, and he let out an exaggerated "Ow!" as he squirmed away. The noise had Athlen turning his head. He spotted Tal and smiled, wide and bright, as beautiful as the sunset on the water.

"Are you going to kiss him?" Isa asked.

"I just puked seawater."

"I don't think he'll mind."

Tal stood with their help. He took a few wobbling steps, but they became more balanced as he went, and his siblings stepped away, calling Corrie to them. She stood, her dress soaked, water wicking up the hem to her hips. She gave Tal a smirk as she passed him.

"Athlen?" Tal asked, falling to his knees next to Athlen's hips. "Are you . . . can you . . . do you have legs?"

Athlen's smile turned fond. "Yes. When I woke, I was in the ocean with legs, but I turned to this form," he said, sweeping his hand down his body, "to swim to shore. Are you all right? Your brothers and sister pulled you from the waves, and I didn't want to intrude." He twisted his fingers together. Tal rested his hand over Athlen's.

He was alive. Athlen was alive. He was perfect. "Yes. I ache all over. And I drank too much seawater. And I'd like a nap. But otherwise I'm fine."

"Good. I was worried. I don't know what she asked of you. What you had to do."

Tal bit his lip. "I may have doomed my descendants. I gave her my blood."

"Tal—"

"I'm sorry. I . . . I couldn't let you go. Not when there was a chance. I know you didn't want me to interfere. I know giving her my blood was reckless. But, Athlen, I—"

Athlen grabbed the front of Tal's shirt with his hand and tugged him down into the surf. Tal toppled easily, falling to his back as the waves rolled over his feet and legs. Athlen hovered over him, his tail a gold-and-red arch. He cupped Tal's cheek in his webbed hand, then pressed his mouth to Tal's in a tender kiss.

"You're my beloved," Athlen said, his voice a vibration against Tal's lips.

"And you're mine."

They kissed, and kissed, and Tal would've thought it a fairy tale if not for the sand in his collar, and the water in his boots, and the ache of his body. But he wouldn't trade it for anything else.

"I think I lost the shark's tooth," Tal said when they broke for breath.

"I'll find you another." Athlen bumped his nose to Tal's. "I'll find you a thousand if that's what you want."

"One will do."

Athlen laughed and kissed him again.

Tal sank into it—happy, loved, and unafraid.

20

"Are you nervous, Tally?"

Tal stiffened. He ran a hand through his hair. Athlen tsked and smoothed it down with his hand. "No. Should I be nervous? Are you nervous?"

"I'm not nervous," Kest said, though his constant straightening of his waistcoat and the fiddling with his buttons belied his statement. He blew out a breath. "I'm not nervous."

Athlen peeked around the curtain that separated them from the crowd. "Oh! There's Dara!" he said with a smile. "And a lot of other people wearing so many different colors."

"The colors of their kingdoms," Tal said. His hands shook. Despite being integral to the planning of the whole event, and asserting when and how he wanted to make his speech, he was still nervous. He'd not had the experiences his siblings had, and this was his first foray into public politics. But he was certain that announcing himself and revealing his magic was the right thing, and he'd been adamant that he'd speak for himself and not hide behind his mother or sister. However, all the planning and the assertions didn't mean he wasn't anxious. "Ambassadors from the entire continent are out there, and a few of the islands sent representatives as well."

"Well, you invited them all," Kest said with a smirk. "I would've been fine with a small wedding."

Athlen took Tal's hand and squeezed. "They're here to meet you."

"To test me," Tal sighed. He rolled his tense shoulders. "To speak with me," he amended. "I'm sure they'll have questions, and they'll want assurances. Maybe even demonstrations."

Kest gripped Tal's shoulder. "We'll all be with you. It's a good thing, Tally. You'll be fine. And there are guards everywhere. Also, you're made of fire. No one will try anything in the home of the last great mage."

"Not great," Tal said under his breath. "Not yet. Still learning."

Kest poked his finger into Tal's chest. "The mage who bargained with the sea witch and lived and is betrothed to the last merman. They're intrigued more than frightened. Trust me."

"I do trust you. I'm just—"

"Nervous?" Athlen smiled. "You'll be wonderful, Tal," he said, allowing the curtain to fall back into place. He kissed Tal's cheek. Tal's signet ring glinted in the light, nestled against the fine cloth of Athlen's shirt. Athlen wiggled his toes against the stone. "Do you want to practice again?"

"Maybe the ending?"

"Go on."

Tal pressed his fingertips to the new shark's tooth hanging from a cord below his collarbones, then cleared his throat. "I was naïve when I left on my coming-of-age tour of my kingdom, scared to be myself, afraid that my family and the people of our kingdom couldn't accept the dichotomy of me, but I'm not afraid anymore. My character is strong. My family is with me. My magic is powerful. I've found someone who loves me for all my parts, not despite them. And I am ready to be a part of the world." Tal rolled his shoulders. "And then I'll light all the torches and candles."

"Don't light anything on fire, if you please," Kest said. "Not on my wedding day, thank you."

"I'll do my best."

"Hey!" Garrett whispered, sneaking in the back door of the waiting area. "I tried to keep her out, but she wouldn't listen to me."

"Move out of the way, Commander." Shay shouldered her way through the door, her dress trailing behind her, getting caught in the hinge.

"Shay!" Isa hissed. "Will you stop? You're ruining your train."

Corrie appeared as well. "Do you have your bouquet, Shay? I can't find it in the dressing room."

"Shay, it's bad luck for Kest to see you before the ceremony." Garrett attempted to squeeze between Shay and Kest to block their view. "You shouldn't be back here."

Shay swatted Garrett with her flowers. "Commander, I say this with utmost respect, but mind your own business. Now, move. I want to see my future husband. He's nervous."

"I'm not nervous!"

"Tal is the one who is nervous," Athlen corrected.

All their heads swiveled in his direction, and Tal rolled his eyes. "Beloved," he said, "that was not necessary."

Athlen grinned. "They're your family. They love you. They're concerned."

"You're a little green, Tally. You're not going to throw up, are you? Should we make the front row move?" Garrett elbowed him. Tal narrowed his eyes.

"Is *everyone* in here?" Emerick squeezed in through the door. He gave Tal a wide-eyed look, still slightly skittish around him, not accustomed to magic brothers-in-law yet. Emerick had been living in the castle for the past few months and was easing into their lives. "The queen is looking for all of you."

"Dearest, this is a momentous occasion, and we're all enjoying it. Mother can wait a few more minutes."

"I'll let you tell her that, dear," Emerick said, straightening his cravat. "She intimidates me."

"As she should," Garrett said.

Tal leaned on the wall, Athlen snug at his side, their fingers threaded together, and he watched his family interact with one another. Months had passed since he'd stopped Vanessa's plot and faced the sea witch. And while nothing had gone back to the normal it had been before he left the castle, he found he didn't want it to. He and his siblings were closer than ever now that he could be his true self with them, now that they didn't take any of their time together for granted. Any concerns Tal had had about Isa's marriage had been resolved by the way Emerick looked at her like she'd hung the moon, and the way she would playfully swoon into his arms.

"You'd be nervous too if you were getting married," Shay admonished Garrett, smacking him with her flowers again, petals flying everywhere.

"Hey, I was going to get married. She said no."

The alliance with Mysten through marriage had dissolved when the bastard daughter gave a resounding no to Garrett's proposal and eloped with her handmaiden and her fencing instructor. The alliance now hinged on an upcoming meeting between Tal and Mysten's king. Thinking about it, Tal broke into a cold sweat.

"I heard there is a sleeping girl in a tower in the kingdom of Alemmeni waiting for a kiss." Kest gave Garrett a cheeky grin. "Maybe you should journey there."

"Tal? You look like you're going to faint." Shay whipped out a handkerchief and dabbed his forehead. "Maybe you should give your speech after the wedding."

"I'll be fine."

When Shay had returned from the border, as soon as she walked under the castle arches, Kest had dropped to a knee and proposed, giving her his ring. She'd said yes, on the condition that she continue to fight under Garrett's command. Kest didn't want it any other way.

Corrie peered through the curtain and wrinkled her nose. "Everyone is restless. We should start soon."

"Goodness!" They all turned to find their mother, Queen Carys, at the door, hand to her throat. Dressed in her finest gown, her crown positioned on her brow, her jewels glittering in the low light, she appeared a vision from a fairy tale, a beloved queen. She smiled warmly, her eyes crinkling at the corners. "Are all my children in here when they are supposed to be other places?"

"We're all in here," Corrie chirped. "Even the extra ones." She jerked her thumb to where Athlen, Emerick, and Shay stood near one another.

"Okay, everyone out save Taliesin and Kesterell." She clapped her hands. "Come along. We have a wedding and a feast to get under way."

The group filed out. Shay gave Kest a kiss on his cheek before

302

whirling away in a sweep of fabric and flower petals. Garrett gave Kest a hug, slapping him on the back. He ruffled Tal's hair on his way out as well.

"You too, Athlen," their mother admonished gently. "And where are your boots?"

Athlen gave Tal a squeeze to his hand and a swift kiss to his mouth. "Good luck. I'll be in the audience. Look at me if you get nervous. And remember"—he dropped his voice to a whisper—"you're not alone."

Tal smiled fondly, full of warmth and love. "Thank you."

Athlen waved as he stepped through the door and began explaining to the queen how he'd misplaced his boots.

Tal sighed. He let his head knock against the stone wall.

"You ready, Tal?" Kest asked, straightening his jacket one more time.

Tal rolled his neck. He relaxed his shoulders. He was a prince of Harth. He was magic. He was loved by his family and by Athlen. He was the last mage, but he was not alone.

"Yes."

He steeled himself with a deep breath, then pulled the curtain aside and walked into the beginning of his new life.

ACKNOWLEDGMENTS

This book exists because at some point in 2017 I thought to myself, "I wonder what it would be like to write a high fantasy fairy tale." These acknowledgments should start with the people who told me that it was a fantastic idea even though I'd never written anything like it before. I'm eternally grateful to fellow author and National Novel Writing Month buddy Carrie Pack, and to my best friend, Kristinn, who both had utter faith that I could write this plotty romance adventure fantasy. They coaxed me along in my word count, read the finished product, and continued to encourage me throughout the process of this manuscript becoming a book. By the time this novel makes it out into the world, it will be a total of four years from inception to completion, which is a long time for anyone to have to field panicked emails about magic systems, potential titles, and nautical metaphors, which they have with more grace and patience than I probably deserve.

Next, I want to thank my agent, Eva Scalzo. Thank you, Eva, for seeing something special in this manuscript and championing it, and for being the 'let's talk via phone' email that I had been striving for ever since I decided I wanted to become an author. And thank you to the team at McElderry Books, especially my editor, Kate Prosswimmer, who worked so hard to bring out all the potential in the storytelling and character arcs and made this book the best it could be. Thank you to the cover illustrator, Sam Schechter, and to the cover designers for this beautiful, beautiful cover. It really has been a dream to work with you all. Thank you for bringing Tal and Athlen's story to the page.

I'd like to thank a group of authors who are not only my friends, but amazing colleagues, and who are my cheerleaders, beta readers, support group, confidants, and convention buddies: Julian Winters, C. B. Lee, Jude Sierra, Laura Stone, & D. L. Wainright.

I'd also like to thank the authors who run the Asheville/WNC Writers Coffeehouse—Beth Revis, Jamie Mason, Brian Rathbone, and Jake Bible—for all their amazing advice and encouragement. Special thanks to Beth for writing a wonderful blurb. I'd like to thank Malaprop's bookstore in Asheville, which is my local amazing indie store and has been so kind to me the past few years. The booksellers are awesome, and if you are ever in the Asheville area, please drop by and say hi to Katie.

It wouldn't be my acknowledgment section without thanking my fandom life mate and fandom twitter pals, who are the greatest when I need a name suggestion or need help deciding on a detail. My Internet family always comes through, and I can't thank them enough for sticking with me this past decade.

I'd like to thank my family, especially my spouse, Keith, and my three kids, Ezra, Zelda, and Remy, who bring joy and excitement into my life every day. Sometimes I'd be okay with a little less excitement. That might be a nice change for next time. I'd also like to thank my brother, Rob, and my sister-in-law, Chris, who account for most of my sales since they seem to purchase multiple copies of my books and then hand them out to their friends. Thanks for that, y'all. Also, Rob is the only person I know who actually reads the acknowledgments. (Hi, Rob!) Also, I want to thank my sisters, Christy and Amanda, who have made the pandemic a little more interesting via memes in our sibling group chat. I would like to thank my niece, Emma, who is always willing to be my assistant at conventions, as well as my other nieces and nephews, who tell their school librarians about their aunt's books and talk them up to their teachers and friends.

Lastly, I'd like to thank everyone who reads this book, whether you purchased it or borrowed it from a library. Thank you for allowing me to entertain you for a few hours. I'm very appreciative of your time. I hope you enjoyed reading Tal and Athlen's story as much as I enjoyed writing it. Until next time, I hope you stay safe and happy.

Thank you.

F.T. Lukens

TURN THE PAGE FOR A SNEAK PEEK AT

So This Is Ever After

I 'd been envisioning what it would be like to behead the Vile One since the old wizard had shown up at my door the day after I turned seventeen and told me my destiny—that I would be the person who ended the dark shadow of evil that ruled our realm. Well, okay, not that specific second because who believes a drunken stranger with a crooked hat carrying around a humming staff? No one. That's who. At least, you shouldn't. That's unsafe.

Let me amend. I'd been envisioning this moment since after we'd had tea and he'd explained a few things and told me about *the prophecy*. Though it didn't feel real, as in very likely, and downright probable, until I pulled a magical sword from a bog and a beam of light shot down from the sky, anointing me with supernatural purpose.

After that, I kept a vision in my head about what would happen when I separated the Vile One's head from his shoulders in the final climactic battle. The cut would be clean. There would be artistic arterial spray, and the disembodied head would roll down the steps of the raised dais and come to rest at the feet of my best friend. Everyone would cheer, and I'd finally be the hero I was prophesied to become. I'd *feel* different. Righteous. Awesome. Accomplished. Finally grown-up.

Unfortunately, as things seem to have gone since the start of this whole journey, that did not happen. Not even a little bit.

Fueled by adrenaline and vigor, I swung my blade for the death blow, expecting to cleanly remove the Vile One's head. Instead, the blunted edge buried halfway through his neck and jarred to a stop on his spinal column. Huh. Who knew that prophesied weapons didn't come ready-to-use? Apparently, magic swords that spring from bogs don't rise pre-sharpened.

Stunned at this unexpected turn of events, I froze long enough to draw attention from the party of questors supporting me.

"Arek!" Sionna yelled from somewhere in the chaos. "Finish him off!"

I wrenched the blade from the Vile One's throat, did my level best to ignore the astonished look on his face, the open mouth, the wide eyes, the gush of blood running down the front of his black robes, and struck again. And again. I hacked at the twitching body, which had fallen backward and slumped on the front of the throne, propped up like a grotesque doll, until I was certain he was dead, and no amount of magic could bring him back.

Finally, the neck gave way and the head plopped onto the ground, splattering like an overripe pumpkin. Dead eyes peered up at me from sunken hollows, and thin lips pulled over yellowed teeth in a parody of a scream. A picture that would surely fuel my nightmares for at least the next few months, potentially the rest of my life.

I had also imagined lifting the Vile One's head by his hair and holding it up as a kind of trophy as all the dark magic he'd used to usurp the throne and control the realm would recede like a fierce tide, sucking itself from the world in a flash of light as the populace cheered. Except, the Vile One was bald, and there was no way I was picking the head up by anything else, because *ugh*.

Also, *nothing happened*. No flash of light. No magical reversal. No swell of victorious music. No fanfare. Nothing.

Huh.

Disappointingly, I didn't feel different at all, other than sticky. And weary down to my bones, and nauseated. There were no cheers from onlookers, though the sound of vomiting was clear over my right shoulder.

I dabbed my blood-drenched face with the hem of my tunic, but only succeeded in smearing the crimson more thoroughly. My chest heaved. My arms ached. I turned, swaying on the steps, and surveyed the chaos of the room behind me. The fighting had ceased. My friends were all upright, scattered around like thrown dice, but alive. Followers of the Vile One, distinguishable by their black robes and neck tattoos, were either dead, fleeing, or kneeling in defeat.

I leaned heavily on the sword—barely resisting the urge to sag right there onto the stone steps, next to the jerking corpse, and take a nap. Instead, I stumbled down to the main floor.

"You okay?" Matt asked. He had soot stains on his sleeves, tears in his clothes, and a cut above his eye that leaked sluggishly. His brown hair was matted to his head with sweat. He smelled like ozone and magic. He held his staff in his hand, the bright blue jewel at the tip glowing like a star, but as we stood together in the aftermath, his power faded.

A late addition to the vision of victory I kept in my head included sweeping Matt into my arms and declaring my undying affection. But as I was literally covered in blood, I didn't think Matt would appreciate a hug at this point, or a grand gesture or even a friendly slap to the shoulder. Not when we were both trembling with exhaustion and ebbing adrenaline.

"Yeah. I'm good. You?"

"Yeah." He grinned weakly. "It's done."

"It is." I ran my gloved hand through my hair. "Super gross, though."

"Oh, definitely. That was, for lack of a better word, vile."

"Good one." I held out my fist, and he bumped his knuckles against mine.

Bethany appeared from around a corner, small harp in one hand, wiping clinging bits of vomit from her mouth with her sleeve. She peeled a strand of sweaty auburn hair from her cheek, cast a look at the throne, turned green, then disappeared again. The sounds of her retching echoed in the eerie silence of the previously chaotic throne room.

Sionna rolled her eyes. She wiped her sword on a prone body before sheathing it. Her brown skin was blood-spattered, but far less than mine. She'd no doubt sharpened her sword. Her black hair still swung in her high ponytail, and the wisps that had escaped framed her face, and though her shoulders slumped with relief, her steps were as energetic as ever. Every inch a warrior. Every inch beautiful. Every inch the reason for many of my inconvenient boners while on this quest.

"I'll check on her," she said.

I cleared my throat. "Good idea."

She left the room through the same arch. Matt and I exchanged a glance. Pretty sure we were on the same wavelength about the boners. Even if we weren't, at least he was still by my side. Thankfully, that piece of my vision was fulfilled. We'd been best friends since we were boys and we'd be best friends forever if I had any say, weird wizards, glowing staffs, enigmatic prophecies, and secret crushes notwithstanding.

"You two okay?"

Startled, I spun around.

Lila stood on the ribbon of purple carpet that led up to the throne. Her soft-heeled boots made little noise when she moved normally, but on the plush, she made no sound at all. With her hood pulled up, her features were partially hidden, but I knew the familiar jut of her chin and the bow of her mouth. She had a bulging sack over one shoulder.

"Yes. We're fine. Exhausted and"—Matt gestured toward the headless form—"vaguely traumatized, but . . ." He trailed off; his eyebrows drew together in consternation. "Have you been looting?"

She shrugged. "A little." She dropped the overstuffed bag at her feet with a loud clank.

"Lila!" I placed my hands on my hips, a difficult task when holding a sword. "Put it back."

"No."

"Now."

"No."

"But—but . . ." I sputtered. "What do you even have in there?"

"Oh, you know, loot, spoils, riches. The usual."

Matt pursed his lips. "That's vague."

She smirked. "Exactly."

"Here you are!" The voice came from behind us, and again, I found myself turning quickly, sword raised. Rion leaned on the heavy wooden doors that we'd barged through mere minutes before. Besides his grimy army, he looked almost untouched from battle. He smiled when he saw us, tipping his blood-smeared sword in acknowledgment.

I relaxed and blew out a breath. "Can people please stop sneaking up on me? I've had *a day*."

"Is it over?" Rion asked, not remarking on my outburst. Instead, his gaze drifted around the throne room until it settled on the body by the dais.

"I think so?" Matt said. "I mean"—he gestured helplessly—"this is it. Right?"

Sionna returned from the adjoining room, her arm looped through Bethany's. Bethany wavered on her feet, but she'd stopped actively vomiting. The entirety of our party now stood in the throne room. We looked at one another, no one speaking, merely existing in the moment of sudden calm after the storm.

I surveyed the group, reassuring myself that we'd all made it, that we were all there and safe. Bethany, our bard, rested against the wall, gaze locked on the broken window across the room, and not anywhere near the bloody neck stump that leaned against the foot of the throne. She was charismatic and magic, essential to our success with her ability to talk her way in or out of any situation. Sionna gripped Bethany's arm, lending her strength. Sionna was a fighter, sleek and deadly, as fearless as she was dangerous. Lila, the rogue, stood on the carpet, loot bag at her feet. She was dexterous and conniving, her past shrouded in mystery, as were her motivations. Matt, the mage, my best friend, my confidant, my secret crush, and wielder of arcane spells, held his staff in the gentle curve of his hand. And Rion the knight rounded out the crowd. He was hulking and strong, older than the rest of us, but barely an adult himself, bound to our group by a sacred oath.

Then there was me. Arek. The Chosen One. The fulfiller of the prophecy, awkwardly standing in front of the throne. Somehow, this ragtag mess of personalities, dubious expertise, and questionable hygiene had come together and completed the impossible. We'd saved the realm. Holy shit. *We'd* saved the realm. *This* was the moment. This was victory.

Lila nodded once sharply, then grabbed her sack and threw it over her shoulder. "Great. Well, this has been fun, but I'm out."

"You're out?" Matt hobbled in front of her. I narrowed my eyes. Matt hadn't mentioned an injury. That doofus probably twisted his ankle when we ran up the entryway stairs dodging arrows. "What do you mean by that?"

She shrugged. "The quest is done. It's over. We won. I helped." She hefted the sack. "I took my reward. I'm out."

"Wait." Bethany straightened from her hunch by the wall. "You can't just *leave*."

"Why not?"

"Don't you want to be here for what happens next?" she asked.

Lila raised an eyebrow. "What does happen next?"

Again, we looked around at each other, silent and unsure. The question hung over the room, like the black pennants that swayed limply against the stone in the slight breeze. Bethany shrugged. Sionna blinked. Rion tapped his fingers on his smudged armor. Matt's mouth tipped down in that funny little frown he always got when he was thinking.

Well, at least we all knew the question, but it didn't look like anyone had an answer.

Perfect.

It was Rion who broke the awkward silence. He cleared his throat. "A new ruler needs to be instated. He," Rion said, jerking his chin toward the body, "was the ruler of our kingdom, as ill-gotten as it was. He killed all the royal family save one—"

"Oh," Matt said, straightening from his impressive lean on his staff, "we should find the princess."

I furrowed my brow. "Isn't she locked in a tower?"

"I think we need to wake her from an eternal slumber," Bethany said, "with true love's kiss?"

"I think that's a different quest." Lila dropped her sack, the contents clanging. "Doesn't she have to let down her hair?"

"No," Sionna said. "We have to guess her name."

"You're all wrong." Matt waved his hand. "We just need to let her out."

"Well, that doesn't sound right," Bethany said, hands on her hips. "Are you sure?"

Matt sighed and dug around in the pouch at his side. "The prophecy—"

The entire group groaned. We all knew the prophecy. We'd all read the prophecy. Matt had lectured us extensively on the prophecy. I could recite the prophecy from memory with my hands tied behind my back while being beaten with sticks by angry gnomes. Well, almost all of it, save for a section that was significantly smudged by wine. But I didn't mention that because it was a sore spot, and as fond as I was of Matt's withering glares, I didn't want to be the target of one at the moment.

Undeterred, Matt yanked the scroll from his bag and flapped the parchment in our direction like he was scolding us. "The prophecy doesn't mention true love's kiss or long hair or guessing names."

"You pulled it out just to tell us that?" Lila crossed her arms and quirked an eyebrow.

Matt's lips twisted into a frown. "I'm making a point."

"Is the point that you're pedantic?" Bethany asked, fake smile plastered on her face despite looking a little green around the gills. "Because we're aware."

"You have vomit in your hair," Matt shot back, stuffing the scroll into his pack.

"Okay, okay." I raised my hands and addressed the group. "Let's all take a moment to breathe."

Lila wrinkled her nose in my direction. "Before we embark on any side quests, there need to be baths all around. And food."

"Hey! I just killed the Vile One." I waved at the decapitated corpse behind me for emphasis. "Cut me some slack."

Rion cleared his throat. "Before I was interrupted, I did have a point."

I gestured at him. "Continue, then."

"So commanding," Matt whispered, snickering.

I bit my lip to keep laughter from bubbling out. I was covered in blood, and some of the castle residents had poked their heads out of their hiding places. Hysterically laughing wouldn't be a good look.

"The point is, with no current royal family to assume the

throne, and with you being the individual who hacked off the head of the Vile One, the job to rule the kingdom falls on your shoulders."

Huh. He said hacker of heads. The alliteration was nice, but there could be a better title in my future. Better nip it in the bud.

I crossed my arms. "Let's not go with 'hacked off the head,' please. And there's a princess in a tower who is the lawful ruler. I'm just . . . a prophetic pawn here."

"Yes, but until she is freed, you are the rightful monarch." Rion nodded to the empty throne.

I shook my head. "But I don't want to be the rightful monarch."

"Arek," Sionna said, pinching the bridge of her nose. "We can't leave the throne open while we complete the side quest."

"But—"

"Do you really want to have to do it all again," Bethany whined while flailing her hands emphatically, "if someone even worse sneaks in and sits there while we're gone and takes the throne?" She clutched her harp tighter and absolutely did not look at the headless body slumped nearby. "Or do you want to suck it up and proclaim yourself king for like a few hours?"

I shot a look at Matt. He shrugged, his expression not reassuring at all. Ugh, I really wanted for this all to be over because I wanted to talk to him in *private* and do the whole confessing thing that had been eating away at me for months. Putting on a dead man's crown seemed the opposite of wrapping up the quest, but I couldn't deny that Bethany's point was sound. I *didn't* want to do this all again.

"I . . . um . . . I . . ."

Rion took my stuttering as acceptance. He unsheathed his sword and knelt on the stone floor. "All hail, King Arek!"

"Oh no!" I held up my hands. "No. Stop that. Don't do that."

Bethany strummed her harp, her pale lips curled into a smirk. "All hail, King Arek," she sang, and with the magic of the instrument, the statement amplified into a chorus of voices. *Bitch.*

The proclamation rang out in the small room, and suddenly, everyone knelt. The few servants who had wandered in at the commotion. The remaining followers of the Vile One. And my fellow questors, my friends, those traitorous assholes.

"Get the crown," Matt said, nudging me with his shoulder, positively gleeful. His lips tugged into a smug grin that stuck to his ridiculous face. He sank to his knees. "Put it on."

"No. It's on the head. The *severed* head. That's disgusting."

"You're wearing gloves. It'll be fine."

"And then what? Put it on *my* head? Fuck that. Gore will get in my hair."

"It's already in your hair. It's all over you."

"Don't be a coward," Lila said. She was the last to kneel, but she did, which was surprising. She even pulled back her hood, revealing the long braids of her blond hair, and the pointed tips of her ears. "Do it."

"Do it. Do it. Do it," Matt whispered, cackling.

Lila reached out and pressed a single fingertip to my arm. "Peer pressure."

"Ugh." I marched back to the head, considered it, and nope. Putting on a bloody crown was not part of the vision. Neither was the whole ruling thing. Absolutely not part of the deal. But for appearances, and until the true heir from the tower was freed, I guessed ruling for a few hours wouldn't be so bad. Especially if it shut up the irritating chants.

I yanked the golden crown off the head. It rolled to the edge of the step and teetered for an agonizing second before toppling off and hitting the stone with a gag-inducing splat. I swallowed down bile, desperately trying not to pull a Bethany in front of my soon-to-be subjects. Knocking the lifeless figure off the dais, I ascended the remaining stairs and stood in front of the throne.

It was ornate, in a menacing way, with terrifying monsters etched into the decoration, and intimidating all on its own. It shouldn't have been—it was only a chair—but I did pause at the idea of plopping down where the guy I just killed used to sit.

I took a breath. "Well, all right then." Despite my misgivings, I placed the crown on my head, turned quickly, and dropped onto the throne. It was not at all comfortable.

I don't really know what happened in that moment, but something in the room swelled, and crackled, then broke over me in a wave of warmth and potential. The hair on my arms stood on end and a shiver traced down my spine. It was like standing in a field during an oncoming storm as the pressure and expectation of something much bigger than myself bared down on me, a reminder of the wonder inherent in magic and in the world, and my place in it. In an instant, I was suffused with the song of everyone who'd come before, and how all roads had led me there, to that place, to that moment, to that role.

It lasted the length of a breath, then evaporated.

The chanting ceased. I squirmed, trying to find a position that didn't twinge my back. All eyes stared at me. Yeah, this was a bad idea. Almost as bad as leaving my house in the middle of the night nine months ago, clutching the prophetic scroll that landed me here with Matt trailing behind me.

"Say something," Sionna hissed.

"Oh." I leaned forward, shaking myself out of a stupor. "Uh. The Vile One is dead. I killed him. So, I hereby assume the throne of Ere in the realm of Chickpea and declare myself King Arek." I licked my chapped lips. "But only until we free the princess from the tower. My rule will be for a few hours. Tops. An interim king, if you will. Yay. Huzzah. And all that."

Sionna snorted.

"Spoken like a true statesman," Matt said with a grin.

Lila rolled her eyes. Bethany, still pale, picked a few strings on her harp, and my words echoed outward, throughout the castle and the grounds.

A round of polite applause followed.

"Can . . . uh . . ." I swallowed. "Can we have the room please? And maybe a cleanup crew?"

The few interlopers scattered, including the last remaining living followers of the Vile One, and soon the room was clear save for us and the dead.

"Did you lot feel that?"

They blinked at me.

"Feel what?" Bethany asked. She clutched her stomach with one hand. "Sick? Because yes."

"No. The magic? Matt, did you do something?"

He furrowed his brow. "Not that I'm aware of."

"Huh." It could have been the release of stress, the receding of adrenaline, leaving me chilled and shaking. But I knew better. After nine months of prophetic fuckery, I recognized the presence of magic. The way warmth and power washed over me on the throne mirrored the prickling shock when Matt used his staff, or the sweep of mystical promise when I touched the sword for the first time in the bog. There was more brewing in the throne room than I wanted to be part of, and the sooner we found the princess and installed her as queen, the sooner I could be done with being destiny's pawn.

I slapped my hands on the arms of the throne and stood. "Well, let's find this princess, then."

"Now?" Bethany asked.

"Now," I said with a sharp nod.

Lila frowned. "But baths and food."

"And rest," Sionna said.

"Now." I pointed to the crown. "Consider it my first act as king."

"Your first act as king is to not want to be king," Matt said, smile lurking around the curve of his mouth. "Sounds about right."

Bethany snickered.

"Come on," I said, descending the dais and striding quickly out of the room. "The sooner we find this princess, the sooner we can put this whole quest behind us."

LOVE BARGAINS ARE A TRICKY THING . . .

And this is not your typical fairy-tale romance.

SWEET & BITTER MAGIC

ADRIENNE TOOLEY

THERE IS NOTHING MORE DANGEROUS
THAN A FAERIE TALE.

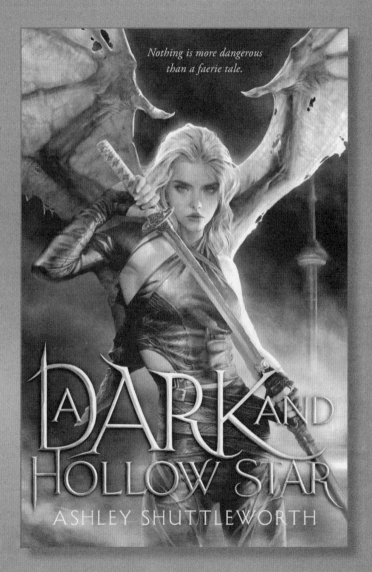

Discover the spellbinding worlds of *New York Times* bestselling author Margaret Rogerson

★ "Sure to appeal to fans of Holly Black, Diana Wynne Jones, and Sarah J. Maas."

—*School Library Journal*, starred review

★ "An enthralling adventure . . . and a world worth staying lost in."

—*Kirkus Reviews*, starred review